MW00834873

Dark Awakening

Karlene Cameron

ISBN 978-1-936556-02-1

Published 2016

Published by Black Velvet Seductions Publishing

Dark Awakening Copyright 2016 Karlene Cameron
Cover design Copyright 2016 R. J. Savage

Printed by Black Velvet Seductions Publishing
A division of Savage Publications

Visit us at:
www.blackvelvetseductions.com

"Tha gach uile dhuine air a bhreth saor agus coionnan ann an urram 's ann an còirichean. Tha iad air am breth le reusan is le cogais agus mar sin bu chòir dhaibh a bhith beò nam measg fhein ann an spiorad bràthaireil."

"All human beings are born free and equal in dignity and rights. They are endowed with reason and conscience and should act towards one another in a spirit of brotherhood."
(Article 1 of the Universal Declaration of Human Rights)

Chapter One

Before you embark on a journey of revenge, dig two graves.
Confucius

June 16, 2012, Seattle, Washington

Caitriona Sinclair knew how she was going to die. She had seen her death countless times since she was a young girl. Each time the vision splashed violently across her mind, she trembled and broke out in a cold sweat. But it wasn't just the images that disturbed her; the loneliness and heartache that ripped through her left her gasping and afraid.

Her death wasn't peaceful, nor was it a sacrifice for someone she loved. Her death was violent and bloody, perpetrated at the hands of a dark, powerful stranger and the blade he so skillfully maneuvered.

She took a deep breath to steady her nerves and reached up to smooth a stray strand of reddish-brown hair from her pale heart-shaped face, blinking several times to clear the remaining imprints from her mind. As with all the other times she'd witnessed her death, she felt unsettled. She had no idea who the stranger was and, more importantly, why he wanted her dead. His face was always shrouded by darkness. The only real discerning characteristic was the tattooed Celtic knot that circled his left upper arm. A chill ran across her body and she began to shiver uncontrollably. She knew the headache wouldn't be far behind - a horrendous parting gift from a vision she was all too familiar with.

Caitriona sank back in the cold, unyielding office chair that had been a permanent fixture in the old building long before she had been promoted to the rather small office. She ran her hand through her long hair, pushing away the nostalgia that threatened to consume her day. Having lost her mother and older sister in a violent car accident when she was only thirteen years old, Caitriona had been raised by her mother's widowed sister. While neither abusive nor uncaring, the woman had seldom shown any great degree of love or affection toward Caitriona. Her aunt was devoted to Christ and had raised Caitriona as only a good Christian woman could; with hours of religious study, prayer and service to others. Once, Caitriona had tried to talk to her aunt about the nightmares and visions that haunted her. Her aunt's horrified expression, along with ensuing hours of prayer and scripture, reaffirmed Caitriona's belief that it was best to remain silent.

It was no great surprise, then, that Caitriona had spent her youth longing for a mother she barely remembered and a father who had disappeared when she turned five. From that fateful day when the car accident stole her mother and sister, she had spent her days in religious hell, longing for a life where she could run through rain puddles, climb trees, and read fairy tales. She learned quickly enough that her aunt could tolerate only so much of Caitriona's "differences." So Caitriona had learned to keep silent, obey the rules, and blend into the monochromatic world around her. This left a tremendous void in Caitriona's life. With no one around to explain what she was experiencing, let alone help her develop the skill she so desperately wanted to understand, she felt like even more of an outcast; an unwanted pebble in her aunt's worn and sensible shoes.

Caitriona smiled as she recalled images of her older sister. Unlike Caitriona, Danika devoured life. She had a penchant for finding mischief. Unconventional and unapologetic, Danika believed that life was a classroom, and nothing should be left unexplored. Despite her free spirit, Danika was disciplined when it came to her music studies. An accomplished pianist by the age of twelve, Danika soaked up the spotlight and never passed up an opportunity to perform. Caitriona smiled, thinking about the way her sister could command an audience. Sloe-eyed with long chestnut brown hair, she had a way of turning heads both on and off the stage.

Danika should have been the one to live that day, Caitriona thought sadly, as memories of the car wreck brought tears to her eyes. Her sister, who had just turned eighteen a week earlier, had gotten her driver's license that afternoon. She had begged their mother to let her drive them to Dairy Queen, a celebration—she had laughed—of a major milestone in life. And one she convinced their mother that shouldn't go unrewarded or unrecognized. Caitriona smiled, remembering the theatrical flair Danika had for even the most mundane of chores. Their mother had finally relented.

It was unusually rainy for that time of year and the roads were slick with rain and oil. The SUV Danika was driving hydroplaned shortly after she had pulled onto the two lane highway. Danika crossed the center line and their vehicle was struck head-on by a motor home. Their mother was killed instantly. A man in another SUV saw the accident and stopped, pulling Danika from the wreckage, but she died later at the scene. Caitriona had spent several weeks in the hospital with multiple broken ribs, internal bleeding, and a ruptured disc. To her aunt's credit, the woman never left her side and provided a stable sort of comfort during her long recovery.

Caitriona sighed and shrugged away the remaining nostalgia. She wasn't even sure that what woke her from her dreams, and hijacked her day vision was anything worth exploring. After all, the yellow pages and online directories were already full of psychics and mystics, all claiming to be able to see future events. Most, she knew, were simply looking for employment opportunities. And the few legitimate psychics there were constantly had to battle a public image that had long since been tarnished.

So, in deference, Caitriona turned a blind eye to her "gift" and concentrated instead on the career ladder she was quickly climbing. At twenty-six, she was one of the youngest marketing executives on the team at Brennen and Dornais, the largest marketing agency on the West Coast. Indeed, her career path had cost her plenty: a lost love, an estranged aunt, and plenty of sleepless nights. But, as an aspiring young marketing executive, Caitriona didn't spend much time lamenting the things she had lost.

"Hey, Cat!" Eric Brockman popped casually into Caitriona's office, breaking her concentration and bringing her attention once more to her work. At nearly six feet tall and broad shouldered, Eric's massive frame filled the doorway. Sandy brown curls made a mocking display of the gel he so generously used to keep them anchored in place.

"You know I hate it when you call me that," snarled Caitriona, but a smile gathered easily at the corners of her mouth.

"Did you hear who won the Amazon account?" Eric questioned, his deep blue eyes sparkling with the excitement of his soon-to-be-told news.

Caitriona arched one brow and gestured for Eric to sit down. "Please don't tell me Brennen and Dornais gave it to Elena and her team?" Caitriona pulled her lower lip under her teeth and grimaced when Eric gave her an affirmative nod. "How could they?" she groaned in exasperation.

Eric allowed his gaze to dip appreciatively to Caitriona's ample breasts as he replied, "You just don't flaunt what you've got, Cat!" Eric chuckled and tossed a stack of papers on her desk before she could admonish him further. "Don't let it eat at you. We've got plenty to concentrate on with the new Matherson account." While Eric didn't allow his gaze to linger long, Caitriona noted that his eyes took in every appreciative curve of her body. At 5'7", Caitriona was taller than the average woman, but she knew this only served to give her an air of authority and power. Perfectly proportioned, Caitriona had a mass of auburn curls that fell seductively over her narrow shoulders. Full lips and emerald green eyes accentuated her beauty and called attention to her flawless ivory skin, finely chiseled cheekbones, and softly feminine features.

Caitriona picked up the papers and quickly scanned the stack for relevant information. "I'll need you to be the lead designer," Caitriona mumbled, not looking up from the stack she continued to scan, knowing Eric wouldn't hesitate. "I'll pull together a team and schedule a kick-off meeting for next week." She dropped the stack of papers back to her desk and looked up, rubbing her temples in an effort to ward off the headache that was on the brink of becoming a full-blown migraine.

"Eric, I'm going to call it a day." She managed a tiny smile that was more perfunctory than sincere, and began gathering documents she would work on later that evening in the comfort of her small downtown apartment, near the edge of the beautiful Seattle waterfront.

"Another headache, huh," Eric asked as he retrieved her computer bag from the hook behind the door and helped pack her folders. He stopped suddenly and looked at her, his eyes filled with concern. "It's the vision again, isn't it?" he questioned, fear making his tone harsher than what she knew he intended. At her silence, he heaved a rather breathy sigh and took a seat across from her in the padded office chair she reserved for visitors.

"Cat, you really need to get in and see a doctor. The headaches are becoming way too frequent; which means the vision has become more frequent," he said as more of a statement than a question. "I don't like this." His concern was etched visibly in the furrow of his brow. He continued stuffing papers into her bag and, vacating the uncomfortable chair, retrieved her sweater from the hook behind the door. "Do you at least want some help getting home?"

"Thanks, Eric, but it's a short bus ride. I promise I'll be fine. I'll even call you later tonight and we can talk about the details of the Matherson account." Caitriona smiled reassuringly at Eric's scowl and slung her bag over her shoulder, taking the sweater he proffered with one arm. He walked with her to the elevator in uncomfortable silence, concern still visible on his handsome face. Caitriona had known Eric since undergraduate school at the University of Washington. Together they had shared many late nights, dreams of the future, and steaming mugs of coffee. One particular night after several shots of tequila and rounds of Corona, Caitriona had confided in Eric about the vision. At first he didn't believe her, but after witnessing an episode that left her nearly writhing in agony from the debilitating aftereffects, he no longer questioned her honesty or integrity. Instead, he had helped her focus on the details, pulling out the smallest minutiae to aid her in piecing the puzzle together. Over the years they had shared many theories about the vision, but despite counseling, sleep therapy, and hypnosis, the vision continued to haunt her dreams, and more recently invaded her waking thoughts as well.

Eric touched her shoulder, locking deep blue eyes with emerald green. He had been drawn to her from the moment they were paired together in chemistry at UW. Her sharp mind and even sharper wit had endeared her to him in a way no other woman ever had. While Eric soon stood out as the stronger academic, Caitriona impressed her professors with her visionary prowess, and later blazed a professional trail, through hard work, a tenacious attitude, and an uncanny ability to know when to take risks.

While she and Eric had, at one time, explored a brief romantic interlude, Cat didn't feel drawn to him in the same way he did to her. She was restless and searching for something that she could neither articulate nor understand herself. And so she distanced herself from any close relationships. But regardless of how much she continued to push Eric away, he followed her career path relentlessly and positioned himself in companies where they could partner together in work.

Eric punched the elevator button for Cat and squeezed her arm affectionately as the elevator doors hissed open. Caitriona smiled reassuringly and saw the worry still etched in his handsome face. She started to say something, but the doors began to close and the pain in her temples grew stronger. She relaxed against the back of the elevator, glad to be calling it a day.

Outside, Caitriona tilted her face to the warm mid-afternoon sun and inhaled sharply; willing the pain in her head to go away. While her apartment was just slightly over three miles from the office, she was in no shape to walk. Deciding the bus was a better alternative, she scooted quickly across the street to wait at the already crowded bus stop. She didn't have long to wait and was relieved when the city bus pulled alongside the gathering horde.

Caitriona pressed sharply against her temple to quell a surge of pain that was threatening to burgeon into a full-blown migraine. She groaned inwardly as she stepped onto a standing room only bus. As she swiped her bus pass and the requested fare was subtracted from her balance, she caught sight of two men who looked like they would be more comfortable in an Aston Martin than the crowded Metro. Both men were striking, with well-developed arm muscles that strained against their white collared Armani shirts. Before she had a chance to reflect further, she was gripped with another searing flash of pain that brought her hands up sharply to her temples; a vain effort on her part to subdue the ember-hot pain shooting through her brain.

Caitriona sighed again as she realized that the chance of finding a seat on the over-crowded bus looked slim. She eyed several passengers in seats closest to her, but all of them looked away, not eager to offer her their coveted vinyl thrones. Caitriona breathed deeply and closed her eyes, willing the bus driver to get her home quickly. She wanted nothing more than to pull on her favorite sweats, pour a glass of wine and relax in the comfort of her plush but aging sofa. Instead, she took another cleansing breath and closed her eyes against the pain. The doctors had been unable to find any cause or provide any treatment for the unbearable headaches. Short of shots of Demerol for pain and electrical pulses to stimulate the nerves, the doctors had been unable to offer any permanent comfort or relief. What made it even more confusing was that the headaches became worse right after a "vision." *Some "gift"*, she thought absently.

She rubbed her temples again and briefly considered getting off the overcrowded people mover, but knew the few minutes she would spend standing would be infinitely better than walking, so she resolved herself to her fate and pushed forward until the stream of humanity stopped and the young girl whom she was following turned to face her, signaling they had reached standing capacity. Caitriona smiled wanly at the young girl and turned to face the front of the bus, shrugging off her pack and placing it at her feet. She looked up and caught her breath as her gaze settled on the giant before her. The man she had spotted earlier had gotten on behind her. He was huge. Not fat, but all hard lines and muscles. He was easily 6'4" and dominated the space around them. *Formidable*, she thought wryly as she allowed her gaze to move approvingly over his broad shoulders, muscled arms and thighs, and the tightness of his firm buttocks. *I bet he has no shortage of women at night.*

As if sensing her eyes on his back, the man turned sideways so that he could face her. His gaze swept her body quickly before meeting her inquisitive stare. Caitriona dropped her gaze and fished in her pocket for her cell phone, needing a distraction to keep from staring at the hulk of a man standing before her. She swiped quickly through her email and Facebook posts with one hand while the other hand held the strap that was positioned uncomfortably above her.

Caitriona could literally feel the stranger's eyes on her, exploring her curves unabashedly. She felt an undeniable exchange between them, almost as if an electrical current were dancing between them. She refused to look at him, but could still feel his eyes lingering on her small form, burning their way across her body. His friend said something to him and he turned to acknowledge him. Caitriona was glad for the interruption and slyly looked up through dark lashes, noticing the smile that reached his eyes as he replied to his friend.

She gauged him to be in his late 30s; tiny lines edged his eyes and he had the faintest hints of salt and pepper beginning to streak his neatly trimmed beard. His hair was mesmerizing: jet black and full with soft curls forming at the ends. It reached nearly to his shoulders and was tied back with nothing more than a leather thong. *Warrior.* The thought came to her as she took in his masculinity and mannerisms. This guy was all man. An intricate tattoo peeked from under his loosely buttoned shirt and she wondered how much of his body was covered by the arresting ink. A flash of the mysterious stranger from her earlier vision invaded her thoughts but she pushed it quickly away. *Don't be ridiculous*, she thought angrily; *not everyone who sports a tattoo is out to kill you.* But the thought that this could be her deadly stranger wouldn't leave her.

She glanced at him again, noting how his expensive yet tasteful clothes hinted at the muscles underneath. His powerful physique stretched taut the cotton cloth that did little to hide the masculine form beneath. His pants were more like trews, she thought absently, and then mentally chided herself as she pictured this man at home as captain of a large clipper. *I bet he's part of the Pirate club here in Seattle.*

As the bus pulled away from the curb, she braced herself for the jarring ride home. Caitriona was not a big fan of the Metro, but did acknowledge that, in a city where parking was at a premium, it was better to brave the bus line than to go broke paying for overpriced, oversold parking.

She didn't have much time to ponder this last thought as the bus driver slammed on his brakes suddenly, and she was flung violently forward. A collective gasp was heard from the riders as they struggled to maintain their balance and keep from landing on the floor.

Caitriona realized she was still standing and the dark-haired man-wall in front of her was to thank. He caught her easily by the waist, his arm tightening in response, bringing her body alarmingly close to his. Caitriona's body immediately warmed, heated by the way he held her to him, possessive and confident; as if he had every right to keep her pinned to him as long as he liked.

Caitriona tried to regain her composure quickly; her rational thoughts being pushed away in favor of the wicked, wanton images that flooded her mind. His high-end designer clothing alone was worth admiring. Precisely cut to showcase broad shoulders, trim waist and long, well-muscled legs, the fitted charcoal blazer lent him an air of power and wealth. The jacket was worn over a white collared silk shirt, open at the collar to reveal black chest hair and tawny skin, and fitted khaki pants. But it was the way he filled the space around him merely by standing there that caused a soft gasp to escape her lips.

"Are ye alright, lass?" he said, his Scottish lilt giving him an even greater sexual advantage in Caitriona's book.

"Yes, thank you. I'm fine," she said a little too breathlessly. She hoped he hadn't noticed. He smiled at her and shifted his weight, his arm still possessively around her. She dropped her gaze, unsure of what to say and acutely aware of the uncomfortable silence that was beginning to stretch before them. Caitriona, still shaken, replied, "I'm sorry."

"Dinna be," he said with a seductive half smile. He still held her firmly by the waist, sexual energy rolling off him in sheets.

Caitriona could feel him hard and unforgiving beneath his clothes. She pushed slightly against his hard chest, but he still held her tight against him. He locked steel grey eyes with her emerald green ones, paralyzing Caitriona with that single stare that inextricably connected them. She suffered a fleeting moment of déjà vu, feeling as if she had known this man in another life, and wondered briefly again about her vision. Sadly, she felt his hands drop from her waist, leaving an electrical trail as they slowly left her body.

Caitriona was brought back to her surroundings and out of her hypnotic trance as she once again registered the presence of the other passengers. She was acutely aware of her modest but professional attire and the heat that rose to her cheeks. The brown, pinstripe skirt she wore hugged her curves appreciatively but was bereft of any designer label. A sea-foam green blouse added a hint of color and complimented the deep emerald hue of her eyes. She fidgeted nervously with the buttons of her shirt, wishing she could be anywhere other than on the bus and under the penetrating, electric gaze of the man before her. It wasn't the first time in her life that she wished she had more of an interest in fashion.

His eyes dipped appreciatively to the valley between her breasts, and she thought she saw a faint smile dance quickly across his masculine features. *Get a grip*, she admonished herself silently. *Men like that don't look at girls like you.* Having been raised by a religious zealot, she was taught that vanity was one of the greatest sins. As a result, her wardrobe consisted primarily of simple muslin and cotton dresses, practical loafers, and unassuming handbags; a far cry from what the other girls her age were sporting. While she retired the muslin when she left her aunt's home to go to college, she still found it difficult to spend money (and even time) on a wardrobe that was as meaningless and shallow as many of the men, and women, she met.

Caitriona turned around and tried to tune out the cacophony of voices that were going on animatedly about the most recent traffic issues involving Metro drivers. As the bus once again jolted in and out of traffic, Caitriona's thoughts turned to the man who stood just mere inches from her. The feeling that she had seen him before wouldn't go away, but she couldn't pinpoint her concern - unless he was the man from her vision. The thought left her feeling unsettled.

A sharp pain suddenly wracked her head from the base of her skull to the spot behind her eyes. She cried out and clutched her head, immediately regretting her outburst.

"Are ye alright, lass?" he asked for the second time that day. Concern was clearly visible on the stranger's face. She shook her head quickly, the sudden motion reminding her that the pain had not dissipated.

The man placed his hand on her arm and in that instant, a flash formed in the back of Caitriona's mind: a quick image of the man before her on a horse, a sword at his side and an army behind him. Like many of her other visions, it moved quickly across her mind and was gone almost as swiftly as it began. The pain wracked her head again and she moaned softly.

"It's nothing," Caitriona replied softly. "But thank you for your concern." She reached to get her pack, noting that the bus had once again started its downtown journey and was closing in on her destination.

Caitriona was thankful for the short ride to her home and was even more grateful when the light traffic allowed the bus to make better than usual time. She sighed and considered getting off at an earlier stop five blocks from her weathered apartment building. The thought of some fresh air and a chance to escape the hordes of people sounded like a good idea. Deciding she didn't feel up to the walk, even a short one, she waited patiently as several in front of her exited the bus. Those who weren't getting off quickly took possession of the recently vacated seats.

"It certainly doesna seem like nothing, lass," the man-wall chided her as the bus pulled forward again slowly, "Perhaps I can at least see ye home?"

"Truly, I'm fine," she said again. "My stop is the next one." She motioned to the window as the bus pulled up alongside the curb, and the kneeling bus stooped to let her off. The two gentlemen got off with her, as did many others who were standing. Many of them would simply reboard and, if they were lucky, find seats for the rest of their journey.

Caitriona exited the bus, mustering a smile for the bus driver as he shut the bus doors. As he started to pull away from the curb, she noticed the man-wall conversing with his friend in hushed tones. They glanced in her direction, making her feel uneasy. "Can I help you find something?" she called out to the two men, deciding it was better to acknowledge their presence, in the hopes she could redirect their attention.

"We are looking for someone," stated the smaller of the two men. Of Asian descent, he spoke perfect English, which indicated he'd most likely been born in the States. The Scottish man-wall eyed her inquisitively, but otherwise said nothing. His companion smiled amicably and extended his hand to Caitriona in a warm greeting. "My name's Lee," he stated simply, gripping her hand firmly and flashing her another smile that showed perfectly even, white teeth. His thick, jet black hair was cut short and framed his angular face rather nicely. "This is Duncan MacKinnon," he nodded to the man-wall, who acknowledged her with a slight dip of his head.

Caitriona couldn't take her eyes off the man-wall's deep, steel grey eyes that once again found her own. Caitriona eyed the men warily and instinctively took a step back, piecing together her exit plan in case she had to fight or get away. Sensing her uneasiness, both men stepped back, giving her the space she needed to feel more secure.

"I'm afraid I don't know too many people in this area," Caitriona stated. "Perhaps you can check over at the market." Caitriona gestured behind the men toward Pike Place Market. "Several of those merchants have been around for decades."

Caitriona turned away from the two men and started to walk quickly toward the steps leading to her apartment when the Asian man interrupted her. "Thank you, miss. But we were hoping you might have a directory." Caitriona turned, the pounding in her head igniting the short fuse she had on her temper. She started to say something impudent, but he interrupted her again, "It shouldn't take too long, and then we'll be on our way."

"You two don't have cell phones?" Caitriona stated as more of a fact than a question, eyeing them quizzically. At their apologetic shrugs, she sighed and said rather tersely, "Stay here and I'll bring the phone book out to you." *Who wears Armani and doesn't have a cell phone*, she wondered with suspicion.

Caitriona dug around in her laptop bag for the keys to her apartment as she began climbing the steps. Unlocking the door quickly, she slipped inside and kicked off her shoes. The large bay windows overlooking the Puget Sound provided ample light, so she opened the blinds and raised them in order to take in an obstructed view of the bay. Sighing heavily, she opened a kitchen drawer and removed the three-inch-thick directory and ran back outside, leaving her door slightly ajar.

Both men got up from where they were sitting on the bottom step, and thanked her for the use of the directory. "You can just leave it on the step. I'll get it later," Caitriona stated. The man-wall looked like he wanted to say something and thought better of it. Caitriona slipped quickly back inside the apartment and bolted the door; her inability to remember where she had seen the man-wall giving rise to her growing suspicion.

Sinking wearily into the love seat facing the windows, she closed her eyes and took a deep breath; the uncomfortable encounter with the strangers already fading from her mind. Rearranging the pillows, she stretched out on the love seat, curling up into a ball in order to accommodate its shorter width. Sighing contentedly, she pulled a light blanket across her legs and drifted off to a restless sleep.

***

Caitriona was running. She knew there was something chasing her, but she didn't know who or what it was. She knew only she had to keep running. As she ran, images kept surfacing; disturbing faces of people she ought to know but, try as she might, she simply couldn't put names to any of them.

Somewhere in the distance a red light continued its monochromatic blinking, casting eerie shadows on the walls around her and causing her to feel disoriented. Uneasiness quickly spread over Caitriona and she found herself running in circles, unable to exit the maddening race. A pair of steel grey eyes flashed into her vision, bringing a sense of familiarity and security. The feeling passed quickly and there was nothing but darkness engulfing her once again.

Caitriona felt something brush against her arm. She screamed and tried to move, but her legs refused to budge. The air felt heavy and her lungs burned as she tried to inhale deeply. She could feel the blackness engulf her, threatening to pull her under. But under what she didn't know. Then there were hundreds of hands reaching out to her, touching her, trying to pull her toward them. The scream tore from her lips and escaped into her waking life.

***

Caitriona felt the rumble in her bones long before she heard it. As the movement continued to grow, Caitriona became aware of a panic that was growing in her as well. As her eyes fluttered open from her, now forgotten, dream, she struggled against the darkness that enveloped her. *Had she been asleep that long*, she wondered. Darkness had somehow snuck in without her awareness. She struggled to escape the heaviness that threatened to keep her in her dreams. She fought to open her eyes, blinking rapidly to push the weightiness from her lids.

The rumbling grew deeper this time and shook the chandelier, until its dainty crystals sang a melody that belied the current danger. Caitriona forced her eyes open at last and sat up, hastily throwing off the cover; her fear growing more visible as she realized what was happening. *Earthquake*, she thought frantically; paralyzed as heirlooms, dishes, and other items were tossed carelessly to the floor by the growing tremblor.

Caitriona managed to stumble toward the door frame, throwing open the front door to better brace her slight form within the thick, solid beams of the door's structure. She cried out when a splintering crack brought a portion of the ceiling plaster crashing in around her. *This isn't happening*, she thought wildly. She pulled her arms over her head instinctively to protect herself, cringing as more of the building began groaning under the earth's growing assault.

Around her the apartment's weathered bricks began crumbling and collapsing; one of them landing loudly on the phone book the two strangers had left on the apartment's now debris littered steps. The rumbling continued as light poles swayed and crashed thunderously to the ground. Transformers began exploding, and everywhere the sound of screaming and sobbing could be heard.

Surely this should have ended by now, Caitriona thought, as dust and debris littered the air, making it impossible to breathe. Caitriona looked up in time to see several telephone utility poles sway, break and fall away, executing a man caught in the electrical giant's swaying tendrils. The shaking intensified, slamming Caitriona against the door frame as the rolling motion combined with a horizontal jerking forward and back. The building, stressed in its foundation, bucked like a mechanized bull in a cowboy bar. The clamor of car alarms and sirens pierced the air, while all around her the cacophony of destruction polluted her senses. *Shit, this is really bad.* The thought filled her with dread.

Suddenly, Caitriona heard a terrifying wrenching noise. Glancing behind her, she found the source of the noise. The entire west side of the apartment building was collapsing, pulling residents, pets and bystanders into the burgeoning heap of rubble gathering below. Caitriona felt the ground give way beneath her. Clawing with her hands, she frantically tried to reach out and grab onto something in order to keep from slipping into the abyss below. Dust and plaster choked the air, burning her lungs and clouding her sight. She managed to pull herself onto a long, thin board as the floor below her gave out.

Caitriona heard the screams and could smell the blood that permeated the air. She tightened her grip on the thin board and wondered how long until she was pulled under the sliding apartment building. Another violent shake passed and she could hear metal scrape against metal as the support beams succumbed to the forces of nature. This time there would be nothing to hold her. She squeezed her eyes shut as two steel beams gave way and a large piece crashed inches from her. A metal rod that had been torn free pierced her thigh.

The force of the rod caused her to exhale sharply and cry out with pain, fear and frustration lacing her breath. Blackness threatened to engulf her as a wave of nausea overtook her. She tried once again to reposition her hands and reaffirm the tenuous hold she had on the board. The temblor had reluctantly ceased its shaking, and the sounds of death lingered in its place. From somewhere below her, a car alarm rent the evening air with its piercing wail. The pain in her leg was growing unbearable. She cried out again, even as she tried to suck air into her dust-filled lungs. Caitriona squeezed her eyes tight shut, trying to block out the death and destruction that surrounded her. She knew she had to fight through the pain and pull herself to safety.

Sobbing in frustration and anger, she suddenly felt strong arms lift her from the debris, careful not to cause any more damage. Caitriona tried to focus on her rescuer, but, whether from the smoke, or from blurred vision, she couldn't make out more than a tall, muscular stranger. She tried to assist in her rescue, but the tiny effort she put forth caused her to nearly pass out.

"Be still, lass." The words were commanding, yet gentle. Caitriona glanced at her rescuer and noted a rather large Celtic knot peeking out from beneath his white collared shirt. She squeezed her eyes shut again; she had seen this symbol somewhere before. Caitriona tried to stand, but cried out when she noticed the rather large gaping hole in her thigh where the rod had penetrated. She sagged against the stranger as warm rivulets of blood ran down her leg.

"It's a wee cut is all, lass," he lied in a rich Celtic brogue. "Let's get ye out of here and then see about bandaging that leg." He gave her a reassuring smile as the apartment building again shifted beneath them. Caitriona fell back against the stranger's arms, succumbing to a pain filled sleep, secure in the knowledge that he would indeed see her to safety.

Chapter Two

Do not dwell in the past; do not dream of the future, concentrate the
mind on the present moment.
Buddha

Caitriona awoke to bright lights on white walls. Instinctively, she shielded her vision from the intensity of the lights; the sensation reminding her of the striking noon-day sun after hours of the dull office lighting she had become accustomed to. She rubbed her eyes slowly, blinking away the last remnants of sleep, as she tried to adjust her eyes to the intensity of the lights.

She had no idea where she was. That much was clear. It looked as if she were in some sort of hospital, but the medical displays looked foreign to her. *Think,* she chided herself gently. She tried to recall the last few hours. She had been caught in an intense earthquake and must be in a hospital, perhaps an overflow room where they placed newer technologies for more serious injuries. She touched the bandage on her thigh; the memories flooding her mind like a tidal wave of pressure.

She should have died, and probably would have, had it not been for the stranger who carried her from the razed building. She hadn't gotten a good look at his face, but he carried himself with a countenance few people possessed. His arms had been powerful and had easily borne her weight. His hair was black, thick, long and wavy, yet a few strands of silver were visible in the dark mane. She remembered a band of Celtic knots tattooed around his upper arm, which somehow complimented the man's thick brogue.

God, why can't I remember anything more, she thought with trepidation. Her thoughts were jumbled and none of the pieces seemed to fit together in the right order. Caitriona touched her forehead where a bandage was covering what she presumed would be a rather ugly wound. *That could explain why I can't remember anything,* she said more to herself in an effort to ward off the unyielding panic that was threatening to overtake her. She raised herself cautiously to her elbows and looked around. The room was spacious, with two other hospital beds in somewhat close proximity. They were both empty. On the wall behind her, panels of lights kept a pulsating beat and provided the only sound in the otherwise noiseless room.

She placed her feet slowly on the floor and sat for a moment, squeezing her eyes shut, willing the blackness to disappear. As she regained her focus and the room quit spinning, she was dimly aware of a solitary figure working on one of the instrument panels in the outer room. The woman obviously hadn't noticed her, or was unconcerned. Either way, Caitriona needed answers and this woman appeared to be her only source of information.

Pushing herself up from the sterile, cold medical bed, Caitriona braced herself as a wave of blackness passed over her, and the pounding in her head built to a throbbing crescendo. She became acutely aware that the panels behind her had stopped flashing and the room had become eerily quiet.

"You mustn't try to stand yet," said the solitary woman from across the room.

Caitriona pressed her fingertips to her temples. Some pain killers were definitely in order.

The woman came closer and placed a steadying hand on Caitriona's arm. "Please, just try to rest. You've been through quite an ordeal." The woman flashed Caitriona a sincere smile, showing even, beautifully white teeth. Although older than Caitriona by about twenty years, the woman had aged gracefully, with a complexion that belied her current age. Her eyes were an amazing color of aqua green, and heavy strawberry blonde curls hung halfway down her back. Effortlessly, she eased Caitriona back onto the exam bed.

"Where am I?" asked Caitriona. The pounding refused to abate and the short exertion had left her breathless and lightheaded.

"There will be plenty of time for questions later," replied the woman. "My name is Doctor Fiona MacKinnon. Please, you must try to rest."

Caitriona didn't want to lie down; at least not here. Something didn't feel right. She closed her eyes and then opened them slowly, willing the pounding in her head to subside. "If you could just get me some Tylenol, I'm sure I'll be alright," Caitriona said as she became aware of a slow, dull ringing sound that seemed to emanate from the medical equipment and panels lining the exam room.

"MacKinnon," she said, pronouncing each syllable slowly. "I've heard that name before." Caitriona brushed the hair from her face, closing her eyes as she tried to recall the memory.

"I see our patient has awakened," said a somewhat familiar voice from the doorway.

Caitriona glanced up to see a striking Asian man peering at her from the doorway. His smile was enchanting and reached his eyes. Tiny laughter lines framed his eyes, evidence of one who found life amusing and enjoyed sharing it with others. He came over and extended his hand to Caitriona in a warm greeting.

"Caitriona, this is Lieutenant Commander Lee Tadeo," said Dr. MacKinnon, giving the new arrival a look that was more cautionary than warm.

"I'm in a military institution," Caitriona said hesitantly, staring at the Lieutenant Commander's outstretched hand, before accepting it in greeting. "You're the man from the bus stop," she continued. Dr. MacKinnon and the Lieutenant Commander glanced at each other, but otherwise were careful not to confirm or deny her assumptions.

"The Commander will be in to talk with you shortly," Lieutenant Commander Tadeo replied cheerily. "He is busy at the moment, but asked me to personally welcome you." Lee flashed another grin before moving next to her.

"Welcome me where?" Caitriona asked, fear making her voice seem unusually high pitched. She placed her hand over her eyes. The headache was becoming unbearable. "Please, can someone just tell me where I am and how badly I'm injured?"

Dr. MacKinnon stepped to the other side of the bed across from the Lieutenant Commander and adjusted the monitor so the lights ceased their incessant blinking. "Caitriona, you've suffered an injury to your head and to your leg," Dr. MacKinnon said as she carefully removed the small bandage that covered Caitriona's right temple and brow. "The injuries are not life threatening, but you do need to rest." She looked at the injury and carefully pulled the bandage back in place. She eased Caitriona gently to the pillow and carefully removed the bandage around her leg.

Caitriona closed her eyes and tried to gather her thoughts. *This place is wrong*, she thought wildly, fighting back the panic that threatened to overtake her. Opening her eyes, Caitriona looked cautiously from one face to the other as Dr. MacKinnon finished examining her leg, removing the bandage around her thigh. *Why would she remove the bandage*, she thought; the edges of her memory still hazy. She reached down to touch her thigh, but the doctor pulled the blanket around her legs, effectively cutting off her efforts.

"Who is in charge?" Caitriona asked with more bravado than she felt.

Lieutenant Commander Tadeo looked at Dr. MacKinnon and flashed Caitriona a rather guarded smile. "The Commander will be in to see you shortly, Caitriona," Lee said. "Until then, please accept our hospitality and rest. In fact, you must be hungry. I'll have something brought to you at once." He opened his mouth as if to say something else, but instead, merely nodded toward the doctor and walked purposefully from the room.

Caitriona watched the man's quick departure, noting the guarded expression he gave the doctor. "How did he know my name?" Caitriona asked, doubt edging her voice. "I don't believe I've ever met you before, and I'm pretty sure I didn't introduce myself on the bus." A sharp pain at the base of her skull made Caitriona grip her head, willing herself not to be sick. Dr. MacKinnon reached out with a strange, oblong looking instrument and lightly touched it to the base of Caitriona's neck. The pain subsided immediately. Caitriona lowered her hands slowly and opened her eyes, tears brimming beneath the surface.

"That was a pain reliever I just administered," said Dr. MacKinnon. "You shouldn't feel anything for several hours, but if the pain returns, please let me know. I can adjust the dosage." Caitriona took full advantage of the relief she felt and swung her legs to the floor, standing shakily. She hastily blinked back tears as she tried to regain the upper hand. Dr. MacKinnon moved quickly to Caitriona's side, concern evident in her aqua green eyes.

"I'm tired of not getting any answers," Caitriona spat vehemently, fear giving her courage she didn't feel. "Where is this Commander you both speak of, but who couldn't be bothered to see me himself?" Caitriona demanded.

"Please, Caitriona. Just try to ..."

Caitriona reached out quickly and, with a flawlessly executed martial arts move, pinned the doctor's left arm behind her body in a vice-like grip. Dr. MacKinnon gave a startled yelp and arched her back, trying to relieve the pain. Caitriona's grip grew tighter as she forced the doctor to her knees. "Now I'm going to get a few answers," Caitriona said in a low, even tone, surprised at how well she controlled her voice despite the trembling she felt inside.

"Where am I?" Caitriona tightened her grip just slightly to give emphasis to her words. The gesture had the desired effect as Dr. MacKinnon cried out with pain.

"I can't answer any questions, Caitriona," Dr. MacKinnon panted between bursts of pain. "Please ..." Her words trailed off as Caitriona struck the back of the doctor's neck with her free hand, dropping her into an unconscious state. "Then we will just have to find someone who can," Caitriona muttered. She pulled the edges of the hospital gown further around her body and was thankful that her slender form made it easy for the gown to close. Still, Caitriona looked furtively around the room for any signs of her clothes.

With time against her, Caitriona abandoned the search, pulling the drawstrings of the gown around her waist. She moved to where she had seen the doctor and the Lieutenant Commander enter the room, and was nearly toppled by the Lieutenant Commander as he entered bearing a tray of food. Without hesitation, Caitriona pushed past him, hooking the back of his calf with her right leg, toppling him effortlessly and bringing a heap of meats and pastries raining down upon him.

Lee quickly bolted to his feet and turned to face his opponent. "Caitriona, no one here will hurt you," he said softly. "Let's just sit ..."

Caitriona spun and brought her right foot in contact with his jaw. She heard his expletive as she bolted for the door, which had thankfully remained open. Out in the hall, she barely paused long enough to hear him call for reinforcements before she broke into an all-out run, the pain in her leg strangely muted, considering the hole she had seen earlier. Whether caused by the Lieutenant Commander's call for help, or an alarm she had somehow triggered, when she fled the room, the hall went suddenly dark, and an ambient red light cast the hall in eerie shadows. She had a vague sensation of déjà-vu and realized she had played out this scene in her earlier vision-dream. An ear-splitting alarm brought her back to the present and left her in no doubt that soon the corridors would be teeming with men searching for her.

Caitriona fought through her panic as she realized she could very well be on a ship and escape was futile. Her heart was beating wildly, drowning out even the cacophony of noise emanating from the alarm. She continued running with no thought as to direction. The corridors were a series of turns and mazes that left Caitriona breathless and discombobulated. She forced herself to slow down. Leaning momentarily against the wall, Caitriona pressed her hand to her heart, gulping in deep breaths of air. She had to think. The Lieutenant Commander had clearly been of Asian descent. North Korean, perhaps? Was she in the middle of a political battle? Had she been taken captive only to be displayed on a North Korean station proclaiming Americans as the infidels they surely knew them to be? She pushed this thought away. After all, the doctor was clearly not Asian. There must be another explanation.

Caitriona could hear footsteps behind her and began running again, furtively looking around for a place to hide as she turned down one corridor and then another. She inhaled sharply as she realized this would probably not end well.

"*Is leor din!*"

Caitriona spun around at the commanding authority that was audible even above the wailing of the alarm. She stared at the tall, imposing stranger. His presence clearly bespoke his position. Without being told, Caitriona knew this was the Commander; the man-wall who had held her upright earlier when the bus had unceremoniously slammed to a stop. He exuded authority. The steel grey of his eyes penetrated her emerald green ones as she met his stare with an unflinching candor. As with their first encounter, his look sent an electrical pulse through her body, heat rising instantly to flush her soft ivory cheeks.

Caitriona's heart was beating so fast she thought it would leap from her chest, but she managed to rein in her emotions and appear in control. "I want answers," she said with more confidence than she felt. She took a step backward instinctively, only to be brought up short against the wall - a tactical error on her part that gave her adversary the upper hand.

"Ye are nae in a position to demand anythin', *Alainn.*" Duncan MacKinnon spoke softly in a thick brogue. His eyes followed the rise and fall of her breasts beneath the simple cotton hospital gown she wore, and his gaze lingered on the disarray of red-brown curls that reached nearly to her waist. He stepped closer, closing the distance between them quickly, rather like a makeshift game of cat and mouse.

Caitriona was in awe of the giant that stood before her. He towered a foot or more above her, with broad shoulders and muscles that lent him a powerful air. His beautiful steel-grey eyes seemed to sparkle with an unmannered amusement. He had traded the earlier, tailored suit for a uniform of sorts that did little to conceal his muscles. She realized how small and vulnerable she was. There would be no way past him and, in a physical match, it would be no contest. "What do you want from me?" she whispered breathlessly. She was dismayed to see that her breathing was giving away her physical limitations. She inhaled sharply, determined to take a deep breath and still her nerves. Yet she felt as if the narrow corridors were closing and the air was becoming thinner.

The Commander closed the distance yet again and, this time, Caitriona pushed away from the wall in an attempt to get around him. Without effort, he brought his arm around her slender waist and pulled her close. Caitriona trembled against him and tried to push away. He only held her tighter, searching her deep emerald eyes.

"*Ciunas,*" he said softly.

Caitriona didn't recognize the language, but felt strangely comforted by the strength in that one word. She looked directly into his steel-grey eyes, noting her own, scared reflection mirrored within them. It wasn't enough, however, to stop the fear that penetrated her. She freed one arm from between their pinned bodies and tried to slam the heel of her palm to his chin. Duncan deflected the blow easily and chuckled softly, "Ye've had some trainin' in the martial arts, lass, and ye have the heart of a warrior. But ye've no need for that here. Ye are safe."

Caitriona realized she must have been hurt worse then she had originally thought. Her breathing was much more labored than usual and the headache was returning. She felt light headed and, for a moment, leaned into the warmth and strength of the Commander's arms. The hardness of his chest, however, was enough to jolt her back to reality. She tried to raise her knee quickly to his groin, but he was too fast - and too accomplished. He spun her around so that he held her firmly in front of him, her arms pinned securely behind her back. Duncan chuckled softly.

Blackness threatened to engulf Caitriona as her breathing became even more labored. Duncan loosened his hold on her and lifted her up against him, her knees crooked over his left arm, her head lolling against his right, and swept her into his arms. Refusing to give up, she beat her fists against his chest, but the blows were ineffective, like the annoying bites of a mosquito. *"Ciunas,* Seer. I am nae here to hurt ye." She struck one more time, then her eyes rolled upward and she went limp.

***

Duncan held Caitriona effortlessly as she slumped in his arms. He marveled at the firmness of her muscles and simultaneously delighted in the softness of her skin. Her face was pale and her breathing labored. The atmospheric conditions of the ship were far less than what the girl was accustomed to on her home planet, and he worried that any sort of physical adjustment would take more time than he had.

He maneuvered his way easily through intertwining corridors; Caitriona's slight frame nestled comfortably in his arms. He passed the medical center with hardly a pause, before continuing to his quarters. The girl would be safer in his quarters, and he would be better able to help her adjust, he reasoned. He knew he should take her to the medical center, but an overwhelming need to be near her, to protect her, kept him focused on his quarters. He shifted her slight weight in his arms and could feel the soft outline of her breasts as they brushed against his chest. *Mine,* the single word echoed through his mind as he felt the now familiar charge that pulsed between them.

Duncan entered his spacious quarters, the metal door retracting automatically as he neared. Once inside, the door closed quietly behind him, while the lights automatically lit the interior in bright light. "Dim lights," Duncan said softly, so not to disturb his charge. The lights dimmed automatically as the computer recognized his voice command and complied with the request.

He crossed the room to his sleeping quarters and laid Caitriona on the massive four poster bed. She groaned slightly and rolled to her side, bringing her knees up to her chest; whether for warmth or comfort, Duncan didn't know. He pulled a day blanket across the top of her, smoothing the tangled locks from across her forehead before retreating from the room.

"Connect me to the medical center," Duncan said in a low voice. The computer complied immediately.

"Duncan, where is the girl?" Fiona's voice was mildly disapproving over the intercom system.

"Relax, Fi," Duncan growled. "She's restin' in my quarters. She'll need some attention, though. Her breathin' is still verra labored and her sleep is restless. Are ye alright?" Concern laced his voice.

"Only my pride has been seriously injured," she replied hastily. "I'm on my way. And try not to frighten her." She was gone before he could retort, and Duncan was left with only the soft breathing of the girl whose future he had managed to change within a matter of hours. What had he done? He had broken his sacred oaths, destroyed a young woman's life, and sentenced himself and his men to a life of hiding—or death—if they failed in their quest.

To further complicate matters, he had no idea how he was going to elicit the lass's help. He could always use force, but he stopped short of the idea; physical force on women had never appealed to him. Besides, the young lass was no match for his physical strength. He would succeed only in frightening her. He needed to gain her confidence though, and quickly. There simply wasn't time to soothe her fears and gain her approval.

"Dr. MacKinnon requests entry," said a softly feminine, computerized voice.

"Allow entry," Duncan said as the door retracted to allow his sister entry to the room.

Duncan nodded to his sleeping chambers and motioned his sister to follow him. He watched as his sister crossed to his charge's side and proceeded to run a long cylindrical medical device over her previous injuries. *Goddess, what had they done*, he mused silently, momentarily suffering an attack of morality.

Finishing her scans, Fiona packed away her instruments and motioned for Duncan to follow her from the room. "She will be fine, Duncan. It will simply take her some time to adjust to the atmospheric conditions of the ship. On top of that, she has a serious head injury and is recovering from three broken ribs and a deep puncture wound to her thigh. We'll simply have to take it slow for now."

"Fi, ye know better than anyone that we dinna have the luxury of time." Duncan brushed a hand through his thick black hair, pausing before facing his sister. "We will be home in six weeks. Will she be ready to face the council then?" He had devoted his life to the cause, and had never allowed one ounce of regret to ever cross his features, and yet now, standing in front of his sister, he knew he looked every bit his thirty-eight years.

"She'll be well by then." Fiona said softly. "I've given her a sedative that should help her sleep."

Duncan smiled wearily at his sister and sighed, glancing over his shoulder at the girl who slept in his chambers, unaware of how he would obtain her help in the days to come. "Let me take a look at you, Duncan," Fiona admonished slightly. "You haven't slept well in days, and I'm sure you've neglected your nutritional needs as well."

"I'm fine, Fi." He used the childhood endearment he had given her when they were younger. Both of Scottish descent, Fiona had chosen to adopt the English dialect, connecting more with the heritage of her foster parents. While Duncan fully embraced his Celtic heritage, he often slipped in and out of the Gaelic language, his brogue becoming more pronounced with his emotions. Although both siblings had grown up together, neither knew their biological parents. Each was a product of genetic engineering: Fiona engineered for her acute intelligence and further trained in medicinal science, and Duncan engineered for superior strength, military strategy, and intelligence. Although both were products of the New World Order's quest for genetically engineered superiority, each was loyal to the Templars' quest for freedom, and had carried the secret since their early teens. Both envisioned a world free of tyranny, structure, and the Order's rule; where all could live in harmony, free to choose their own path and raise families that were not predisposed to genetic selection and genetic engineering.

Fiona searched her brother's face for signs that he was lying. Finding none, she gestured·to the girl in her brother's sleeping chambers. "Keep her warm and let her rest. It's what she needs right now. I've repaired all the physical damage, but the emotional scars will take some time." Fiona embraced her brother and gave him a light kiss on the cheek. He returned the kiss and watched as she exited, leaving him once again to his own dark broodings.

Chapter Three

The injury that we do to a man must be such that we need not fear his vengeance. Steve Perry

Brady Hawkins self-consciously pushed the wire-rimmed spectacles that sat askew on his face farther up his nose. He hated wearing them; they were a constant reminder of his imperfection, and the very thing the New World Order sought to eliminate. A chemical accident three years ago had nearly blinded him and, while doctors were able to save both eyes and even restore vision to his right eye, he was still nearly blind in his left eye. The glasses allowed him to see perfectly, but were an ever present reminder that he was now damaged goods.

He sighed heavily, staring intently at the reading monitor that had delivered today's status to him. His outfit in the New World Order army had found another rogue band of Dwellers and had exterminated them on sight. This marked a hundred and sixty-one useless eaters that his group of highly-trained soldiers had eliminated in the course of a month. He knew they were making progress, but the war was slow and regardless of the victories they had scored, the Dwellers were fierce in their resolve to live apart from the Order and in accordance to the old laws. He shook his head absently, seemingly unaware that his spectacles had once again slipped down the bridge of his nose.

Hawkins focused his attention on the latest missive that would give their organization an edge. He was acutely aware of the Templars' efforts to time travel. What he wasn't sure of was their reason. As a result, he patiently allowed the group to continue with their secret mission as he watched and waited for events to become clear. He had long suspected that the Templars existed and that they were sympathetic to the Dwellers; the name given to the men and women who were not genetically engineered and who lived outside the Order's laws. The Dwellers had succeeded in randomizing their residences and had gone underground in an attempt to find protection from the Order's rule.

But the Order was ruthless in its drive to extinguish imperfections, and Hawkins took great pride in the number of kills he and his men had personally executed in the past year. Nearly five thousand Dwellers had been executed under his watch; a number that no other army had been able to top. He smiled, pushing his glasses back up his nose, squinting at the report he spent hours reading.

The Dwellers disgusted him. Their constant pursuit of freedom and disgusting sexual acts of procreation further infuriated him. Hawkins sat down in one of the camp chairs and stirred the fire with an iron poker as flames sparked and grew taller. His musings became dark and he longed to travel to Hitler's time and join the ranks of the superior few that had put Hitler's notion of perfection in motion.

Hawkins set the poker down next to his chair and once again punched up the report on the electronic device he carried with him. He scanned the missive quickly, a smile forming at the corners of his mouth. This next assignment would be a rare one indeed. He and his men had been hand selected to find a weapon the Templars were hiding. The report didn't provide much information, but Hawkins knew the intelligence was only a matter of time. They would leave at first dawn and raid an underground Dweller habitat; an action that would serve to flesh out the miscreants. He would round up every child and torture and execute each one until the Dwellers provided him with the information he was after. And once he was confident they had shared everything with him, he would gas them all in the very chambers they called home.

Chapter Four

Those who cannot remember the past are condemned to repeat it.
George Santayana

Caitriona snuggled deeper into her covers, finding solace in the warmth that caressed her body. She was dimly aware of the rich aroma of coffee invading her sleep. Caitriona stretched languidly and slowly opened her eyes. Panic gripped her as she struggled to find familiar settings. Images of a tall, dark stranger rushed suddenly into vision as memories of the previous night came flooding back.

Caitriona sat up with a start, flinging the warm cover from her body as she frantically searched for an exit. A slight pounding at her temples reminded her to move more slowly and she squeezed her eyes shut tight against the pain.

"Ciunas," Commanding, yet warm; Caitriona found succor in that one word, and looked up at the man who was responsible for saving her life.

"Where am I?" she asked softly, her heart beating loudly as she struggled to find familiarity in the new surroundings.

"Catie, lass, ye're onboard a military starship." Duncan softly let the weight of his words register before continuing. "Ye willna be harmed," he softly emphasized, handing her a steaming mug of coffee.

Caitriona accepted the coffee, breathing deeply of the thick, hickory aroma. "Military starship?" she questioned, arching one brow, her eyes moving around the room, straining to find a window, taking in the rich furnishings and unusual art. "You mean, like on Star Trek?" Her heart was beating faster. *Why in the world would the military want to hold me?*

Duncan chuckled softly at the reference to "Star Trek," the science fiction cult classic that had captured television viewers for nearly five decades. "Aye, lass, something like that, although I'm afraid without the conveniences of 'beaming' in and out." Duncan sat down in an oversized leather chair near the bed and poured himself a cup of coffee, his eyes never leaving her face. Propping his feet up on a small round ottoman, he watched her expression carefully. Caitriona merely pulled the covers up snugly around her small frame and sipped the steaming mug of coffee. The warmth penetrated her body and helped ease the ache in her head.

"Catie, I need to tell ye some things that ye may find hard to believe," said Duncan softly. "But ye must remember one thing; I will never lie to ye, lass. Never."

Caitriona was uncertain where this was headed. Twenty-four hours ago she had never met the man, let alone bundle her faith in him. Not giving away the internal war she was waging, she only looked at him and arched one eyebrow, questioning his integrity.

"Computer, release all images," Duncan said suddenly. There was a soft hum as the art that had adorned the walls disappeared, and beautiful views of the stars overtook the room. Caitriona's gaze swept the area, her mouth parting in silent appreciation and wonder. She stood, letting the covers slip to the bed, and crossed to the nearest window, handing the coffee to Duncan as she moved past him. She reached out, as if to touch the stars, but instead met only resistance beneath her hand. Caitriona's eyes grew big as she pushed harder against the invisible shield.

"'Tis a force field that willna allow ye to pass beyond it," Duncan said, crossing to her and pulling her small hand into his; the warmth of his hand immediately chasing away the chill. She looked into his eyes, astonishment clearly visible in her soft features.

"But it looks transparent," Caitriona protested.

"Aye, it is … to some degree," Duncan replied. Caitriona turned to stare at the stars, pulling her hand from his, immediately missing the strength and warmth of the brief contact.

"I don't understand," Caitriona said, wrinkling her brow. "Am I on a spaceship?" The question was more of a statement, but Duncan nodded affirmatively, waiting for the information to be absorbed.

"I didn't think commercial space travel was available yet," Caitriona stated slowly, Duncan's silence giving rise to her growing panic. She shook her head slowly, stepping backwards in an attempt to disengage herself from the information that was unfolding before her like the denouement in a mystery novel whose twisted ending was completely unexpected.

"No," Caitriona stated simply yet forcefully, as the realization of where she was begun to register. "I want to go home ... now!" Her eyes were like emerald daggers as panic welled up within her.

"Catie, lass, I canna do that," Duncan replied evenly.

"No!" She said again, more emphatically. Tears were beginning to brim beneath her eyes and she blinked several times to clear them. She pulled her upper lip beneath her teeth and bit hard in an effort to quell the fear and emotions that were making their way, unbridled, to the surface.

Caitriona spun around, refusing to let Duncan see the fear and tears brimming beneath the surface of unshed emotion. She had to ask, but fear caused her to inhale sharply instead, her body trembling. He placed his large hands on her shoulders, the warmth from his hands like a searing iron where he touched her. She couldn't control the trembling, "What year?" she asked quietly.

Duncan's reply was soft but firm, "'Tis the year 2212, lass."

Caitriona slid to the floor, tears flooding her face, no longer denying the anguish and loneliness she felt. She cupped her face in her hands and sobbed openly, the pain and fear finally finding an outlet through the tears that made their way, unchecked, down her cheeks.

"Caitriona, I ..."

"Get out!" She spat.

"Caitriona, we need to talk ..."

Caitriona raised her eyes and glared at her abductor. "The only thing we need to discuss is how I'm getting home."

Duncan shook his head, his silence telling her everything she needed to know.

***

It was late evening when Duncan finally dared return to his quarters. Caitriona hadn't moved from the floor. She lay curled in a ball, her hair a glorious cascade of autumn colors that accented the soft ivory of her skin. Her sleep was restless and he noticed her eyes were swollen from crying. He stood staring at her for several minutes, once again cursing the fates that had brought them together. He had to find a way to gain her trust and, more importantly, the use of the rare gift she possessed.

He sighed heavily, knowing there was no turning back. But his emotions were raging. What had he done? She was barely more than a child, drawn into an intricately woven political battle that spawned several centuries. Would she ever understand? Would she ever forgive him?

Duncan ran a hand through his thick hair, acutely aware of how drawn he was to the girl. He felt a fierce need to protect her and to share his world with her. He also knew it went deeper than that. He felt pulled to her, as if they were joined by something larger than this time, this place.

He bent down and scooped her slender frame effortlessly into his arms, reveling in the feel of her. She whimpered softly and snuggled into him, her hospital gown parting slightly to show delicate curves that tantalized him with a sweet promise of something more. *Ach, she is beautiful,* he thought. He laid her gently on the bed, once again covering her with thick blankets for warmth. She turned from him and snuggled deeper into the covers. When her breathing had once again become deep and even, he retired to the outer rooms, lost in his own private thoughts of politics and war.

Duncan's private quarters opened onto the bridge, which he cursed silently, as his bridge officers would have heard most of the exchange between him and the girl earlier that day. On a starship there was little privacy and, as Commander, this was even more evident. Duncan sat down wearily in his chair, staring at the stars as they streamed past the large starship.

The space program had been initiated late in the twenty second century, after the near annihilation of the human population. The Church, backed by the fanatical group the New World Order, was at the backbone of the destruction, but few knew of this. Led for countless centuries by prophets and men of God, the world had put their trust in a God and a church that had long ago abandoned them. Indeed, it wasn't until late in the twenty-first century that scholars and archeologists began to piece together and uncover the biggest conspiracy that ever existed: The Bible was fiction; its priests, powerful men ruled by greed and power, and Jesus Christ merely a man. *Albeit a man with special gifts,* Duncan thought.

As millions followed the teachings of the Church blindly, their power grew. But only a handful of men, the Templars, knew the fallacy of what the church preached. Powerless after centuries of hiding, the Templars could do little to stop the false prophecies and teachings of the Church. As the Church grew in power, they sought out the Templars and nearly succeeded in destroying them. Only some of the Templars had survived and had gone into hiding, carefully preserving their lineage and their secret until they would one day again be powerful enough to stop the Church and preach the true message.

Duncan got up and walked over to a panel on the wall and pressed a button. Immediately, the large, oval shaped panel slid from view and, in its place, was a view of the stars sliding past at light speed. Duncan ran his hands through his thick hair and continued to gaze at the stars, wondering what his life would have been like had the Templars succeeded in their mission thousands of years earlier. *We would be living in a much different world*, Duncan thought wistfully. Perhaps he, and others like him, would have been free to choose their own path and live their own lives, free of religious persecution, tyranny and the New World Order.

Nestled comfortably into Duncan's oversized sleeping unit, Caitriona stirred softly, intruding into the solace of his thoughts. He glanced over at her still form; her deep, even breathing indicated she was in a sound sleep. *Better tae rest now, Alainn. Ye will need yer strength in the days that follow.* Duncan closed the viewing panel and retired to the lounge in the outer room, his charge unaware of the destiny she was about to fulfill.

***

Caitriona paused to listen for the footsteps she knew were right behind her. Up ahead, she could see daylight and hear the faint sound of ocean waves. *Freedom*, she thought frantically. Her legs felt heavy and she could barely pull herself up the long stone stairs that stretched upward and curved out of sight. *I must have gone deeper than I thought*, she mused, her hands sliding along the cold wet stone which provided no warmth or solace for her flight. Nor did she have any conscious understanding of where "deeper" was.

She paused for a moment; her breathing much more labored, when she heard footsteps behind her - closer now, as if they were not bound by any sort of physical limitations. Caitriona quickened her steps, gasping for each breath as the spiral of steps continued its ascent. Panic gripped her, but she was unsure why. She knew only that she had to reach the top before the darkness behind her overtook her.

The light from above became stronger and she knew she was getting closer. The sound of waves crashing against the shore also became more distinguished and gave her renewed energy to continue her exhausting pace. As the steps became deeper and more treacherous, she looked down and saw that the near-transparent dressing gown she was wearing was becoming entangled around her ankles, hindering her progress and slowing her efforts. She tugged at the sheer garment, and gave a startled cry when she felt something heavy push her from above. Her arms flailed out from her side, grasping for something to hold onto, yet finding nothing but cold, smooth stone as she started to fall. The stairs evaporated suddenly into nothingness and she realized she was plunging through ice cold water to her death.

***

Caitriona gasped in her sleep, wincing at some unseen terror. Duncan was alert immediately and crossed the room, quickly closing the distance in several strides. He was unsure whether to wake her. She seemed to be having a nightmare. *Or was it more than that?* Duncan rested his hand lightly on her forehead, noting the damp locks and the beads of perspiration that lingered on her skin. He brushed her hair away from her face, aware of the worry that was evident in the crease of her brow. He touched her arm lightly and she awoke suddenly, sitting up and clawing at his hand. He could see clearly that she was disoriented and frightened. Quickly, grasping both her hands in his, Duncan pulled her close, the hard lines of his muscles lending her strength against the lingering fear her nightmare brought.

"*Alainn*, ye are safe here," he spoke quietly the Scottish endearment that meant "beautiful one" in Gaelic, his thick brogue invading the silence. Caitriona was terrified, her eyes darting around the room to find the hidden terrors that lurked in the shadows. She tried to force her hands away from him, kicking at the covers in an effort to free herself and flee her unseen terror.

Duncan held her hands more tightly, placing both between their chests as he leaned in close. Her body trembled uncontrollably and her breathing was short and shallow. "*Alainn*, it is nothing more than a dream. Ye're safe now, lass." He could feel her begin to relax against him as his words calmed her tremors.

Duncan released her hands tenuously and pulled her to him, one hand stroking her hair. After several moments had passed and her breathing had once again returned to normal, he pulled away slightly to look into her eyes, his own face reflected back.

"It seemed so real," Caitriona's voice was barely a whisper as she placed her head against his hard chest.

"*Ciunas*," his voice was equally soft and Caitriona nestled closer. Curled in his arms, Duncan could feel the soft beating of her heart and her jasmine scent intoxicating his senses. After several minutes, he felt her body grow heavy with sleep, her hands falling gently against his chest. He kissed the top of her head as the sweet arms of sleep claimed his charge once again that night.

***

Duncan had remained with Caitriona until he was certain she was sleeping peacefully, and had then slipped quietly from the room and retired to the outer chamber where he spent a somewhat restless night. Images of Caitriona's teary face and sorrow filled eyes invaded his dreams, dispelling any notion of sleep.

Filling a cup with steaming coffee, Duncan sat down at his desk, his thoughts turning to the young woman sleeping in the other room. He hadn't anticipated the intense emotions that had coursed through him.

"Lieutenant Commander Tadeo requests entrance," stated the feminine computer voice, startling him from his persistent musings. Duncan gave the instruction to enter and looked up as his first officer and best friend since childhood entered his quarters.

Lee gestured toward Duncan's sleeping quarters and arched an eyebrow. "What are you planning to do with her, Highlander?" Lee used the familiar endearment he had given his friend when they had first met at the Global Academy nearly twenty years ago. They had bonded instantly, and later realized each was a Templar, infused with their traditions and beliefs since childhood. It had been a natural friendship and one that grew stronger over time. A lifetime of guarding their secret, covertly fighting their enemy, and relentlessly pursuing an elusive notion of freedom had bonded each man to the other for life. Both genetically selected and bred for their physical endurance, fighting abilities, and intelligence, they each stood in stark contrast to the other. At 6'6", Duncan towered over his friend by at least nine inches. Lee, while shorter than Duncan, proved to be exceptional with the sword and bow. Both men had become expert fighters during their time in the academy and had risen quickly to the top of their class in academics. Of Korean descent, Lee embraced his roots, proudly utilizing his inherited skills in battle.

"What I was sent here to do in the first place," Duncan replied wearily. "Goddess, help us all." Duncan removed the leather strap that kept his hair tied neatly back and ran a hand through the errant locks. He had retired his outer jacket so that strong muscles were clearly visible through the form-fitted shirt he wore underneath. A Celtic tattoo encircled his upper bicep and lent him a roguish arrogance he neither embraced nor dissuaded.

"Duncan, tell me you are not developing feelings for the girl?" Lee asked him. His English was perfect, without a trace of the Asian dialect that was prevalent among his people. "We knew the mission would not be easy, and that people's lives would be altered," he paused before emphasizing his next remarks, "perhaps permanently." Lee moved to a chair closer to the desk Duncan was seated behind. "And we also know how important it is that we succeed. You can't let anything get in the way of that … or anyone," his friend softly emphasized the last word.

Duncan stood and began pacing the floor, casting a glance at the lone figure who lay curled in his bed. "She doesna' even understand why she is here. How am I supposed to gain her trust when she sees me as the enemy?" Duncan stopped pacing to face his friend, deliberately not sharing the extent of his earlier encounter with Caitriona.

"I don't know, my friend, and I don't envy your position. But we all have a job to do and the lives of thousands depend on us," Lee reminded him. "Let her into your world, Highlander, but keep in mind we have a mission to complete; that we have been sworn to complete. She is frightened and alone … and most likely doesn't realize how valuable she is. Help her to see her worth…and the worthiness of our cause." Lee ran a hand through his dark, neatly clipped hair and then smiled a precocious and somewhat impish smile. "And whatever you do, don't frighten her!" He clapped his friend on the back in an encouraging embrace. "I've got to go check on operations." Lee walked toward the door and then turned toward his friend. "Duncan, we have trained a lifetime for this mission. We have to succeed." With that, Lee turned and left the warrior to his own dark thoughts.

Chapter Five

Indeed, history is nothing more than a tableau of crimes and misfortunes.
Voltaire

Caitriona awoke once again to the rich aroma of coffee and a tray of warm pastries placed on the nightstand next to her bed. Stretching languidly, she let out a sigh and reached for a scone, realizing she hadn't eaten since boarding the starship. Her stomach rumbled in appreciation of the tasty treat and she ate another eagerly before reaching for the coffee.

Looking around at the richly furnished room, she ran a hand through her tangled hair, wishing she could shower and change her clothes. Her face was still swollen from crying and emotionally she was still unsettled. There were so many unanswered questions that she feared she wouldn't even know where to start. But one thing she was certain of … she needed answers if she was ever going to find a way back home. Feeling more resolved, she placed the coffee mug on the table and climbed out of the oversized down bed, looking around for her clothes.

"I can draw ye a bath, and bring ye some fresh clothes," said a deeply masculine voice from behind her. Caitriona turned around to see the commander staring at her intently. His hair was no longer tied back but hung loose over his shoulders in thick, heavy waves. There was a shadow on his face that hinted at the full beard that would eventually take its place. His tunic hung open at one side, providing a nice view of hard, even muscles, while slightly wrinkled trews bore evidence that he had slept very little.

"When can I leave?" Caitriona's voice once again held more bravado than she felt.

"*Nior, Alainn*," he spoke quietly, but firmly.

She turned from him and took the cup of coffee from the tray, letting the warmth of the cup ease the tension she felt. She could feel him behind her, but she refused to turn and meet his steel-grey eyes.

They remained like that for several minutes; the silence nearly impalpable. He broke their reverie first, his voice hard and clipped. "We have things we need to discuss, Catie."

"Aye," she mocked and turned forcefully, nearly spilling the coffee she held in her hands. "I want answers! No, that's not really true. You can keep your damn answers and your secrets. I just want to go home." She met his gaze, fire blazing in her eyes.

"I canna do that," Duncan met her scrutiny, refusing to back down.

"Cannot, or will not?" Caitriona asked tersely. She broke the intensity of their gaze first and slumped wearily to the bed, determined to try another approach. After taking a deep breath, she tried again. "Why me?" she asked, lifting her gaze to lock with his beneath long, thick lashes. "Was I simply in the wrong place at the wrong time, or is there a reason for this abduction?"

Duncan sat down beside her and took the cup from her hands, placing it on the tray beside the bed. He reached for her hands, his thumbs lightly caressing the tops of her knuckles. The gesture sent shock waves across her body and ignited a fire deep in her belly. Her heart beat faster as he captured her gaze and held it locked in his own. She pulled away from him abruptly, unsure of her feelings, yet knowing she wanted and needed answers.

"*Alainn*, you were nae an accident," Duncan replied softly. "Indeed, you are a rather … rare prize." His gaze wandered appreciatively over the curves of her body before returning to her emerald eyes that were now ablaze with fury.

"You'll have to do better than that, Highlander," she used the endearment Lee had given him mockingly. "I want answers." She paused. "And then I want a way home." She drew her knees up to her chin, her eyes challenging him.

Duncan ignored her latter request. "I will answer all your questions, Catie. I have nae wish to keep anythin' from ye." He stood up quickly, putting distance between them. "*Alainn*, ye have certain … gifts that will be most beneficial in our fight for freedom." He paused, his words sounding heavy against her ears.

"Catie, the earthquake that shook yer home was part of a much larger plot to reduce the world population and put an organization called The New World Order into power," Duncan said.

"I've heard of them," Caitriona whispered, her brows furrowing in deeper concentration. "I thought they were largely a government conspiracy theory or some group that had been dislodged centuries ago."

Duncan chuckled lightly at her loose reference to history. "From yer perspective, I ken how ye would think that. No one was aware of how powerful the organization was until shortly after the 9.7 magnitude earthquake, and attempts to rebuild failed. In fact, rumors started circulating that a group had the power to create seemingly natural disasters that were anythin' but natural. Their agenda was to reduce the world population and slowly shift the balance of power in their favor."

At her inquisitive nod, Duncan continued. "And aye, they shifted the balance alright, and they managed to do it so quietly, so unobtrusively, that millions sat back silently and watched the slaughter, powerless to stop it and even more powerless to change course. In less than a year, the world population was reduced by 4.2 billion people. Those that remained were fearful and eagerly clung to any word, any hope of a brighter, safer future. The president became merely a puppet figure, controlled by the Order and manipulated by a handful of men in great power.

"The economy collapsed, famine was rampant and lawlessness reigned for the next fifteen years. Slowly, as the Order started to exert its authority, they offered a message of hope and peace to the people who remained. Ye have to understand, *Alainn*, this was a time of unrest and desperation. People would have clung to any sort of hope or salvation, and The New World Order provided people with just such a hope."

"What people didn't realize, however, was that they were being carefully manipulated by those verra people that offered them hope. At first, the new laws seemed reasonable. People complied willingly in exchange for a future that promised peace, health, enhanced productivity, and technological advancement.

"But, as time progressed, the Order's agenda became more apparent and included population control and genetic selection. Imagine, Catie, no economy, and scarcity of food. As the Order united countries and nations, they were slowly carving out their own agenda; one that included a master race that made Hitler look benign."

Caitriona sat fascinated at the historic revelations that in her time hadn't yet happened. She encouraged Duncan to continue, shivering slightly as the morose pictures he conjured were vivid reminders of the tyranny she escaped.

"Soon after the Order started to assert itself, a leader emerged from that group; Matthew LeConway. This man carved out an edict that left no doubt as to the objective or goals of the Order: eliminate those who were not essential to the preservation and continuation of the master race. For the next fifty years, genocide was rampant, and even as millions were being slaughtered, the Order was ensuring future generations would be intelligent, beautiful, strong and talented. In short, a master race was being carefully engineered.

"When LeConway died, his successor, Brady Hawkins, continued his quest, putting his own twisted spin on the Order's goals. He began using genetic selection to ensure only those with desired traits were brought into the world. Since the fiduciary system had collapsed, people worked instead to ensure their own survival and to further the Order's cause. The Genetics were brought up in cities rich in technology, education, and fine foods. They had the best of everythin' and were taught that genetic engineering was the only way to preserve their way of life.

"What the Order didn't realize was that the Dwellers were slowly growin' in number, backed by many of the master race who longed once again for equality and the right for all people to live their lives as they choose."

"Wait a minute. You lost me," she interjected. "Who are the Dwellers?"

"They are people forced to live outside the cities—often underground—simply because they are seen as genetically inferior. They are the ancestors of non-genetics who escaped the Order's persecution and went into hiding. Most of the Dwellers have lived their entire lives in an elaborate system of underground tunnels and chambers, carefully guarded and kept hidden from the Order's despotic massacres.

"There are Dwellers and Genetics alike that dinna want to live under the Order's oppressive rule any longer. But we are too few in number to overtake the Order. They are simply too large, well-supplied and, because of their technology, they are always one step ahead of us. We need a competitive advantage in order to level the playing field."

"So what does all this have to do with the fact that you kidnapped me?"

Duncan arched one eyebrow but refused to rise to the bait. Instead, he reached over and refilled her coffee, pouring himself a second cup as well. After he had set the pitcher on the table, he continued with his story.

"Plenty, but first hear me out." He raised his hand slightly, indicating she should hold any further comments. "*Ach*, Catie! The New World Order was the largest conspiracy ever manufactured and, while millions denied it could ever happen, it did! Generations before me have pushed for genetic selection, to the fatal detriment of billions." Duncan stood and moved quietly to the viewing screen, staring out at space as countless stars streamed by the ship in a shower of brilliant white light. A slight tic in his lower jaw bore evidence of the fury that his historical account invoked.

"Genetic selection started quietly late in your century. Once President Obama reversed the edict banning stem cell research, a flood gate was opened for scientists and researchers to experiment with science, and eventually genetics was taken to a whole new level. Parents concerned with debilitating and fatal diseases used genetic selection to screen for those diseases. Imagine being able to eliminate the possibility that your child would be born with Downs' Syndrome or Huntington's disease? The old would no longer be predisposed toward Alzheimer's. It was amazing technology that, unfortunately, opened the door for the New World Order."

Duncan turned to look at Caitriona, who sat quietly at the edge of the large bed, her hands folded lightly around her coffee mug, captivated by his story.

"Of course, it wasn't long before technology advanced enough to where we could genetically select the qualities we wanted in a child. And, while moral dilemmas played out in the media, the New World Order sat back quietly, pushing their own agenda through propaganda, intimidation, and growing popular consent. Catie, lass, they are not unlike your period's Hitler, building the master race he once envisioned. Only the New World Order wasn't alone. Backed by the Church, they were able to manipulate the masses and push their agenda even further. By the year 2180, the Order had managed to attain what your century worked so hard to eliminate: segregation. Only this new segregation wasn't based on color. Oh no, our century was far too enlightened for that. The Order crafted a race of intelligent, beautiful, and talented individuals who would have everything: power, status, prestige. And of course, they crafted a race of servers to ensure the elite's survival."

He paused, allowing Caitriona a chance to digest what he had said. Caitriona stood, and walked toward the outer door, her dressing gown breaking the silence as the material rustled beneath her. "Slavery," she whispered incredulously.

"Even now, Catie, most Genetics dinna want to admit what they ken to be true: The New World Order was behind mass genocide, genetic selection, and now genetic engineering. They are doing all this to build a master race that will serve their needs. In your century, think of the natural disasters that claimed millions of lives." When he noticed her quizzical look, he explained further. "All were set in motion by the New World Order. Famine, drought, earthquakes, hurricanes, and more; all manufactured by the technology the New World Order had in place."

"You can't expect me to believe that a group of people were responsible for creating hurricanes and earthquakes, can you?" Caitriona responded.

"Aye, Catie. Global warming was blamed for many of the disasters, when in fact, there was technology that caused seismic reactions and seeded clouds to massive proportions, all while denying rain to regions the New World Order wanted to eliminate."

"Africa is a perfect example, Catie. By denyin' water tae the region, the Order ensured that the inhabitants literally starved tae death. And, thanks tae a humanitarian effort by the US, their sufferin' was prolonged. When the people didna die quickly enough, the Order created civil unrest among the citizens. Eventually, the entire population was eliminated."

Caitriona sank back onto the bed, the weight of his words resting heavily on her shoulders.

"And who kens how far back this goes; the Mayans, the Incas? How many other civilizations have fallen victim tae the Order and the Illuminati? It has to stop." Duncan searched her inquisitive green eyes and softened his voice, "We have to stop it." He emphasized the first word.

"I don't understand how *we*", she stressed the word mockingly, "can possibly undo or change what's been done," Caitriona replied.

Duncan walked over to the computer panel and adjusted the settings. Immediately, the view screen came to life and displayed a series of images from earth's ancient history. Caitriona recognized the pyramids, Stonehenge and a host of other pre Christian images.

"In your time, scientists and archaeologists searched for the answers to puzzling mysteries: the pyramids, Stonehenge, Biblical miracles, and more. There were many theories, but it wasn't until late in the 20th century that they started tae piece together these mysteries by exploring facets of magic." Duncan watched her face carefully, but she only arched one eyebrow, so he continued.

"The Merovingian bloodline … what do ye ken about that?"

"That's Jesus' bloodline … or supposed bloodline. It's never been proven …" Caitriona paused, looking up at Duncan. "It was?" she asked breathlessly.

"Aye, *Alainn*, in the year 2094. There were a group of uncovered scrolls, much like the ones found in Nag Hammadi in 1965 that finally laid rest the claim.

"So Jesus was just a man?" Caitriona asked tenuously, unsure of where the conversation was heading.

Duncan shook his head. "Not exactly. It turns out that while Jesus was just a man, he did possess a genetic trait that set him, and his descendants, apart from his contemporaries." He paused again, watching for her reaction. "Jesus possessed magic."

Caitriona looked at Duncan, her eyes searching his, looking for some indication that what he had said was a joke. She opened her mouth to speak, but was too blindsided by this new information to formulate a thought. Duncan took that opportunity and continued.

"If ye think about what magic is, it's really nothing more than increasing probability through manifestation of will. This is not theory or parlor tricks. In fact, it was Einstein who figured out that everythin' has an element of energy to it, and that by matching the frequency of the reality one wanted to its energy, that reality would be realized.

"Jesus had that ability. He possessed a unique genetic trait that allowed him tae concentrate his will better than most and tap into the underutilized areas of his brain. The end result was that he was able to perform miracles through the concentration of this will."

"So he really did turn the water to wine?" Caitriona asked skeptically.

He chuckled softly and raised his hand to cut off her next comment. "The magic I am talking about is nae related tae illusions and parlor tricks, but rather the direct result of manifestation of will. Let me try tae explain this in a different way." Duncan thought for a moment and then started again. "Suppose ye are just startin' out in yer career. Ye ken the path ye want tae take and the position ye eventually want to achieve. Ye envision yourself as a leader, taking the next role and the next set of responsibilities until ye find yerself on the career path ye envisioned. Did ye get there by fate, chance, hard work, or through a manifestation of your will?"

"I don't know, Duncan, that's a pretty big stretch." Caitriona got up and walked to the view screen, her brow slightly furrowed as she contemplated the arguments Duncan was presenting. "It seems more probable to me that Jesus was simply a man, nothing more. Even the evidence we had in the twenty first century pointed to that." It was her turn to wave him silent as she wrestled with the ideas Duncan was surfacing.

"Then how do ye explain the Gnostic Gospels that were found in 1945?" countered Duncan.

Caitriona arched one eyebrow, surprised at the reference to the Gnostic gospels, a series of 52 texts that were the source of controversy among scholars in her time. These Gnostic Gospels were thought to be non-canonical chapters that scholars believed were at odds with what was considered canonical Biblical text. "I don't deny they exist, but doesn't that simply substantiate the fact that he was an ordinary man and not some God-like persona with magical powers?" She paused, sinking to the edge of the bed, allowing him the chance to counter.

"Aye, *Alainn*. But, if we tie back in the magical attributes we now know existed at that time due to genetic DNA labeling, we get a much different picture of Gnosticism and pagan practices." He paused as she wrestled with this latest information, watching the furrow of her brow deepen with his revelations.

"Scholars now believe there were descendants both before and after Christ who carried the genetic code for magical abilities. These ancestors were the original pagans ... the ones that crafted spells, healed the sick, and built incredible monuments. As others were born without the gift, the balance of power shifted. The non-gifted were truly afraid of their gifted brothers and sisters and thus shunned Paganism as a dark, satanic art. Eventually, those Pagans who did not denounce their beliefs were executed.

"And it didn't end there. The non-gifted eventually needed a way to control the masses, particularly those who were gifted. So they created Christianity, burying any evidence of Jesus' magical abilities." Duncan paused and took a sip of his coffee. Caitriona stared into her coffee mug, dimly aware that the dark brew was growing tepid. What Duncan suggested contradicted everything Caitriona had been brought up to believe. The idea that magic not only existed, but at one time had been prevalent, was incomprehensible. Caitriona placed the coffee cup on the night stand and stood up, running her slender fingers through the dark mass of curls that hung heavily over her shoulders. She turned and faced Duncan, concern etched deep in her brow.

Duncan continued, watching her carefully. "Since Paganism was the true belief at the time," he continued, "the Church had to have some way to convince the masses and control their behavior. Their strategy was to start at the top by convincing the Roman Emperor Constantine that Christianity was the only way to true salvation. It worked. By 313 AD, Constantine had completely given up his Pagan beliefs and embraced religion and the notion of Christianity. That was the turning point. After that, the movement took flight and made even greater strides."

Caitriona sat back down in the high backed leather chair, curling her legs under her and tucking the folds of her dressing gown in around her legs. Absently, she twined a strand of hair around her finger, letting the dark curls fall carelessly from her fingers. "Okay. So assuming what you say is true, I still don't see what this has to do with me or the connection to magic."

"Remember the Gnostic Texts?" At her affirmative nod, he continued. "Those texts contained the Gospel of Phillip, which openly describes Jesus' relationship with Mary Magdalene as an intimate one. A bloodline was born from that union: The Merovingian blood line – the descendants of Christ. It is through that bloodline that the traits and gifts of magic were inherited. Catie, ye're descended from that line." He took both of her hands in his, and she became aware suddenly of the charged air that subtly passed between them.

She dropped her eyes from his penetrating gaze and pulled her hands from his. She shook her head. "This is all too hard to believe, Duncan." His touch elicited feelings she didn't understand and didn't want to explore.

"And I'm nae askin' ye to embrace it all right now," he replied softly. "Just keep yer mind open to the possibilities and hear the rest of my story. I told ye when ye came on board that I wouldna lie to ye, lass, and I will keep that promise." He cupped her chin in his hand, tilting her face so that he was gazing into her eyes.

Caitriona nodded her head, unsure of why she placed so much trust in a man she barely knew. "Okay," the single word was barely more than a whisper. She needed space from this man and the intense feelings he invoked.

Duncan poured more coffee for both of them and continued his tale. "So with the advent of Christianity, the Order now had a way to control the masses and ultimately gain control and power. If the masses kent there were those among them that had great power, then the Order's vision of world dominance would never come tae fruition."

Caitriona turned away from his penetrating gaze and spoke softly, "Why not just seek out those with magic and rule over them? It seems to me that if you control the ones with magic, then you control the masses ... and the outcome."

"Nay, *Alainn*. It's not quite so simple. The New World Order wants to eliminate the world of magic. They know that if the non-gifted were to find out that Jesus possessed magic, then they would lose the control and dominance they've sought to build over countless generations.

Caitriona reached up to rub her temples. What Duncan was saying was almost too incredible to believe. And could she really have a tie to magic? Is this what the visions were; a genetic tie to an ancient bloodline, centuries old? "From where I stand it just all seems rather preposterous," she said.

"And people used to believe the world was flat," he replied tersely. Duncan stood up, gesturing to the bathing chamber in the far left corner of the room. "I think we can continue this discussion at another time, *Alainn*. I have had some things brought in for ye and will draw a bath for ye as well. I am certain ye will want to digest much of the information I've shared with ye, and get yerself cleaned up." He gestured for her to follow him from the room.

"Wait," she said softly, not quite ready for their conversation to be finished. "Your army is well-funded then?" she asked.

"Not quite, *Alainn*." Darkness spread across his features. "Technically, I am part of the Order's army." At her concerned look, he continued quickly. "But there are those among us, myself included, that feel personal freedom is a right, and the right to live as we choose should be granted to each individual. Alas, we are small in number though, and need a strategic advantage if we are to win our freedom."

Caitriona locked green eyes with grey and chose her next words carefully. "That would make you a traitor."

"Aye lass," he said "and one of the worst. Do ye ken what they do to traitors in the twenty third century?"

She shook her head, a shudder shaking her slight frame.

"Let's just say death would be a welcome reprieve."

Duncan turned his back to her and crossed to the bathing chamber, indicating she should follow. Her mind was whirling with this latest information. *Just how many traitors did the Order have,* she wondered. *And what advantage did she provide? Was it of value to the Order? If so, perhaps she could trade with the Order for passage home.* For the first time since coming on board the twenty third century starship, she felt as if she might have some control.

Her ponderings were cut short as Duncan motioned her into the spacious bathing chamber where a large sunken Roman tub was the room's most enticing feature. The tub was layered in a material she wasn't familiar with but looked to be made of a polished stone composite. Pleasant adornments created a charming, yet masculine atmosphere. Adjoining the bathing chamber was the lavatory, much more functional in nature and absent the adornment of the bathing chamber. Deep, plush towels had been laid over one edge of the tub and all sorts of scented soaps and bathing accoutrements, including a toothbrush and a small amount of paste, were left at her disposal. She had not expected twenty third century accoutrements to be so simple in design, nor void of branding. It was a refreshing break from the bombardment of advertising so prevalent in her century.

A gown of rich chocolate and turquoise had also been hung in the chamber. Caitriona reached up and touched the soft fabric, noting the way the colors overlapped. The gown dipped low in front with beaded straps that crossed in the back, providing a very sexy fit. Undergarments, shoes, and even hair accessories had been considered and placed in the room for her to use.

"I guess they don't have jeans in the twenty third century," Caitriona quipped as Duncan finished drawing the bath. Already, lavish bubbles were beginning to grow in size and would eventually threaten to spill over the strange tub. Duncan stared at her as he turned off the water with a wave of his hand and then stood. "Clothing is a sign of status, *Alainn.* The gowns that have been made for you are reserved for Genetics. You will need to wear them, or we risk the Order's unsolicited attention." Caitriona nodded slowly, her mind racing. She watched as Duncan pulled two large towels to the edge of the tub. Glancing once more around the small room to ensure she had everything she would need, Duncan left, allowing the door to slide shut behind him.

Caitriona released the breath she didn't even realize she'd been holding. She undid her dressing gown and pulled the hospital gown over her head. Lowering herself slowly into the hot, steaming water, she inhaled the jasmine and lily-scented water. The hot water helped ease the tension from her body and she leaned back to let the silky drops envelop her body.

The morning's conversation and events of the past forty-eight hours weighed heavily on her, and the water felt like silk as it caressed her body languidly. Caitriona closed her eyes, letting a small sigh escape her lips. Before she allowed herself the opportunity to fully relax, she scrubbed every inch of her body with the jasmine scented soap. Washing her long tresses with a matching scented shampoo, Caitriona held her breath and submerged herself, rinsing the soap from her hair as she did. Surfacing, Caitriona wiped the water from her eyes and leaned back against the tub. As the water lulled her thoughts, Caitriona allowed the past two days to gently drift from her mind.

Duncan's masculine body drifted across her inner vision and a slight smile tugged at the corners of her lips as she recalled the way he had conversed with her easily this morning. She enjoyed their deeply intellectual conversation and the way he sought her opinion and input. She sunk down lower in the tub, allowing the water to swirl just below her chin. Thoughts of the friends and colleagues she had seen only days earlier left her feeling empty and alone. She missed Eric's smile and the way his concern for her always showed on his face. She wondered if he had died in the earthquake or if he had survived and had tried to find her.

Caitriona breathed deeply and pushed the memory from her mind. Practicing a relaxation technique her mother had taught her, Caitriona pushed all thoughts from her mind, focusing on each deep, even breath until her mind was a blank slate and she was in a fully relaxed state.

Caitriona first saw the image as a backdrop across her inner vision. Reaching out with her mind, she tried to bring the image into focus. The more she tried to focus, the cloudier the image became. As she allowed her mind to wander away from the image, the picture became clearer. Eventually, the image cleared and she was surrounded by the vista, almost as if she had become part of the scene that was unfolding around her.

She had never seen the man in her vision, but a rather striking scar wove its way down the left side of his face. His eyes penetrated right through Caitriona's, leaving her apprehensive and cold. Despite the hot water, Caitriona shuddered and a small moan escaped her.

Wanting desperately to see more, Caitriona once again reached out with her mind; trying to bring the image closer until it became unerringly clear; the clarity and movement so intense, Caitriona felt like an active participant in the scene. Caught up in what she was experiencing, Caitriona's focus was drawn toward the menacing figure that lurked just beyond the shadows. Drawing closer, the man gestured with his left arm to an expanse of nothingness that was as black as the midnight sky. He sneered and pointed again, this time showing a child bereft of any arms, crying in the lonely expanse. Caitriona cried out, visibly upset at the terrifying turn the image had taken. The man in the image now had another child by the hair and was busy cutting out the child's eyes. Blood was pouring over his hands, slowly blazing a trail over the dry desert ground. Caitriona could taste the vile mixture in her mouth. She screamed, striking out with both arms at the horror that was now part of her world. Her arms struck something hard. Raising her hands, she tried to strike her assailant. This time her attempts not only met resistance, but were restrained.

***

Duncan wanted to check on the girl when he first heard her slight cry, but wanted to give her privacy and space. Instead, he continued the aimless pacing he had been engaged in moments before he was distracted. He was uncertain if he had gotten through to Caitriona earlier in the day. There was so much information that he needed to share with her, but he knew he had to proceed slowly and with a good deal of caution and patience. Remarkably, Caitriona was adjusting well to her surroundings. He still didn't know how likely she was to embrace their cause, but he was encouraged by the fact that she was inquisitive and hadn't yet shut him out.

Duncan discontinued his pacing and glanced at the closed chamber doors. *Had she cried out?* He thought. A hollow scream pierced the air, and he activated the door quickly, slipping easily into the room. Caitriona's eyes were wide with fright and she was flailing wildly at an unseen terror. He crossed to the tub and took hold of her arms, pinning both her small hands easily in one of his. "*Ciunas*, Catie!" He cupped her chin with his free hand, trying to get her to respond to the sound of his voice. Trapped in her terror, Caitriona didn't respond.

She tried to pull her hands from his. It was clear he was only agitating her further so he withdrew his hands and knelt next to her, trying to shake her from her vision. Her flailing had splashed water on the floor and the water clung to his trews, instantly soaking him. Standing, he reached into the tub and plucked her small frame effortlessly out of the water, cradling her naked body close to him. Caitriona pushed against his chest, but he remained steadfast in his resolve. Pulling a towel over her naked body, he spoke softly, trying to get her to return to him.

Caitriona's eyes fixed suddenly on his face and her body relaxed in his arms. She scanned the room quickly with her eyes, "Lights, lights," she beat softly against his chest. He had carried her from the bathing chamber into the darkened bed chamber and realized she was disoriented. "Computer, lights." He spoke the command quickly and softly so as not to frighten her further. As the room sprang to light, Caitriona scanned the room quickly, tears brimming beneath the long lashes, searching for hidden terrors in the still dark recesses of the room. Finding none, she relaxed against his chest once more. "I don't know what happened," the words came out in a choked sob. He pulled her closer in his arms, her arms circling his neck and her head resting softly on his shoulder.

"*Ciunas*," he whispered again. She shuddered in his arms and they both became aware of her naked form beneath the towel. He placed her gently in his bed, keeping the towel securely over her body. He pulled the blankets close around her and sat down next to her, pushing her wet hair away from her face. Tears continued to stream down her face and her lower lip trembled uncontrollably. "Tell me," he commanded softly, leaving no room for argument or disagreement.

He could tell she was distraught, but he had to get her to talk to him. He was fairly certain she had just had a vision and he was eager to know more.

"It's never been like that before," Caitriona spoke softly, the uncertainty in her voice giving him pause.

"What do you mean?" Duncan asked. He poured a cup of hot tea from the carafe that was next to the bed and pushed it into her hands. "Drink this."

Caitriona took the tea but merely stared into its dark depths. He pushed a strand of hair from her face and watched as she chewed her lower lip, her brow furrowed in concentration.

"Catie, why was this time different?"

"I don't know. I don't know how to explain it," she said softly, her eyes still focused on the cup of tea she held in her hands.

Cupping her chin in his hand and tilting her face to meet his gaze, Duncan searched her eyes. "But it was different, aye?"

Caitriona nodded as a shiver shook her small frame. "Usually the images aren't so clear, and they usually move across my mind so quickly that I'm unable to see fully what they are."

"What did ye see, *Alainn*?"

Caitriona recounted the vision for him, trying to include as many details as she could remember. "It's more of what I didn't see," she stressed the last word, her voice quivering with the effort of holding back her tears. "I was there, Duncan. I have never felt terror like that." She dropped her eyes to her lap as the tears came unchecked. The muscle along Duncan's jaw tensed as she hesitantly related the horrors that, in her mind, were as clear as if she had participated.

"*Damnu!*" Duncan exclaimed when she had finished. He stood up and began pacing, lost in his own thoughts of war and politics.

Caitriona pulled her bottom lip between her teeth, worrying her lip as she watched his anxious pacing. At her look of concern, Duncan stopped his pacing and returned to her side. Placing his hands on her shoulders, he forced himself to take a deep breath. "Catie, why do ye think this time was different? Why do ye think the images were so much clearer?"

She dropped her eyes and rubbed her temples. Seeing her distress, Duncan took the cup of tea from her hands, the heady brew already growing tepid.

"I don't know. I was much more relaxed this time, and I suppose I wanted to have a vision. I wanted to know if what you said was true." She stressed the last part of the sentence, her eyes remaining fixed on her lap. "I've never been able to control what I see, but I think it's because I've never had much of a reason." She leaned back into the comforts of the oversized bed and closed her eyes. "Could it be that the intensity of my desire to have a vision defined the clarity and continuity of the vision?" Seeing the fatigue and pain in her eyes, he started to say something when she cried out suddenly, cradling her head in her hands. Her wet hair clung in clumps to her bare shoulders.

Duncan crossed to the communication center and activated the viewing monitor. Immediately, Fiona's face was on screen. "Fi, I think she's had a vision, and is nae handling it so well."

"Understood. I'm on my way."

Duncan turned from the viewing monitor and looked over at his charge, her brow was wrinkled and her skin was ghostly white. She had leaned back into the pillows and appeared to be asleep.

Duncan crossed to her side and placed the back of his hand lightly across her forehead. Her eyes fluttered open, but it was clear she was having difficulty focusing. She allowed her eyes to close once again, and he picked up the now discarded towel and began drying the ends of her hair, wishing his sister would hurry. As if in silent answer, the familiarized computer voice requested that the doctor be allowed entry. Duncan gave the appropriate approvals and turned his attention back to the girl lying in his bed as his sister quickly approached her still form.

Taking a long, cylindrical object out of her bag, his sister held one end over Caitriona's forehead and slowly moved the instrument the length of her head, watching the instrument's small panel closely. "Her cerebral cortex is under severe pressure, Duncan. I can administer some pain medication, but I'm not sure what the underlying cause is. These readings weren't present when we first brought her on board." Fiona took out a cylindrical tube, pressing it lightly at the base of Caitriona's neck until she heard the familiar hiss and slight pressure that indicated the medicine had been administered.

Almost immediately, Caitriona's eyes opened and she looked from Duncan to the doctor. "I can't do this again," she said breathlessly. "The images were too real. It's as if I were there experiencing the horror that man inflicted on those children. And," she paused as if trying to find the right words, "I could swear he saw me; that somehow he knew I was there."

Duncan looked at his sister and then back at his charge. Her face was still quite pale and he could see the pulse at the base of her neck throbbing.

"I believe the man ye saw in your vision is Brady Hawkins, although I am unsure of the symbolism or the meaning of the vision." Duncan paused, worry visible on his face as his charge remained pale and quiet in the midst of the oversized bed. She rubbed her temples slowly, once again closing her eyes, and he wondered briefly what else she hadn't told him.

Fiona administered a sedative before Caitriona had a chance to protest. Duncan watched as her eyelids grew heavy and she drifted to sleep. Duncan placed another blanket over her and sat down next to her.

"*Samhach, Alainn,*" Duncan whispered softly, not taking his eyes off Caitriona's still form. His sister touched his shoulder lightly, interrupting his thoughts and reminding him of her presence.

"Duncan, she will sleep now," Fiona reminded him gently. "We should let her rest. I will come by again later this evening to check on her." She paused before leaving him with one final thought. "If we move her to the medical center, I can care for her and monitor the visions." Duncan refused to look at his sister, and instead simply shook his head. He wasn't ready to dismiss his duty to his charge. Besides, he knew he had garnered a breakthrough of sorts in regards to the young woman's vision. If she was able to go this deep, she may be able to go deeper still, and ultimately use her gift to aid their cause.

"Very well," Fiona said, rather disapprovingly. "You know where to reach me, brother." She packed her instruments into her small bag and made her exit quickly, leaving Duncan to watch protectively over the young woman who had witnessed the horrors of his century within 48 hours of being extracted from the only world and peace she had ever known.

Chapter Six

*Do not belittle or disregard those who are different than you, for
without them you would cease to be special.*
Anon

"You realize how fucked up this is, right?" Caitriona spat angrily.
Duncan's explanation of his century's gross misuse of genetic
engineering was unconscionable. He opened his mouth to say something,
but she waved him silent. She didn't want to hear any more. She had
always assumed that future generations would be much more enlightened,
tolerant and peaceful. But the tale Duncan wove was nothing like what
she had imagined.

Caitriona took a deep breath and closed her eyes. On top of
everything, she was physically and mentally exhausted. For nearly a
week, she and Duncan had spent countless hours trying to channel her
energy and tap into the gift he was certain she possessed. Frustrated,
tired, and angry, Caitriona could feel the unshed tears rimming her
emerald eyes, but she refused to give in to the swell of emotions. It was
easier to get angry.

"So, it would appear that by your century's definition, I am rather
unremarkable," Caitriona quipped. She met his steely gaze; irritated that
in this century there was nothing about her that would have ensured
her preservation.

Duncan shook his head. "Nay, lass, and I think ye ken that," he said,
his thick brogue becoming more pronounced with his barely checked
frustration. Caitriona dropped her eyes from Duncan's, exasperated
with her warring emotions and uncomfortably aware of how physically
attracted she was to him.

She exhaled loudly, turning her thoughts to her own century and the
people she had left behind. She still found it incomprehensible to think
she would never make it home. While she complied with all of Duncan's

questions, she never lost an opportunity to question the technology that had brought her here and why they simply couldn't reverse what he had done. She was convinced there was a way home—she had merely to ask the right questions—and find a benefactor willing to invest in her dream.

Duncan stood up and walked to the large mahogany desk, sinking into the high backed leather chair that had molded to his body over the past year. His fingers rapidly tapped out a series of commands on the glass-top display, and a holographic image of Earth appeared above the table. Duncan gestured to the egg-shaped chair that sat facing his desk, "Please sit, *Alainn*." His eyes followed the graceful way she moved as she delicately sank into the chair across from him. The layers of her deep magenta gown provided a rich backdrop to her ivory complexion. Her russet curls had been swept atop her head where several rogue tendrils dared to escape the otherwise perfectly coiffed hair. She had chosen a brown gemstone, which nestled in the valley of her breasts, drawing his attention to the rise and fall of her chest with each soft breath.

Duncan tapped out a series of commands and the holographic image of earth changed to a kaleidoscope of images portraying 20th century iconic culture. Some of the images, like World War I and images of iPods and computer developments, Caitriona recognized. Others moved past her vision in a dissonance of sound and color. "Hold image," Duncan said softly as the instruments rushed instantly to do his bidding. Caitriona stared at the technology that was so clearly beyond anything in her century's arsenal. He had chosen to hold the image of what was now present day earth. Towering buildings made of a material she had never seen sprang from a ground that was nearly barren of any vegetation. Aircraft flew through the sky, seemingly at odds with the other sky vehicles. Caitriona stared at the image, wondering how she would ever acclimate to this strange, new world.

"We are desperate to undo what the New World Order has done, *Alainn*," Duncan stated softly. "While we appear to be at peace," he tapped out a series of commands and the images were quickly replaced by scenes of celebration, the arts, and community gatherings, "there is open war against all that belongs to the realm of magic. Most won't even acknowledge that it once existed, for fear of retaliation and persecution. But myself, and others like me, know that if we can bring back our magical abilities, we can confront the Order and win back our freedom."

"I'm but one person, Duncan. I don't see how I can possibly affect the change you need. I don't even know how to use ...," she hesitated slightly, "my gifts." She smoothed the folds of her gown, feeling rather uncomfortable in the rich, silk material that clung gloriously to her curves. Over the past several days, she had often wished to exchange the luxurious garments for a sturdy pair of blue jeans and comfortable cotton T-shirt.

She shifted restlessly and felt Duncan's eyes on her. She felt uncomfortable thinking of herself as "special." She had spent most of her life trying to blend in with her surroundings. She refused to believe she had a "gift" that would make a difference in this man's fight.

Duncan sighed heavily but continued his lesson. "As the Order grew in size and power, they began developing technology that could scan a person's genetic code and determine instantly if they were genetically superior. People who did not meet these new, exacting standards, and those who were found to have the genetic trait for magic, were eviscerated, without trial and without justice. This is the world we now live in, Catie. We spend our lives looking over our shoulders. The Order is tenacious, their technology pervasive and deadly. Our people live in caves that have become their salvation and their only sanctuary. While the Order will preach superiority, perfection, and obedience, there are others who live with the fear of death, persecution and oppression. We are no longer free to live our own lives, marry those we love, or build a life through hard work and dedication. These directives are left to the Order and the elite few." Duncan paused, watching her wrestle the information he was giving her.

"Your fight is not mine, Duncan," Caitriona said hesitantly. "I will not get involved in your war." Wide, emerald eyes locked with steely grey ones. The muscle in his jaw flexed, evidence, she knew, of the anger he was controlling.

"*Damnu, Alainn!* Do ye think I enjoy seeing what this is doing to ye? Do ye think I sleep well at night knowing that I've condemned ye to a life of solitude? But I see no other way."

An uncomfortable silence stretched between them.

"The only question now, Commander, is what you will do with me, since I am not a willing participant in your war. Will you kill me?" She refused to back down and kept her face locked with his. "There are times when I wish you would," she spat angrily. Seeing the anger on his face, she didn't stop. "I suppose you hadn't thought about that," she sneered at him. "You just assumed I would jump on board this...this crusade of yours, with little regard to my own feelings or wellbeing. You miscalculated then, Commander. You may as well dispose of me now." She stood abruptly, facing him, arms akimbo, challenging him to carry out her wish.

"Make no mistake, Caitriona. I have a mission to complete," Duncan retaliated. "We have technology that will force you to comply. Don't make this any harder on yourself than it already is."

Caitriona's face was pale and, despite her brave front, she was trembling uncontrollably. Willing herself not to cry, she glared at him, the emotional exhaustion of the past seven days finally catching up with her. Emotionally and physically spent, she no longer cared what they did to her. She simply wanted it to be over. "Do what you must. You'll get nothing more from me." As she turned to leave, Duncan reached out and grabbed her arm, pulling her toward him, an icy expression settling across his lean face.

"I should have expected nothing less from you," she spat, her eyes challenging him to remove his hand. "Assuming I can even give you what you need, you still haven't told me what will happen to me once this war of yours is over ... or even when it will be over."

"Caitriona, your skills will always be of service to us," Duncan said pointedly. "It will be necessary, however, to keep you isolated from society, so you don't contaminate the time line."

She stared incredulously at her captor for several minutes, disbelief plainly evident on her delicate features. "What?" She shook her head slowly, backing away from him. "So let me make sure I completely understand. You need me to predict future events through visions that I can neither control, nor understand?" When Duncan started to interrupt, she waved him silent and continued. "And then, when your war has been won—against a foe I've never met, and a cause that means nothing to me—then I'll be carted off to some dark corner of the earth so I won't change the timeline; which you've already done by bringing me here. Have I pretty much summed it up?" She mocked him, and the cause he spent a lifetime fighting. At his continued silence, she realized suddenly there was something more he wasn't telling her.

"What else, Commander?" she stressed his formal title, rage welling up inside her. "What haven't you told me?"

"Ye will need to share a bond," he stated simply.

"What do you mean, 'I will need to share a bond?'" she asked tentatively, not liking the turn the conversation was taking.

"Ye will need to be linked emotionally to someone, a handler, who can guide ye and care for ye." He watched the emerald green eyes narrow to tiny slits as she ascertained this latest threat. He continued; the relief to be disclosing the entirety of his plan evident on his face. "He will be able to feel your emotions, know where ye are, know if ye're hurt or even if ye're in danger," he said more softly.

Caitriona could only stare at Duncan in disbelief. "No." She shook her head slowly, the realization and understanding of what he said becoming clearer. "No," she said again more emphatically. "This isn't happening. I refuse to have any part in this!" She backed further away, nearly knocking over her now vacated chair in her haste to retreat from his crazy, half-baked scheme. Her heart was beating wildly and she could feel the adrenaline rising in her to an almost alarming height.

"*Is lior din*," Duncan said, rather sternly. Caitriona had no idea what the Gaelic words meant, but his tone told her he would tolerate no further arguments or outbursts.

She rubbed her palms against her dress, noting for the first time how clammy her small hands had become.

"Sit, Caitriona," Duncan said again; this time more calmly but still with the unmistakable air of authority that was evidently as much a part of him as any of his other organs.

"Is there a physical bond as well?" she asked almost hesitantly, fearing the answer.

It was Duncan's turn to be surprised. "No," he said as emphatically as her earlier demonstration had been. He saw the relieved look in her eyes and continued, hurriedly. "The bond is there to protect ye, *Alainn*. Ye will na share a physical bond," he added.

"An emotional connection that is neither solicited nor warranted is every bit an assault as any physical rape," she stated tersely, through clenched teeth. "Surely you must see that."

Caitriona suddenly felt lightheaded. She wanted so desperately to pinch herself until she awoke to the familiar surroundings of her modest waterfront apartment.

"Everything we have established has been done to ensure your safety and protection," he stated, reaching out and grabbing her arm to halt her impending departure.

"What if the thing I need protection from is the person, or people, who would threaten my personal liberties and freedoms?"

Duncan ignored the jibe. "It won't be like that, I give ye my word."

"Your word?" Caitriona stressed the last word incredulously. "Your word means nothing." She laughed bitterly, pulling her arm away from his grip.

"I am nae the enemy, *Alainn*." The last statement was little more than a whisper.

"From where I sit, that's exactly who you are. You've kidnapped me, threatened me, and are holding me against my will. How does that not make you the enemy?"

"There is far more at stake here than ye understand. This war must be won and we will stop at nothin' to ensure victory."

"I didn't ask for any of this," she said petulantly. She didn't care.

"I ken. And I am sorry," he said almost sadly. "But this isna about ye." His look pierced her heart. "It would nae have mattered who we brought forward in time. This war must still be fought. And it must be won," he said tersely. "At any cost and at any sacrifice," he added more quietly.

Caitriona dropped her gaze. She was finding it hard to process everything he was telling her. She was merely a pawn in his war, a symbol of freedom and change for his people. He would fight for her and protect her, as would her handler. But not because either of them cared for her, but because of what she meant to their people and their cause. He saw her as nothing more than a weapon in his arsenal of tools.

"How many have died as they've battled for your cause, Commander?" It was more of a statement than a question. At his blank look, she continued. "I'm not sure you'll ever set aside your hatred for each other." She turned her back on him and ran from the room, not hearing his final remarks.

"We will Caitriona ... with ye."

Chapter Seven

We are more disturbed by a calamity which threatens us than by one which has befallen us.
John Lancaster Spalding

Caitriona could feel the shift in the starship engines as they came out of warp speed. While subtle, the shifts and mechanical rumblings no longer alarmed her. Five weeks on the starship and she had gotten used to the plethora of sounds that were ever present on their journey home. Caitriona walked to the view screen of her modest accommodation and stared intently at the scene before her. She didn't think she would ever grow tired of the beauties of space. How different her life was now.

Caitriona sank down into the comfortable, plush settee and continued to stare out the view screen at the stars that seemed to hang in a black puddle of ink, her thoughts once again turning to Duncan. After their last heated exchange, both had refused to back down on their respective positions. Caitriona still clung to the hope that she would one day go home, and Duncan held steadfast to his mission and in seeing her safely to her handler. While neither acknowledged that the six weeks was rapidly coming to a close, each managed to set aside their animosity for one another and work together to quickly close the history gap that, for Caitriona, still persisted.

As such, she and Duncan continued to have daily discussions around history, geography, politics, and religion. He was rapidly trying to educate her on 200 years of history, which for her, hadn't even occurred.

Caitriona brushed a stray strand of hair from her eyes and took a deep breath. Try as she might, she still couldn't grasp the idea of time travel and how they had ended up returning to the correct year, yet light years from earth. From what she had gathered, they had entered a wormhole but because of the hole's instability, they were brought several light years away from their intended target, hence the six week journey home. Caitriona had also gathered that travel via wormholes was extremely dangerous and rarely attempted. Because of their instability, the hole could collapse at any time, crushing those inside. Caitriona shuddered, knowing her abduction had been at the risk of all these men's lives.

Caitriona sighed audibly and instead focused on the present, endeavoring to learn all she could. She plied the crew with questions and enamored herself to them with her own intrigue and zest to learn, never giving up hope that someday she would return home to her own time.

As the weeks passed, Caitriona made it a point to get to know each of the eleven crew members on board the ship. She quickly developed a rapport with Lee, Duncan's second-in-command, and spent several hours a day training with the master swordsman, trading her knowledge in Hapkido for his knowledge of swordsmanship. She found his companionship easy, and in the weeks she had been onboard, had developed a comfortable friendship with him. While Caitriona had spent several years in Seattle, she had grown up in Washington D.C., a place full of history, politics, and intrigue. Her mother had insisted she learn self defense and so she had started Hapkido lessons at the age of four. While she had suspended her training for nearly a year after the accident, she eventually found her way back, the strenuous workouts a refuge from her otherwise mundane life. By the time she had left for college, she had achieved a rank of second degree black belt. The lessons had never been put to practical use until her escape from the ship's medical facilities. Now, Caitriona found herself as mentor and teacher to the man she had confronted earlier.

The crew was also eager to learn about Caitriona's time and hear firsthand experiences that to all of them had been nothing more than words in a history book. As the days continued to pass, Caitriona became more comfortable with the atmospheric conditions on the ship and found her strength had fully returned. She hadn't had any more visions, and the terrible headaches that resulted from her earlier visions seemed to be in a state of rare hibernation.

But it was Duncan's behavior that puzzled her the most. While they met daily to discuss his century's politics and status, he had become slowly more distanced from her. The warmth she had first seen in his eyes no longer reached his smile; indeed, he rarely smiled. The laughter that had laced their earlier conversations and infectiously found a path to her heart was now absent. And the closer they came to Earth, the tenser and more withdrawn he became.

So Caitriona focused her attention instead on learning all she could about the twenty third century: the culture, people, political issues, fashions, and more. And what she learned disturbed her. Money was no longer a driving factor. Genetic engineering ensured the continuation of the master race, and things that were once familiar to her, no longer existed: fast food, shopping malls, automobiles, and churches were all relegated to pages in the history books. The absence of football, entertainment, and television pointed to a civilization bereft of any social escapes or community. Caitriona pictured, instead, a sterile world of human drones more focused on technology, education, and space exploration than humanity, feelings, and love. Duncan had emphasized repeatedly that individuality was pushed aside in favor of serving the New World Order and the greater good.

More confusing to her, though, was the class structure that was firmly engrained in twenty third century society. "Genetics" were the upper class; they were the elite master race the Order had created to rule the world. These people were genetically engineered for a number of desirable traits including beauty, intelligence, strength, and talent. Each child who was genetically bred was designed for a specific purpose or job that furthered the Order's cause. Children were raised in group settings—foster holds—never knowing their biological parents and always with the understanding of their place in society.

Conversely, "Dwellers" were a rogue group who still clung to biological values and fought for freedom and the rights of all people to live harmoniously as they chose. Dwellers were considered a risk to the genetic population since they were not sterilized and produced children through natural means. Because Dwellers were hunted by the Order, many had gone underground or deep into unpopulated areas to avoid detection. Protection of their children was a top priority since they were most vulnerable and often hunted by the Order.

While Genetics clearly lived a life rich in technology, medical advancements, and worthwhile contributions, another group of genetics, "Lessers," were bred to serve the needs of the Genetics. These Lessers were granted some freedoms and were educated alongside Genetics.

However, once these children reached the age of sixteen, they were sent to work in labor positions to serve Genetics. They were brought up with the acute understanding of their role in a society designed to favor Genetics.

Caitriona had grown up in a world long known for conspiracy theories and anti-heretical teachings, but the thought that the New World Order was no longer a conspiracy but fact, astonished her. To think that a single entity could actually bring about the enslavement of the world and destruction of two thirds of all life on Earth, was incomprehensible.

On the surface, twenty third century earth sounded like a veritable utopia. Disease, cancer, and other fatal and debilitating illnesses had completely been eliminated. With the advent of genetic engineering, doctors were able to identify the genes that caused predisposition to certain illnesses and debilitating diseases, and could simply eliminate those genes. Over time, geneticists also discovered that criminal behavior was genetically predisposed as well. Eventually, scientists were able to identify that gene and eradicate the unwanted behavior. The result was a perfectly behaved society and citizens that no longer feared rape, murder, and violent crimes. In its place, doctors learned to isolate more desirable genes and select those that would lend themselves to the creation of a master race.

Despite the appearance of a utopian society, the Order's secrets were dark and not all citizens embraced the New World regime. Gone were values of freedom, and the foundation from whence the Constitution was built upon. E Pluribus Unum was still the basis of the New World Order, but under the Order's rebellious and sickening ideals, it had been replaced by another meaning entirely. Thus, the Order had imposed a new regime; one that did not embrace the democratic values the United States once held in high esteem. In fact, Caitriona learned that, while many nations had finally embraced their unique differences and come together to serve as one, the Order ensured that the direction they were following maintained the missive they clearly established centuries earlier.

During one of their more heated arguments, Caitriona had pressed Duncan on why she had been chosen from among countless ancestors that surely possessed a stronger tie to magic than her flailing abilities. The answer had left a cold place in her heart: she had no family and her place in her time period was not marked by any significant contributions.

From that point forward, the relationship between her and Duncan became more strained. An ever present reminder that she was nothing more than an obligation to him, she spent her days avoiding him and her evenings longing for the warmth of his earlier smile. And, while her days were filled with history lessons, fencing, music, and friendship born of the crew, her evenings were spent in quiet solitude and her own equally quiet musings. She spent more and more time with Fiona, enjoying the older woman's easy affection and genuine warmth. They developed a strong friendship that provided comfort to Caitriona during the long voyage back to Earth. Each day, Fiona worked with Caitriona, teaching her patiently how to meditate, clearing her mind in order to focus on the images which would allow her to bring better clarity to the visions. Fiona was convinced that eventually, with proper training and time, Caitriona would be able to call the visions at will. Fiona also insisted on regular brain scans in order to monitor any changes in Caitriona's cerebral cortex. While Fiona tried not to express too many of her concerns to her, Caitriona knew that her friend was concerned she was being pushed too fast in an effort to further the Templars' cause. As such, she had insisted on monitoring Caitriona's physiological changes, promising to report any dramatic alterations to her brother.

As days turned into weeks, Caitriona's resolve to return home only strengthened. While she had pressed the crew about their passage through the wormhole, they had not been willing to share much beyond what she already knew about wormholes: they provided passage to other times, were unstable at best, and required superior navigational abilities in order to traverse their boundaries safely. Still, the fact that Duncan and his crew had not only found a wormhole, but had been able to travel safely to her time and navigate back to his, gave her a small glimmer of hope that she would one day find a way home.

For now, she resolved to play along, knowing that her chance of returning home was dependent on her ability to find someone who possessed ample resources and strong navigational abilities. And she wouldn't find that person by sitting in her quarters and lamenting her fate. If she possessed any sort of magical abilities, she hoped her latent talent would help her find a way home. If not, she was forever destined to live a life of solitude, willing or not.

Chapter Eight

Be he a king or a peasant, he is happiest who finds peace at home.
Johann Wolfgang Von Goethe

Caitriona watched from the large forcefield windows as the Falcon docked at the orbiting space station. She wasn't aware of the hum of the engines until they powered down, and there was an eerie silence that followed. Outside the station, she could see mechanical robots working on the structural integrity of the space station, providing an even deeper feeling of isolation.

She felt Duncan's presence long before he ever made a sound. Not bothering to turn around, she continued to stare out at the space station, a small shudder of apprehension shaking her slight frame. Duncan walked over to her. She could hear him inhale and a slight smile tugged at the corners of her lips. She deliberately took her time getting ready this morning, choosing a scented soap of cherry blossoms and wild orchids. The folds of her russet colored dress fell softly to the floor and accentuated the deep green of her eyes, while her auburn curls fell alluringly over her shoulders and down her back.

Duncan touched her shoulder softly and she trembled at the electricity that ran through her body. He did that to her and she could no more deny her feelings for him than she could the very air she breathed. He caressed her hair gently before he turned her to face him. Her eyes were like glass with the shadow of unfinished sleep just beneath the aqua surface.

"It's time for us to go, *Alainn.*" His voice was harsh and clipped. Caitriona smoothed the folds of her gown and brushed a stray curl from her face. Clasping her hands nervously in front of her, she allowed Duncan to guide her down the corridor. As they approached the air lock, Caitriona slowed. All eleven crew members were waiting. Over the past six weeks, Caitriona had come to know each one; they were like an extended family, and she was surprised to realize how deeply she would miss them.

Lee stepped forward and saluted Duncan, his formality and serious expression leaving no question as to how he felt about their mission. Both men wore the military uniform that clearly bespoke their rank. Caitriona noted the way Duncan's shirt and tunic strained against his muscles, his kilt leaving little to the imagination. A plaid tartan that bore his family's crest, a broadsword, and dress shoes completed the ensemble. His dark hair had been tied back in a leather thong, and the military cap she had so seldom seen him wear was now pulled low over his brow. He had shaved that morning and the sandalwood scent of him was intoxicating. He looked every part the dashing Scotsman.

"We will be right behind you, Duncan." Fiona hugged her brother warmly, and then kissed Caitriona lightly on each cheek, her smile encouraging. "We will see each other again soon, my friend. I promise." Fiona shifted the medical bag she was prone to carrying to her shoulder and stepped back so the two could pass.

As the airlock hissed open, Duncan guided her through the narrow opening. As soon as they were through, the doors hissed closed again and Caitriona felt the isolation of the space station. "Come, lass. A shuttle is waiting for us." Duncan took Caitriona's cold hand. He raised her hand to his lips and pressed a warm kiss to the back of her hand. Pulling her closer, he tilted her chin up so that he was looking into her eyes. "I promise ye lass, I willna let anythin' happen to ye."

"You can't promise that, Commander." She turned away from him, not wanting to get lost in his eyes. Her heart was beating so loudly, she felt certain he could hear it above the sound of his voice. She dropped her eyes to the floor and pulled her hand from his. He touched her lightly on the elbow, guiding her forward once again. At the shuttle bay, he punched in a series of codes on the command screen and the shuttle hatch door slowly lifted. Gesturing for her to enter, Duncan followed her on board.

The shuttle was comfortable but not spacious. Designed for short distances, the shuttle could accommodate up to sixteen passengers across two long bench seats, but on this trip only Caitriona, Duncan, and his navigation officer, Gavin, occupied the small ship. Duncan stepped into the command chair and took control of the helm while

Gavin moved toward the rear of the ship to take control of operations. Duncan motioned for Caitriona to take the seat next to him. Pulling the seatbelt tightly around her, he fixed her with a roguish grin and said, "I like you in restraints." Before she could reply, he strapped himself into his own seat and began quickly punching in codes. The little craft soon hummed to life.

Caitriona relaxed against the high backed chair and closed her eyes. Taking a deep breath, she tried to calm her nerves and still the rapid beating of her heart. "Catie," Duncan's deep voice was reassuring. She opened her eyes, mesmerized by his smile. "Ye may want to watch this, lass. It's like nothin' ye've ever experienced." He grinned like a mischievous child.

"Commander, you're cleared for take-off," came his navigation officer's clipped voice.

"Aye."

Duncan grinned even wider, effortlessly keying in a few more codes. The outer bay doors opened suddenly and the runway lights lit the darkness with a soft, eerie glow. Duncan brought the ship into position so that it was aligned with the open doors. "Breathe out, *Alainn.*"

Before Caitriona could question him further, the shuttle lurched forward and she was pressed back into her chair. She felt as if she couldn't breathe, but then they were clear of the doors and they seemed to be floating in space. Outside the station, the stars seemed to hang in their midst. Remembering to exhale, Caitriona breathed out suddenly and immediately felt her stomach begin to settle. Looking around her, she was captivated by the wonders of space. The stars were so brilliant she felt as if she could reach out and touch them. Ahead of her, the Earth looked peaceful, still and calm. She was in awe of the planet's beauty and felt overwhelmed by the expanse of space.

"How long will it take to reach Earth?" Caitriona whispered.

"About ninety minutes, lass." Duncan looked out at the expanse of space, and Caitriona wondered what was at the source of his thoughts. "I know it's an incredible view, lass, but we need to review our cover story. The earth is a far different place now, and an outsider will be noticed, especially one with such special … skills."

"Duncan, you've prepared me well," Caitriona said, almost bitterly. "I will play the dutiful wife, speak only when necessary, and trust no one." She paused before nearly whispering, "And when this is over?"

The question hung in the air as Duncan refused to answer. They had been down this road many times and it inevitably ended in fierce arguing. "Once we are at Dunrobin Castle, ye will be safe. The staff and residents are loyal to our cause."

"And then what, Duncan? I'm not what you think I am. I can't help you."

"You still don't realize how valuable you are." He turned and looked at her, searching her emerald eyes. "It's ironic that I have the one thing you so erringly lack; faith in you."

Duncan turned back to the control panel and continued navigating the small craft. She knew he was reacting to the fact that, in the weeks prior to their departure, he hadn't been successful in helping her master her gift. Truthfully, she wasn't certain why she wasn't able to call upon her gift or hold the images she did see. Caitriona knew he thought she was just being obstinate, but she truly didn't have any idea why she hadn't been successful. As a result, she became frustrated and lost confidence.

Caitriona stared out into space as stars seemed to rush past the small craft, bent on some destination that she could neither see nor understand. Duncan input several more commands into the console and the small ship slowed. Turning to Caitriona, he repeated his last statement. "Even now, lass, ye still have no idea how valuable you are." His words settled uneasily around them both as Caitriona searched his steel-grey eyes for answers. "Just because I havena been able to help ye lass, doesna mean ye are nae the one we seek."

"What if you've made a mistake, Duncan? Are you so arrogant that you will not admit to your own fallibility? And when you finally realize you have made a mistake, what will become of me? I'm not merely a pawn in this game you play, but flesh and blood too."

He ignored her statement, focusing instead on the commands and the gait of the ship as it responded to his touch. After several minutes, he turned to face her. "There has been nae mistake," he said softly. He palmed her cheek and brushed his thumb lightly over her cheek bone. "Ye are nae mistake." They stayed like that for several seconds until Caitriona pulled away, effectively breaking the tension in the small craft.

"Tell me about Dunrobin Castle," she said softly, no longer wanting to be under the penetrating scrutiny of his smoldering gaze. He straightened and leaned back in his chair, his eyes lighting up as he began to talk animatedly about his ancestral home. They spent nearly an hour discussing the castle, its hidden passages, historical references, current inhabitants, and the surrounding land. Caitriona was eager to see the home Duncan so dearly loved, and to explore the crags and cliffs that surrounded the castle walls. As she was about to ask him about the significance of the castle's name, a jarring hitch in the engines caused her to catch her breath and dig into the arm rests of her chair. She glanced quickly at Duncan, who immediately bent over the controls, although he appeared relaxed and unconcerned with this latest development.

"Hang on lass, it may get a wee bit bumpy, but 'tis normal." The engines groaned, while the hull shuddered, belying his earlier statement.

"How are ye doin' back there, Gavin?" he questioned his navigation's officer through the communicator that was embedded in the chair.

"I've got it under control, Commander," replied Gavin, his voice even and composed.

"Then why haven't we started our descent?" Duncan growled, a little too tersely.

"I don't know sir," the officer stated. "I'm switching to manual control now." The hull gave a slight shudder while the engines hummed a rather loud protest. Duncan unbuckled his safety restraints and squeezed her hand, "Stay put, lass. Looks like Gavin may need my help after all." He smiled a lopsided grin and was gone.

The ship shuddered again and Caitriona gasped. There was a violent pitch to the port side and Caitriona was grateful for the restraints that kept her firmly in her seat. Trying to quell the panic that was making its way to the surface, Caitriona dug her nails into the arm rest of the shuttle chair. Another violent pitch and the engines groaned, causing Caitriona to shut her eyes tight. She had always found air travel to be unsettling, and this new experience did nothing to quell those fears.

"Catie, lass, I know it's a bit unsettling, but we're going to be fine," Duncan said through the communicator, as if he had been able to read her thoughts. Caitriona squeezed her eyes tight as the ship shook violently. "Caitriona?"

"I'm here," she stated quietly, amazed at how tiny her voice sounded next to the hum and vibration of the engines.

"We'll be on the ground shortly, *Alainn*," Duncan sounded calm and sure of himself. Caitriona took solace in that thought.

Glancing out the shuttle window, she saw flames shooting out behind the engines and noticed they had already entered the atmosphere.

Caitriona could see the ground getting closer and wondered what it would be like when they hit. Just as she was sure they would burst into a fiery ball, the engines were reversed and they slowed abruptly. The ship's engines ceased their grinding, rumbling emissions and settled into a slow, droning hum. She felt a slight lurch as the shuttle touched ground and the engines powered off. Duncan came back to her seat just as she was unbuckling her restraints.

"Fear not, lass," he said quietly. Caitriona allowed him to help her out of the seat. Tucking her hand into the crook of his arm, he placed his free hand over hers and squeezed encouragingly. "Welcome home, Catie," he said softly. She stared blankly at him, knowing in her heart she would never forgive him and that home would never be this time.

Chapter Nine

We shape our dwellings, and afterwards our dwellings shape us.
Winston Churchill

Duncan had set the shuttle down in Edinburgh, Scotland, one of only sixteen cities in the world that still remained. Caitriona soon discovered that even the term "city" was not really indicative of the way these people lived. Although Duncan had prepared her for the idea that technology only persisted in these cities, Caitriona was overwhelmed by the stark differences between twenty third century life and twenty first century life.

Taking the arm Duncan proffered, Caitriona was careful to hide her intrigue and appear as if she had been here many times before. They had spent countless hours rehearsing her cover story, and now she knew she had to deliver a believable performance or her life would be in jeopardy. The Templars had arranged for Caitriona's picture and false genetic code to be uploaded into the Order's main computer system. To further solidify the story, Caitriona had been coached by Lee and Duncan daily so that she almost began to believe she was from Chicago and had been trained in the performing arts where she met Duncan when he attended a concert at the Metropolitan. Theirs had been a whirlwind romance which had prompted Duncan to apply for permissions to wed. The story was believable enough as long as no one dug too deeply or asked Caitriona to give a performance. The ruse, she knew, would also allow Duncan to keep her close.

Duncan leaned in and kissed her cheek lightly, brushing the back of his hand lightly down her face - a loving gesture a husband might make. His hand lingered slightly before dropping to cover her hand that was looped loosely through his arm. He gave her an encouraging smile as they exited the shuttle.

Duncan navigated them both quickly through several corridors, Caitriona's layered skirts billowing out behind her as if engaged in a hearty game of tag. Duncan glanced at Caitriona, squeezing her hand gently. She knew he was aware of her anxiety through the quickening of her pulse. She looked stoically before her and refused to look at him, concerned that if she did, he would see the fear and anger that bristled near the surface.

At the top of a long, circular staircase, Duncan was met by two men, both in their late thirties, strikingly handsome with classic blonde hair and blue eyes. Caitriona silently wondered if they were both genetically engineered and had had their attributes chosen for them.

"*Mo cridhe*, Caitriona," Duncan introduced the two men to her, both of whom bowed their heads slightly in greeting. Duncan gestured with his free arm, indicating the two men should lead the way. As they descended the spiral staircase, Caitriona stole a quick glance at Duncan. His jaw was rigid and a slight tick in the lower left corner was the only evidence of his mounting tension.

The four of them followed the staircase to the main floor where the two escorts stepped aside and motioned Duncan toward the far checkpoint. "Commander, we'll need you both to go through the monitoring station." The shorter of the two men gestured to the station at the far end of the platform.

"Since when do Genetics test someone on the High Council, lads?" Duncan gave a short chuckle and appeared relaxed. Coming to a stop, he faced the two security officers. "Why all the security?"

"We've had problems lately with Dwellers, Commander," the taller of the two men responded. "There's been a breach in security and the council is worried the genetic base may have been compromised or even contaminated."

"Why wasn't I notified about this?"

"You've been away on your honeymoon, sir. The council was planning to brief you once you returned." The taller man once again motioned to the monitoring station at the far end of the corridor. Caitriona glanced at the station to see people passing beyond a steel grey bar, their casual, unconcerned demeanor evidence of their elevated station. She wasn't entirely certain what would happen if she were to try and pass beyond the mechanical sentry. Did an alarm sound? Would she be neutralized right there, or would she be carted off to some modern day laser protected jail cell? She managed a slight shudder and stepped instinctively closer to Duncan.

Duncan placed his arm around her shoulder, drawing her in tight. "This is an outrage!" Duncan kept his voice low and even, but the look in his eyes gave no room for argument.

"Sir, we have our orders … no one," the young officer stressed the last two words, "is to be excused." He motioned once again to the scanning equipment.

"Verra well." Duncan leaned over and brushed a light kiss against Caitriona's forehead. As he did so he whispered, "Trust me."

Caitriona tried to search his eyes, but he had already withdrawn and was escorting her to the scanning equipment.

"Go ahead of me, *mo anam*. I'll be right behind you." He flashed her an even white smile that she simply couldn't read. Not knowing what to do, she passed quickly through the scanning arch. An ambient glow reacted quickly and seconds later she was staring down the barrel of what she assumed were several modern day weapons. Caitriona gasped and instinctively raised her hands over her head.

"Stand down," Duncan shouted to the other officers. "Stand down." Confused, the men lowered their weapons as their superior officer stepped forward with a smaller instrument. "Run the scan again. There's been a mistake," Duncan said.

"These machines do not make errors," the lead officer stated.

"Walt, we've known each other for years. I'm asking ye as a friend and colleague, as one married lad to another, run the scan again."

Walt arched one eyebrow, but motioned for Caitriona to walk back through the scanning equipment. She complied quickly and this time only the fluorescent glare of the station's white lights lit her way.

"Instruments are not infallible, Walt," Duncan smiled politely at the young officer. "I know my wife, and I can assure ye, she's nae a Dweller."

"My apologies, Commander. We have strict orders not to let anyone through who doesn't pass the scan. Hawkins has been adamant that we adhere to protocol. I'm going to need to send for one of the drones. We can do a quick DNA scan. It shouldn't take long." He withdrew a small communications device from the belt he wore at his hip and pushed a series of numbers to open the communication signal.

"Ye'r just doin' yer job, Walt." Duncan clapped the officer on his shoulder and leaned in close. "But do ye really want to bother Hawkins with this? You and I both ken what Hawkins will do if he feels his time has not been well spent." Walt nodded slowly and closed the communication channel.

"It does seem silly to bother him with this," Walt added. "Let them pass," he said rather loudly, his voice laced with nervous anticipation.

Duncan bent to kiss Caitriona's cheek. Her heart was pounding so loudly, she felt certain the officer and his men could hear it through the layers of material she wore. She took a deep, steadying breath, feeling as if the walls were closing in around her. Duncan seemed suddenly very far away, and his words were deep and indistinguishable, like an old 45 that had been slowed down on the turn table.

The ashen look on her face must have given her away, because Duncan quickly grasped her elbow to steady her.

Caitriona smiled wanly at Duncan as he led her past the checkpoint and down a long corridor.

"Commander, I wasn't expecting you until tomorrow," said Brady Hawkins, the high commander for the New World Order's army.

"*Damnu,*" Duncan swore softly under his breath. Masking his emotions, Duncan turned to face the highest ranking officer in the New World Order, saluting as was the custom.

"Sir," Duncan stated brusquely.

Hawkins nodded at him, his eyes traveling the length of Caitriona's body. He licked his lips, a sneer forming as Caitriona shuddered.

"I understand there was a bit of a commotion at the screening area," Hawkins said, his eyes never leaving Caitriona.

"Aye. A malfunction in the equipment."

"Hmm. It's unusual for our equipment to malfunction." He pronounced each syllable in the last word as if he was unfamiliar with the way it rolled from his lips. "I'd heard you'd been granted approval for a biological mating." He pulled a handkerchief from his shirt pocket and wiped at the perspiration that had gathered on his upper lip.

"Aye," Duncan said. Caitriona heard the edge in his voice and stepped closer to him. She didn't like the way Hawkins assessed her as if she were the last morsel of food at a dying man's dinner. Duncan's grip around her waist tightened and she hoped he would cut this little reunion short. As if reading her thoughts, he said quickly, "In fact, we were just going to Dunrobin Castle for the celebration."

Hawkins nodded appreciatively. "I wouldn't want to keep you then."

Duncan saluted and started to steer Caitriona toward the exit. "Commander," Hawkins shouted after him.

Duncan turned and acknowledged the older man with a slight nod of his head.

"I assume you and your new bride will be attending the festivities tomorrow night?" At Duncan's hesitation, he added, "I'm sure it would not go unnoticed by those in command if you weren't there to share the victory."

Duncan merely nodded. Taking Caitriona's arm once more, he steered her toward the exit. She winced at the slight increase in pressure and stopped, pulling her arm away from him. She started to protest, but suddenly Duncan's mouth was on hers, teasing her lips apart. She pushed against his chest, but his hands caught hers and held them tight. He sucked gently on her bottom lip until a moan escaped her lips and she gave in to the feelings his kiss evoked. Just as she started to thread her fingers through his hair, he broke off the kiss, brushing an errant strand of hair behind her ear. Leaning close to her ear he said, "Behave yourself, *Alainn*, and dinna do anythin' foolish. We are being watched." She could only stare at him, her lips bruised from his passionate assault. She had one thought as he tucked her arm back through his - *I am not the only one who needs to behave.*

***

Hawkins watched as MacKinnon pulled the girl to him and covered her mouth in a searing kiss. The young beauty seemed surprised - too surprised for a new bride, Hawkins thought absently as he watched the kiss deepen. He imagined his own tongue dancing with the young woman's as she writhed naked beneath him. He groaned inwardly. He watched as MacKinnon eventually broke the kiss, whispering something that was lost to Hawkins. The girl only stared at him with her big doe-like eyes and nodded.

Hawkins watched as the young warrior escorted his new bride from the building. MacKinnon was hiding something, Hawkins thought absently. That much was clear. And this was just the sort of mystery Hawkins enjoyed unraveling … and he knew just where to start.

***

Duncan knew he had startled Caitriona when he'd captured her mouth. But he needed a distraction to stop his charge from blowing their cover. He could sense the girl's anger and had anticipated her trying to seek Hawkins' help. At first he felt his charge stiffen beneath his gentle, probing assault. But gradually she relinquished to his ministrations, parting her lips and leaning into his kiss. His tongue lightly raked her teeth as he softly nipped at her bottom lip. She groaned outwardly, her hand sliding around his neck and pulling him tighter to her. Duncan needed no further encouragement. He pulled her bottom lip gently against his and relished the way her mouth responded to him.

Duncan broke off the kiss first and leaned in close to her ear, "Behave yourself, *Alainn,* and dinna do anythin' foolish," he warned through gritted teeth. "We are being watched." He brushed his lips against her cheek and glanced at Hawkins who was eyeing the pair quizzically. Duncan saw the flush that rose to her face as she stood back and adjusted the bodice of her gown. He watched as her fingers trembled, noting the fullness of her now-bruised lips. *Had he imagined her response? Mine.* The single word reverberated through his mind until he thought his brain would explode. *What am I thinking?* He admonished himself. *There could have been a thousand different ways to silence her - why choose a kiss?* But even as he thought it, his body betrayed him. He could still taste the sweetness of her lips and feel the hitch in her breath as she opened to him. *Nay,* he thought again. *It was the only thing to do.*

***

Caitriona concentrated on getting her breathing under control as she admonished herself for her rash behavior. *What has gotten into me?* She mentally chided herself. *Am I that easily distracted that I should forget he's the enemy?* She looked deep into his eyes, but the mask he wore so easily, like any other piece of clothing, was firmly in place, giving nothing away. She dropped her gaze and allowed Duncan to tuck her arm into his elbow and walk her outside.

Once outside, Caitriona turned her face to the warm noonday sun, closing her eyes slowly and allowing her fear to all but dissipate in the warm promise of the day. Opening her eyes slowly, she glanced around at her first look at twenty third century Earth. Caitriona drew in her breath sharply, shocked at what she was completely unprepared to see. She wasn't looking at an Earth torn apart by war, conflict and poverty, but rather a beautiful paradise. Lush green vegetation and rolling hills seemed almost virgin-like, as if a painter had rolled his brush generously in the paint and stroked the canvas in broad, artistic strokes.

The quiet was uncanny. There were no cars to pollute the air or the senses. People were walking among the buildings and, save for the modern architecture of the infrastructure and the occasional sky vehicle, Caitriona would have sworn they had traveled back in time, to a simpler, more peaceful place that no longer existed in the twenty first century.

Allowing the warmth of the sun to push all thoughts from her mind, Caitriona was brought out of her musings by Duncan's gentle but persistent squeeze on her shoulder. She was reminded quickly that, regardless of the beauty, this planet was more hostile than twenty first century Earth and she needed to never lose sight of that fact.

An interesting air vehicle glided to a stop in front of them, slowly touching ground. The doors opened sideways, allowing Caitriona to climb easily aboard the small but sturdy craft. Duncan climbed in beside her, leaned back in the comfortable reclining seat and closed his eyes. Caitriona wanted to ask him a myriad of questions but was afraid to voice her thoughts out loud. Instead, she sank back in the seat next to him and allowed her gaze to follow the scenery as the shuttle lifted slowly and then accelerated rapidly as it navigated easily between buildings and other sky vehicles.

Duncan invited no conversation as he pulled his hat lower over his brow, folded his hands across his midsection, and closed his eyes. Caitriona continued to watch the countryside, mesmerized by the buildings and how quickly they retreated from view.

Caitriona said nothing and eventually leaned back in the plush leather-like chair. There was no driver, and Caitriona noted the vehicle ran on an "auto-pilot" setting. Wanting to understand this new world, Caitriona hesitated just slightly before engaging her abductor.

"Do you want to explain to me what just happened back there?" Caitriona asked quietly.

"Aye, *Alainn*." Duncan took a deep breath, opened his eyes and tapped out a series of commands on the wall next to him. Immediately a screen appeared which showed a directional route.

"Confirm route," said a computerized voice. Duncan finished tapping out another series of inputs and leaned over to take Caitriona's hands in his own. Leaning in close, as if to kiss her cheek, he whispered in her ear, "Freedom is something my people have never known. We canna continue blind tae the Order's perversions. We have tae find a way tae defend ourselves. If ye were scared today, ye'd do well tae remember that. Had they caught on tae our ruse, ye would already have been dead.

There is zero toleration for any genetic deviations."

Caitriona gave a slight shudder and pulled away from him. She was no longer sure of her feelings when she was near him. He was intoxicating, to say the least. He was powerful, confident, and sure of his cause. But she also saw a dark side in him, one that allowed him to disengage his feelings and allow the ruthless warrior within to be unleashed.

"We can talk further when we reach the castle," Duncan interrupted her thoughts. Caitriona resumed her almost hypnotic review of the landscape, still struggling to acclimate herself to this strange new world that boasted zero tolerance for any sort of diversity. She continued to watch for any signs they were nearing their destination, but as far as she could see, there were simply overgrown fields of heather, craggy rocks, and caves; a landscape held pristinely virgin from the people who once, long ago, polluted her with an overabundance of technology, effluence, and garbage. *We are indeed a scourge upon the Earth*, she mused to herself.

Caitriona saw the castle long before she felt the engines powering down. She looked over at Duncan and noticed the almost giddy excitement in his eyes for the home he loved so dearly. The shuttle touched down slowly on a strip of land about fifty yards from the outer castle walls. Caitriona was in awe of the stone giant which Duncan indicated had been handcrafted in the late 14th century and was now the only dwelling to still stand near what used to be Inverness.

Duncan motioned to the hatch that was opening and got up to escort Caitriona from the ship. Once she was safely on ground, the space shuttle closed its hatch automatically, hummed softly as it lifted into the air, and then sped forward, the automatic pilot accurately charting its next course. Once gone from view, it was difficult to find any traces of technology in the bustling little community. Caitriona once more lifted her face to the sun, allowing a tiny smile to light her features. The sun felt warm on her skin and everywhere the smell of heather invaded her senses.

Duncan had explained to her that the large castle was originally built sometime in the late 14th century, although the earliest written records mentioned 1401. The castle had an outer curtain wall—popular at that time—stretching around the castle on either side of the heavily fortified outer gate-house. Caitriona could see arrow slits on both sides, with a crenellated parapet that she knew would have allowed defenders of the castle an advantage when shooting. At the top of the gate-house, behind the parapet, there was an allure, a small walkway that allowed access between the parapets. She also noticed several sharp shooters strategically positioned in guard stations along the allure; an ever present reminder that they were never alone.

As she and Duncan emerged from the gatehouse into the outer court of the castle, Caitriona noticed the various domestic buildings that lined the entrance and stretched away unimpeded to the west. The buildings surrounding the courtyard resembled those of a Tudor manor house style, and Caitriona noticed large gatherings of people rushing about to get their work done. The Great Hall was to the east, while a bell tower and a minute oriel window rounded out the courtyard scene.

Caitriona couldn't believe what she was seeing. It was as if she had suddenly awakened in the 14th century. *How could this have happened,* she thought incredulously. As they neared the outer wall, people waved a friendly welcome to Duncan and shouted greetings. Duncan waved back and shouted Gaelic greetings in return. The smile that had been absent Duncan's face for so long had suddenly reappeared lightening his earlier dark mood. He turned to look at Caitriona, who had begun walking slower as she continued to marvel at the twenty third century. "Tis beautiful, isn't it?" Duncan waved at the expanse of heather, hills, and vegetation that extended as far as the eye could see.

Caitriona nodded, turning absently to look behind her as she saw a small circular probe about twenty-four inches in diameter, appear suddenly out of nowhere and hover in the air slightly behind them. Duncan placed his hand at the small of her back and guided her forward, brushing a kiss on her cheek as he whispered, "Hawkins," with a terse growl. "I will explain once we are in the castle." She allowed him to guide her the rest of the way until they entered the Great Hall amid a throng of people, all talking excitedly and enjoying the myriad of discussions taking place in the amply built room. Large marble pillars supported the half dome which allowed for couples and groups to gather.

Caitriona turned to see the probe follow them a short distance and then, just as quickly as it had appeared, it shot straight up about fifty feet, then paused for a brief second before snapping forward and disappearing from view. Caitriona didn't have much time to ponder this strange occurrence. Upon seeing the couple, an older man raised a marble chalice and saluted them, "To the bride and groom!"

"Here, here!" Others in the room took up the chant. Caitriona felt a slight heat rise to her cheeks as she became the center of attention, especially under such a ruse. Duncan reached for two chalices, offering one to Caitriona as he saluted the throng of people. His eyes scanned the room rapidly. Sighing, he leaned into her and whispered, "The Order's men are here. We will need to continue our ruse a little longer, I'm afraid."

"To returning home safely to friends and family," Duncan said loudly, delivering a believable performance. There were even more congratulatory cheers and people moved excitedly toward them to offer hearty congratulations and a chance to talk to the bride and groom.

"Duncan, lad, where are yer manners?" said a rather stout woman with graying hair and an ample bosom that had long ago succumbed to gravity. She pushed her way to the front of the group and kissed Duncan soundly on both cheeks. "Yer bride must be exhausted by her travels. Have ye na decency, boy, tae offer her a room and a chance to freshen up a wee bit?" Duncan embraced the woman good naturedly and turned to offer an introduction to Caitriona.

"This is my Aunt Lenore. She is my father's youngest sister and has had the great misfortune tae raise me," said Duncan, grinning wickedly from ear to ear. "Any of my bad habits, ye can blame on her."

"Ach," she admonished, slapping him lightly on the back. "Come, lassie, I'll show ye to the bed chambers so ye can freshen up a bit." She placed a hand on Caitriona's arm and started to escort her from the room when Duncan interrupted her mission.

"It's all right, Aunty," said Duncan. "I want the pleasure of being the first to escort my wife to our bed chambers." He gave her a wicked grin and allowed his eyes to openly explore Caitriona's small frame. Before Caitriona could react, he guided her toward the grand staircase at the other end of the hall.

"We will be down in time for dinner," Duncan tossed back over his shoulder with a slight chuckle as he and Caitriona ascended the steep staircase. At the top of the staircase, Duncan scooped Caitriona into his arms, unexpectedly causing her to squeal. The guests down below chuckled in amusement and gave robust encouragement to the long night ahead. "They'll nae' be down for dinner, I can guarantee that," came a deep older voice from the throng of people. Others laughed and went back quickly to their drinking.

Duncan set Caitriona back on her feet when they reached the chamber doors. She adjusted her skirts, not wanting to look him in the eye.

Pushing open the massive oak doors, Duncan motioned for her to enter the room. Caitriona entered, her eyes widening at the plush and elegant surroundings. A large, oversized bed filled with goose down and feathers was the most distinguished piece of furniture in the room. Pillows of every size in rich earth tones beckoned the couple to relax. Colorful tapestries adorned the walls while thick, elegant rugs removed the chill from the floor with their plush warmth. A huge fireplace divided the room nearly in two, allowing warmth to be enjoyed from both sides. Two plush chairs and a matching divan created an inviting sitting area, while a dressing table and matching armoire of rich cherry wood rounded out the furnishings. A Monet and Renoir painting complemented the earlier furnishings and Caitriona couldn't help but wonder if they were originals.

Caitriona turned to Duncan, who had already begun piling more wood on the crackling fire. "It's beautiful." Her unanswered question hung in the air between them.

"I'm afraid as long as we are posing as a married couple, we'll be sharing these chambers," Duncan said, once again seeming to know her unspoken thoughts. "Once our unintended guests have departed, I can have yer belongings moved to another room." He didn't look at her but continued to focus on the flames of the fire.

"I understand," she whispered, shocked that her own words sounded too much like rejection.

"I'll take the divan," he said a little too brusquely. "I've spent many a night there and find it rather comfortable." Caitriona walked over to the divan, running her fingers over the textured material. She glimpsed his arched eyebrow but otherwise he said nothing.

Walking to the open window, Caitriona stared out at the scene below her, wondering how a civilization hundreds of years beyond her own time could, in many respects, be hundreds of years before her time. She felt like Alice and wondered if she would eventually find the rabbit hole to emerge in her time once again.

Duncan broke her quiet reverie and brought her thoughts back to the present. "I've got some business tae take care of that will keep me away the rest of the afternoon and into the early evening," he said. "I'll have tae ask that ye dinna leave the room until I return. While ye are safe here, *Alainn*, there are also many dangers if yer secret were tae become known. If ye have need of anythin', please use this device." He pressed a small, raised circular chip into her hand. "Just press the center and either I or my sister will respond."

Caitriona nodded her head and inspected the chip before placing it on the table. "I thought you said the people at the castle were loyal," she asked solemnly.

"Aye, the residents and staff are quite loyal. Unfortunately, many of the people ye just passed downstairs are nae residents," he said. "Most are from Edinburg and are guests of the Order … here under Hawkins' orders for our wedding celebration. Just stay put for now, and ye'll be safe enough." Duncan crossed to the chamber doors, pausing before he turned to face her. "Caitriona, we are nae' animals. But we have done things we would never have imagined doing. When the day comes, we will be ready and we will take back our freedom!" Not waiting for a reply, he left the room; Caitriona's stunned silence following him into the approaching gray afternoon gloom of the highland hills.

Chapter Ten

Sometimes by losing a battle you find a new way to win the war.
Donald Trump

Brady Hawkins slammed his fist against the large metal frame of the solid gray steel door that was closed, allowing him unfettered privacy. He had received irrefutable evidence that MacKinnon had acquired a new weapon to aid him in his crusade. While he had spent the last several weeks trying to surmise the extent of MacKinnon's cunning, he simply wasn't able to track down MacKinnon's newest weapon. Indeed, MacKinnon seemed far removed from the uprising he was purportedly leading, having just taken a new bride. Hardly seemed like the actions of a man caught up in waging a coup.

Regardless, perhaps MacKinnon's new wife would prove useful; in several ways, he pondered sadistically. He recalled the red headed beauty and wondered if her passion ran as hot as the temper redheads were famous for. Perhaps he could use the girl to get to MacKinnon. After all, love unions were extremely rare any more, and reserved only for those holding high rank; a testament to the career MacKinnon had built and the success he had enjoyed. As such, she would be a rare possession indeed. Something MacKinnon may be inclined to come after. And when he did, he would capture MacKinnon, torture the girl until he found this new "weapon" MacKinnon had supposedly recovered, and expose him for the traitor he knew him to be.

Replaying the scene at the screening station several weeks ago, Hawkins was unsure how MacKinnon had so quickly manipulated the screening equipment so that the girl was able to enter a second time without causing alarm. He had paid a guard dearly to manipulate the equipment to give a false reading. He had then given the young guard explicit instructions to hold the girl until he arrived. But something had gone wrong and the girl had walked right through the screening station. The bigger question was not *how*, but *why*. Perhaps he had been wrong about MacKinnon leading the resistance fighters. After all, his latest actions spoke more of a man devoted to science, than war. Hawkins' intelligence told him that MacKinnon had just returned from a deep space flight where a doctor and psychologist on board the vessel he was piloting had been exploring the effects of deep space on the human body. Of course, that is what the communiqué told him. Hawkins knew MacKinnon's space missions provided him a solid cover if he were indeed the leader of the resistance party and exploring facets of time travel.

But his intelligence had also failed to dig up any real facts on the girl MacKinnon had wed. Supposedly, she came from a small community outside of Chicago. The two had met when MacKinnon was sent to settle a dispute related to his lands. While MacKinnon was in Chicago, he had attended a performance at the Metropolitan and, reportedly, had fallen in love with the girl the moment she stepped on stage. By the end of the first act, MacKinnon was already applying for the proper credentials and permissions to wed.

Hawkins had his men check the girl's profile; she was a Genetic, bred for superior intelligence and musical talent. She was in the last few weeks of her fostering at Chicago when she and MacKinnon met. The remote community was home to hundreds of talented musicians who fostered there under the talented hand of Grand Maester Aulay, an artful composer, musician, and singer. A fast courtship and an exchange of paper work, and the Commander had been granted permission to wed the girl. But Hawkins wasn't stupid. He knew papers could be forged, information planted, and truths concealed. He would be wise to send a small team to investigate their story.

Hawkins stopped pacing and stared out the window at the activity below him. The New World Order had taken command of the capitol in Washington, DC nearly fifty years earlier. Most of the city had been deserted by then, the Smithsonian museum long forgotten by its meticulous caretakers and inquisitive citizens. Grass had grown into cracked staircases and abandoned doorways; the structure's once emblazoned beauty now relegated to the past and to the memories of those who walked her halls. The artwork, books, and documents that had once brought the past to life now lay scattered throughout abandoned buildings, the rich history they once provided now consigned to the elements and dust that weathered and cracked their former beauty.

Hawkins preferred to spend his time in Germany, but met regularly with his officers at the Order's headquarters in the US. At present, the Order's military leaders occupied the White House, the men having destroyed the plush tapestries, furnishings and paintings that had once lined the great home. Peeling paint and wallpaper provided further proof of the Order's disdain for beauty; theirs was merely a quest for the Order's cause that all men serve the Order and the greater good of the Order's command. Hawkins' commanding officer chose this location because of its historical importance; he wanted the people of earth to recognize his power and authority. By choosing this location, he knew it sent a message to the people that freedom and self-expression would no longer be tolerated. To emphasize this point, Hawkins' men scourged the Statue of Freedom that for over 300 years had remained atop the Capitol as a symbol of the freedom guaranteed to all Americans under the constitution.

The door opened softly behind him yet Hawkins did not turn around. His command post was heavily guarded so he knew it could be none other than his second in command, Harry Billinger. His second in command was fiercely devoted to the Order's cause. As such, he killed at will; many times for only a slight suspicion of treason or espionage from those he sought. Because of the various torture devices he had acquired, he had earned the nickname, Harry the Horrible.

Billinger closed the door and stood waiting to be acknowledged. Hawkins knew his men had learned many years ago to tread softly around him lest they rile his rancor to an unearthly level. Without turning, Hawkins said, "What news do you bring from the Southern army?"

"The front lines have collapsed," Billinger stated flatly. "We were unable to penetrate the perimeter."

Hawkins clenched his fist, working hard to maintain his composure and his temper. The Southern army was vastly inferior to his own Northern army that repeatedly scored more deaths than any of the other troops. However, each army was his responsibility and the defeat the Southern army routinely experienced did little to lighten his already dark mood. He turned to face his second in command, his brown eyes hard and his lips pulled into a tight, thin line. He could sense Billinger's unease and knew the man was probably counting the seconds until he was dismissed. "Where are the armies now?" asked Hawkins.

"The men have fallen back and have regrouped south of the Mexican border," stated Billinger. "They are waiting for new orders."

"Damn it," thundered Hawkins, his fist striking the weathered cherry wood of the desk he had just vacated. "We should have had them by now! We have the best armies, yet these vermin continue to evade our patrols and strike down our men! Kill the man in charge and move his second to the command position. Make sure he understands his orders. I do not want to hear of failure again!"

Billinger saluted brusquely and backed quickly out of the room. Hawkins continued his rhythmic pacing, fury evident in his reddening face. The Dwellers were useless eaters. Contaminants to the Master Race, they threatened to keep the world from achieving the mission his ancestors had put into motion over a thousand years ago. He simply couldn't let anything or anyone disrupt their cause.

Chapter Eleven

Exploration is really the essence of the human spirit.
Frank Borman

Caitriona paced the large room, pausing every so often to warm her hands by the fire. She was angry that Duncan had left her in the room like a caged animal. Looking out the window at the bustling activity below, she suddenly wanted to be out among the action and enjoying what was left of the magnificent highland day.

Giggling like a schoolgirl, she crossed the room and quietly opened the large chamber door. Glancing up and down the hall, she suddenly remembered the chip Duncan had given her and ran to the small nightstand to retrieve it. Grabbing the disk hurriedly and closing the door softly behind her, she made her escape down the long hall; apprehension causing her heartbeat to accelerate and her pulse to quicken.

The guests were still indulging noisily and singing hearty drinking songs; their infectious laughter making Caitriona giddy with excitement. Not wanting to be seen, she ran quickly past the grand staircase, looking for the servants' stairwell she knew would be present in a castle this old. She barely noticed the grand furnishings, paintings, or elaborately carved architecture as she made her way toward the servants' staircase. Pausing at the bottom of the stairs, she peered cautiously around the corner, unsure of what she would do if she were caught. *As far as anyone knows, I'm the mistress of this castle, so why am I sneaking around?* Forcing herself to appear poised, she passed through the large kitchen, noting as she did the blend of technology and antiquated tools. *This is a curious place,* she mused, once again feeling like Alice in a very strange Wonderland.

Seeing her target in sight, Caitriona picked up her pace and had just made it to the back door when a young girl about sixteen years old spotted her. "M'lady, I'm sorry to be so tardy with your tray of food," the young girl said quickly, dipping her head slightly to Caitriona. "I promise I'll have it for you shortly. It's just that Cook hurt herself and delayed everything."

"It's fine ..."

"Anna," the young girl supplied.

"Anna, that's a pretty name." Caitriona noticed the girl began to blush. Classic blonde hair and blue eyes, petite figure and beautiful, even teeth, made Caitriona wonder if the girl had been genetically engineered with these traits or if she was simply the offspring of beautiful parents. Realizing Anna was still watching her, Caitriona sought hastily to find a response that wouldn't arouse suspicion. *Suspicion for what*, she wondered?

"Anna, please don't worry about the tray of food," Caitriona said. At the look of alarm on the girl's face, she hastily added, "I am going to go out and enjoy the fresh air. When I return, I'll accept your most gracious hospitality."

The young girl beamed her approval and nodded, allowing Caitriona to make her escape outdoors. Despite the chill and the now threatening, overcast skies, Caitriona felt exhilarated. Pulling at the tartan shawl she had grabbed tighter around her shoulders, she shivered as the chill from the damp air penetrated the thin wool shawl and invaded her bones. Realizing that people were beginning to stare at her, she headed quickly in the direction of the cliffs she had seen earlier that day.

As she quickly left the security of the castle grounds, she noted the absence of any people outside the walls and wondered why there weren't more people spread out in the surrounding areas. Stopping several times to admire the view and breathe deeply of the lavender and heather, Caitriona lost track of how far she had wandered. She had chosen to follow the path along the cliffs, enjoying the sound of the waves crashing against the rocks below. The wind tore through her shawl, but she was unaware of the cold; her thoughts focused on her new surroundings. Behind her, she could still see the castle, although it looked much smaller and she could no longer see the outer walls or dwellings that lined the inner castle wall.

Caitriona didn't know how much time had passed; it was difficult to tell the position of the sun because of the dense cloud cover that had crept quickly in. Deciding she didn't want to get too far from the castle, she chose to sit for a few moments before starting back. She was certain if she didn't rest too long, she could make it back before night fall. She walked closer to the cliff's edge and chose a rather large rock to sit on, stretching her long legs out before her. Sighing, she looked out at the ocean, mesmerized by its almost hypnotic movement. Before her, the sun was beginning its westerly descent, the clouds seeking to mask its brilliance before its final disappearance over the horizon. Caitriona breathed deeply of the fresh ocean air, a painful reminder of her hometown and the salty sea-air that permeated the Seattle waterfront. Lost in her musings, she didn't hear the man approach her from behind.

"Well, look at what I've found," said a gruff voice, several feet beyond her resting point.

Jumping to her feet, Caitriona suddenly questioned her judgment in venturing so far from the castle unescorted. Seeing no one, she said with more bravado than she felt, "What do you want? Show yourself!" Trying to find the source of her phantom visitor, Caitriona scanned the rocks and various hiding places, but still saw no one.

"Ye're a feisty lass, that's fer certain," the man chuckled. Caitriona peered in the direction of the voice and saw movement in some dense vegetation next to the rocky crag, just beyond her line of sight.

Caitriona considered making a run for the castle, but even if she could outrun the man, she'd never have the stamina to make it all the way to the castle. Deciding she was better off utilizing the fighting skills she had mastered over several years of careful study and preparation, Caitriona placed her arms akimbo and challenged the man once again to show himself.

Emerging from behind a recess set deep within the face of the cliff, the man walked slowly toward her. Caitriona noted that he walked with a slight limp, had yellowing teeth and solid streaks of gray in an overgrown beard. *He couldn't possibly have been genetically engineered*, she thought, noting the scars on his face that bore evidence of adolescent acne. She wondered if he was a Dweller, especially since he had emerged seemingly from nowhere.

"Think ye're too high-n-mighty for the likes of old Max, eh, girly?"

Caitriona instinctively took a step backward. She stumbled as her foot came up against the rock she had just vacated. She cried out as she tumbled backward. Max chose that opportunity to spring forward. He was surprisingly agile and grabbed her by the arm before she could regain her footing. Grinning wickedly, he suddenly dropped his hold on her arm and grabbed her hair instead, yanking her painfully to her feet.

"Ye damn Genetics think ye own the world," the old man snarled, dragging her toward the opening in the cave. "I wonder what they'll think when we carve ye up and send ye back to them in little pieces." He cackled with apparent delight at his own devious musings.

Caitriona clawed at his hands, but she was no more effective than a fly caught in a spider's web. Unable to gain an advantage, Caitriona tried to shift her weight to break his hold. Max tightened his grip, firm in his resolve to drag her into the caves. Crying out again, she knew her situation was getting desperate. Max pushed her roughly down into the dirt and kicked her hard in the ribs. Caitriona doubled over, clutching at her abdomen as she coughed violently. Tears welled up in her eyes and she fought hard against the wave of nausea that overcame her. She tried to get to her feet, but he kicked her again, this time landing a blow to her jaw. Darkness engulfed her as she struggled to keep conscious.

"Ye damn Genetics want depopulation? Why don't ye start with yer own first!" He spat at her and walked into the cave. Caitriona was vaguely aware that she was alone. She couldn't think, and she was quite confident she had a broken a rib or two. Max reappeared at the cave mouth, carrying a large broadsword. Caitriona cried out and tried to inch away from the crazed man.

"Ye think there are too many of us *useless eaters*, on the planet, eh, girlie? Ye think we are an infection that's destroyin' the planet, when it is ye and yer kind who have created this hell we live in. Yer damn Order wishes to eliminate us so they can have the world to themselves!" Max was getting more agitated as his diatribe continued. Caitriona looked around for a weapon of some sort, wishing she had had the foresight to bring a knife from the kitchen.

Remembering the chip Duncan had insisted she carry, she felt around in her pocket and pulled it out, careful not to alert Max to her movements. Pressing the center button, she hoped it was all that was needed to summon help, and that her rescuer would arrive before Max had completed his singular deadly mission.

Max continued with his rant, seemingly unconcerned that she was inching further from the cave opening. "The war on our minds and bodies has been long, monstrous, and incomprehensible to most," he ranted noisily. "The war for our souls, though, aye, that is just beginin'.

Many have been deceived, but none of ye wants to see the truth. Seek the truth fer yerself and it shall set you free!" He emphasized his words by swinging the broadsword in a wide arc. As he brought the sword down, Caitriona managed to roll away from the sword's deadly aim. She wasn't quite fast enough, however. The sword caught her on the side; a painful burning ripping through her body. Caitriona gave an astonished yelp and tried once again to pull herself upright. Collapsing against the pain, she cried out in fear.

"What is your filth working on these days?" Max asked angrily. He was hovering over her, his broadsword red with her blood. He propped the weapon next to his leg. "With their deep connections, there's no tellin' what weapons or diseases they have been workin' on in secret fer all these years."

Caitriona realized he was a guerrilla, fighting for the oppressed against the powerful. Hearing voices coming from the cave, she glanced in the direction of the cave opening and saw approximately thirty people emerge from the cave. They eyed her warily, circling her as they cast cautious glances toward the sky.

"Max, what have you done?" hissed a younger woman who walked with a slight limp. "We can't risk exposure of the cave, you moron!"

"We should kill her," said another man, eyeing Caitriona's movements with interest. "Aye," the crowd chimed in. "We can dispose of her body in the ocean," stated the woman who originally seemed to question the old man's motives, yet now seemed bent on killing Caitriona as well.

"Please don't," Caitriona pleaded with her captors.

They were unsympathetic and merely looked at her with undisguised disgust. Max raised his sword and walked over to her. Kicking her once more, he raised the sword above her head. Closing her eyes, tears streaming down her cheeks, she continued to push her body back away from him, sobbing hysterically. *This isn't how I'm supposed to die*, she thought absently.

"*Is leor din!*" Duncan's voice was explosively loud over the ocean waves and general commotion of the other Dwellers. Max turned to look at Duncan, who was charging up to the group, his large stallion lathered from the hard ride.

Max turned his focus back to his captive, raising the sword once more, deciding the Highlander was not a threat. "Stand down, Duncan. This doesna concern ye, lad," he stated.

"Stop!" Duncan dismounted quickly from his horse and drew his sword. He was a commanding presence with his broad shoulders and warrior's stance. Next to him the stallion snorted impatiently, tossing its head in agitation. "It is ye who will stand down, Max, or I will kill ye." Duncan snarled the last sentence, raising his broadsword in one hand above his head while his other hand panned out in front of him to motion the crowd back. Caitriona tried to raise her head, but everything blurred before her. Struggling against the heaviness she felt in her lids, she had only one thought before darkness overtook her; *Duncan had come for her.*

***

Duncan was acutely aware that Caitriona had slipped into unconsciousness. He had quickly assessed her condition and knew she had been severely injured. He swore beneath his breath but remained focus on the threat before him. What was Caitriona thinking? Did he nae command her to stay in her room? Once again, he had sorely underestimated his willful charge.

"Move away from her, Max," Duncan growled tersely. Max considered the Highlander and then snarled, "Ye've never been one of us." As he swung the sword, Duncan didn't hesitate but thrust the blade quickly. Max staggered back, his sword falling inches from Caitriona's now still form. Blood gushed from the lethal wound Duncan had inflicted to Max's heart. Clutching his heart in an attempt to stop the bleeding, Max looked down at his blood soaked hands, the disbelief on his face clearly evident as he shifted his gaze from his soaked tunic to Duncan's stoic reserve.

Some of the Dwellers who had gathered at the cave front now drew weapons of varying sizes and faced Duncan. Eyeing them warily, Duncan swept the bloody broadsword before him, "She is yer Seer, ye fools!"

The hush that followed was deafening. All weapons dropped noisily to the ground and some of those who had gathered dropped to one knee, not wanting to look at the Highlander. "Duncan, we had no way of knowing," stated the woman who had not dissuaded the group from their earlier, deadly plan.

Scooping his now unconscious charge into his arms, he noted her slight wince as he placed too much pressure on the damaged ribs. "*Damnu!*" he exclaimed loudly. "*Is lior din!*" he growled at the gathering crowd. They stepped back instinctively as he wrapped his cloak protectively around her.

"She should nae have come here, Duncan," said a tall, lean man who had bravely approached the warrior. "Ye ken there is a war amongst our people, lad. Why was she nae warned of the dangers?"

"Ye would have killed her! We agreed from the onset, we were done with the killing," he yelled angrily at the mob. "How can we move past our differences when yer answer to anythin' is more bloodshed?"

"We can't risk the cave, you know that," said Rowe, the youngest in the crowd, who had stepped forward with some clean rags and some water. She was all muscle and dark tattoos. Her mouse-brown hair had been shaved close to her scalp on one side of her head, but left long on the other side. The remaining hair was pulled tight across her scalp and braided in thin, tight corn rows that cascaded down her back. The effect was stunning in a brutal and animalistic way. "Think of the children, Duncan! We have to think of their safety!"

Duncan looked at his charge, whose breathing was labored and slow. Blood coated her dress and hair and dark bruises were already gathering along her cheeks and eyes. He couldn't risk the location of the cave by contacting his sister, yet he knew his young charge needed medical attention.

"Rowe, can you heal her?" he asked the young woman who had brought the bandages, and was already wiping blood from Caitriona's face. "I can," she stated simply. "But it won't be as fast as what your doctors could manage. We do have some supplies and instruments, but not many."

Duncan nodded his agreement. "We should get her inside. We risk much by standing out here." He adjusted his arms under Caitriona's legs and back carefully to support her as gently as possible. As he shifted her weight, she cried out and her eyes fluttered open.

"Dinna fash yerself, lass. 'Tis a wee scratch, is all." He was certain she could hear the worry in his voice. He shifted her weight once again, wishing he could take away the fear, pain and desolation he knew she felt. He brushed his lips against her forehead. Feeling her relax against him, he whispered soothing words to her in his native tongue until she slipped into a troubled sleep once more.

Chapter Twelve

Hope is necessary in every condition. The miseries of poverty, sickness and captivity would, without this comfort, be insupportable.
William Samuel Johnson

For the next several days, Duncan watched as Caitriona drifted in and out of consciousness. She seemed vaguely aware of his presence, and, for his part, he rarely left the young woman's side. He was furious with himself for having left her alone so soon after arriving at Dunrobin Castle, and even more irritated that he had sorely underestimated her stubbornness and wretched determination to free herself from her perceived imprisonment.

Duncan sent a message to his sister and father through the communicator he had given to Caitriona earlier. Being careful not to give away his position, he merely said they had decided to spend the next few days in Edinburgh, taking in the city. He was hopeful that anyone monitoring the frequency wouldn't be suspicious and think to check the shuttle logs. His father had understood immediately and had simply asked if they wanted "company." It was his father's way of asking if they needed help. After assuring his father they would return shortly, he had ended the communication and disabled the unit to ensure no one would trace the signal.

The next several days Duncan spent by Caitriona's side. He changed her bandages, allowing Rowe to relieve him only when he needed rest. Caitriona continued to drift in and out of consciousness. She tossed restlessly, and he wondered what demons she wrestled that left her bathed in sweat. For the most part, she seemed unaware of where she was and what had happened. While none of her wounds were life threatening, the antiquated tools and medicines the Dwellers had on hand were inadequate to speed up the healing process. Regardless, Duncan could not risk disclosing their location simply to have the Seer healed in a matter of minutes compared to weeks.

Duncan grimaced with the thought of how much time he had lost. The council was meeting in less than three weeks and he still hadn't made any headway in eliciting Caitriona's help and tapping into the special gifts he knew she possessed. To exacerbate the problem, he blamed himself for the fact that Caitriona had almost died. He had acted irrationally and carelessly in leaving his charge alone. *Damnu,* he thought, running a hand through his unruly hair. *Her handler would not have made such a grave error.* He winced at the thought of the dark-haired handsome young French man who would soon guide and share in Caitriona's life. Duncan knew he had erred by letting his feelings for the lass get in the way of his mission. He should never have left her so soon after arriving at the castle, but the encounter with Hawkins had not sat well with him. It was no accident that Hawkins had been at the screening station. Duncan wanted to know why.

"Penny for your thoughts, Duncan?" Rowe asked as she entered the small, dark chambers with fresh linens and water. The torches in the room cast long shadows against the wall. At his silence, she changed the subject. "You must be exhausted. I can watch over her while you go rest." The young woman set the supplies down on the nightstand and placed the back of her hand against Caitriona's forehead.

Duncan shook his head, running his hand once again through his long, dark hair. Stretching, he took the fresh bandages from the nightstand and began undoing Caitriona's wraps. "I'll stay with her, lass," Duncan said wearily. "Have there been any sightings?" He was referring to the drones the Order regularly sent to the countryside to track down Dwellers and eliminate their homes. As such, most of the Dwellers had gone underground long ago to escape a life of hardship and tyranny. Those who were found were pressed into servitude for the Order and sterilized so as not to contaminate the genetic population. Children, the elderly, and the sick were simply killed on sight.

"None recently," she said. There was a rather uncomfortable silence as Rowe deliberated on how to approach the next subject. "Duncan, Max acted alone when he went after the girl. Had we known she was the Seer, we never ..."

Duncan's stony gray eyes were like a blade as he interrupted her apology. "Even if she were nae the Seer, when will the killing end,

Rowe? I've proven myself loyal to this cause. We agreed there would be no more killing."

"Duncan, the children … we couldn't risk anyone finding this location. You know that," Rowe placed a hand on his shoulder and met his steely gaze. "There is renewed hope among our people now that you have brought the Seer. We are prepared to guard her—with our lives—if necessary." Rowe picked up the old bandages and prepared to leave the room. "I'll bring you some food. You need to eat."

When Rowe had left, Duncan looked at the restless woman who carried the hopes of an entire nation, "The Goddess give us all strength for what must be done."

***

Caitriona awoke hours later to darkness and shadows. How long had she been out? She had to find Duncan. She sat up quickly and groaned. Her head felt as if it would split in two.

"Relax, Seer. The danger is past," said Duncan, his brogue thick with emotion.

Caitriona sat up and squinted, her eyes struggling to adjust to the darkness. Duncan sat in a big mahogany chair, watching her. He kicked his boots up onto the scarred oak table and relaxed back into the oversized chair.

Lowering herself back down to the pillows, she closed her eyes and inhaled sharply. The room smelled of spice and sandalwood and everything Duncan. Releasing her breath, she opened her eyes slowly, noting Duncan's deep scowl and relaxed position. He had bathed and changed into casual riding clothes, his deeply tanned skin making his white shirt seem brighter. She tried to push herself up on her elbows and paused as a wave of dizziness washed over her.

"Rest, Seer," Duncan said abruptly. "You will need to regain your strength quickly if we are to return to Dunrobin."

"Duncan, I didn't …" she abruptly quit speaking when he waved her silent.

"I dinna want an explanation," he said angrily. "It's clear ye think of yerself as a prisoner. Ye will have yer wish, Seer." He pushed himself up from the chair abruptly and was at her side in two strides. "From now on, ye will be under locked guard. Ye will not be allowed any freedoms save for the ones I grant ye."

Caitriona glared at her captor, challenging him with her eyes. "I am not some possession you can keep under lock and key, Commander. I will not be treated as such! I never asked for any of this, and I refuse to play the part you've cast for me in this … insanity!" She pushed the covers away from her and swung her legs over the edge of the bed. Fully intending to leave, she stood, the pain in her temples a harsh reminder of the trauma she had suffered days earlier.

Duncan merely watched her, and she realized suddenly he felt secure, knowing the perimeter was locked and there would be nowhere for her to go. His nonchalant, detached attitude rankled her even more, reminding her that she was every bit the prisoner and at his mercy.

Realizing she was wearing only a thin camisole and panties, she cast modesty aside and instead searched out the room for the remainder of her clothes. Duncan followed her movements motioning with one finger in the direction of a large trunk. Caitriona glared at him but retrieved her clothes hurriedly and began pulling them on. The pain in her head was building to an excruciating climax, but was nothing when compared to the pain that was building in her rib cage. Pressing her hand to her side in an effort to quell the ache, Caitriona winced, leaning over slightly to catch her breath.

Duncan continued to eye her like a cat who had just found a mouse and was relishing the game that was about to be played. A slight smile tugged at the corners of his lips, infuriating Caitriona even more. Crossing to the door, she tugged at the door knob, thankful for a piece of old fashioned mechanics that enabled a more graceful exit from the room. Finding the door locked, she whirled back to her captor and spat angrily at him, "Unlock this door at once!"

Seeing the fury in her eyes, Duncan motioned toward the bed. "Sit down, Seer." She glared at him, refusing to follow his instructions. The pain in her side caused her to inhale sharply, but she pushed it away, her anger taking center stage.

"Do not bark orders at me, Commander," she stressed the formal title. "If you'll recall, I have something that you need." She tilted her head slightly to the side, a sardonic smile playing at the corners of her lips.

"And we will be the recipients of your very special gift, with or without your consent," Duncan stated menacingly. "Now sit down. And do not challenge me again."

Caitriona glared at him but returned to the edge of the bed. Glancing down at the pain in her rib cage, she noticed blood was beginning to soak her bodice. She touched the growing stain, staring incredulously and wondering why there wasn't more pain. Duncan got up quickly and pressed her back against the pillows, ripping open the front of her bodice and camisole so that he had quick access to the source of the bleeding. Looking up at Duncan, she suddenly felt nauseous and closed her eyes against the dizziness.

Crossing the room quickly and unlocking the door, Duncan yelled out into the long hallway. "Rowe, I need help, now!" he thundered, his voice echoing through the cavernous chambers. Rowe appeared quickly and wasted no time assessing the damage. "She's reopened the wound," she stated tersely. "Damn it, Duncan, what was she doing out of bed?"

"Can you repair the damage?" Duncan asked, ignoring Rowe's question.

Caitriona felt like she was a bystander at a crime scene. She listened, detached, to the order's that flew from Duncan's mouth, while Rowe worked to stop the bleeding.

"I'm not sure," Rowe placed a clean bandage directly on the wound and applied pressure. Motioning for Duncan to continue applying pressure, she ran from the room. Returning quickly with her medical bag, she evaluated the damage. She turned to the worried Commander and shook her head. "Duncan, I can try to close it again, but she really needs your technology, now. I don't have the tools needed to close the wound properly. If we don't get her the advanced help she needs, she could bleed to death. Your sister should treat her."

"We can't move her, Rowe. She'd never survive the ride back to the castle, not to mention the suspicion we would arouse."

"Duncan, she will die if I'm unable to stop the bleeding." She stared at him, both locking eyes. Caitriona fought back the blackness that was already threatening to take her. She knew, even without looking at her two guards, who would win this battle.

Duncan took his cloak from the hook by the door and turned to face Rowe. "I'll bring my sister."

"But Duncan, the risk …?"

"Will be a moot point if the Seer is dead. Take care of her, Rowe. Our very existence depends on this."

"The Goddess be with you," she said as he left the security of the cave without another look at Caitriona.

***

Duncan rode hard and made the trek to the castle in less than twenty minutes. It would be nightfall before he would be able to find his sister and gather the supplies they would need. The castle was quiet as most of the occupants had long since retired to their sleeping chambers. Duncan's father was seated near the fire in the Great Hall, drinking a brandy as he stared blankly into the fire. Seeing Duncan, he got quickly to his feet and greeted his son warmly.

"Duncan, what news do you bring?"

"The Seer has been injured," Duncan stated hurriedly. At his father's questioning look, Duncan continued quickly. "I will have to fill you in later, Father. Right now I need Fiona and we need to hurry."

"Of course, of course," Gawain said. Setting the brandy on a nearby table, Gawain activated his communicator and sighed when he heard Fiona's smooth voice on the other end.

"Father, is everything alright? It's unusually late for you to be opening communications," Fiona asked, concern lacing her voice.

"Fi, Duncan's returned - alone," Gawain told his daughter. Duncan added in a rush. "I need you to bring your medical equipment and join me for a ride. I'll fill you in when you're here."

"Understood," she stated quickly. Duncan heard the familiar hiss of the communication link being severed and knew his sister would be downstairs shortly. "Have we aroused any suspicion?" Duncan asked.

"None. As far as anyone knows, you and the lass have been locked in wedded bliss," he gave a slight chuckle at the memories the tale conjured. "Duncan, how bad is she?"

"Two cracked ribs, internal injuries, and head trauma," he stated.

Gawain inhaled sharply. "There is too much riding on this, son. Will she recover?"

"Aye, but we'll need to hurry," Duncan began pacing, impatient for his sister to arrive.

As if on cue, Fiona came down the stairwell carrying her medical kit and a small overnight bag. She had dressed quickly, choosing to wear a dark jumpsuit that was typical of those in her profession. The outfit hugged her shape nicely, accenting each curve. Sweeping her reddish-blond hair into a pony tail, she secured her hair quickly and gave her brother a tight hug.

"We'll return when we can," Duncan told his father. Fiona gave the old man a quick hug and kissed his cheek lightly.

Outside, Fiona reached for her saddled mare; a pure line Appaloosa that had been given to her as a gift by her father several years earlier. The mare tossed her head and snorted derisively, upset by the stable hand who had interrupted her nightly feeding. Fiona swung up easily, years of practice and experience making her appear a natural. She clicked her heels and patted the mare's golden mane. Duncan swung himself easily onto his mount, and together they set off into the cool darkness of the night, the moon casting the only light as they navigated the castle grounds and disappeared deep into the Highlands' shadows.

***

"Caitriona, I'm here, lass. Listen to me." Duncan brushed a strand of matted hair from the Seer's face, noting the yellow and purple bruises that darkened her brow. Fiona opened her medical kit quickly and scanned Caitriona's injuries, inhaling as she surveyed the readings on the instrument panel. Caitriona groaned slightly, helplessly trying to push the instruments away as Fiona worked to stop the bleeding and close the wound.

Duncan watched as Fiona removed several instruments from her bag, never ceasing her patient ministrations. Holding a small instrument about the size of a ball point pen, she used the tiny laser to close the wound. Her hand steady, it took several passes until the wound began to close and fade from view. Administering some pain medication to the base of Caitriona's skull, Fiona wiped the perspiration which had beaded on Caitriona's forehead during her treatment. Eyeing her work, she released a sigh and turned to face her brother who continued to pace worriedly in the small room.

Fiona straightened and closed her bag, carefully replacing the instruments that were as much a part of her as the very air she breathed. Arching one brow, Duncan said nothing but was relieved when Fiona stated his charge would recover. "She needs rest, brother," Fiona said as he remained staring at Caitriona. The covers were drawn around her body and he watched the labored rise and fall of her chest as she succumbed to a drug-induced sleep.

At the silence that pervaded the room, Rowe came forward and touched Fiona lightly on the arm. "You must be exhausted, Fiona," she spoke softly. "Let me show you to your quarters. You can rest for the night and decide in the morning if the girl is well enough to travel." Fiona allowed herself to be led from the room, casting one last glance at her brother, whose concern was visible on his handsome features. Once the door was closed and the room emptied of its occupants, Duncan went to Caitriona's side and sat next to her on the bed. He closed his eyes and inhaled sharply. He had almost lost her today.

Duncan opened his eyes slowly, taking in the subtle beauty of the girl who openly defied and challenged him. He touched her cheek lightly, marveling at the soft, silken texture of her skin; *like corn starch*, he thought absently. He bent to press a kiss to her forehead, wanting in that single gesture to right her world and erase the struggles she had already faced.

At her soft moan, he drew back hesitantly and watched her face for any sign that she might awaken. Feeling his arousal growing, Duncan stepped away from the bed and took up the methodic pacing that had kept his thoughts at bay for the past several hours.

"Duncan," the soft, hesitant sound of his charge's voice brought him out of his musings and quickly to her side. He sat down next to her and pressed her hand between his palms.

"*Ciunas*, Seer," he said quietly. "Ye must rest. No more fighting, lass."

Caitriona stared at Duncan, her eyes a mystery to him. Beneath the dark lashes, the remnants of the dark bruises Max had inflicted were just beginning to fade, thanks to his sister's instruments and gifted ministrations. "I am sorry." A tear traced its way slowly down her battered and bruised face, reminding Duncan of how he had failed his charge.

Duncan reached out and wiped the tear with the back of his finger, allowing his hand to linger for just a moment before he retracted it and placed it in his lap. His emotions were dangerously close to being out of his control. He took a deep breath and exhaled slowly, willing his thoughts to places other than the woman lying in the small bed.

"'Tis I who am sorry, *lass*," Duncan said softly. "I have failed ye. I promised ye would be safe and yet I've allowed my anger to put yer life at risk." His voice was husky with emotion. Caitriona mustered a wan smile through the shallow cuts around her mouth that were just beginning to heal.

"I am stubborn, Duncan," she said softly. "You are trying to keep me safe and yet I obstinately refuse to abide by your wishes. I'm just so confused here." Her voice broke and the tears that were pooling at the surface of her eyes now spilled over her thick lashes in unimpeded streams. Duncan reached out and brushed the tears away with his thumb. His own feelings were at war with his sense of duty and loyalty to his mission. He had never counted on developing such strong feelings for the girl, but he had. He wished fervently that there was some way he could still fulfill his mission yet allow the young lass to go home.

There was a light rap at the thick wood door, which startled them both from their somber interlude. Without waiting for an invitation, Rowe pushed her way in bearing a tray of dried meat, berries, and breads. "I see our patient is awake," Rowe said. Duncan swore softly beneath his breath at the untimely intrusion.

Setting the tray on the table nearest the bed, Rowe bent to examine the nearly healed wounds. "This is healing nicely," she said to Duncan, noting the relief that passed briefly over his dark features. "I have brought you both something to eat," she stated, nodding at the tray of food that had already begun to fill the room with the rich scent of freshly baked bread. Duncan realized it had been a while since he'd last eaten, but he was more concerned that his charge eat and begin to restore her strength. The council was meeting soon and he was duty bound to ensure her safe arrival.

Rowe poured a glass of water and offered it to Caitriona, who took the glass in both hands. She took several sips before handing it back to Rowe. Duncan had piled a plate with the fresh bread and hand churned butter. His charge's stomach growled noisily and he laughed heartily, much encouraged by her apparent appetite.

After his charge consumed two thick slices of the buttered bread, Duncan eased her back against the pillows and he and Rowe stepped out of the room.

Duncan pulled Rowe away from the door and motioned for her to keep her voice low. He was still concerned that there had been no patrol sightings. "It doesna' add up, Rowe," Duncan said, his deep brogue more pronounced with the effort it took to keep his voice low. "We've made three trips from the castle in the last week and there hasna been so much as one probe." The low flying cylindrical drones were the Order's robotic sentries. Designed to cover the countryside and penetrate dense areas, the drones were adept at finding non-genetics and relaying the coordinates instantaneously to the closest base camp. Armed patrols could then be dispatched in a matter of minutes, eviscerating those who had not had a chance to disappear below ground. "Something's nae right," Duncan growled. His military senses were on full alert.

"We've had guards patrol the outer perimeter since the Seer was first brought inside. There's been nothing amiss. Nothing is out of place," Rowe insisted.

"Ye ken as well as I do that the Order regularly patrols this area," Duncan replied tersely. "The fact that we havna seen the drones in over a week is nae an accident."

"What are you suggesting?" Rowe asked hesitantly.

"We're being watched," he stated firmly. Rowe shook her head and started to protest but he waved her quiet. "The Order knows we're here and that we have the Seer. They're baiting us."

"What do you suggest?"

"The Seer needs to regain her strength rapidly. She will have to be moved, and quickly. She is endangering all of you by staying in the caves," Duncan's voice trailed off to a low whisper as he mentally calculated how long it would take until he could safely risk moving his charge.

Rowe nodded. "Duncan, she is still too weak to be moved," she said hesitantly. At his look of mounting fury, she hastily added, "You know that as well as I. I know the risk is great but if she dies from her injuries our one remaining hope dies with her." Rowe waited while the weight of her words settled around him like a heavy cloud.

"Three days, no more," he said tersely.

She nodded again. "I will see to her care myself," she assured him. "Is there anything else we can do?" she added hesitantly.

Duncan could sense Rowe's concern at the timeframe he had given her. Running his hand through his thick hair, he sighed heavily and locked eyes with the young Dweller. "Nay, it's in the hands of the Goddess now."

Chapter Thirteen

Healing is a matter of time, but it is sometimes also a matter of opportunity. Hippocrates

Duncan spent the next three days tending tirelessly to his charge. He was encouraged by her progress, but it was still slower than he had anticipated. Her appetite didn't favor long journeys that required strength and stamina, and she seemed to be withdrawing into a self-made prison that went far beyond the walls of her room.

Her sleep was almost always troubled and she tossed restlessly until she awoke with a start; her breathing ragged, heartbeat racing, and tears pooling in her sorrow filled green eyes. Caitriona said nothing but seemed to draw strength from his embrace, and so he continued to hold her close, shielding her unseen terrors with a strength that only he possessed. During the first two days in the cave he tried to encourage her to walk, and spent time introducing her to the men, women and children who dwelled within the massive cavern. She smiled, shook hands, and greeted each with a kind word and a thank you, but Duncan noticed she tired easily and her smile never quite reached her eyes. The cave was killing her.

On the morning of the third day, Duncan asked Rowe to help escort his charge to the bathing chamber. He was certain she would feel better after a long, hot bath. He would then let her know they would be leaving. He was uncertain if she would find it a welcome relief or if she would recognize that she was again moving closer to her destiny.

Duncan pushed open the heavy oak door and found Caitriona standing in front of a fire that was nothing more than a soft glow of nearly burned out embers. The room had taken on a slight chill, but Caitriona seemed unconcerned, staring into the dying embers. "It will happen in the caves. This is where it begins." Caitriona stared intently at the embers before her but appeared lost in her second sight.

"Where what begins?" Duncan asked softly, not wanting to disengage her from the vision.

"War. There will be a great war." She began to tremble, but Duncan remained still, determined to allow the vision to play out.

"Tell me what you see, *Alainn,*" Duncan probed gently. He could see she was clearly beyond this world, lost in a dimensional depth only she herself could understand or comprehend.

"If you don't take chances," Caitriona said in a hushed whisper, "you won't be alive." Her body shuddered and Duncan noticed the deep emerald of her eyes had become dull. Although she turned and looked right at him, he knew she was no longer seeing him.

Caitriona raised her right arm and drew an arc with her index finger. "There is a great army that will cover the land like an infestation of ants. No one will escape their destruction. When they leave, the people will look to one leader for strength and direction. That person is surrounded by protectors and friends but doesn't want this role," Caitriona's voice trailed to a small whisper as she concentrated intently on the image that Duncan knew was unfolding in her mind.

Duncan touched her arm softly, but Caitriona's vacuous stare assured him she was consumed in her vision. "Catie, who is it? Can you see his face? I need to know who he is." His voice, although gentle, was insistent and penetrated Caitriona's dark world.

"There are too many people near. I can't see if it's a man or a woman." Her hands began to push at ghosts that appeared only in Caitriona's world.

"You have to try, Caitriona." Duncan squeezed her arm more intently.

"The people don't want me here. They are keeping me from this person, shielding him from me." Caitriona gave a startled cry and stumbled backward. Duncan steadied her as she protected her face from an unseen foe. "I can't be here anymore. They know I'm here." She cried out and suddenly came out of her hypnotic trance. Duncan wrapped his arms around her and motioned for Rowe, who had entered the room silently during Caitriona's vision, to retrieve the blanket that had been cast to the bottom of the bed. He took the blanket from Rowe and folded it gently around Caitriona's body, his gaze taking in the way she watched his movements. He held her close to him.

"Duncan, this person is someone of great importance," she said tiredly. "That person is the one needing protection. I don't know why I know this, but I do. That person is the one who will lead your people to freedom."

"Caitriona, were there any clues to his identity, anything that might be used to track him down?"

"No. it was more of a feeling, Duncan; strong emotions that pulled at me. I don't even know if it's a man or a woman but I could feel the power literally emanating from him. It was strong, like nothing I'd ever felt before." He stared down into her emerald eyes, noting the way her auburn hair lay tangled against her cheeks and forehead.

"We will talk more," he said abruptly, pushing her away from the heat of his body. "Rowe will take you to the bathing chamber and help you into some traveling clothes." At her look of surprise, he added quickly, "It's not safe for you here anymore, *Alainn.*" He stood and walked swiftly to the door. "We leave within the hour," he stated tersely, and quickly fled the room.

***

Caitriona watched as Rowe followed Duncan from the room. She could hear their low whispers just outside the massive oak door. Sighing softly, she glanced around the room; noticing the uneven stone walls that comprised the architecture of the inner cave chamber. For the first time since she'd regained consciousness, she took the time to notice her surroundings. The room was spacious, but sparsely furnished. A small table with one rickety wooden chair pushed all the way in, an old trunk and the large mahogany chair Duncan had occupied earlier were the only furnishings in the room. What the furnishings lacked in quality was made up for in the delicately embroidered cloths that covered the weathered wood of the table. Small torches were recessed to allow the smoke to dissipate through small openings in the cavern walls and ceiling. The light cast eerie shadows across the room, illuminating what would otherwise have been impossible to see.

Caitriona felt a momentary flicker of panic as the room seemed to grow narrow and dark. She closed her eyes tightly and leaned further into the pillows, glad for the warmth of the goose down comforter that enveloped the small bed. *No windows. How do these people live,* she wondered? And suddenly Caitriona imagined a life bereft of sunshine, birds, flowers; everything that had made her world enjoyable. She shuddered involuntarily and continued her dark, brooding thoughts, as she drifted off to a troubled sleep full of dark prisons and darker beings.

Caitriona awoke much later to Rowe's movements around the room. *So much for "leaving within the hour,"* she thought to herself, stretching languidly. She suspected Rowe had something to do with the additional time, and she was grateful the young woman had intervened on her behalf.

"I was just getting ready to wake you," Rowe said, handing Caitriona a warm dressing gown and soft deerskin slippers. Caitriona donned the proffered items hastily and allowed Rowe to help her from the bed, grateful that she'd be able to soak in a tub. She allowed Rowe to escort her to the bathing chamber, noting as she did that the pain in her side was receding. She was looking forward to a nice hot bath and was dimly reminded of another bath in which strong arms had plucked her from tepid water and terrifying visions. She felt her cheeks get hot with embarrassment and hastily pushed the thought away.

It was a rather short walk to the bathing chamber, for which Caitriona was relieved. Allowing Rowe to help her remove her dressing gown, she sank down into a massive stone bath that was heated by natural means. Steam rose in steady puffs that fogged up the small chamber and made it difficult to see. Lavender and chamomile had been added to the water, diminishing the harsh smell of the sulfur, and Caitriona selfishly allowed herself to indulge in the warm water and relax. Rowe had left a selection of soaps and salts at her disposal, and she made short work of cleaning up the grime that was the result of nearly one week in recovery. The bath made her feel human again, and, after washing her hair two times, she sank back in the tub and closed her eyes. She loved the way the natural springs massaged her feet and back lightly.

After fifteen minutes in the languid water, she heard someone enter the chamber. Assuming Rowe had come to help her dry off and get dressed, she sighed, dismayed that her time in the natural stone tub had come to an end. She stood up reluctantly, but dropped quickly to the safety of the tub when she heard Duncan's appreciative sigh. She glared at him, keeping her arm firmly over her chest, which was still partially exposed through the cloudy water.

"You, sir, take far too many liberties," she said haughtily.

Duncan laughed softly and said, "Relax, *Alainn*. Rowe was busy and this is clearly a task I excel at." He opened the big bath towel in front of him and held it out so that she could step into it.

"I will gladly wait for Rowe," Caitriona tossed back "or you can leave the towel on that chair and leave at once."

He wiggled the towel in front of her, clearly enjoying his position. He winked at her and said, "If it helps, I will simply turn my head. But I must insist that you remove yourself at once, *Alainn.* We need to be on our way. We have already spent more time here than I had intended." He danced the towel in front of her again, an impish grin softening the hard lines of his face.

Sighing in resignation, Caitriona motioned for him to turn his head, waiting until she was certain he was affording her at least some degree of modesty. She stepped gracefully from the tub and wrapped the proffered towel hastily around her body, ensuring he stayed true to his word and kept his eyes averted. With the towel safely in place, Caitriona started to move toward the door, but Duncan pulled her to him before she could make good her escape. Looking into the steel grey eyes above her, she was acutely aware of his hardness pressed against her body. The arm around her waist tightened, bringing her hard against his chest, while his other hand reached up and brushed the matted, wet locks from her face. Duncan stared deep into her emerald green eyes.

Caitriona wanted to get lost in his embrace. There was something powerful about this man, something safe and warm; something potent that connected them to each other. She wanted to feel the touch of his lips on hers again and wondered briefly what it would be like to know the full pleasure of being with a man so powerful, so hard, and so incredibly sure of himself. Her heart was racing as the heady rush of Duncan's stare penetrated her world and threatened to dissolve any thread of sanity that remained. Duncan leaned closer to her, his eyes searching her own emerald depths. She wanted desperately to feel his lips on hers, taste the very depths of him, and explore his mouth with her tongue. That world would never be. She shifted her weight and dropped her eyes, determined to put some distance between them both.

***

Duncan wondered if the girl wanted him as badly as he needed her. His body gave evidence to the need that boiled inside him. But he simply couldn't read her emotions. Still, she made no effort to leave. Her eyes were locked with his, searching for something. She shifted her weight and withdrew her gaze. In an impulsive gesture of pure masculinity, he pulled her close against his body. She gasped but did not try to resist. His free hand encircled her waist. He could feel the heat of her through his clothes and wondered briefly what it would be like to explore her body in ways he had only dreamed of. She parted her lips, inviting him to explore the sweetness of her mouth. Her lips were full and tempting. Needing no further invitation, his mouth captured her lips in a crushing kiss that demanded more. Duncan allowed his tongue to taste the sweetness of her own, exploring the smoothness of her teeth and the texture of her tongue. He lost himself in her, allowing himself this moment - no thoughts of war, the New World Order, or his mission.

***

Caitriona leaned in to Duncan's kiss. She delighted in the feel of him, all hard lines and muscle. His tongue took her mouth, demanding and sure. There was no urging or coaxing or teasing. It was an assertion of ownership and she willingly surrendered to it. She reveled in the feel of his tongue over her teeth and the masculine taste of whisky and spice. His mouth sucked lightly on her lower lip, causing butterflies to surface in her again and again. At last, he pulled away and she was left with a longing that had very little to do with the fact that it had been several years since she'd been with a man.

***

His hand brushed a rogue curl from her forehead and lingered caressingly on her cheek before encircling her waist once again. He wasn't about to let her go; not yet, but he had only one idea of how this could end. He had no right playing with this young woman's emotions. She was his charge and he was duty bound to see her safely before the council. He had taken her from her home and entombed her in a time, and country, that was vastly different from her own. She needed him as protector, confidant, and friend, not as a lover. She shifted her weight against him and the slight pressure against his manhood reminded him of his burgeoning need. He disentangled himself from her abruptly and moved to the door. "I will send Rowe to help you get ready," he said roughly. "We leave within the hour." And with that, he closed the large oak door, leaving Caitriona alone with her thoughts and the memory of his kiss.

***

Caitriona felt the tears form long before they coursed freely down her cheek. She had followed Rowe hastily back to the warmth and safety of her personal chambers and, dismissing her only friend, she threw herself across the bed, irritated when she felt hot tears fall down her cheeks. Swiping the back of her hand across her cheeks, she took a deep breath and resolved to put the memory of Duncan's searing kiss behind her. She felt inadequate. After all, had she been genetically engineered like the women in Duncan's time, he would have found the idea of kissing her much more palatable. As it was, she was genetically inferior, a master of nothing valuable in this world, and a burden to him; an ever present reminder of his precious mission and his duty to his people. She felt the tears well up again and blinked several times in an effort to keep them at bay.

A knock at the door interrupted her self-indulgent pity and she mumbled a quick "come in" before turning her back to her visitor.

"Duncan said you would be leaving shortly," said Rowe, concern evident in her voice. "I've brought you some fresh clothes and boots that will make the walking and riding easier for you." She placed the clothes on the bed.

"Thank you, Rowe," Caitriona said quietly. She didn't trust her own voice not to crack under the emotional duress. "I can manage by myself. Please tell the Commander I'll be out shortly." Rowe arched an eyebrow at her friend, at the use of Duncan's formal title and the swollen, red eyes that looked at her from beneath long lashes.

"I'll be right outside should you need anything," Rowe said, and reached out impulsively and squeezed the young woman's hand in a friendly gesture of kindness. It was enough to dissolve the small sliver of resolve that remained. The door barely closed before Caitriona sank deeper in the covers, no longer caring about the torrent of tears that coursed freely down her face.

Chapter Fourteen

All journeys have secret destinations of which the traveler is unaware.
Martin Buber

The sound of Marcie's hooves on the softened earth provided a hypnotic backdrop to the quiet that otherwise did little to disturb the lush hillside. Caitriona leaned forward slightly in the saddle, her buttocks and inner thighs sore from the day's ride. She had no idea how much farther Duncan intended to ride, but pride would not allow her to ask. They had ridden the better part of the day in stony silence, neither daring to break the stillness that had occupied them on their ride.

Duncan rode slightly ahead of her, vigilantly watchful for any signs of disturbance in the Highlands, one hand resting lightly on the broadsword he kept loosely in the scabbard at his side. From behind him, she admired the perfect line his body created with the horse. He was at ease on the majestic stallion, an Appaloosa with sleek muscles and the coloring to prove its heritage.

Her own mount was a delicate white mare with sure footing and light steps. Most likely of Arabian breeding, the mare needed little direction and, as a result, Caitriona found herself beginning to doze under the hypnotic and rhythmic gait of the young horse. Bringing herself upright as she found her head lolling forward, Caitriona forced herself to shift once again in the saddle, the effort to stay awake becoming more difficult. She thought about asking for a bio break but knew it would only buy her a few minutes and the thought of climbing in and out of the saddle was less than desirable.

With a heavy sigh, she tried to focus her attention on the beautiful, lush landscape. They had been traveling east since they left, and she could no longer hear the ocean waves. The cliffs had also disappeared and had been replaced by fields of heather, dense trees, and an occasional expanse of undergrowth. Vastly different from her native western landscape, she enjoyed the gentle slope of the hills and the panoramic scenes that stretched before her like incredible works of art on muted canvas backdrops.

Lee had joined the two shortly after they left the safety of the cave. He rode close behind them, watching for anyone who might decide to follow the trio, an archer's bow slung casually over one shoulder and a next-generation gun holstered at his hip. She felt safe amongst her escorts, yet unsettled by the fact that they were always watchful, aware that terror could be around any corner, tree, or rocky crevice. Lee trotted past her suddenly and caught up to Duncan. She could hear the two exchanging words, but couldn't make out what was being said. Sensing something was about to change, the mare perked up her ears and picked up her pace, causing Caitriona to pull a little too tightly on the reins. She had no desire to ride any closer to Duncan than she needed.

Seeing that the two men were deep in discussion, Caitriona's gaze was inexplicably drawn upward toward tiny clouds that were beginning to gather. She watched, mesmerized as the clouds grew in size, their shapes becoming odd creatures and objects in the otherwise blue-grey sky. Transfixed on the images before her, she was barely aware that the clouds had become ribbons of color and were now swirling and shifting around her. She felt Duncan's presence, hardly noticing that he had ridden to her side. She wanted to touch him and draw him in, but she was powerless to move her limbs as the vision consumed her.

"I know," she stated simply, her hands dropping to her sides as she looked past Duncan and addressed her phantom attendant.

"What do you know, Catie?" Duncan reined his mount close to her and touched her shoulder lightly.

Caitriona blinked as the colors before her began to take shape and substance. She no longer saw or heard Duncan but could feel his presence near and somehow she drew strength from that knowledge. The swirling colors became suddenly less dizzying as Caitriona locked on the darkest ribbon and willed it to reveal itself. Brady Hawkins' scarred face leered at her.

"You have power in you that you are not even aware of, you silly girl," Hawkins spat angrily at her.

"You are wrong," Catie said quietly. Hawkins was standing before her now, as clearly as if she had been suddenly transported to another place. Her body began to tremble. *She had to find Duncan*, she thought absently. *Why had he left her?*

Hawkins twisted his face into a sardonic smile that served only to accentuate the deep scar on his cheek. "You can't hide behind your protector," Hawkins replied. "We know you and our numbers are great. The next time we meet will not be through the veil of your powers."

"Then heed this warning, Hawkins," Catie's voice dropped to an almost inhuman sound. "Should you cross my path or threaten those I care about, I will kill you."

"A meaningless threat from a mere girl who has yet to realize the full extent of what she is." His laughter was mocking and ugly; a harsh sound that was a reminder of the sadistic stories Duncan had shared. Caitriona shuddered, fueling Hawkins' bullying power even further.

A dark shape began to form next to Hawkins and Caitriona recognized the impressive bulk of her protector. "Duncan," she whispered breathlessly.

"I'm here, lass," Duncan brushed the cascade of auburn curls away from her face but she didn't register his touch. Duncan's horse snorted and tossed his head, sensing the other worldly magic that had formed around the young woman.

Caitriona reached out to the phantom Duncan. The ribbon had extracted itself and she now saw him in full detail. Duncan was in irons, his clothes bloody and torn. Matted blood had dried on his face and his hair was tangled with blood, dirt and leaves. Caitriona gasped and reached to him, her hand grasping at air. Hawkins' ethereal laugh penetrated her soul and caused her slight frame to shudder uncontrollably.

"You won't be able to save him, Caitriona," Hawkins hissed wickedly. "In the end, his death will be on your hands and your gift will be mine." She watched, horrified, as Hawkins raised his sword and beheaded her lover. Duncan's head rolled to her feet, where a horrified expression on Duncan's severed head burned deep into her memory.

***

Duncan had been watching his young charge since she had stopped her mount several yards back. Only vaguely aware of what his first officer was telling him, he kicked his heels suddenly against the horse, maneuvering the great steed quickly to where Caitriona still remained transfixed on the wispy-thin clouds awash on the stark blue canvas.

Lee rode up beside him, motioning for Duncan to remain where he was. "Leave her, Duncan," Lee told him. "She is no longer here with us in this world."

For the first time, Duncan noticed the cloudy film that settled over Caitriona's eyes. He saw her ghostly pale reflection in the late afternoon sun and drew in a deep breath, unsure of his next move.

Duncan felt helpless as he watched the Seer wrestle with the contents of her vision. He wished fervently that he could share the visions with her or remove them from her completely. He hated watching her suffer through them, and the physical aftereffects as well. He winced, knowing that her handler would share a connection with her that would allow him to assist the Seer in managing her emotions. He would be able to help her in ways that Duncan could not even comprehend.

Lee's hand on his arm kept him from shaking his charge until the vision released her. Her face had taken on an even paler hue and he worried unremittingly over what it was that had visibly shaken her. Gasping, Caitriona pitched forward suddenly in her saddle, dropping the reins, the vision having finally relinquished its hold. She brought her fingers to her temple immediately and cried out.

Lee steadied the mare and retrieved the now forgotten reins as Duncan pulled alongside his charge's mount and touched Caitriona's elbow lightly.

"I'll be fine," she croaked.

"What did ye see, Caitriona?" Duncan demanded, his tone much sharper than he had intended.

"Hawkins," she whispered, not elaborating on the details. "Please, can we talk about the details later? I'm tired and my head hurts."

Both men exchanged glances and turned their horses around. Duncan gave the stallion a slight tug on the reins, and a quick click of his boots against the horse's rib cage sent the stallion trotting off into the overgrown vegetation.

***

Caitriona was simply too tired and in too much pain to care where Duncan was headed. She desperately wanted a warm bed and a dark room. She couldn't remember the last time a vision had left her in this much pain. She thought about telling Lee she needed to rest. Before she had a chance to gauge his mood, he turned his mount toward her and motioned for her to stay where she was. "Duncan will return shortly," he stated. "There should be a small shelter that is well hidden from the trail. We will rest there for the evening."

Caitriona sighed and dismounted. She tied the horse to a nearby tree and noticed that Lee remained astride his horse, his eyes ever watchful for movement in the nearby brush. Caitriona stretched her legs and arms, enjoying the feel of the land beneath her feet. Already, the sun was beginning to paint the sky in beautiful shades of magenta, pink, and gold. She sighed, wondering if they would reach the safety of the shelter before dark descended upon them. She hoped the shelter had some sort of bathroom facility as it had been several hours since she'd had any chance to relieve herself. Looking around for an area that might provide some level of privacy, she felt the rumble of a horse's hooves before she heard them. She looked worriedly at Lee who motioned for her to get out of sight. Crouching low behind the overgrown vegetation, she finally exhaled when she saw Duncan ride into sight.

Duncan rode directly to Lee, bringing the stallion around so that his back was toward her. Coming out from her hiding place, Caitriona walked to the mare and pulled herself back into the saddle, the effort sending sharp pain shooting across her skull. Rowe had provided her with a pair of riding pants that hugged her small frame and made traveling much easier. While she missed the deep color and rich fabric of the gowns, she appreciated the freedom she gained while wearing the riding gear, unhampered by the large skirts and folds of fabric.

Caitriona strained to hear the conversation between Duncan and Lee, but, whether by nature or by design, the men's voices remained low and Caitriona decided she was merely a "passenger" on their journey. Irritation beginning to set in, she brought the mare quickly between the two men. Duncan's stallion snorted derisively and he patted the horse's thick neck, instantly calming the agitated animal.

"So what's the plan?" Caitriona asked rather pointedly, frustrated by their exclusion of her.

Duncan turned to her and she could see the worry etched across his brow. She didn't care. She was tired and her patience was growing thin.

"Am I simply not to know the plan?" She locked her green eyes with his grey ones as she tried to control her mare's impatience. "I'm afraid, Commander, that I've never been very good at following; unless, of course, I have complete confidence in the leader," she challenged.

"There is a shelter not more than six hundred yards in that direction."

He nodded into the thick, dense Highland vegetation. "We will rest there for the night." Caitriona touched her heels to the mare and turned her sharply in the direction Duncan had indicated. "And, Madame," Duncan's tone was sarcastic as he stressed the more formal title, *"to change your mind and follow him who sets you right is to be none less free than you were before."*

Feeling the heat rising to her cheeks and thankful for the darkening skies, she retorted haughtily, "I see you are familiar with the works of Antonius. It is good to see that such works have not been forgotten in the twenty third century and that you have somehow taken time from kidnapping young women to acquaint yourself with their ideals. You would do well to heed the wisdom found in his words." Caitriona pushed the mare forward into a quick trot, a slight smile playing across her face for the second time since setting foot in this strange century.

Chapter Fifteen

Love is composed of a single soul inhabiting two bodies.
Aristotle

After seeing to the horses, ensuring the perimeter was secure and that there were no visible tracks that would lead an enemy to their location, Duncan entered the small one room shelter and found Caitriona fast asleep on the undersized but clean, bed. He opened the last drawer in the small chest of drawers that stood like a solitary sentry at the far end of the room and pulled out a rather old, but clean, wool blanket. Duncan had used the old shelter during many of his hunting trips and had often left additional provisions and blankets.

Laying the blanket gently over Caitriona's body, he took great care not to wake his charge, despite the fact that he wanted to learn more about the vision she had undergone earlier that day. Lee had admonished him for pushing the young woman too far and too hard, and he knew his friend was right. Duncan had been at war with his emotions for the better part of the day. The memory of the kiss he and Caitriona had shared had caused him to grow uncomfortable in the saddle and he cursed himself for allowing his emotions to gain the upper hand.

He pulled the blanket around her small frame, taking in the way her riding habit hugged her curves. The dark color accentuated the pallor of her skin and reminded him that she was still not one-hundred percent well. Today's vision had clearly taken a physical toll as well. While she had not complained during the long day's ride, he knew she needed rest. He worried that she would not be able to withstand the scrutiny or the tests of the council. Indeed, he knew he'd have to push Caitriona to continue riding if they were to make the council meeting in four days.

To address the problem, Lee offered to ride ahead and stall the proceedings, buying them a few more days. In truth, Duncan simply wasn't ready to discharge the girl into the care of her handler; a young man who had trained since boyhood for his role as watcher and protector of the Seer. If Lee were to ride on without them, it would also give Duncan time alone with the girl; something he both relished and feared.

Caitriona stirred slightly in her sleep, drawing the covers from him and coiling herself into a tight ball. She sighed softly and he wondered if he were at the center of that sigh or if there were another man—a lover perhaps—that she had left behind. He chased the idea from his mind; the thought of Caitriona being touched by another man did little to lighten his mood.

Deciding that the location of the shelter was secure enough for a small fire, Duncan placed the kindling carefully in the fireplace and coaxed a small flame to life, enjoying the warmth and soft glow of light that was afforded him from his efforts. Lee had effortlessly caught two small rabbits earlier that day and Duncan had skinned and gutted the animals quickly before coming inside. Spitting both rabbits on the same turning fork, Duncan set the spit so that it would cook the rabbits evenly.

Regrettably, Lee would not be joining them for the dinner he had so efficiently procured. After a heated exchange with his long-time friend, Duncan had reluctantly agreed that Lee should ride ahead and stall the council proceedings. While he was relieved that his time with his young charge would be extended, he also felt the weight of this latest setback.

Using the large mitts that were near the fireplace, he turned the meat carefully, enjoying the delicious aroma that permeated the small cabin. Caitriona stirred slightly, and he glanced at her wondering if he should wake her. He knew the food would help her regain her strength. Testing each rabbit to ensure it was thoroughly cooked, he removed both carefully from the flame. He then placed all the meat on a single plate after pulling it from the bones. Crossing to the bed, he touched Caitriona's shoulder gently. For a fleeting second he considered jettisoning the idea of eating and instead giving into the temptation to taste the sweetness of her sumptuous lips.

Caitriona blinked her eyes slowly and relaxed visibly when she saw him sitting next to her. "Smells good," she said groggily, rubbing the sleep from her eyes.

Duncan noticed the color still had not returned to her face, and there were dark circles under her eyes that mixed with the almost healed bruises from the attack on her nearly two weeks ago. Placing an arm beneath her, he helped her sit up and pushed the plate of food onto her lap. "Courtesy of Lee," he said softly, brushing the hair from her face.

Caitriona stared at the plate of food for several seconds and Duncan wondered if she was having another vision.

"The vision was different this time," Caitriona said softly, rubbing her temples to ease the ache that he knew had been building for hours. "They're less scattered, more focused." She dropped her hand to her lap and raised her eyes so that she was looking deep into his steel-grey ones. He wanted to pull her to him and lose himself in her touch. He pushed his feelings aside and instead focused on his mission.

"Did you see faces?" Duncan's voice was hard.

"I saw Hawkins ... and some others, but it's difficult to put a name to anyone when I don't know who they are," she said. He could tell she was deliberately withholding information from him. Caitriona pushed the plate of food aside, stood up and walked toward the fire. They both were silent for several minutes. Next to Caitriona the fire popped and hissed as she traced the fire's flame with her gaze.

"I think you should eat and get some sleep." Duncan stood and walked to the door, the sound of his boots echoing on the stone floor.

"Yes, maybe you're right," Caitriona said, stretching her hands out toward the fire.

"I'll be outside if you need anything." Duncan paused at the door, wanting to say more, but afraid of pushing her farther from him. He started to leave.

"I'm sorry." The apology was barely a whisper.

"For what?"

"For not being what you need - what you thought I was."

Duncan thought he heard her voice break with emotion, but he didn't acknowledge her feelings. The pain and emotion of the last two weeks tore at his heart, but he had a mission to complete and an entire population was depending on him to do his job. He simply couldn't afford to indulge his personal feelings.

"Get some sleep, Seer."

Duncan, I don't think I can do this,"

"Yes, you can." He walked over to her and cupped her chin in his hand, raising her eyes so that he was looking deep into the emerald green lagoons. Her lips were full and intoxicating, tempting him to taste the sweet nectar of passion he had tasted once before.

"You don't know what it's like to live this way." Caitriona was fighting back tears. "I hate it. Everyone I've loved, I've lost." The last two words were barely a whisper. She lowered her eyes as a tear rushed past her eyelashes to fall in a mocking display of feminine betrayal.

Duncan wondered if she were including him in that statement. Goddess, how he hated who he had become. He placed her small hands in his.

"It won't always be like that."

"You don't know that. You can't promise that."

He said nothing but sat next to her as she took up her place on the bed once again. He pushed the plate of food in front of her and waited as she wrestled with her own inner demons.

At her invitation, he tore off a piece of the rabbit and savored the juicy game. It had been too long since he had last eaten, but at the moment his only thought was for the beautiful, intriguing woman next to him who had stolen his heart. She had eaten several pieces, the succulent juices and grease coating her fingers. She looked around for something to wipe them on. Duncan seized that opportunity and captured her small hand in his. His eyes never leaving hers, he took her index finger and, pressing it to his mouth, gently sucked the tip, his finger tasting the saltiness of her skin mixed with the gamey flavor of the rabbit.

Caitriona inhaled sharply, her lips parting and her head tipping slightly back. A small shudder shook her.

Duncan released her hand reluctantly. "Nay, *Alainn,*" Duncan whispered hoarsely as his hand reached out and lightly caressed the expanse of auburn curls which cascaded freely over her shoulders. Staring at the brilliant green eyes that occupied his dreams and invaded his waking thoughts, he leaned closer, bringing their lips mere inches from each other. "Dinna deny this, lass."

***

Caitriona was getting lost in the feel of his tongue on her fingers. Her stomach fluttered as she gave into the sensations Duncan's ministering evoked. She groaned softly and pushed the plate from her lap, the now forgotten meal growing cold. An earlier memory of the searing kiss they had both shared invaded her memory and brought her back to the cold reality that this interlude would end terribly. She trembled at the thought. Caitriona was losing herself. She had no desire to become an amusement for him. She tore her gaze from the steel-grey eyes and tried to push herself away from him, but her efforts were brought up short against his solid, well defined chest. She slapped his face hard, the resounding crack giving evidence to the force behind the blow.

Duncan stood immediately and rubbed his cheek. "Ouch. That actually hurt," he stated in astonishment.

"I didn't think anything hurt you," Caitriona spat vehemently, being careful to avoid his penetrating gaze.

"No. There are some things," he said slowly. "The irrefutable disinterest of a beautiful woman, for instance," Duncan replied warily.

The silence that followed was nearly deafening and complete. Caitriona dropped her gaze but could feel the intensity of the grey eyes still on her. She had a feeling she knew where this interlude was leading, and she wasn't certain she could stop it; or that she wanted to. She shifted in the bed, deciding she should get up and put some distance between herself and the lovely expanse of masculinity that delighted her senses. She rolled to the opposite side of the bed.

"Wait," Duncan said. "I can't just walk away from this ... from you." His eyes found hers.

She looked up at him from under long lashes, willing herself to be anywhere but under his intense scrutiny. She brought her hand unconsciously to her face, her index finger caressing the place where his lips had claimed hers earlier in the cave. If she was being honest, a part of her desperately wanted to feel his tongue, demanding and insistent, exploring hers. Instead, she scrambled to the opposite side of the bed and pulled the blankets hastily around her for added warmth and protection. "I suggest you take some time, sir, to remember your duties and commitments," stated Caitriona. "Seducing me is not part of your duty. You would do well to remember that."

Caitriona abandoned the blankets and got to her feet, crossing quickly to the door, wanting nothing more than to leave and never return. She was too angry to cry; which suited her mood perfectly. Duncan stopped her when she reached to open the door.

"Madame, I will never again cross those boundaries," he paused, his eyes finding hers, "until you invite me to do so." Caitriona opened the door quickly and fled outside, the cold air a welcome distraction from the still lingering heat of their exchange.

Chapter Sixteen

Man never made any material as resilient as the human spirit.
Bernard Williams

The days melted into two weeks, yet their time at the cabin passed quickly. Duncan was pleased the Seer was regaining her health and credited her fast recovery to the time they spent climbing the Highland hills and exploring the land. For the most part, the tiny cabin had become home. Duncan had unpacked their saddle bags, quickly stashing their extra clothes in the small dresser and putting away the remaining provisions they had been carrying. A nearby river allowed the two to bathe, wash their clothes, and bring water to the house that could be boiled for drinking.

As the days sped past, Caitriona's strength returned, as did her fiery spirit. Duncan knew the Highlands were responsible for breathing new life into the young lass and he continued to encourage her progress. Carving two rather long tree branches into faux swords, he had eagerly continued the sword lessons Lee had exchanged with her during their time on the ship. He was pleased to see she was a quick study and she had even, on one occasion, caught him off guard.

While their days were filled with comfortable friendship, nothing more was ever said of their brief interlude in the cabin. Her words had cut him to the quick; largely because there was a ringing endorsement of truth to them. How had he become so carelessly obsessed with this woman that he was willing to put duty and obligation aside in favor of a brief, seductive interlude? It was apparent she still considered herself a prisoner.

Even as the thought crossed his mind, he pushed it aside knowing there had been some feeling from the girl when he had kissed her in the cave. Indeed, rather than pull away, she had pressed her body against his and the soft, unmistakable moan of a woman who had been too long denied brought the heated memory back to the surface.

Now, each kept a respectable distance and limited their conversations to politics, war, the weather, and the progress Caitriona was making in her recovery. Duncan kept a watchful eye on his roguish charge, taking great care not to cross the line he had so carefully drawn. He was pleased to see the color had returned slowly to her face, and under his care and hearty cooking she began to gain back some of the weight she had lost.

But he knew their time together was coming to an end. They would need to leave for the council soon and once there, he would be duty bound to relinquish his charge to the council and ensure her safety and trust to another man. He scowled at the idea of another man sharing the Seer's life, learning the way she tilted her head to one side when she was confused or the way she put forth a brave façade when trying to cover her emotions.

For Duncan, the nights were agonizingly long. With only one bed in the tiny cabin, he was adult enough to acknowledge they needed a comfortable place to sleep, so he put aside his feelings for his charge in favor of a restful night of slumber. As such, he spent an inordinate amount of care ensuring the invisible wall that divided the narrow bed was never breached, remaining true to his word and not revisiting his passion for her again.

After a week in the remote cabin, Lee returned to tell them the council had agreed to reconvene in three weeks. Duncan felt that after another week in the Highlands, and in his watchful and guarded care, his charge would be ready to travel and face the council. Lee and Duncan had spent much of that afternoon discussing their plans, growing silent whenever Caitriona approached. It wasn't as if they didn't trust her, Duncan simply didn't want to burden her with the details of their war. Toward nightfall, Lee said goodbye, promising that he would see them both again shortly. Duncan noted his friend's tired eyes, but saluted and watched as his friend and comrade rode off into the fading sun.

Duncan gave Caitriona her space, allowing her time alone to climb the hills closest to their cabin in order to enjoy the beauty that Scotland provided so freely. He imagined she could almost forget who she was and the bleak destiny that lay before her when she stared out across the vast expanse of heather and wild flowers.

On the evening before their departure, Duncan spotted Caitriona half way up the closest knoll. She was sitting on a rather large rock just watching the sun beginning to fade from the sky. The pastel colors of the fading sun were in stark contrast to the darkening skies. He watched as she absently picked the field flowers that spread like a carpet around her, twining them together in a delicate chain of glorious color. For not the first time in his life since meeting his young charge, he silently cursed the Templars and the oath he had taken to further their cause.

***

Caitriona didn't need to turn around to know Duncan was behind her and that he was coming to deliver the news she had so vigorously pushed from her mind the past two weeks. She didn't want their time together to end, but knew Duncan had other tasks to complete, and other duties to fulfill. In a few days, her life would be handed over to a young man who had spent his entire life with the knowledge that he would one day be her protector; that he would forgo his own needs to share an emotional bond with a woman he had never met. She shuddered and drew the shawl closer around her shoulders. She would not, could not, allow that to happen.

"We leave tomorrow at first light," Duncan said quietly, interrupting her thoughts.

Caitriona nodded silently, refusing to speak or turn in his direction. He walked up beside her and sat down next to her. She continued staring at the landscape, trying to see the view of his homeland through his eyes. She wanted to open up and share with him, but knew that to do so would inevitably invite an unwelcome invasion of the boundaries each chose not to cross. So instead she sat quietly, waiting for him to speak. Several minutes passed and she watched the sun begin to fade from view. Darkness would soon settle around them both and with it the loneliness that was an ever present reminder of duty and sacrifice.

When the last of the sun faded from view, Caitriona stood up to make her way down the hill. She had come here many times during the past couple of weeks and could easily navigate the narrow trail by moonlight. She was grateful for the darkness that concealed the anguish on her face. She would miss the serenity of this place.

"Caitriona, wait." Duncan's plea was more a question than a request. Caitriona stopped and turned slowly to face her guardian. She saw the doubt and longing in his eyes, and what remaining will she had left crumbled and dissipated with the passing sun.

Caitriona touched his face tenderly, tracing the outline of his lips with her forefinger. She locked green eyes with grey but saw nothing reflected with the pitch black darkness of night upon them. After all these weeks of guarding her feelings, she wanted—needed—to feel the heat of his lips under hers. She reached her hand behind his neck pulling him closer. "Yes," she whispered breathlessly, a smile tugging at the corner of her lips. Duncan needed no further invitation. His mouth found hers with crushing urgency.

Caitriona was as eager and desperate to feel his tongue inside her. She gently sucked on his tongue, moaning when he nibbled gently at her lips, his hands fisting in her hair. She pulled reluctantly away, caressing Duncan's hair as it fell across his shoulders. "In all the many ways I envisioned my life, I never imagined this," she stated simply.

"I've been imagining little else from the first moment I saw ye," Duncan's eyes shone darkly as he lowered his head. Arching her body to meet the demands of his mouth, Caitriona's hand grabbed his head and lifted it. "No more imagining," she replied huskily. Duncan groaned and slipped the shawl from her shoulders. Tugging on the drawstrings of her simple gown, he pushed the gusseted fabric hurriedly from her slender form. Caitriona trembled as the garment slid softly to the ground.

"What's wrong?" He frowned.

Caitriona stiffened, aware of the electricity that had suddenly sprung to life and danced across her skin. "I don't know," she said breathlessly, wondering if he felt the current like she did.

He stroked her breasts absently with feather light fingers until her gasp provided the resolution he was seeking.

It was far easier to ignore his words than his fingers. "It doesn't matter. Don't stop."

"*Alainn*, stopping is the farthest thing from my mind this evening." His fingers grazed her stomach, making her heart beat wildly against her rib cage. The cool night air danced across Caitriona's body, raising the skin on her flesh and causing her to shudder.

Leaving her clothes where they fell, Duncan scooped Caitriona into his arms. She relished the way her curves fit his body, recalling a similar time several months earlier when he had carried her into his quarters on the ship. Caitriona nestled against him, feeling safe and at peace for the first time since coming to this strange land.

Duncan traversed the knoll quickly and pushed the cabin door open gently with his foot. Crossing to the bed, he deposited Caitriona in the middle; the invisible barrier no longer a consideration. Duncan tugged his shirt over his head and allowed it to fall carelessly to the floor. Caitriona's appreciative gaze followed the outline of his well-defined muscles and sinewy hardness as he climbed onto the bed. Reaching for him, she allowed her hand to trace a path her eyes had only momentarily left. Her pulse quickened at the sight and touch of him. A flash of memory crossed her mind; a tattooed arm and muscled hardness. She frowned but pushed the memory away. The eerie feeling she had earlier crept back over her, but, once again, she ignored the intrusive memory; her body more interested in the sensations Duncan's hands invoked.

Caitriona pressed the length of her body against him, undulating softly as his legs twined around hers. She felt his body respond as her hand traced its way lightly down his flat stomach to rest at the waist band of his trews. Propping herself on one elbow, she tugged at his trews, willing them to disintegrate in her hands. Duncan laughed softly, brushing her hand aside as he made short work of the fabric that provided the only remaining barrier. Duncan discarded his trews hastily and pulled her against him, the hardness and length of him pressing against her thighs.

Caitriona pushed hungrily against him, her hand finding the dark area below his navel, her fingers lightly teasing the hair around his shaft. Duncan's eyes were bright as he grasped her head and captured her mouth, his tongue gently teasing her lips apart, caressing and demanding until she inhaled sharply. As her hands reached for the hard length of him, he gently but firmly grabbed both wrists in his right hand, pinning them to the pillow.

Duncan shook his head and nibbled softly on her exposed neck. "Not so fast, *Leannan*...lover," he said, translating the Gaelic word when he saw the inquisitive look on her face. "I want to love you ... slowly."

Caitriona moaned softly as his lips captured her nipple, teasing the rosy peak until it became hard and long under his skilled ministrations. She had never thought about sex as anything more than the physical release between two people. Clearly, she had had physical relationships with men, but she was unaccustomed to the intense feelings she was experiencing with Duncan. Every nerve in her body felt as if it were on fire, begging for a release only Duncan could provide. She gasped again as he released her hands and found the soft place between her legs, his fingers expertly teasing her folds apart before sliding deep inside her. Her feelings for him were becoming inextricably bound with her body's responses, his fingers and mouth tying them together in complicated, agonizing knots that threatened to snap and disintegrate beneath her.

"*Leannan*," he whispered, stroking the folds of her flesh with his fingertips. Her body shook with unspent need as her hand gripped his and encouraged him to explore deeper. "Be still." He continued his slow ministrations until once again, he claimed her wrists, keeping them firmly pinned to the pillows, his engineered strength no match for her own.

Giving in once again, Caitriona relaxed against him, her legs parting, encouraging his soft, but unrelenting, exploration. He positioned one muscular leg over hers, effectively pinning her body beneath his. She arched slightly beneath his touch as his fingers began a rhythmic caress. She could feel the slickness of her body's desire giving in to his touch as his fingers kept up their maddening pace. She moaned, her body undulating against his hand as he teased her body and took her to unexplored heights. She could feel her release building and trusted where he was taking them both. He released her wrists, convinced, quite rightly she knew, that there would be no further attempts to distract him now.

Catching his face in her hands, she kissed him long and deep, opening her legs further, inviting him into her, body and soul. Duncan needed no further invitation, his throbbing erection an indicator of his physical need for her. Withdrawing his hand, Duncan hesitated slightly, searching her emerald eyes; for what, she wasn't sure. Positioning himself above her, he thrust suddenly into her, her gasp of pleasure smothered as his lips found hers and their tongues danced in unison to the thrusts of their bodies. Caitriona arched her back and met every hard thrust, delighting in the pleasure he gave. She locked her legs around him, savoring the feelings of being so completely stretched.

He brushed the hair from her face, his eyes reaching for her soul. She could smell her arousal on his hand and inhaled deeply of the musky scent that filled the air. She wanted even more of him; wanted to feel his passion spilling into her. Everything else faded away as she concentrated only on this moment, this man and her need. She could see the intensity building on his face and knew they were both close.

"Duncan." His name was a moan on her lips.

He answered her passionate call with an intensity of his own, his demanding pace increasing; the length of him stretching and filling her completely. Duncan grabbed her wrists once again, his muscles straining with the effort it took to control his passion. "Let go, *Leannan*," he said huskily.

The passion in his voice was her undoing. She exploded around him, the slick evidence of her arousal coating him and mixing with his own desire. Tremors shook her body as the aftershocks sent ripples of pleasure throughout her body. For once, the aching need that enveloped her whenever he was near was satiated. The electricity that danced between them, released. She sighed contentedly, enjoying the feel of him inside her. Releasing her hands, Duncan kissed her eyelids, whispering Gaelic to her as she floated back to him and her heart returned to normal rhythm. When she finally mustered the energy to open her eyes and look at him, he had his warrior's mask of indifference once again settled across his face. She literally felt the warmth leave his body as he pushed himself off her and pulled her next to him.

"Sleep now, *Leannan*. We can enjoy each other again later," he stated, his fingers trailing through her hair.

Caitriona touched his lips with her fingers. "What's changed?" she asked softly, pushing herself up on her elbows so she was looking at his dark mask. He folded his hands beneath his head and looked up at her, his expression guarded.

"Nothing's changed, *Leannan*," he said softly, but the warmth that had been in his voice was gone and the hardness of his features once again settled over him like a well-polished armor.

She could literally feel his change but said nothing, determined to bring him back to her ... to this moment. Caitriona studied him with the same intensity he had lavished on her earlier. Her fingers traced the outline of the Celtic tattoo that covered his upper forearm while her mouth inched its way down his flat belly to his tapered hips. Again, she had the nagging feeling that her recurring vision was somehow tied to this man. The thought disturbed her and she pushed it away again, determined to ignore the invasive reflections until another time.

She turned her attention once again to the well-muscled man before her. Duncan's body sported several deep scars and she ran her fingers lightly over each, memorizing every puckered line and silently cursing the bastards who had done this to him. She shivered at the thought of all the battles he had fought, and the ones he would fight still in her defense.

"I don't want you to go to war for me, Duncan." Her voice shook with anger, her eyes narrowing. "I can't stomach the thought that you could be hurt, or killed, for me."

"A sacrifice I will gladly give if it means keeping you safe and seeing my people freed." At her pained expression, he stroked her cheek and added, "I'm a warrior, *Leannan*; genetically engineered to be the very best."

"No. You may have been made to fulfill that role, but that is not who you are," she said quietly. "You're a leader, a starship commander, a man who's filled with compassion for his people's well-being." She paused, searching his eyes. "You're a lover," she said more softly, "my lover."

The words were not lost on Duncan. Pulling her into his arms, he caressed her hair for several minutes before he spoke.

"Nay, *Leannan*. I have been a warrior longer. It is what I was created for." He captured her mouth in a searing kiss effectively silencing anymore questions.

She pulled his tongue deeper into her mouth, sucking gently. Breaking the kiss first, she inched her way down his body, suddenly wanting to explore more of him in her mouth. Stopping at the dark triangle of hair that framed his manhood, she cupped his balls softly, feeling the weight of them in her hand. Duncan groaned and sank back against the pillows. She smiled seductively, knowing she did that to him; that she alone was able to break through his dark thoughts and bring him back to her.

His erection pressed against her hand, begging for inclusion in her sultry ministrations. Pulling her hair over her shoulder, her eyes never leaving his, she took the length of him into her mouth. She swirled her tongue around the head as she sheathed her teeth and began a slow, sensuous rhythm with her mouth that left them both panting.

She took her time exploring the saltiness of him that mixed with her own desire. She had never known how sensual it could be to know a man so intimately, and greedily continued her efforts until her jaw was all but aching from the girth of him. Withdrawing slowly, she bent lower and took one of his balls in her mouth, sucking gently, enjoying the weight and feel of him in her mouth. Her hand took over on his shaft as his whole body stiffened beneath her, heralding his imminent release. His breath hitched in his throat as he fisted his hands in her hair and arched his body.

A growl suddenly tore from his lips as he pushed her from him and rolled her so that she was pinned beneath him. Pushing her legs roughly apart with his knee, he barely hesitated before slamming into her, the force of the thrust driving her into the mattress. She arched her back to meet his demands. Gone was the gentle lover who only moments before had tenderly stroked her flesh and brought her to orgasm. She cried out and wrapped her legs around him, drawing him in even tighter, meeting his thrusts inch for inch.

"Ach, *Leannan*," Duncan growled, his breath hitching in his throat as his muscles contracted with the effort it took to control his release. "Come with me, lass," he ground out between thrusts.

"Duncan," she said hoarsely, unanswered need lacing her voice.

Pushing the hair from her face, he inhaled sharply and slowed his demanding pace. Sliding one arm under her back, Duncan picked her up and rolled her again so that she was on top and in full control. Not missing a stroke, she opened her legs further, taking him deeper inside of her. She could feel his erection growing and pulsing inside her. Arching her back, she placed his hands on her breasts relishing how their two bodies fit perfectly together. His hands held her hips in place while she grew accustomed to the sensations this new position afforded her. After several seconds had passed, he began teasing her nipples lightly, groaning when she slowed her pace, her hips undulating in a slow, rhythmic motion she knew would drive him mad.

Guiding her hips, he encouraged her to ride him faster, groaning with the pleasure her movement induced. In time, Duncan found the frenzied pace he had relinquished earlier and, driving hard, brought them both over the edge.

Collapsing on top of Duncan, Caitriona remained there for some time, her ear against his chest, listening to the steady beat of his heart. She sighed contentedly, the rhythmic beat making her drowsy. She stayed that way until she felt Duncan grow soft. Rolling off of him, she drew the covers to her chest and nestled against her lover. She was uncertain if, or how, this would change their relationship. But she was certain of one thing: her life was somehow intricately entwined with this man's heart … and his war.

Chapter Seventeen

War does not determine who is right - only who is left.
Bertrand Russell

Hawkins was close to victory. After weeks of monitoring MacKinnon's transmissions, one of his officers had intercepted a rather cryptic communication that had garnered Hawkins' attention. His cunning and tenacity was rewarded as his men investigated and discovered that, not only had MacKinnon left the castle with his new bride, but that her paper trail had indeed never checked out. His lips curled into a sneer as his men reported that, after several days of being uninvited guests at the fostering hold where Caitriona had supposedly grown up, there was no one there who could remember the girl. Despite the fact that she appeared in the hold's registry, not one person could remember the red-headed beauty.

Hawkins wanted to be there when he captured MacKinnon. He was tired of getting reports from his seconds; he wanted to see the hatred in MacKinnon's eyes and the fear when he slowly tortured the woman MacKinnon proclaimed to love. A slight frown crossed Hawkins' features as he realized the marriage was most likely a ruse and the woman was undoubtedly under MacKinnon's protection. *But why,* he pondered. *Why protect the woman? What did she possess that garnered the attention of one of the highest ranking officers of the Templars?* Hawkins couldn't shake the feeling that the woman played a much larger role than he had originally surmised.

No matter, he thought absently. Torture MacKinnon's true love or torture his valued property, the result was the same: he would enjoy watching the torment on MacKinnon's face as he brought him to his knees and to heel. And perhaps, when he was finished with the girl, he would indulge his own sadistic pleasures with her.

Hawkins removed his glasses and rubbed the back of his hand across his left eye. The ache behind his eye was growing stronger and more painful, and he knew it wouldn't be long before what remained of his vision became spotty and blurred. He sighed outwardly as the computer announced his second in command.

"Enter," Hawkins spoke the one-word command brusquely, hoping his second had better news to report today. Hawkins had sent several patrols in search of MacKinnon. While he didn't expect to find the man locked in wedded bliss at Dunrobin Castle, he did expect that his men would be able to persuade the occupants to provide valuable information. He put his glasses back on and turned to address his second in command.

Harry Billinger entered the room quickly and saluted his commanding officer with the appropriate touch of his right hand over his left breast and then out in front of him at face height, an emulation of an earlier period in time when Hitler ruled. Hawkins saluted as well and indicated the man should stand at ease. Billinger shifted his feet apart and rested his hands behind his lower back.

"What news do you bring?" Hawkins asked rather shortly, the ache behind his eyes beginning to grow more pronounced.

"MacKinnon and his bride were not at the castle," the man stated tersely. "Gawain said they were visiting the surrounding farm holds and would be gone several weeks."

"And you accepted this as truth?" Hawkins asked, irritation beginning to lace his voice.

"As you are aware, sir, MacKinnon holds high rank among the Order and we are not at liberty to use persuasion tactics on our own." At Hawkins' look of disgust, Billinger added hastily, "There are those in power that do not believe the man is a Templar. Until we have proof, we must tread lightly regarding his property and his holdings."

Hawkins slammed his fist down on his desktop, causing the papers he was scrutinizing to flutter carelessly to the floor. "And the other patrols? What news do they bring?"

"Not all troops have reported yet, sir. We received credible information while in the field that MacKinnon and the girl were spotted on the crags. If we assume MacKinnon is the leader of the resistance army, there is a good chance a Dweller community is somewhere nearby. We have sent men to scour the countryside for signs of habitation."

"What about the drones?" Hawkins countered. "Why have you not sent the drones?"

"The drones would raise suspicion, sir." Billinger countered. "We need to remain discreet and allow the malefactors to weaken and reveal their position."

"Very well," Hawkins resigned. "I want a report as soon as the second and third troops have reported."

Billinger nodded, saluted and exited the hot and stuffy command room. Hawkins knew his second in command was glad to be away from him and the wrath he was famous for unleashing on a whim. While MacKinnon had so far proven elusive, he knew it was simply a matter of time before he caught up to the man and the secret he so carefully guarded.

Chapter Eighteen

Ultimately we know deeply that the other side of every fear is freedom.
Marilyn Ferguson

Duncan lay in bed listening to the rise and fall of Caitriona's breathing. The evenness of her breaths told him she was in a deep sleep. He brushed the back of his hand instinctively across her cheek, tracing the contours of her face to the hollow of her neck. His body tensed when he heard a sound in the woods. Immediately alert, Duncan propped himself on one elbow, careful not to awaken Caitriona. He heard the sound again, closer this time. Duncan rolled away from Caitriona and got out of bed, noting the cold chill that had settled upon the room. He donned his trews quietly; his military senses on full alert, fearing what his instincts already knew to be true.

Duncan quickly crossed to the window and carefully lifted the edge of the curtain, the embroidered edge belying the danger that awaited mere feet from the sanctuary of the cabin. Scanning the outline of trees, Duncan counted four shadows in his immediate line of sight. "*Damnu,*" he cursed softly. Finding Caitriona's riding habit, he crossed to the bed. He bent close to her ear so as not to startle her. "Get dressed," he whispered urgently, handing her the clothes she had washed at the stream the day before.

Caitriona's eyes were immediately alert and she hastily took the clothes he had laid next to her. She pulled the dark, button up riding blouse across her shoulders, buttoning the shirt clumsily as she struggled to see in the darkness. Duncan put his finger to her lips, cautioning her to keep quiet. He could see her fear as she stood up and pulled the riding pants on, the memory of their love making hours earlier still fresh in his mind.

"Follow me," Duncan whispered. Caitriona swept her hair into a pony tail as she hastily followed Duncan to the outer room. There, she tugged on her riding boots, struggling to keep the boots from clacking on the hard wood floors and giving away their position.

"Stay close," he cautioned. At the look of concern in her eyes, he pulled her close, his mouth crushing hers in an urgent kiss that left him breathless. Reluctantly, he pulled away. "Everything will be fine, lass, I promise," he added tucking his broadsword into the scabbard at his side.

Caitriona trembled uncontrollably but followed him to the back door. He pushed the door open just far enough for them both to slip quietly out into the dark night, Duncan's right hand never moving from the gold gilded handle of the gleaming sword. Mercifully, the door opened silently, providing him and his charge with a covert escape.

Caitriona stayed close. Duncan was assured of his step and knew the way, despite the lack of moonlight and the darkness that engulfed them. Time passed agonizingly slowly. They made very little progress as Duncan led them both just a few steps at a time and then stopped to listen. This pattern went on for almost fifteen minutes. At one point, Caitriona tensed suddenly against him and gasped aloud when she saw a soldier thirty yards to her right. His back was to the two fugitives. Duncan pulled Caitriona quickly to the ground, the familiar heather a perfect cover in the dark, cloudless night. When he was certain the danger was past, Duncan once again motioned for Caitriona to keep silent and follow him.

Duncan had easily spotted the four men from his vantage point in the cabin. What he wasn't sure of was how many men Hawkins had diverted to the cabin. As such, Duncan decided to face the enemies he knew rather than risk running into more if he chose to move away from the cabin. He had to assume the cabin had been surrounded by Hawkins' men. His only option was to use the darkness to his advantage and creep through the heather and low lying brush until he reached the safety and cover of the forest some two hundred yards ahead of him. He also had to assume that for Hawkins to come after him, he must have realized the information on Caitriona was false. Duncan sighed. This now meant open war.

Once they reached the shelter of the trees, Duncan picked up the pace, but continued to be on alert. He could feel Caitriona's presence behind him, but knew he would not rest until they were safely with the council. He used the crag and bluff ahead of him as a guide, continuing to push them at an ever faster pace through the woods.

Suddenly, a shout rang through the forest followed by more shouts, excited voices and the pounding of boots and horses' hooves. "*Damnu*," he cursed for the second time that night. "Run," he said to Caitriona, pushing her ahead of him to shelter her from the dangers that would be fast approaching.

Duncan's options were rapidly diminishing. They would lose this foot race; it was only a matter of time. He had only one option, and it was a long shot. "Right, go right, Caitriona," he shouted. She veered suddenly to her right and continued to push through the undergrowth and trees. Ahead, Duncan could see that the trees grew thinner and knew they would soon leave the tiny thread of safety the forest provided. It couldn't be helped, he thought frantically, his genetically engineered intelligence already in over-drive to find a solution.

Behind him, he could hear Hawkins' men getting closer. He could tell Caitriona was beginning to fatigue. Her steps had slowed and he watched as each breath she drew became more labored. She clutched her side and he knew sharp pains were likely dancing across her abdomen and back with the effort it took to keep going.

Duncan could almost feel the roar of the waves against the rocks before he saw them. He pulled Caitriona to a sudden stop in front of him as the cliff's edge loomed large before him. Duncan held her hand tightly and began pulling her forward. He could feel her body shaking uncontrollably, but his mind was still racing in a million different directions, trying to calculate their chance of survival with each solution.

"Caitriona, trust me," he said, his voice soothing and quiet, yet able to cut through the din of the crushing waves below them. She glanced back at the woods, the soldiers getting closer with every second. Duncan cupped her chin and forced her to look at him. His thumb brushed across her lips, grey eyes locking with green.

Caitriona's nod was barely perceptible. Duncan's mouth was mere inches from hers and he watched as she sucked her upper lip in tight; a brave facade she donned when she was terrified. From the woods, he could hear shouting as the Order's soldiers approached. Duncan's hand cupped the contours of her face, the back of his other hand sliding slowly, lovingly across her neck. Caitriona leaned into him and let out a sob. He kissed the top of her head and tilted her chin to look into the emerald depths that were now visibly scared. Across her shoulder he saw the first soldier emerge into the clearing. Pushing Caitriona behind him so that he shielded her body with his own, he faced their adversaries.

As if on cue, two dozen men emerged from the woods, their crisp uniforms in stark contrast to the deepening night sky. Each man leveled a small laser on Duncan, who watched as the tiny red dots grew to the size of one perfectly round golf ball sized shape once all sights had been locked on their target.

"Drop the weapon, Commander," Hawkins hissed, his voice low yet audible above the crush of the waves.

Duncan drew the sword slowly from its scabbard and tossed it to the ground in front of him. He could feel Caitriona's body trembling behind his and he swore silently beneath his breath. He mentally calculated the distance between the cliff edge and the shore below, trying to account for the slope of the cliff and the rocks below. He would need at least three feet to clear the distance to avoid being crushed by the rocks. And even if they were to safely clear the cliff's edge, the waves would surely drive their bodies back against the rocks.

"Now step away from the girl." Hawkins' voice had an edgy quality to it that Duncan didn't like. This was a man known for his treacherous cruelty and brutality.

"Let the lass walk away, Hawkins," Duncan's voice was steady, resolute. "If ye harm her, I swear to ye, I will kill ye."

"On the contrary, MacKinnon, we have no intention of harming her." He licked his lips provocatively and Duncan became more feral, a low growl emanating from him. Duncan was glad his charge was not able to see the lecherous leer that spread across Hawkins' face. "You, on the other hand, I have no such misgivings over. Do you hear that, Caitriona?" He chortled gleefully, raising his voice to ensure she heard his words. "Your lover's entrails will soon be spread along the bluffs. I'm sure the crows and vultures will be quite delighted with my gift."

Duncan glanced over his shoulder at his young charge, whose hand had flown to her mouth. He saw the crashing waves below him, noting the foamy water that appeared as merengue against a deep chocolate pie. His charge shivered; whether from cold or fear he didn't know, but instinctively he pulled her closer.

"Stop this madness," Caitriona shouted, stepping from behind Duncan. He reached out instinctively to pull her back but stopped short when he saw the fire in her eyes. "I will go with you … willingly, but he walks away free, with no threat of pursuit."

"You are hardly in a position to negotiate," Hawkins spat.

"Indeed, I am in every position to negotiate." She glanced over her shoulder at the cliff's edge not more than six feet away. "I would rather die than watch you kill someone I care about." To emphasize her point, Caitriona backed up closer to the cliff's edge. Duncan reached for her but she pushed his arm away and whispered, "I trust you; now trust me."

"How very touching, Caitriona. But we both know, this marriage is a façade," Hawkins hissed at her. "He no more cares about you than he does the day. Step aside and come with me. I will shower you with riches you have yet to dream of. And I will help you return home. That is what you truly desire, is it not?"

Duncan turned and faced his young charge, noting the determined set of her chin and the bold, almost defiant determination in her eyes. He gripped her hand tightly and she squeezed it reassuringly, a slight smile tugging at the corner of her lips.

The lasers still leveled at Duncan, he smiled at Caitriona, knowing what was in her heart. He only hoped his calculations were correct, and that they would clear the bluff before he was eviscerated.

"Time's up, MacKinnon," Hawkins stated tersely, pushing the wire-rimmed glasses farther up his nose. As if sensing what the two were about to do Hawkins yelled above the crashing ocean waves, "I know you won't jump, MacKinnon. You'd never risk the girl's life."

"Perhaps," Duncan said evenly, his eyes never leaving Caitriona's. "But are ye willing to …" His words were cut off as Caitriona gripped his hand more tightly and, turning ran for the bluff's edge. Duncan pulled her forward as they left the edge of the bluff, hoping it was enough extra force to clear the rocks below. He could hear the soldiers powering up their weapons, but then they were over the edge. Caitriona had inadvertently let go of his hand as soon as they were in the air and, as fast as they were over the edge, he suddenly felt the water and was plunging toward the bottom.

***

Caitriona didn't think. She simply moved. As soon as her feet left the ground, panic welled up inside her. The scream that she was certain would erupt got stuck in her throat. An eternity seemed to pass as she was free falling through the air, and then the ocean rushed up below her, grabbing her legs and pulling her in.

She hit the water with such force that it expelled the air in her lungs. An intense panic gripped her as she fought her way to the surface to get air. She began frantically kicking her legs, her arms unwilling participants to aid in her escape. Panic consumed her as she realized she was sinking farther to the bottom. With no more air left in her lungs, she inhaled deeply only to suck icy water into her mouth and lungs. The water burned her throat as it began filling her lungs. She could feel her throat getting smaller and smaller. *This is what it is like to drown*, she thought absently. She looked up and saw the surface which seemed miles away. No longer in a state of panic, she felt only peace and a fierce need to sleep. Her body felt heavy as she continued to sink deeper, watching the surface get farther and farther away. Her last thought was that this wasn't how she was supposed to die.

***

Duncan drew his legs to his chest as he hit the water. As soon as he felt the cold water, he began using his legs and arms to pull himself to the surface. Clearing the water, he shook his head to remove the salty water from his eyes and looked around for Caitriona. The moonless night was making it difficult to see anything.

"Caitriona," Duncan shouted into the depths of the night. His keen eyesight searched the shoreline for any signs that she had made it safely ashore. Fearing the worst, he kicked his powerful legs out behind him and dove back into the foamy undercurrents. On his third attempt, he thought he spotted her familiar cascade of auburn curls. He dove again, the persistent opposition of the waves a hindrance to his rescue efforts.

His tenacity was rewarded as he reached for her sinking body and pulled her toward the surface, her vacant eyes filling him with fear. Duncan pulled Caitriona's lifeless body onto the rocky beach. He was grateful for the moonless night which provided adequate cover from the soldiers. He knew, however, it would only be a matter of minutes before the Order sent a drone to track their position. He had to work quickly. Turning Caitriona on her side, he noted how cold her skin was. His hand found her wrist and checked for a pulse which was faint at best. Her lips were blue and her matted hair clung to her battered body like seaweed to a barnacled boat.

"*Ach*," he cursed silently as he tilted Caitriona's head back and placed his hands just above her rib cage. He covered her mouth and pushed air into her lungs while his hand counted out the rhythmic pumps to stimulate her heart. *How long had she been unconscious*, he wondered, panic giving rise to the fear of losing her. "Breathe, *Leannan*." He continued the rhythmic ministrations, all the while praying to the Goddess, hopeful she would answer his fervent prayers.

***

"My little bird, you shouldn't be here," the woman said, her voice soft and soothing in the darkness. "You must return to him now." Caitriona peered in the direction the voice was coming from, but saw only darkness and threads of somber colors that swirled into a mist that neither dissipated nor grew in size. The woman's voice seemed familiar and she was certain there had been another time, another place where she had heard the endearment whispered.

"I don't want to return." Caitriona's reply sounded small and hollow in the vastness of space. "I like it here. I feel happy … and safe."

"But there is much work for you to do, my little bird," the voice said, as the somber colors began to grow more vibrant. "And it is not your time. You know this."

Caitriona noted the way the auburn and magenta threads were beginning to grow into lighter shades of lavender and pink. The hypnotic movements of the thread were dizzying, yet exhilarating at the same time. Caitriona watched as the ribbons danced and moved all around her, beguiling her. "The man will protect you." The colorful apparition spoke the words in a sing-song melody that was soothing. "He is yours, little bird. You need to go to him now."

Caitriona sighed, mesmerized by the ever-growing swirls of brilliant color.

"I think I will stay here instead," she sighed contentedly. The swirls of color grew more brilliant and began to take on depth and substance. From the colors, a woman emerged, her pale skin in stark contrast to the darkness that swept around her. Her hair was the color of a brilliant sunset and hung in loose waves that reached nearly to her buttocks. She was absent the entrapments of any physical clothing but did not seem aware of this in the way most people are. Indeed, the absence only served to lend a more ethereal quality to the woman.

Caitriona blinked, certain she was imagining the woman before her.

Finally, realization washed over her. "Mama?" It was more a question than a statement. Caitriona reached out to the vision of her mother that stood before her. Caitriona's mother took her hand and pressed it to her cheek. The warmth coursed through Caitriona's body and she choked back a sob.

"Caitriona, you must listen to me now." She kissed the back of Caitriona's hand, her lips strangely cool yet comforting. With her free hand, Caitriona wiped the tears now running freely down her cheeks. She could taste the saltiness their trail left behind. "You don't have much time. You must leave this place and go back to finish your work."

"I don't know what it is I'm supposed to do," she implored her mother.

"When the time is right, you will know. You are gifted my child; use those gifts. Your father and I could not protect you, but there is one who has been given to you as protector and guardian. Don't shut him out."

The woman started to lose substance, the shape of her body losing form to the brilliant colors that had earlier stood in its place.

"Mama, no! Don't go."

"*Return to him, little bird.*" The command was strong, but more in Caitriona's mind rather than outside of it. "*It is time.*" Caitriona started to feel herself being pulled toward the cold darkness. She reached out once more for the comfort of the woman who had left her life years ago, but felt nothing. With a retched sob, she fought against the darkness that threatened to engulf her. Her fight was short lived as she eventually felt herself being pulled into a dark, cold void.

Her lungs burned from the effort it took to force air into them. She tried to move, but it felt as if a large rock were placed on top of her chest. She started to panic, trying to free her arms from the terrible weight. As if by design, she felt the boulder move suddenly, and she began expelling water violently.

Duncan rolled her quickly onto her side to help her expel the water from her lungs. When the racking, violent coughs had subsided, he pulled her close and smoothed the tangled hair from her face. She could see the worry etched in his face and wanted nothing more than to wipe the lines and uneasiness from his handsome features.

Realizing she had come very close to dying, she clung to Duncan, drawing strength from his warmth and nearness. The vision of her mother and the feelings she had experienced were dissipating slowly, but left her unsettled and frightened.

"Can you walk, *Leannan*?" Duncan's breath was soft against her skin. She nodded, not quite trusting herself to speak. The encounter with her mother was still too fresh in her memory and she wanted to hold it close for as long as possible.

***

Duncan breathed a sigh of relief when Caitriona began coughing. Pulling her to him, he held her for several minutes, allowing his own fears to dissipate with each passing minute. Finally, fearing for their safety, he helped her to her feet, wishing he had dry clothes for them both and a safe shelter to turn to. The council was still a good three days' walk ahead of them and, in Caitriona's condition, the trek would most likely take even longer. He needed to find a way to get help, but with the Order flanking their every move, it wasn't likely to arrive any time soon.

Duncan put his arm around Caitriona's waist so she could lean on him for support. He knew they had to put the shoreline behind them in quick order, lest they become more vulnerable to the Order's drones. Aside from the near death experience Caitriona had just endured, she also bore several new cuts and bruises from their escape into the sea.

Caitriona began to tremble, her teeth chattering noisily in the silent night. Duncan wrapped his arm around her protectively, drawing her in close. He needed to get her out of her wet clothes and into something dry. Dawn was just beginning to break; the silver-grey light beginning to outline their surroundings. Ahead, he saw the faint outline of a doe and knew there would be fresh water nearby. As a boy he had climbed the hills, scouted the coastline, and been throughout the forest many times. He knew the area well and, more importantly, knew there was an entrance to the Dwellers' hidden sanctuary in the nearby Bolsa cave. He and Lee had often retreated there when they were playing truant from their lessons; a welcome respite from the growing obligations the boys were inundated with each day. Duncan looked at Caitriona and brushed the back of his hand against her cheek. They would have to move quickly, but he was confident they could reach the caves before the sun made her early morning debut.

Duncan set out at a brisk pace, pulling Caitriona along behind him. After several minutes, she cried out and fell against him. He could see the fatigue in her eyes. The hollowness of her cheeks and dark circles beneath her eyes bore little resemblance to those of the woman he had brought aboard his ship nearly three months ago, and with whom he had been intimate just hours before. Not for the first time since he set out on his mission, he cursed the man he had become and his role in his century's uncertain future.

Placing his hand behind Caitriona's knees, he scooped her effortlessly into his arms. She was too startled and too exhausted to protest. Instead, she settled her head against his chest, her hand resting lightly below his collar bone. Duncan picked up his pace once he noticed his charge's steady breathing. His military prowess was on full alert, as were his genetically engineered senses. Ahead, out of range of normal human vision, Duncan saw the outline of a doe drinking from a stream. He knew he was headed in the right direction and merely needed to reach the stream in order to follow it to the ocean and the cave's secluded entrance. He shifted Caitriona in his arms; but more as a precautionary measure to ensure her slumber. Her slight frame was hardly a burden to the powerfully built soldier.

Duncan picked his way among the dense underbrush, carefully avoiding any rogue branches that might scrape and awaken his charge. While he could have reached the cave in less than an hour, he had to backtrack several times in order to avoid the Order's men and the invasive drones that now littered the air. He knew the next wave of soldiers wasn't far behind and those men would have better training, deadlier weapons, and greater numbers.

Nearly two hours later he reached the entrance to Bolsa Cave; its smoky, gray-granite columns a welcome sight after spending the last hour covering his tracks. At the entrance to the cave he brushed his lips against Caitriona's cool lips, noting the salty taste of sea that still lingered from her time in the cold, dark ocean. Her eyelids fluttered open and. for a fleeting second he saw the disorientation and fear in her eyes, but once her eyes found his, she settled into his arms.

"I need to set ye down, *Leannan*. Can ye stand?"

She nodded, allowing him to set her on her feet. She was ice cold and her damp clothes clung to her small frame.

He kissed the top of her head lightly. "Dinna move. I'm not going far."

He receded to the dark interior and was swallowed by the blackness of the cave. His hands roamed the cave wall, trying to find the latch he knew existed. After several minutes, he could hear Caitriona moving in his direction. "Duncan," she called softly. Her voice echoed his name through the cave, sounding small and empty against the dense, cave walls. "Duncan," she called again, this time a little louder, her voice laced with fear.

"*Ciunas*," Duncan whispered in her ear, the darkness having masked his movements. She sighed softly and leaned against him. "Say nothing and follow me." He could feel her nod and so he released her, placing her hand on his back as her guide. The iciness of her hand broke through his wet shirt and he could feel her body trembling through that simple touch.

He led her to the very back of the cave and ran his hand along the cave wall. He knew there was a mechanism that would release the stone entrance. The Dwellers had created the entrance nearly fifty years ago as a secure way to reach the coastline, thereby allowing them access to the ocean's abundant supply of fish, crab, seaweed, and kelp. At length, he was rewarded with an audible click as his hand found the hidden spring. In front of him a granite wall swung slightly inward, revealing a long dark corridor beyond. Duncan reached behind him to take a hold of Caitriona's hand, ensuring she would follow him into the cavern. Once inside, his hand moved quickly along the cold stone wall until he found the matching mechanism that closed the door from his side.

When he was certain the stone door had closed, he took Caitriona's hand and led her down the dark corridor. The dirt floor was smooth and hard, indicating the corridor was heavily used. The path sloped down gradually and, after several minutes, Duncan knew they were beneath the ocean floor. Soon the corridor began to widen and he saw a faint light ahead of them. As they drew closer to the light, he noticed there were torches burning in sconces set deep within the cave walls. They had reached the inner living quarters.

Caitriona stopped suddenly and tried to free herself from Duncan's grip. Sensing the source of her concern, Duncan wrapped his arm around her waist and pulled her close to him. He knew the memory of her earlier attack and her first encounter with the Dwellers was likely causing her some fear. Her head nestled right below his chin and he held her close, trying to ease the tremors that wracked her body. After several minutes, he lifted her face to his. In the soft light of the torches, he could see the worry in her face and absently tucked a matted lock of hair behind her ear.

"Ye will be safe here, *Leannan*. I promise ye this." He bent and kissed the top of her head.

"I can't shake this feeling, Duncan," her eyes implored him to turn around.

"I promise," he said again.

She nodded, but he couldn't see the conviction in her nod. Hearing movement up ahead, he pressed her to the wall and motioned for her to be silent. His enhanced hearing had picked up the sounds of an approach about fifty yards away. He reached for his broadsword and grimaced as his hand came up empty. Cursing softly, he withdrew a smaller blade from his boot. Motioning for Caitriona to stay behind him, he made his way cautiously deeper into the tunnel. After about twenty yards, he softly called her to him. Leaning in close to her ear, he whispered, "Stay here, lass. Dinna move until I say it is clear." She nodded, and he squeezed her hand reassuringly.

After several minutes, Duncan once again called for her to join him. Caitriona made her way quickly through the corridor until she was reunited with Duncan. Two Dwellers, who were tasked with patrolling the passages, also joined them.

Each man was armed with a long sword and an array of twenty third century weapons. Forming a single file, Duncan's party quietly moved the length of the corridor until they reached the large open chamber that was used as the main dining area. Here the stone became smoother, the walls lined with carved wood or painted Celtic knots.

Along the back wall a stone seating area held pillows of nearly every size and color, in a beckoning array of cushioned invitation. The chamber had brightly colored floor tiles that were formed into a large, intricate Celtic knot. The simplistic elegance was at odds with the cave's hard angles and primitive design. By all accounts, these people lived simply, with little adornment, but here, hidden in the cavernous depths of their caves and tunnels, was a cornucopia of cultural treasure.

Duncan's gaze took in the long dining table that had been set for the morning meal. The polished oak table held a steaming array of pastries and meats as well as mugs of hot coffee. An older woman, grey hair just beginning to dust the sides of her temples and brow, rose quickly, pulling a blanket from a nearby chair and wrapped it around Caitriona's shoulders. "Come, Duncan," she motioned to the table. "Sit and eat while your chamber is being prepared." She guided Caitriona to the table and placed a mug of coffee in her hands.

"Thank you, Beatrice," Duncan replied, kissing the older woman lightly on each cheek before accepting the mug of coffee she placed in his hands.

"We received word from the scouts about your escape, and I'm afraid we feared the worst." She glanced at Caitriona who sat staring absently into the fire, watching the smoke as it was sucked easily through the stone vents. "Will the lass be needin' a healer, Duncan?" she whispered anxiously, as Caitriona barely pressed the mug to her lips.

"Some food and rest, Beatrice, is what she needs now," he replied, crossing to where his charge sat. He pulled the blanket closer carefully around her damp clothes. Duncan thought she still seamed uneasy but shrugged it off as nothing more than emotional and physical fatigue. As if on cue, a young girl with a curly mop of sandy brown curls and freckles that dotted the bridge of her nose came into the sitting room and reported that the sleeping chamber had been prepared.

"Which room do you have us in?" Duncan asked Beatrice as he piled a plate with pastries and meat pies.

"The one at the farthest end of the West corridor, Duncan," Beatrice replied. "It will be quietest, since it is farthest from the common rooms. I will send the healer once she finishes her rounds." Duncan nodded his agreement, touching Caitriona's shoulder lightly, breaking her silent reverie. Caitriona pushed her chair back absently and, clutching the still-steaming mug of coffee in her hands, followed Duncan farther into the cave's interior.

Once inside their spacious sleeping chamber, Caitriona set the cup of coffee aside and let the blanket slide to the floor. Flinging her arms around Duncan's neck and pulling him close to her, she said, scolding, "Let's never jump over a cliff again."

He gave her a lopsided, mischievous grin before kissing her soundly. "Ever," she emphasized again.

"You seemed like you needed more adventure," he said playfully, pulling his wet shirt from his head, noting the color that was slowly returning to his charge's heart-shaped face.

"I may have to rethink that wish," she replied haughtily, rubbing her arms in an effort to ward off the pervasive chill from the damp cavern interior.

"Agreed, Madame! I will take 'leaping-from-cliffs' off any future lists that involve adventure." He crossed the room to an old trunk that sat at the base of the large four-poster bed. Popping the spring on the rusted lock, he reached inside and withdrew a wool blanket, trousers, and two shirts.

"I can always count on Beatrice to have a spare set of clothing—although I'm afraid it's far from the height of fashion," he explained at her inquisitive look. "Here," he tossed her a pair of trousers and a grey cotton button up shirt. "I'm sure the previous owner won't mind," he grinned mischievously.

Caitriona took the offered items and the blanket. "Turn around," she motioned with her hand when he looked confused.

He chuckled softly. "I forget how modest yer century was," he replied, but complied with her request.

"I'm not sure I've ever heard anyone refer to the twenty first century as modest," she responded glibly, pulling her soaked shirt over her head and removing her bra as well. She kicked off her boots, tugging off her pants and undergarments as well. She wrapped herself in the wool blanket and sat on the edge of the bed, the coarse wool scratching her soft skin. "OK. You can turn around."

Duncan did as he was told, his eyes scanning the length of her. "Are ye hurt?" he asked, his earlier playful demeanor replaced with the more serious countenance he nearly always wore. "I saw cuts on yer arms and legs earlier." At her hesitation, he added, "I willna leave, lass, until I'm certain yer injuries are na life threatening."

"And I suppose you simply won't take my word for it?"

Duncan shook his head and watched as Caitriona resigned and pulled the wool blanket away from her calves. He muttered a string of curses in his native tongue. A deep cut on her left shin would most likely leave a scar unless they reached the council and the benefits of his century's more modern technologies. He reached for a nearby bandage and, soaking the cloth in clean water, gently washed away the dried blood. After securing the bandage, he quickly scanned the rest of her for any more visible signs of injury. Pushing a lock of hair from her eyes, he noted the stubborn resolve of her chin and the fire that lit her emerald eyes.

"*Tha gaol agam ort*," Duncan said softly, the hypnotic lilt of his Scottish brogue filling the space between them. His hand reached out and cupped Caitriona's chin. She eyed him quizzically, and he knew she was waiting for a translation from his native Gaelic tongue. "I love you, Caitriona." The words were simple, laced with a lifetime of unspoken need, desire, and understanding. "I have loved you since the day you came aboard my ship. Goddess help me, I tried not to." His voice echoed his need.

"*Tha gaol agam ort,*" Caitriona replied back, incorrectly placing the emphasis on the first and last syllable. Her mispronunciation drew a soft chuckle from Duncan before his mouth captured hers in a fierce kiss that left him wanting more.

Caitriona let the blanket slide from her shoulders as she released her hold on the scratchy cloth and traced the line of Duncan's chin lightly with her finger. She pushed her breasts brazenly against the sinewy hardness of his chest, sighing softly when she spied the sudden response she was able to evoke. Duncan released the drawstrings surreptitiously, allowing his trews to fall freely to the stone floor, the length of him freed from the imposing prison of his trews.

Ach, she is beautiful, he thought. Despite the cuts, bruises, and tangled mass of auburn hair, she glowed from within. Duncan pushed an errant curl away from her eyes as his other hand lightly traced the outline of her breast. He was rewarded with a soft moan as her hand captured his, pulling his finger to her mouth and sucking softly. He inhaled sharply, pushing his knee between her thighs. The electricity fairly danced between them, the ever present charge he had felt from the beginning begging for release.

Caitriona wrapped both arms around his neck, her fingers tangling themselves in his thick hair as she pulled his leather thong free and allowed the length of his hair to spill across his shoulders. The length of him pressed against her wetness. His need ran deep and he pushed against her.

He entered her gently, his hands squeezing her buttocks and caressing the curves of her body. She arched her back, pushing against him and taking him deep within her. He groaned, his body relenting to the sensuous tempo they both shared. He reveled in their lovers' dance, each moving in sensuous rhythm with the other.

Wrapping his arms around her, he rolled them both suddenly so that Caitriona was straddling him. A soft sigh escaped her lips as she rocked her hips slowly against him, undulating as she sought to take the full length of him. Duncan put his hands on her hips and increased his tempo. He could feel the clenching of her vaginal muscles as she sought to pull him deeper inside her. He groaned, increasing his tempo as she arched her back and allowed him to imprison each breast in tribute to their mesmerizing lovers' dance.

Duncan captured one nipple, flicking his tongue expertly across the sensitive tip until it hardened and Caitriona's groan nearly undid him. She laced her fingers through the thick expanse of curls that now fell tantalizingly over his shoulders. Guiding his mouth to her other nipple, she encouraged him to tease the nipple to hardness as she continued a steady undulation with her hips, a dance only he and his lover would rehearse. His hand dipped lower, tracing a path from nipple to belly as he marveled at her soft skin and firm muscles. She gasped as his fingers dipped to her secret spot, a moan escaping her lips when he found the little nub that had hardened with her rhythmic efforts and his expert touch.

Caitriona pushed her hips forward, allowing him even greater access to her clitoris. All his thoughts of war and politics were abandoned as this one primal need took over and drove his actions. He pushed the hard length of him deeper into her, filling her and stretching her until her moans nearly undid him. Duncan groaned and locked eyes with her, knowing at this moment that he would never be able to release her to her handler.

Duncan reached up and grasped the back of her neck, pulling her face to his. He needed to feel her lips on his, her tongue entwined with his, and needed to know she was as pulled to him as he was to her. His lips gently caressed hers, while his tongue danced and gently probed hers. He opened his eyes and saw the rapture building on her face; the freedom that comes from abandoning one's inhibitions and giving power and trust to your lover.

"Look at me, Caitriona," he said huskily, her name like a prayer on his lips.

She opened her eyes and instantly locked her emerald green orbs with his. He was overwhelmed at the intensity of her gaze, her emotions unchecked and clearly on display. She kissed him soundly, her eyes never leaving his, her tongue expertly capturing his. He broke their kiss, his hands finding her hips and increasing their tempo. She groaned, her own release building, his need to feel her shatter around him driving him to even greater frenzied heights.

"Catie, lass," he groaned, his hips driving an unrelenting, maddening rhythm. "Now."

She arched her back, her own release pulsating through her in crashing waves that she continued to ride as Duncan's own orgasm shook his body, filling her with his own spent need. He stayed in her for several minutes while he enjoyed the afterglow of their spent union, relishing the way her body locked neatly with his own.

Duncan finally broke the silence, his weighty declaration a shroud that hung between them. "I never meant to fall in love with you, Caitriona," he said softly, almost apologetically. His hand softly caressed the curls that clung to the faint perspiration still present from their intense love making.

Caitriona nestled closer to him and sighed contentedly.

"But I promise ye this, lass, I willna let anyone come between us." His hands ceased their stroking and he pulled her tighter to him, claiming her as his. He held her like that for several minutes, listening to the rise and fall of her breath and the way their hearts beat almost in unison.

After several minutes, Duncan rolled off of Caitriona. He pulled her close and stared for several seconds at the longing that was evident on her smooth, heart-shaped face. "For a Seer to truly realize her powers, she must be balanced." Duncan's hand stroked Caitriona's arm lightly, his fingers softly tracing the tear-shaped birthmark that had been the harbinger of her destiny.

"Yin and Yang," Caitriona whispered.

Duncan nodded, knowing she would feel his action even though she couldn't see him in the dark. He kissed her softly on her forehead. "We discovered several years ago that although women carried the genetic code for magic, the male was needed in order for a Seer to focus that energy. Without that balance, the Seer will go mad. The energy becomes too great to control and eventually consumes her. She is left as nothing more than a shell, dangerous to herself and those around her as the madness takes over. We call it the awakening."

"You will balance me, then," Caitriona stopped his caresses, threading her fingers with his. "We will complete each other and the only way I shall ever go mad is from your kisses." She grinned up at him, but stopped short when she met his eyes.

"What is it? You're not telling me something," she said, concern lacing her voice.

"One has already been chosen for ye and that canna be undone."

"What do you mean?" Caitriona disengaged her hand and raised the flame in the hurricane lamp that had been placed on the nightstand.

Duncan's face was hard, the grey eyes now cold.

"He is a strong match, Caitriona. He has prepared for this since he was a wee lad. He is a genetic, bred for superior intelligence, strength, and physical endurance. He will not only keep ye safe, but can provide a channel for yer magic and ..."

"No!" Caitriona cried, staring into the hard grey eyes. "This is insane. I won't be handed over like ... chattel. You can't force me to do this. Not now."

"I won't need to force you, Caitriona. When the awakening begins, ye will seek relief. It will feel as if a thousand knives are dancing in yer head. The headaches ye've been having are precursors; they will only get worse."

"I don't believe you. You don't know that it will happen to me. I've been here for several months already and aside from the headaches I feel fine. I rarely even have any visions. Maybe you are mistaken about my ancestry ... maybe ..."

Duncan touched her arm, bringing an end to her suppositions. Green eyes met determined grey ones and a face that remained hard. Reaching out to her, he pulled her to him so that she was nestled in his arms. He could see unshed tears beginning to form behind her eyes and he hated himself for having allowed himself to fall in love with this woman.

She closed her eyes as the tears slipped quietly down her cheeks. He brushed them away with his thumb and pulled her tighter against him, his head resting on top of hers. They stayed like that for several minutes before Duncan pushed her away so he could see her face.

"I have no right to ye, *Leannan*. I am a warrior, bred to fight battles. My mission is to see ye safely to yer handler, nothing more."

"No." The single word was but a breath on the cold night air, its finality clear. Caitriona pushed away from Duncan. "When you first mentioned the bonding on board your ship, you never said I wouldn't be able to choose my partner." He heard the grief in her voice and noted the hard slant to her green eyes. The crease in her brow bore clear evidence of her warring emotions.

"What more would you have me do, *Leannan*?"

"You ask that as if my opinion matters. In reality, we both know that I will remain underground, locked in your stone chambers and guarded like a bird in a cage until your precious council decides I am no longer needed."

Duncan wasn't about to argue with her. He would see her safely to her handler, and it would tear him apart to watch her emotionally bond with another man. But if it meant keeping her safe and free from the Order's tyrannical persecution, he would see this mission through to its heart wrenching conclusion.

Chapter Nineteen

The first step toward success is taken when you refuse to be a captive of the environment in which you first find yourself.
Mark Cain

Caitriona woke suddenly, pushing away the nagging fear and foreboding that had settled over her sometime during the night. The down blanket clung uncomfortably to the perspiration that dampened her skin. She pushed the covers from her body and took deep breaths of the cold cave air into her lungs. She sighed softly, relishing the way the cool air danced across her body and brought goose flesh to the surface. She glanced at Duncan, who was lost in his own world of dreams. She brushed his hair lightly from his face, thinking of several devilish ways she could wake him. With a slight smile, she decided to let him rest while she went to the cave's outer chamber to make some tea, their earlier conversation an unsettling reminder of her bleak future.

Being careful not to disturb her lover, she slid from the bed and pulled on the borrowed clothes Duncan had handed her earlier, the memory of their love making bringing a blush to her cheeks. Dropping a kiss lightly to Duncan's forehead, she crept quietly from the room. She needed time to think; time to process the information Duncan had revealed and sort out her next move. Foolishly, she had assumed Duncan would want to bond with her. She felt the heat rise to her cheeks as embarrassment washed over her. *How could I be so stupid*, she chided herself. She was nothing in this century and to this man; an unremitting reminder of his duty and obligation. And yet, he had professed his love for her. Would he really be able to hand her over to another? She wasn't sure she wanted to know the answer.

She shivered as she made her way through the interior of the cave's passage, the familiar sconces providing an ever vigilant lighted escort as she made her way to the keeping room. The cave's dark interior did nothing to lift her spirits and she ran her hands briskly over her arms to bring some warmth to the cold limbs.

She knew she was getting closer to the keeping room, yet she did not recall the corridors being quite so dark. The Dwellers were vigilant about keeping the common rooms well lit. Caitriona slowed her steps, her uneasiness growing more pronounced. Making up her mind to return to their room and alert Duncan she turned abruptly only to come up against a hard, cloaked body. She started to scream but a hand clamped down hard over her mouth, preventing any further effort on her part. She tried to claw and bite, but her assailant simply ignored her attempts like an indifferent horse swatting at a persistent fly.

The hooded stranger wrapped his free hand in her hair and yanked hard. Caitriona reached up to untangle his hand from her hair. Unsuccessful, she tried using her legs to slow their progress, but the smooth dirt floor of the cave offered no traction. At the opening to the cave, the cold air jolted her senses and renewed her efforts. Growling, her captor stopped and pulled her up short in front of him. A dark hood kept her from seeing her assailant's features, but the narrow slits in the hood allowed her to make out a pair of cold, soulless brown eyes. Without any warning, he brought his knee up sharply to her stomach. She crumpled immediately, trying to force air into her lungs. She didn't have the strength or air capacity to scream, even though her captor had now removed his hand from her mouth. Clutching her middle, which was now shooting sharp daggers of pain throughout her body, she tried to stand. When his fist connected to her temple, she succumbed to the pain and darkness that quickly enveloped her.

***

Duncan woke to a cold void next to him where Caitriona should have been. Instantly on alert, he tossed the covers from his body, barely noting the cold air as it grazed his naked form. His eyes noted the absence of Caitriona's clothes, and he swore lightly under his breath. Quickly donning his pants and shirt, he crossed the room to a nearby armoire which housed an assortment of weapons. He scanned the various blades and chose a heavy long sword, lamenting the loss of his broadsword earlier at the cliff. Strapping a shorter blade into the scabbard he wore at his upper thigh, he left the room, checking the nearby chamber facilities, hopeful that he would find her there. Seeing no sign of her, he moved quietly from the room and down the long corridor toward the inner chambers and the keeping room.

Someone had doused several of the sconces, casting the corridor in dark shadows. Duncan's genetically engineered vision adjusted to the darkness quickly, searching the shadows for signs of trouble. When he saw the absence of any light in the east corridor, he cursed silently and reached for the sword at his side. Every ounce of his military training told him the caves had been breached and Caitriona had been taken. Hearing footsteps coming toward him, he shrank back against the far side of the corridor ready to attack. The footsteps were accompanied by a growing light, and judging by the uneven gait, he knew that whoever was coming was not military. Nonetheless, he stayed at full alert, ready to engage as the men drew closer.

As the first man reached the corner of the corridor, Duncan moved with precision, capturing the man in a vise-like grip around his neck while quickly and deftly disarming him. Spinning him around so he could face his adversary, Duncan recognized the man as Brennan, one of the young smithies who lived among the dwellers.

"Commander," the man croaked out. "We're under attack."

Duncan released the young man, who had broken out in a cold sweat at coming face-to-face with the powerful Highlander.

"Who?" Duncan growled the single word.

"We dinna ken, sir," Brennan said brusquely, rubbing the tender spot against his throat. "The breach was deliberate and planned. Whoever it was, found the entrance you and Caitriona used. Several of our guards have been killed, but the sleeping chambers have nae been disturbed. It's as if they were looking for something specific."

"Or someone . . ." Duncan replied more to himself. "Have ye seen Caitriona?"

"Nay, sir. I was comin' to warn ye when ye stopped me here."

Duncan was already moving back the way he came. "Call for reinforcements, Brennan. They have the Seer."

Brennan's reply was lost on Duncan, who was already covering the corridor in long strides, his heart beating wildly and his warrior instincts already preparing for the battle ahead.

***

Caitriona rubbed her hand across her temple in a vain attempt to stem the throbbing that threatened to drag her back into the darkness that held her prisoner. Her entire body felt heavy as if she were chained to a weight that refused to allow her any purchase. Fighting against the lethargy, she tried to open her eyes and wondered why they refused to cooperate. Another sharp pain seared across her temple and she let out a soft moan, wishing Duncan could hear her. A cold breeze danced across her skin causing her to shudder uncontrollably. Fear getting the better of her, she rolled to her side and tried to push herself up on one elbow, her eyes finally freeing themselves from their black prison.

At first, the light made her squeeze her eyes shut but slowly she forced them open, the memory of her abduction rushing back to her, leaving an outbreak of fear and confusion in its wake. Her mouth was as dry as cotton and tasted of blood. Pulling herself upright, she took inventory of her condition. Her clothes were filthy and bore several tears. Where there were rips, she noticed deep cuts that most likely would have been worse had her skin been exposed. She winced and tried to pull the remnants of the cloth away from the cuts where skin and cloth had fused together. Deciding it would be better not to re-open the wounds, she moved her arms slowly in front of her. Reasonably confident that her wounds were superficial, she stood, mentally taking note of her confined quarters and the absence of any furnishings.

Spotting a large oak door at the end of the room, she crossed the room in three easy strides and pulled at the oversized brass door knob. Locked. She tried again, banging futilely on the wood panels in an effort to garner attention. She kicked at the heavy oak panels with her boot and was quickly reminded of how stout and heavy the door was. Frustrated, she looked around for another means of escape. The room was dimly lit from one small torch that hung well above her reach. The room was bereft of any furnishings or objects and appeared to be no larger than an oversized closet. There were no windows. Caitriona sank to the cold wood floor, her heart beating wildly and her vision becoming narrow as the walls threatened to close in around her.

The enormity of the situation and her abduction began to take hold. She had no idea where she was, what time of day it was, how long she had been here, or what might have happened to Duncan. Giving into the fear and desolation that wracked through her, she let the tears course freely down her cheeks, forging a trail through the dirt that had caked into her skin. A sob tore from her lips and she no longer cared about fronting a brave facade.

Caitriona swiped a hand across her eyes and quickly got to her feet when she heard a key turn in the massive lock. Her heart beat wildly with the trepidation of meeting her abductor. When the door pushed open, two armed soldiers entered the small room, their laser weapons leveled at her ominously. Hawkins strode in after the guards, a sardonic smile creasing his effeminate and rather plain features. The pale white scar, which she had seen many times in her vision, stood in stark contrast to the pink, overly flushed hue of his face.

The room was suddenly too small. She felt the walls creeping toward her as the bile rose in her throat. *Death is a better alternative,* she thought frantically. She rushed for the door only to be stopped short by Hawkins, who grabbed a handful of her hair and pulled her around in front of him. She cried out and clawed at his hands. Hawkins drew his free hand back and slapped her hard across her face, making her head reel from the blow. She tasted salty metallic blood.

Fighting back a wave of nausea and willing herself not to faint, she glared at Hawkins. "What do you want from me?" she spat.

He grinned lazily and leered openly at her, his eyes lingering on the rise and fall of her breasts. "I'm afraid, my dear," he chuckled softly, "that you are to suffer the same fate as all those who show genetic inferiority; unless, of course, we can come to some arrangement." Caitriona pulled her shirt closer around her throat instinctively and spat in his face. The guards powered the lasers, making it clear there would be no further outbursts.

"You will learn to obey, Caitriona," Hawkins hissed as he wiped the back of his hand across the spittle that dripped slowly down his face.

"I would sooner die," she replied defiantly, slowly articulating each word. Her voice was icy cold, her green eyes like daggers.

"*Ma chéri,*" he said, his false French accent at odds with his twisted, perverted masochism. "You will soon learn we have methods of torture that are worse than death;" he chuckled softly as his eyes swept appreciatively over her body, "torture so horrific that you would pray for death."

Caitriona lunged for the door. This time the blow Hawkins dealt her knocked her to the ground, a black and purple bruise beginning almost instantly to mark the point where his fist made contact with her cheek.

"Now we are going to find out what all the fuss is about you," he drawled, snapping his fingers. Another soldier entered the already crowded quarters and opened a medical supply kit. Caitriona stood up and eyed the men wearily. Her face hurt like hell, but she knew it would be nothing compared to what these animals were capable of.

"Go to hell," she spat, fear giving her more courage than she felt.

The soldier worked quickly, removing various vials, rubber tubing, and a single syringe. The reality of what they were going to do was not lost on Caitriona. She took another step backwards, only to have the hard paneled wall stop her short.

"Hold her," the soldier said to Hawkins in an obviously bored monotone. Hawkins grabbed her left arm and pulled it in close to his body, neatly spinning her so that he held her in front of him with her arm tucked tightly at his side. Caitriona pushed against him, nearly vomiting when she felt him grow excited behind her.

Hawkins lowered his head near her ear and licked the side of her face. He purred in the self-satisfied smugness of one who knew he had won. Caitriona shuddered, again willing herself not to faint. Remembering her training in the martial arts, she relaxed her body and waited until she could feel the slightest give in his hold. She didn't have long to wait. What came next was almost instinctive for Caitriona. She raised her foot and brought it crashing down on his instep at the same time her elbow connected with his solar plexus. She took advantage of her release by spinning quickly around and kneeing him in the groin, a satisfied feeling washing over her as she bore witness to his furious expletive and saw him crumple like a rag doll.

Hawkins no longer a threat, she turned to face the other three and knew the odds were stacked against her. She could feel the lasers pointed at her and hear the electric charge as they finished powering up. "No weapons," Hawkins belted through clenched teeth.

It was all she needed. Planting a low round-house kick to the first guard's knee, she quickly did a spinning back kick and connected with the second guard's temple. He fell to the ground, unconscious. The medic looked unsure of what to do and Caitriona seized that opportunity to make her escape.

Caitriona had cleared the door when Hawkins threw himself against her, taking them both to the ground in a tangled heap of limbs. She struggled to regain control, but her physical strength was no match for his. Planting himself on top of her, he took the knife out of his boot top and quickly sliced the palm of her hand. She screamed in terror and pain. Hawkins held the knife below her eye, "Move again, and I will carve your eye out and send it to your lover. I only need you alive; not necessarily in one piece," he hissed at her.

"Bryans," he yelled, "bring the vial; we're going to take a different approach."

Hawkins eyed the rise and fall of her chest greedily as he easily held her pinned against him.

Bryans pulled a new vial quickly from his kit and stepped across the fallen soldiers to where Hawkins and Caitriona lay tangled on the floor. The blood from the wound Hawkins had caused was running down her arm, pooling on the ground beside her. Bryans uncapped the vial and held it under the stream of blood, watching as the vial began slowly to fill with the dark red liquid. Snatching the vial from the young medic's shaking hands, Hawkins placed the vial against the open wound and pushed hard. Caitriona screamed again, the pain causing the corridor to spin darkly before her.

When the vial was full, Hawkins thrust it back to Bryans and hauled Caitriona to her feet. Caitriona cradled her injured hand, pushing it hard against her body to stop the flow of blood. She felt nauseous and trembled uncontrollably, her green eyes challenging Hawkins. Without warning, Hawkins slapped her hard across the face. The force of the blow caused her head to roll forward and hang limply before her. Hawkins gestured to the two guards, who had now regained consciousness and hurriedly came to make amends for their earlier lack of judgment. The guards quickly supported her weight between them, holding her arms back as she threatened to collapse.

Hawkins grabbed a fistful of the auburn locks and pulled her face up so that he was staring into her eyes. She glared at him, refusing to give into the pain or fear that raged through her. Instead, she tried to use her legs to strike out at him, mortified when she barely managed more than a slight gesture in his direction. Chuckling cruelly, he slapped her hard again and then punched her firmly in the stomach. The last blow sent her over the edge and she expelled the contents of her stomach on the ground in front of him.

Hawkins stepped back glaring at the woman before him. He removed a perfectly starched white handkerchief from inside his breast jacket pocket and ran it cruelly across her mouth.

"See, *ma chéri*. I am not an animal."

She spat a stream of blood at him, satisfied when she saw it splatter on his polished black shoes. Once again, she made a suggestion for a vacation destination, "Go. To. Hell."

"I can break you before you can blink, *chéri*, and I will then do to you all the nasty things your imagination has conjured up." Hawkins gestured angrily to the two soldiers. "Take her to my quarters and secure her."

Caitriona tried again to prevent her jailers from taking her away, but she was too weakened from the beating Hawkins had dealt her. As the soldiers dragged her struggling body past him, Hawkins landed one last blow to her temple and Caitriona gratefully succumbed to darkness.

Chapter Twenty

Bravery is being the only one who knows you're afraid.
Franklin P. Jones

Riley McPherson swiped the dirt from her face as her older brother Charlie led them in a hearty game of follow-the-leader through the dark underground passages. Born underground, the two had rarely been to the surface, except at night and only under the watchful eye of their da or grandda. Charlie didn't mind as he had been taught at an early age that dangers lurked above ground. Besides, he and his sister had grown up in a family full of love and affection. He had no desire to leave his family or risk alerting any of the Genetics to the location of their underground haven. So he and Riley remained safe, loved and cared for deep within the recesses of the earth. Stalagmites and stalactites had been their gardens, while natural springs that flowed deep within the earth had provided nourishment. Food was foraged top-side by men trained as warriors and hunters. Stocks were piled high and rationed carefully to ensure there were ample stores even in difficult times.

The two wound their way through the lower catacombs and tunnels; as familiar with the caverns as they were with the nearly two hundred people who lived in the caves and this community. Most of the inhabitants were Dwellers, but some Genetics lived here as well; committed to freedom and the belief that all people should be free to live life on their own terms. In the caves, the inhabitants were not defined by their genetic attributes; all lived together as one, united in the same goal to fight tyranny, oppression, and the New World Order.

As the two youngsters came running around a corner, Charlie abruptly stopped, pulling his sister in close beside him. Something did not feel right. Charlie had a unique empathic ability to sense strong feelings. What he felt made him uneasy. Usually there were voices in the corridors, but today it was strangely quiet. Charlie put his finger to his lips, motioning for his sister to be still. She gripped his hand more tightly, fear emanating instantly from her pale face and large dark eyes. Charlie walked slowly to the end of the corridor and peered cautiously around the corner, his sister clinging fearfully to his tunic. As soon as Charlie peered around the corner, he knew what was wrong. The torches that generally hung on the stone walls and illuminated the darkness had been doused. No one in the community would have doused the flames unless the Order had penetrated the caverns.

Charlie knew he and his sister had to get back to the elders and alert the community. They would know what to do, and could gather the warriors who would defend and protect their close knit family. Charlie glanced at his sister to see tears filling her dark, almond eyes. He tried to reassure her with his silent plea, but Charlie felt the unease and knew he had to get them both safely back to the others.

Grasping his sister's small, cold hand in his, he made his way cautiously back through the corridor they had only moments before been playing in. An ear-piercing scream rent the silence and Charlie stopped in his tracks, drawing his sister in close. She started to cry and he glanced sharply at her to get her to stop. Rubbing the palm of her dirty hand across her tear-stained face, Riley tried to take a deep breath. Charlie wished they were back near the elders and in their da's strong arms.

Charlie pulled his sister tightly to him. He knew he had to find the others, but he also knew that to do so might mean walking into danger. Instead, he backed slowly down the corridor with his sister in tow and into the darkened recesses of the lower chamber they had just vacated. Riley hesitated, but Charlie knew they would have a better chance of hiding in the shadows than being in the light. Another scream rent the corridors and Charlie stopped abruptly, trying to discern where the scream had come from. The corridors and chambers were often quite deceptive in distributing sound. Because of the varying levels and how the corridors intertwined, it was nearly impossible to tell where each sound originated. But having grown up in the tunnels, Charlie was adept at navigating the elaborate system and discerning the sometimes eerie noises that emanated from the caves.

He continued to listen. Sobbing could now be heard along with swords, and the unmistakable sound of boots and the clanking of metal against metal. Charlie pulled his sister deeper into the darkened tunnels. He knew where he had to go. The "whispering stone" was only two levels below them. He and Riley often went there to listen in on conversations in the main chamber. Standing near the stone, one could hear conversations that took place in the great hall. No one but the two children knew about the "whispering stone". They often came to the stone near holidays and festivities to hear what gifts or surprises would be in store for them. Charlie made his way there now. If there were soldiers in the great hall, he would be able to hear their conversation and know the extent of the danger. Perhaps he could put together a plan with the help of the cave's warriors. He shivered from fear, but resolved to be strong. Riley needed him and besides, warriors were not afraid. With a resigned breath, Charlie squared his small shoulders and motioned for his sister to follow him.

Making their way into the stone chamber deep underground, the children huddled together near the whispering stone, their heads tilted to one side, fervently straining to hear what the Order's soldiers were saying. Charlie held his finger to his mouth indicating Riley should keep quiet, her incessant shuffling a distraction in the otherwise quiet room. Charlie was frustrated. Most of what the soldiers said Charlie didn't understand. But gradually, he realized the soldiers had slaughtered several in their community and sentries were still patrolling the corridors, seeking survivors. He was glad his little sister was too young to understand the conversation.

Charlie placed his small ear over the pin sized hole in the whispering stone. The acoustic effects of the half dome shape allowed those in the dome to hear conversations in the keeping room. Charlie hated the Order's soldiers for what they did. His small hands clenched into fists and he fought back several tears. *Soldiers don't cry*, he reminded himself. He had to remain strong for his little sister. He shifted his weight and pressed even closer to the whispering stone, the voices becoming clearer.

"That son-of-a-bitch MacKinnon made it too easy for us," scoffed one of the Order's soldiers.

"Aye, I wouldn't have let that pretty lady out of my sight for an instant," said another, his words slightly slurred.

"We should find MacKinnon and kill him. Imagine our reward if we delivered the traitorous bastard's head on a spike."

"Our orders are to bring the girl to Loch Liobhann," the first soldier spat angrily. "Alive." He dragged the word out slowly as if testing its meaning.

"What do we do about the others?"

"Hawkins will send more troops to gas the chambers. What we don't butcher on our way out will be dead by nightfall." He spat a stream of tobacco on the floor.

Charlie straightened his head and looked at Riley who had moved to a corner of the room and was staring at him through large, almond-shaped eyes. She had stopped crying, but her tears had left streaks down her dirty face. Her eyes that were usually so full of life were fearful and red from crying. She trembled uncontrollably.

Charlie walked over to his little sister and knelt beside her. "I have to report to the Commander what I've heard." At her look of alarm, he continued quickly. "He will know what to do. He will send others to help us."

She shook her head violently, her small hands clinging to his arm.

Charlie hugged his sister to him and raised her chin so that she was looking at him. "Do you remember what Da said about the lady Commander MacKinnon had brought to the caves?" At her slight nod, he continued. "Then you remember he told us that we all had a duty to protect her? Da said she is very special."

Riley ran the back of her hand across her face, sniffing loudly. She nodded her head, a tremor shaking her small body. Charlie wished their mother were here.

"I know which room the Commander is in," Charlie said. "I will go there quickly and tell him what we've heard. He needs to know the pretty lady he brought has been captured."

Riley shook her head again, clearly distraught. But she didn't say anything. Charlie hadn't heard his little sister utter a word since the soldiers started their killing. She grabbed his arm and tightened her grip almost painfully. He knew from her touch she didn't want to be left alone.

After several moments, Charlie finally acquiesced. He hugged her to him again and said softly, "All right. We go together. But you have to mind what I tell you and keep very quiet."

She nodded her approval and slipped her cold hand into his. Together, they left the safety of the whispering stone, fear something he could ill afford to indulge.

***

Duncan returned to the sleeping chamber he had shared with Caitriona. This time, he surveyed the surroundings carefully, looking for any clues as to Caitriona's abduction. He took one of the sconces from the chamber's wall and backed carefully into the corridor. He scanned the ground, hoping to see her familiar footprint, but because of the vast numbers of Dwellers who roamed the halls, it was impossible to discern Caitriona's step from any others. As he continued toward the keeping room, he paused at the junction. Soldiers' boot prints were clearly etched into the dirt floor. He leaned closer to the dirt floor, his eyes not missing the long brush strokes that were indicative of something being dragged.

A sound from one of the inner corridors caught his attention and he quickly doused the sconce. His hand on his sword, he pressed himself against the wall and waited. Duncan decided there was one person, possibly two, moving in his direction, but the footsteps were softer; absent the usual shuffle of the Order's troops. Animal, perhaps, he thought anxiously. Not taking any chances, he moved quickly into the adjacent corridor that would loop around and connect with the passage he had just left. He wanted to come up from behind the trespasser and gain the advantage. Moving quickly, he paused only long enough to listen for the earlier scuffling, sure of his strategy.

Emerging into the main corridor, well behind the intruder, Duncan moved cautiously. He stopped only when he heard the interloper stop. He knew this would be the best opportunity he would get. Springing forward, he brought himself up short as he nearly toppled two small children that were pressed against the shadows. He placed his finger quickly to his mouth, indicating the children should remain silent.

"Commander," the boy exclaimed in a loud whisper.

Duncan recognized the boy as Jocelyn's younger brother. While Jocelyn normally worked in the medical facility, she had been preparing for her handfasting the day Caitriona had been brought to the healing chamber.

"Where is yer family?" Duncan asked, concern evident in his gruff voice.

"I think they're dead," Charlie replied, choking on the last word. Duncan reached out and pulled the two children to him. "Stay close ... and dinna give up hope."

"Sir, we were coming to find you," Charlie said solemnly. "We overheard the Order's soldiers. They've taken the bonnie lady to Loch Liobhann."

Duncan said a silent prayer to the Goddess for this small miracle of information. "Ye're sure?"

"Aye. They said she is to be taken alive and given to Hawkins." Charlie repeated carefully what he had overheard at the stone.

"Ye have done well, lad." Duncan ruffled the young boy's hair who, for the first time that day, smiled. "Let's get ye and yer wee sister to safety. Do ye ken where the others are?"

"I think they are also dead, sir," Charlie said hesitantly. Duncan could see the effort it took for the lad not to cry. "The soldiers said they had what they came for, but they would send others to gas the chambers."

Duncan nodded, already devising a plan. He had to get the children topside and to Castle Dunrobin, but he also couldn't waste time escorting the children there himself. *Damnu*, he cursed silently, and not for the first time that day. He had to find Brennan.

"Keep behind me and stay close," he ordered the children, his voice harsher than he had intended.

The children obeyed immediately and fell in step behind Duncan. He chose his way carefully through the corridors, ensuring the children remained close behind. Several times he paused, listening intently to the echoed wails and groans that cascaded through the corridors. A couple of times, he heard the young lassie behind him sniffle, but for the most part, the children kept quiet and remained obedient.

After several minutes, Duncan reached the cave front. The usually well-lit corridor remained shrouded in darkness, its stone pillars like dark sentries that no longer guarded its inhabitants. Duncan motioned for the children to stay put, pausing just long enough for them to acknowledge his orders. He moved quietly and swiftly to the cave's opening, his hand brushing over the cold stones in an effort to find the hidden latch that would release the cave door. As his eyes adjusted to the dark, he realized the latch wasn't necessary as the Order's troops had indeed breached the cave and had left the usually well-concealed door open. *Damnu*, he cursed inwardly. It's not possible that they simply stumbled across this. He made a mental note to dig into this later.

Duncan called softly to the children, who scampered quickly to catch up with him. Together, they moved from the once-secured cave to the vast outdoors. Dawn was just beginning to break, the soft pink and magenta of the first light painting the sky in a glorious canvas of color. Charlie tugged softly on Duncan's trews, pointing to the dense underbrush that bracketed the cave's location. Duncan peered in the direction Charlie pointed, understanding finally dawning ... the Dwellers would be using the underbrush as cover.

"Wait for me to reach the cover of those trees," Duncan said to the children, motioning to the thick expanse of trees. "Watch for my signal, and then I want ye both to race as fast as ye can to where I am. Dinna stop for anything.' Ye ken?"

Both children nodded solemnly, Riley's lower lip quivering. Duncan squeezed her hand lightly and set off at a sprint for the trees. As Charlie predicted, several Dwellers, including Brennan, were taking refuge under the natural cover. Duncan placed his hands in the air away from his sword in case the men had any doubts as to his loyalty. Brennan motioned quickly for the other men to lower their weapons, acknowledging Duncan with a Templar's salute.

After ensuring the area was secure, Duncan motioned for Charlie and Riley to join him. He kept his hand on the gun Brennan had given him, watching carefully as the children ran swiftly from the cave opening to the safety of the trees. Brennan greeted the children warmly, wrapping them in a big bear hug that left them breathless. They grinned up at the grizzled giant and Riley slipped her small hand in his.

"I'll see ye get to the others, lil' lassie," Brennan said, wiping a tear from Riley's cheek. Charlie slipped an arm around his sister's shoulders and gave her a reassuring squeeze.

"Brennan, a moment in private," Duncan nodded to the man and moved a few feet from the others.

"What news do ye bring us, Commander?" the older man asked.

Duncan drew in a long breath that felt like acid scoring his lungs and spoke the words that acknowledged all their fears and would inextricably change their lives. "Hawkins has the Seer. Prepare for war." Duncan's sentences were short, crisp; the despondency of the situation weighing heavily upon him. "I'm going after her. Take the children and get yerself and the others to Castle Lauriston. They are loyal to the Templars and will send word to Gawain and Lee that we will need reinforcements at Loch Liobhann."

Brennan asked few questions, for which Duncan was relieved. Every minute he spent briefing the older man was more time Caitriona spent in Hawkins' malevolent controls. The older man offered him a smaller dirk, which he accepted gratefully and strapped to his left thigh. Adjusting the hilt of his long sword one last time, and checking the charge on his recently appropriated weapon, he clasped arms with Brennan and set out in the direction of Loch Liobhann, the future of an entire population and the woman he loved depending on him.

Chapter Twenty-One

Foolishness is rarely a matter of lack of intelligence or even lack of information.
John McCarthy

Hawkins looked up at the night sky as he felt the first tenuous drops of rain land on his coat. The clouds blocked the stars, creating an even more ominous shroud over the land before him. Buttoning his black wool coat around him, Hawkins removed his glasses and wiped the rain drops from the glass. He pushed the wire spectacles hastily back on his nose and dug in his pocket for his stocking hat. The rain was coming down even harder now and Hawkins knew it wouldn't be long before the heavens unleashed their wrath on the occupants below.

With the stocking hat covering his nearly bald scalp, Hawkins lit a cigar and inhaled sharply. The pungent aroma, mixed with the whisky he had downed earlier, did little to soften his mood. He enjoyed escaping the confines of the camp and the neverending requests that plagued his task filled day. As such, he made a point of taking a walk at dusk in order to clear his head. The demands of the Order often necessitated long hours, but he had finally captured the attention of the High Command and he wasn't about to let up now. *Especially not now*, he thought to himself.

The DNA reports from Caitriona's blood had shown that she was "gifted." He had suspected as much, but Hawkins still wrinkled his nose in disgust. Spitting a stream of saliva into the wet earth, Hawkins took another long drag on the pungent cigar. Any ideas he had previously conceived about taking the girl as his own had been quickly dismissed. The girl was hardly worthy of the riches and prestige he could have bestowed upon her. Still, he mused, she would be a delightful dalliance, if only to prove to the rebellious MacKinnon the superiority of the

Order's strength. He grew hard just thinking about the possibilities; a sadistic smile tugging at the corners of his lips. He was going to enjoy bringing MacKinnon to his knees.

Hawkins took another long drag on the cigar, savoring the flavored leaves. He had already decided to use the girl to get to MacKinnon, but, once he destroyed the recalcitrant leader, he would turn his attentions to the girl. The Order's position was clear; eviscerate anyone who was not genetically superior or who carried the genetic propensity to wield magic. While a noble intention, Hawkins had other plans. The girl's gift could be harnessed and used to support his political agenda. With her "gifted" assistance, he would be able to reap the benefits of hidden knowledge. How foolish the Order was for not seeing what was in front of them and the advantage that it gave them.

Hawkins laughed softly to himself, his grin growing ever wider. His plan was simply too easy. With the girl's soft spot for MacKinnon, Hawkins could control her easily by dangling the warrior right in front of her. In an effort to keep MacKinnon alive she would readily comply … to all of Hawkins' requests. He spat another stream of saliva into the ground, which was now beginning to pool with water. He took one last pull on the cigar and tossed it away carelessly, enjoying the feel of it beneath his heel as he crushed the remaining leaves and imagined grinding MacKinnon's face into the ground. A thunderous explosion rent the air and the rain storm he had expected was finally unleashed. Still, he was in no hurry to get back.

He could just see the outline of the camp down in the valley where his men had established base earlier that day. He had given the order to leave Castle Liobhann in the pre-dawn hour, determined to put as many kilometers behind him as he could. He knew it was a matter of time before MacKinnon came looking for the girl, and he needed to be well ahead of him if he were to put his plan in motion. They had traveled for nearly twelve hours before he finally gave the order to make camp. He wanted to put even more distance between him and MacKinnon, but the sheer size of his army prevented him from moving quickly.

Once they made camp, Hawkins ordered his men to move the girl to his tent, after having guaranteed she was too badly injured to move of her own accord. He smiled broadly at the injuries he had inflicted. He enjoyed breaking her, although it had taken far more than he had imagined. While she had refused initially to yield to his painful tortures, she had finally succumbed when he sliced into the soles of her feet and burned the bleeding flesh. He had enjoyed watching the tears flow down her cheeks and listening to the piercing screams that blended with the cacophony of the Order's camp. It was nothing less than she deserved. She was genetically inferior and would have died at the Order's command had he not stepped in. *Yes*, he mused quietly ... *for now, she suited his purposes nicely ... quite nicely, in fact.*

Hawkins glanced at the Order's camp nestled among the tall trees and expanse of heather. All appeared quiet. He had left several soldiers to guard the girl. The others, he knew, would be enjoying whisky and women ... two perks soldiers of the Order benefited from when they accepted their commission. Starting the long trek back to camp, Hawkins thought he saw movement in the outlying trees. Wiping his glasses on his coat once more, he squinted, eventually attributing the movement to an animal. Nonetheless, he picked up his pace, a sense of foreboding looming over him.

***

Duncan and his men moved quietly through the Order's camp, the cloudy night providing a perfect cover for their covert maneuverings. It had been nearly forty-eight hours since Caitriona had been taken from the Dwellers' cave. He was furious at himself for not ensuring the security of the cave. He had not only jeopardized the Seer's life, but his carelessness had cost the lives of several Dwellers. Had Charlie and little Riley not overheard the Order's plans, the evening might have had a much different ending. As it was, the Dwellers had lost seven men that night, and two pregnant women had been brutally assaulted, raped and then gutted, their fetuses left rotting next to their mother's corpses.

Duncan squeezed his eyes shut against the horrific images that were permanently etched into his vision. Fury drove his actions, his precise military maneuvers a reminder that he had to stay alert and objective if he were to succeed in getting Caitriona back alive. Horrible images of Caitriona's twisted and violated body danced across his vision as he thought about her at the hands of Hawkins and his perfidious lust.

Lee interrupted Duncan's somber thoughts, touching him lightly on his shoulder. His friend had joined him when he'd heard rumors in Edinburgh that the Order had taken MacKinnon's bride. Riding hard, Lee had intercepted Duncan and his three men as they made their way to the Order's camp.

Duncan turned to where Lee was pointing and noticed lights still on in one of the tents near the center of the camp. Duncan knew from previous encounters with Hawkins that the man kept late hours and often insisted on being flanked by soldiers when they made camp. The presence of several hundred soldiers would certainly make their task more interesting, he thought grimly.

With a series of short hand movements, Duncan quickly conveyed the strategic plan to Lee and the three other soldiers who had joined with Duncan on this mission. Their goal was simple; find the Seer and get her out alive. Duncan also had a score to settle with Hawkins, but deliberately kept that objective from his men.

Duncan's entourage left their strategic vantage point first, creeping deftly among the rows of tents until they were in position near the outer rim of the command tent. Most of the Order's soldiers were sleeping off the night's liquor and randy supply of women, too far into their own drunken sleep to notice the men descending on their camp. But Hawkins was neither a foolish man nor careless. He ensured thirty of his best soldiers remained alert and vigilant against any intruders. Duncan knew theirs would be a mission of stealth and cunning, given their small number. Once his men were in place, Duncan and Lee moved quickly toward the well-lit tent, careful not to arouse suspicion. Keeping to the shadows and using the close proximity of the tents as cover, they were able to reach Hawkins' tent without garnering unwanted attention.

Duncan made just enough noise outside of the entrance to Hawkins' tent to alert the soldiers inside. As the two guards exited the tent, Lee and Duncan skillfully surprised the men and quickly snapped their necks. Knowing the remaining guards would check when their comrades didn't return, Lee and Duncan waited. Their patience was rewarded when, three minutes later, another guard emerged, this one much more alert and on guard. Lee drew the man's focus toward him, which allowed Duncan to slide his short blade neatly between the man's ribs. Gurgling his surprise, the man fell to the ground, his life essence pooling before him.

Lee and Duncan entered the large canvas tent cautiously and spotted Caitriona's still form on a cot set toward the back of the tent. Her back was turned toward them and Duncan's breath caught in his throat when he saw the blood stained clothing which had matted and fused to the wounds on her body. His fury blistered the very air around them all. A low growl began at the back of his throat as he crossed the room to her side. Lee kept watch by the entrance.

"Goddess help her," Duncan stated quietly, his cool hand touching her cheek gently. She cried out and curled herself defensively into a ball. Duncan scanned her body quickly, noting the deep cuts made by a knife, the numerous burns, and large, blackening bruises. While none of the wounds appeared life threatening, he couldn't ascertain the internal or emotional damages.

"Duncan, we need to hurry," Lee cautioned.

Bending over his charge, Duncan placed a feather-light kiss against her forehead. She stirred faintly and he could see she was struggling to fight the drowsiness that clung to her. Her eyelids fluttered momentarily and she cried out, pushing her hands ineffectively against his chest. His heart caught in his throat as he imagined the terror Hawkins had inflicted on her. He curled his hands into fists, fury threatening to take control.

"Save your rage, Highlander," Lee warned. "She needs your focus right now; your revenge can come later."

Duncan drew in a deep breath and leaned close to Caitriona's ear. "*Ciunas, Leannan.*"

Those two simple words had the effect he was looking for. She immediately ceased flailing and began to fight in earnest for consciousness. She tried to pry her battered eyes open but he could see that her body wouldn't cooperate. He pulled her hands into his. He kissed each eyelid until she stopped struggling and instead managed a raspy, "Duncan," through parched lips.

Duncan pulled her close to him and drank in the familiar feel of her body. The tears flowed easily down her cheeks, mixing with the dirt and blood that had dried on her battered face. She cried out when he shifted her weight and he let loose a stream of Gaelic.

"I've got ye," he whispered softly against her face. The tears continued their unfettered descent as Caitriona clung tightly to him. "We have to leave," he whispered. "Can ye walk, lass?" She shook her head and nodded toward her bloody, twisted feet. Duncan was fairly certain the bastard had broken them, but he was careful to keep his emotions in check. "I'm going to carry ye then, lass. Keep yer arms wrapped tight around me no matter what happens." Caitriona nodded. Duncan slid his hands under her and settled her quietly in his arms. Caitriona winced at the movement but wrapped her arms firmly around him as he had instructed.

Duncan shifted her weight and crossed the room, motioning for Lee to lead the way. They were met outside the tent by two of Duncan's soldiers who signaled silently that the perimeter had been secured. Deftly side-stepping the carnage the soldiers had left behind, the party made their way from the Order's treacherous camp.

Once they safely cleared the Order's camp, the small group quickly picked up their pace. Lee pulled a crossbow from the sheath on his back watching carefully for any signs of pursuit. Caitriona cried out as Duncan hefted her weight more securely against his shoulder. Her slight frame rested easily in his arms and his engineered strength allowed him to easily traverse the uneven terrain at a brisk clip. His soldiers surrounded him, carefully ensuring safe passage from Hawkins' camp. In less than two kilometers Duncan would reach his remaining army, where he knew his men would be waiting with horses and weapons. Ahead of him, Lee moved quietly, ensuring he remained within visual contact of Duncan's men should there be any unwelcome surprises. The night was fading quickly to dawn and Duncan knew the disappearing darkness would soon leave them at a disadvantage and vulnerable to the Order's eyes and pervasive technology.

Duncan pressed his lips against Caitriona's forehead, noting the fever that ravaged her body. Her eyelids fluttered briefly, but she seemed unaware of where she was or what was happening. Instinctively, he wrapped his arms tighter around her and picked up his pace. He could feel the apprehension in his men and knew they were matching his steps stride for stride. Ahead, Lee suddenly raised his arm, his fingers clenched in a tight fist. Almost as one, the men came to an abrupt halt, drawing weapons quietly and taking a defensive stand. Duncan shifted his charge so that he could hold her with one arm. He dropped his other hand to the dagger at his hip and skimmed his thumb along the hilt. All eyes were on Lee as he continued to scan the darkness for signs of the disturbance that had brought their small band to a halt. Only when Lee was convinced the danger was past did he motion for the group to continue.

As they drew to the edge of the trees, Duncan spotted his familiar stallion and four soldiers, who stood ready to escort the foursome to the safety of nearby Castle Lauriston. Duncan sighed with relief, recognizing the small group for what it meant: Duncan's vast Templar army was hidden in the hills and would provide ample protection should the Order decide to pursue. Duncan also knew this was as far as he could go with Caitriona. As long as Hawkins remained alive, Caitriona's own life would be in danger. His heart ached with the knowledge of what he needed to do ... what he must do. He placed a soft kiss on her forehead and leaned close to her ear, "Remember me, my love." He kissed her again, wondering if he had imagined her response.

Duncan slowed his pace as they neared the horses. Lee found his mount quickly and untied the antsy gelding. Turning to help Duncan settle Caitriona, he was not altogether surprised to find his friend had not yet untethered his mount.

"Take her," Duncan commanded his second.

"Now is not the time, Commander," his friend stressed the title. "She needs you if she is to make it through this." He paused, waiting for his words to register. Duncan's look was hard and unyielding. "You have a mission to complete," Lee added.

"Precisely why I need to do this." Duncan locked eyes with his long-time friend. Lee finally nodded, acquiescing to the unspoken logic his friend provided. Duncan smoothly lifted his young charge into the saddle, settling her in front of Lee. She stirred and started to protest.

"*Ciunas*, Seer," Duncan said softly. "Ye must ride with Lee now. Ye will be safe, *Alainn*. This I promise ye." He kissed her lightly on her forehead before handing the reins to his friend; the memory of a similar promise he made to her a harsh reminder that nothing in life is a guarantee. She would be better off with her handler; a man trained to assist her with her gift, and an army of men to protect her.

Mounting the stallion, he had ridden earlier, he pulled the antsy beast next to Lee. "Take her to Castle Lauriston. It is the safest place. My sister is there already and will heal her. From there, send word and gather the council. We need to prepare for war."

"May the Goddess protect you," Lee clapped his lifelong friend on the shoulder.

"And ye as well."

Duncan pulled his stallion around, setting off at a gallop toward the Order's camp. What he would do now would ensure the Seer's safety for a very long time, and ensure his people their freedom; but it would come at a very heavy price.

***

Lee slowed his gelding to a trot at Caitriona's second cry of pain. He shifted his weight instinctively to reduce the pressure on the woman who remained slumped in his arms, barely conscious. The four soldiers traveling with him reined in their mounts quickly, their orders to provide protection quite clear. For the second time that day Lee cursed the fates, willing himself on the battlefield rather than escorting the Seer to the castle. Lee had been Duncan's friend since childhood. He knew the Highlander would never leave the battlefield until Hawkins was dead.

"Sir, we need to make Castle Lauriston by morning," said the youngest of the four soldiers, as he pulled his mount next to Lee's. "We are at risk of being spotted by the Order's drones if we continue at this pace."

Damned if you do and damned if you don't, Lee thought distractedly, tightening his hold once more on the young woman and urging his mount to pick up the pace. His thoughts once again drifted to Duncan and the man's inextricable attachment to his gifted charge. He also knew his friend well enough to know that Duncan had fallen in love with the girl. Lee had never seen Duncan care for a woman the way he did for Caitriona. Lee also knew Duncan's feelings for the girl would jeopardize the mission. What he didn't know was how far Duncan was willing to let his feelings guide his actions.

Lee pulled the reins slightly to the right as the moonlit trail dropped sharply down a steep embankment. A lesser rider would have missed the turn and ended up at the bottom of the embankment, most likely without a mount. But Lee and his men had traveled these paths many times and knew the familiar ground with or without the moon to guide their way.

Up ahead, the lead soldier pulled his mount to a sudden stop and motioned for the others to follow suit. Quietly slowing their steeds, Lee listened intently to the night sounds, trying to ascertain the reason for MacPherson's concern. Hearing nothing that put his warrior instincts on alert, he waited until MacPherson gave the all clear. He would rest easier once they reached the safety of the castle and he was able to turn the Seer over to her handler. He also wondered how Duncan would react when he saw the two together. Lee saw the look in Duncan's eyes when he passed the Seer to him and knew his friend would never willingly relinquish his charge so easily.

If he makes it out alive, Lee thought. While there was no denying Duncan's warrior strength, cunning and agility, Hawkins' army was vast, heavily resourced, and technologically advantaged. None of this stacked up well for the suicidal mission Duncan had accepted willingly.

For a moment, Lee considered handing the Seer to one of the soldiers but quickly dismissed the idea. Duncan had entrusted the girl's safety to the only other man he knew was equally committed to their lifelong mission. He wouldn't let him down.

Lee's horse stumbled on a loose stone, causing Caitriona to cry out softly. Instinctively, Lee tightened his hold on the girl and slowed his mount to a safer speed. MacPherson noted the change in pace and brought his mount around, signaling to the others to slow as well.

"It won't matter if we outrun the Order's soldiers if the Seer is dead," Lee stated tersely to MacPherson, sensing the younger man's angst at having slowed their pace once again. Acquiescing to Lee's seniority MacPherson fell back into position as the small but determined entourage moved ever closer to Caitriona's destiny.

Chapter Twenty-Two

It is in your moments of decision that your destiny is shaped.
Tony Robbins

Nicolas LaFelle stood at the top of the stone steps leading to the entrance of Castle Lauriston, surrounded by several hundred 23rd century Templars. His ward's rescue from the Order's army meant each side was now in open conflict with the other. Where the Order had once assumed that Templars existed, they now knew the strength of their army and their unwavering mission for freedom. Nicolas knew this was merely the beginning of a long and bloody war: The Templars fighting for individual freedom and the Order fighting to maintain their rigid and deadly controls. Nicolas also knew it would be a battle won or lost in the realm of magic. He just prayed this young woman was indeed the key to their success.

Nicolas ran a well-manicured hand through his short, jet black hair as he watched the small group approach on horseback. At twenty-eight years of age, he was only two years older than the Seer. He could see his ward slumped in the Lieutenant Commander's saddle and wondered briefly if she was dead. But he relaxed when he noticed the Lieutenant Commander pull sharply on his reins and hand the girl gently to the receiving medic. She groaned, the sound reaching him over the din of horses' hooves and the soldiers' orders. His heart beat faster, but he remained where he was. The medics would see to her injuries first. Tomorrow he would introduce himself to his new ward and begin the bonding process with her.

Following the medics as they brought Caitriona into the castle, Nicolas winced when he saw her condition. Several cuts marred her otherwise porcelain complexion, soaking her tattered clothes in blood.

Dark bruises covered her face and her eyes were swollen shut. She was unconscious and pale, her breathing labored and shallow. He was certain she suffered internal injuries as well. He followed the medics and Dr. MacKinnon to the second floor sleeping chamber, staying carefully in the background so as to allow the medical staff room to work.

Nicolas felt helpless but knew that would soon change. Once they were bonded, he would always share a connection to this powerful woman. Her pain would become his, their joys and fears entwined together in an intimate connection few lovers shared. He trembled slightly at the heaviness he felt. While he had trained for this moment since he was a young boy, his charge had not been given any opportunity to prepare for her role.

Genetically bred by the Order for superior intelligence and empathic abilities, the Templars had learned of the Order's experiment in genetically engineering empathic abilities, and had sought actively to recruit him when he was a young boy. The Templars had provided him with additional training, and studies that allowed him to develop his abilities, careful to conceal the extent of his power from the Order's authority. By the time Nicolas was twelve, he had surpassed his classmates academically and had proven nearly flawless in his ability to read human emotion. He had also developed a myopic hatred for the Order and their intolerance for diversity. Once, Nicolas was caught playing with one of the Lessers in the Great Hall. Nicolas had been forced to watch as the Order's soldiers stripped the young boy and shackled him to the whipping post. The boy was given fifteen lashes. When the soldiers were finished, his back was so badly torn his bones could be seen. The soldiers refused to let the healers use medical technology to close his wounds, so the young boy had suffered for weeks under the patient ministrations of his own kind's healers. Even with the poultices and wraps, the healing had been slow and agonizing. Nicolas tried to see his friend but was turned away.

After that day, Nicolas had tried harder to fit in with the other Genetics at his fostering hold. He fought hard to avoid the Order's radar, but the other boys taunted and bullied him for his kindness and friendship to the Lessers. It didn't take long for Nicolas to realize he didn't want to be a part of something as vile as the New World Order.

When Nicolas turned eighteen, he took the Templars' oath and began an extensive training regime that included combat training, meditative studies and history lessons, all with one goal in mind; to one day take his place as the Seer's handler. The Templars had long ago discovered that a male was needed to balance a woman's power; that without this balance, a woman would go mad from the power she held within herself or, if the Goddess had mercy, she would die. These stories had been shared for centuries, since the Templars had never had a gifted Seer to observe. In truth, Nicolas had never known a man to bond with a gifted woman and was unsure what to expect.

A shudder shook his muscular shoulders as the weight of his responsibility settled around him. He had spent the past two years working daily on a technique the scholars had taught him that would enhance the emotional bond between him and his charge. This connection, once created, would not be easily severed. While he was prepared for his own personal sacrifice, he had doubts about his ward's reaction to him and the bond they would soon share.

He glanced at his charge again, noting how pale and frail she looked lying on the large canopied bed. Fiona was bent over the woman, working fervently to heal the injuries the Order had inflicted. Caitriona cried out as Fiona's equipment repaired the skin that had been badly burned. Nicolas knew what the Order was capable of. While he was never permitted in battle, he had witnessed the horrors from the medical center where he had spent much of his time in laboratory tests for his unique ability.

Nicolas winced as he heard his charge cry out for Commander MacKinnon. Fiona brushed a matted lock from the girl's heart-shaped face and gently cleaned the deep cuts. Fiona worked quickly and Nicolas watched as the cuts began to heal and repair themselves with the aid of the doctor's technology. Nicolas closed his eyes and let his mind slowly find Caitriona's. He wasn't terribly surprised at the amount of fear that lay just beneath the surface of her emotions. *Your fear is normal,* Seer, he projected silently, *but there is no place for it here.* He deliberately kept his feelings and thoughts tightly reined lest he overwhelm her. He continued to project warmth and security until he began to feel her fear abate.

He was dimly aware that Fiona was staring intently at him. While he knew Fiona had been prepared for their bonding, he could see and sense how his interaction with his charge unnerved the older woman. He pushed Fiona's emotions quickly from his mind and focused once again on his charge. A slight smile tugged at the corner of his mouth as he felt his charge relax and begin to open to him. He had heard rumors that the Commander had developed feelings for the girl. Perhaps that was why his sister took an instant fascination with his empathic connection to his ward. If the rumors were true, he was only thankful the Commander was not here to witness the exchange.

Chapter Twenty-Three

Sometimes the heart sees what is invisible to the eye.
H. Jackson Brown, Jr.

Caitriona awoke with a start. She was drenched in sweat from night tremors that were reminiscent of another place, another time. Her nightmare was familiar; its chilling tentacles worming and slithering into her waking visions as well as her dreams. Both waking and asleep, she repeatedly saw Duncan in chains, his body a canvas of dried blood and deep cuts. Hawkins' leering face was an ever-present reminder of the treachery he would succumb to in order to secure her. She shivered and tried to shake the morose feelings that had been building since she arrived at Castle Lauriston.

A light knock on her bedroom door pushed the remaining tendrils of the dream from her mind. She pulled the covers quickly across her and settled back against the oversized pillows.

"*Caterine*, may I come in?" Nicolas asked, his voice deep with the effort it took to keep quiet.

Caitriona pulled on a dressing gown that was lying next to her on the bed, grateful that she would not have to be alone so soon with her thoughts. Hastily she bade him enter, noting his disheveled appearance. It was clear to Caitriona that her handler had had little sleep already.

"I hope you don't mind my coming here," he said quietly. "I sensed your fear. Is it the same dream?"

Caitriona nodded, a tremor shaking her slight frame. She sat up taller in the bed and put her head in her hands, rubbing her temples. It had been nearly a week since she had been rescued and brought to Castle Lauriston. While Fiona had healed her physical injuries, her worry and concern for Duncan took a physical toll that Fiona's technology was ill-equipped to heal. To add to her stress, she had been introduced to her handler, a man whose very presence reminded her she was a prisoner in this world. Although he was charming, intelligent and well mannered, she remained guarded in his company, making it abundantly clear to him that she would never agree to the bonding.

Sighing heavily, she pushed the hair from her eyes and squared her shoulders. *Surely Duncan should have returned by now*, she thought. It had been nearly a week and still there was no word from the scouts. After relinquishing her into the care of the doctor, Lee had returned to the Order's camp to assist Duncan. That was the last she saw of him.

Nicolas closed the door behind him and crossed the room quickly. He sat next to her on the bed, taking her hands in his. She looked into his eyes, mesmerized by their brilliant shade of blue. He smiled at her, rubbing the chill from her cold hands.

"Do you want to try again?" He asked softly. Caitriona knew he was referring to the vision training he had started with her earlier that day. Despite her willingness to learn, Caitriona couldn't call the visions at will.

She nodded slightly. She didn't really feel up to the effort, but she wanted something—anything—to take her mind off the horrifying dream where Duncan never returned to her.

"Tres bien, *Caterine*." She liked the way he pronounced her name and she smiled wanly at him. He gave her cold hands another squeeze. She knew he could sense her reluctance and wondered absently how long his patience would last. Her mind wandered to her first day at Castle Lauriston. Once her handler knew she was out of physical danger, he had met with the council to update them on her condition and broker a new meeting. While Caitriona was relieved at the slight reprieve his solicitations garnered, the knowledge did little to lighten the heaviness of her heart.

"Let's try something a little different," he suggested, interrupting her thoughts. At her nod, he climbed up behind her on the large bed, sitting behind her so that her back was resting comfortably against his chest. His legs straddled either side of her and he placed his hands gently on her shoulders. "Relax, *Caterine*," he said softly, a hypnotic lilt to his polished French accent. He rubbed her shoulders, urging her gently to let go of the stress and fear she knew he could feel beneath his powerful hands.

Caitriona leaned slowly into her handler, allowing his hands to massage the tension from her shoulders. She exhaled slowly through her mouth and followed it with a deep, cleansing breath through her nose. She repeated this several times as she allowed her eyes to close and her mind to wander.

She felt the familiar and gentle push of her handler's mind against her own. As always, the nudge, although tender, was an intrusion into her thoughts. She concentrated on the rhythmic beat of Nicolas' heart, matching her breathing to his steady pulse. She sensed the energy around him and felt the familiar nudge again. "Open to me, *Caterine*," he whispered softly.

She sagged against his chest, a soft cry escaping her lips as she remembered an earlier time within her lover's arms when those same words had been whispered with different meaning.

Nicolas used the energy around them both to weave a web of safety, creating a blanket of softness that enveloped her in warmth. Eventually, she began to relax and allowed her mind to go blank. "Think of nothing." Nicolas spoke close to her ear. "Allow the images to surface on their own."

"It's just blackness," she said in frustration.

"Shhh," he coaxed tolerantly. "Patience, Seer. The images will come."

After several long minutes, her body tensed as the first image came into view. She tried too hard to stop the image and, like many times before, the vision raced across her mind.

"Don't force it," Nicolas said. One arm had circled her waist and was holding her snugly against him. "The next time the image comes into view don't chase it with your eyes. Use your inner vision; your second sight to hold it."

"I don't understand what you mean by that, Nicolas." She tried not to let the frustration show in her voice.

Nicolas took a deep breath and exhaled it slowly against her neck. His breath was like warm honey against her skin and for a brief moment she felt safe and almost normal. "When I studied the works of Nostradamus, DaVinci and Michelangelo, each man described his visions as "other worldly" and used his second sight to amplify the images he saw. Do not focus on your natural sight; use your gifts to *see* what isn't there." He stressed the last word, drawing it out until it was merely a whisper on his lips.

She started to protest but he laced his fingers through hers. "Shhh," he said again. He began to breathe with her, encouraging her to regain focus.

The man has more patience than Mother Teresa, Caitriona thought absently, and then berated herself for allowing her thoughts to stray.

She took a deep breath again and started over. This time when the image swam into view, she didn't focus on it. Instead, she focused on the colors she saw swirling at the edge of her mind. As the colors became more pronounced, she began to mentally untangle the ribbons, separating the colors and then weaving them back together, much like she had done when she had seen the vision of her mother. As she did this, the earlier vision came into view, the images gaining clarity as the ribbons of color danced and weaved around her.

"I've got you, *Caterine*," Nicolas whispered softly, his mind locked with hers, providing a layer of warmth and protection that she could tangibly feel. Caitriona winced as she once again unwound the ribbons, and an image of Duncan emerged from the bold colors. Blood ran from an open wound on his muscled thigh. His face was covered in bruises and a large cut above his right eye dripped a steady stream of blood down his darkly bruised cheek. He was astride his stallion but kept one hand on his thigh while the other rested on the pommel, the trust in his stallion evident.

Lee rode next to him. His friend was also heavily injured but rode steadily forward. Duncan's eyes were shifting, constantly searching the terrain ahead, his hand occasionally caressing the hilt of his sword as a lover would his partner.

"It's Duncan," she said hoarsely. "He's badly hurt. We need to help him," she cried.

"Focus, *Caterine*," he admonished. "Let your mind drift to the surroundings. We need to know where he is."

"I don't want to let go," Caitriona cried. "He will disappear."

Nicolas squeezed her hand tightly and forced her mind to open more deeply to his. She could feel the energy pushing against her shield. "Turn away from him and look out in the direction he is traveling. Tell me what you see?"

"No." It was barely more than a whisper.

"He will die, *Caterine*, if we can't locate him. Do this for him."

Caitriona cried out and pushed away from her handler. She climbed off the bed and stood slowly, turning around as if looking for something not quite in her immediate purview. She reached out suddenly and grasped the air around her; almost as if she were trying to touch someone. She was vaguely aware of Nicolas, who had moved in front of her. He took her hand and placed it on his chest, pulling her close against him. She could feel the steady staccato of his heartbeat and drew comfort from his strength.

"Listen to me, *Caterine.* Reach out with your mind; what do you see?"

"It's like the desert. Everything is so dry. And yet ... I feel like I've seen this area before."

"Good. Where have you seen it? Describe it to me?"

"It's near the crags and the caves, only away from the caves. There's heather everywhere."

"Is the heather blooming?"

"I can't see him," Caitriona cried. "He's gone!" She tried to turn in Nicolas' arms but he held fast.

"It's OK, *ma chéri.* Focus on your surroundings. Where is this place? Let your mind drift further. Allow your inner eye to reach beyond the heather and crags. What do you see?"

She paused, her breathing becoming more labored with the effort it took to focus her mind. "There are people several miles away. They are hanging the wash, preparing food. They ..."

"Go on. Pretend you have binoculars and you are able to zoom. Focus on the faces. Do you recognize anyone?"

"Annie is there! I see Annie, and Cook! It's Castle Dunrobin. The castle is beyond the hold dwellings."

"Very good, *Caterine.* Now let go of that image and let your mind drift again. Tell me what else you see."

Caitriona pushed away from Nicolas, and focused her eyes on a point in her room. "There's nothing but blackness," she stated tersely, panic lacing her words.

"The blackness of night?"

"No. I can't see anything," she growled. She was beginning to grow impatient when she saw the faint, familiar swirls of light begin to mist her vision. "Wait." The black swirl began to take shape, the familiar colored ribbons wrapping around her legs and beginning to take form.

She started suddenly as the ribbons gave way to the Order's troops. "There are hundreds of troops, Nicolas. They have made camp. There are tents, structures that can be broken down quickly and moved." She reached out again with her hand but caught only air. "Nicolas, they have drones. I think they are tracking Duncan."

She shuddered as she found herself transported to the midst of the Order's camp. The leering jeers of the men next to her made her skin crawl and brought back memories of the torture she had endured at the hands of Hawkins and his men. She felt Nicolas' strong arms wrap around her. He cupped his hands on her face and kissed her forehead softly.

"You are safe with me, *chéri*. They cannot hurt you within your vision. You are in control." She trembled, her eyes staring into his brilliant blue ones but seeing only the vision instead.

"They have thousands of soldiers, Nicolas. We can't win this."

He ignored her prophecy. "Tell me where the soldiers are, *Caterine*. Are they south of the castle?"

"I don't know. I can't tell," she said, distressed by the turn in her vision.

"Breathe with me, *Caterine*," he said, slowly and evenly, "otherwise, you will lose the image." His voice sounded calm and reassuring. Caitriona took solace in that. "Slowly; deep, cleansing breaths." He exhaled slowly against her neck, his breath tickling the tiny hairs of her nape.

"The images are starting to fade, Nicolas." Her breathing was shallow and ragged. "No!" she cried out, her hands swiping the air in front of her, searching for Duncan's hard, familiar form again.

"*Caterine*, focus," he said sharply. "You need to gain control of your emotions or you will not be able to help him." He guided her to the edge of the bed and placed one hand on her diaphragm. "Breathe," he said again, "from your belly. In." He inhaled, waiting for her to follow his lead. When she had taken a deep breath, he exhaled slowly and said, "Out." She released her breath and repeated the action several times.

"Where are you now?" he asked, this time more softly. He sat on the bed, pulling her next to him.

"Most of the soldiers are hiding among the crags, but their camp is several miles east of that. There are too many of them. We will never defeat them."

"Don't focus on that," he said softly. "The soldiers who are in the crags, can you see any discerning landmarks?"

She gasped, her body going rigid against his chest. "Nicolas, the drones will fire on the castle. I think the soldiers are merely a diversion."

"Good, *Caterine*, very good. Go east to the Order's camp. I need to know how many soldiers you see there. If you are correct, and the soldiers are a diversion, then Hawkins may not be as heavily guarded as we thought."

Caitriona nodded her head quickly and closed her eyes, drawing in a deep breath. She exhaled slowly, struggling to see beyond the drones and militant weaponry. She saw the familiar ribbons of color in a far off corner and reached out with her mind to unwrap the colorful bands. As the ribbons swirled around her, the image of the drones was replaced with an image of Duncan.

Caitriona gasped and leaned into Nicolas. He wrapped his arm instinctively around her tighter. "It will be alright, *chéri*. What do you see?"

"They let him go," she said quietly, her words a mournful whisper in the pre-dawn light that looked like smoke as it fell across her bed.

"Go on." He smoothed her hair from her forehead, keeping his right arm firmly around her waist. Her heart beat erratically against his hand.

"They are tracking him, Nicolas. They want him to lead them to me." She pulled in a sharp breath and opened her eyes, the vision leaving her. "I'm the one they want." She turned to look at Nicolas who met her gaze. "They are doing all of this to get to me. I'm a splinter under Hawkins' nail. He won't give up until he has me. He'll torture and kill everyone until he's found me."

Caitriona gasped and pushed away from Nicolas. "I can't let him do this," she cried. "I can't let any of you do this! Hawkins is mad and will obliterate anyone that gets in his path. He places no value on human life. The man is completely devoid of any type of humanity. He's a monster, Nicolas. We have to warn the others, get to Duncan and secure Castle Dunrobin." She climbed from the bed, immediately missing the warmth of Nicolas' embrace and the calm reassurance he so easily afforded her.

"Where are you going, *Caterine?*"

"We can't just sit here. If they find Duncan, they will kill him."

"Hawkins won't get to you, *Caterine*. Never again," he said, and she wondered if he could sense her underlying fear.

"You can't promise that, Nicolas. No one can. You have no idea what this man is capable of."

He looked hurt at her last remark but kept his voice steady when he replied. "Duncan will never reveal where you are, *Caterine*. His mission is to dispose of Hawkins through whatever means and force is necessary. He will go to the grave before he allows Hawkins near you again."

Caitriona gasped, the tears beginning to pool behind her eyes. She couldn't let Duncan risk his life for her. He had no idea what he was walking into and wouldn't unless.

Caitriona secured her dressing gown around her and bolted for the door.

"*Caterine*, where are you going?" her handler called after her, concern sharpening his voice.

She was already out the door and running down the hall, her handler close behind.

Caitriona ran down the long dimly lit hall and burst through Gawain's private chamber door, clutching her throbbing temples, the headache already beginning to assert itself. Nicolas was right behind her. But she had to get a warning to Duncan and Lee.

Gawain looked up from the drawings he was studying when the two burst into his room. "Nicolas! Secure her; this is not the place or the time for ..."

"Please," Caitriona cried out. "Gawain, it's a ..." Caitriona's legs felt heavy and blackness threatened to swallow her. "Trap," she managed to croak out before darkness overcame her and the strong arms of her handler encased her once again.

***

Duncan reached the Order's camp as the first light was beginning to illuminate the sky and the birds began to herald in a new day. He clenched his fist as the memory of Caitriona's battered and limp body washed over him. He had failed her. He had promised to protect her and recklessly had allowed his feelings for her to overcome his warrior's instincts. And because of that she had suffered at the hands of Hawkins and his men. She had been so frail when he had handed her to Lee, her breaths shallow and labored. He only hoped he had not been too late.

He chose his vantage point above the crags overlooking the sprawled out camp below, noting the two entry points that were heavily guarded. Duncan pulled a sixty-meter dynamic rope from his saddle bag and hooked it over his shoulder and under his right arm. He worked quickly to set his anchors, securing them carefully so that his weight would be evenly distributed on his rapid descent down the cliff.

He scanned the area below him, selecting a drop-in that would be several meters beyond the Order's troops. Duncan tossed the rope down the cliff, ensuring the anchors would hold and that no snags and tangles would slow his progress. He then snapped on his harness and attached his belay device. Securing his long sword over his shoulder, he hooked his canteen to his belt loop and shoved a dagger in his boot. Tying the back-up line in a figure eight knot, he did one final check and moved to the edge of the crag.

Duncan looked over the ledge, noting the soldiers who were just beginning to stir and the faint aroma of coffee reaching his nose. He had hoped to gain a greater advantage by invading under the cover of darkness, but the Goddess had other plans today. Giving the rope one final tug, Duncan pushed off the ledge and allowed his weight to carry him rapidly down the crag's rocky facade. He felt a surge of adrenaline as the ground rushed up to meet him. His exhilaration, however, was short lived as the weight of his mission settled upon him.

His objective was simple. Kill Hawkins.

With Hawkins out of the way, there was a good chance the soldiers would scatter. Most, he knew, were not loyal to the Order: they had been drafted against their will or had been recruited from the ranks of Lessers. Without the Order's resources and support most of these men would no longer support the maniacal regime they had becomes slaves to. But it wasn't just the strategic advantage the Templars would gain with Hawkins dead; in some deep part of him, Duncan wanted Hawkins to pay for the torture he had inflicted on Caitriona. During his ride back to the Order's camp, Duncan had imagined a hundred different tortuous endings for the man … but none would ever atone for what Hawkins had done to Caitriona.

Duncan landed softly and unhooked his lines quickly, pulling the rope into the thick underbrush to hide any traces of his decent. He hadn't considered how he was going to get back. From the moment he left Caitriona in Lee's arms, he knew this was likely a one-way mission. He owed Caitriona that much. Since coming to his world, she had been held captive, beaten, cut, tortured, and had nearly drowned. She didn't belong here and, somewhere deep inside him, he knew that. But he also knew he had a mission to complete. *One thing at a time*, he berated himself.

He stopped abruptly when he detected movement in the trees a hundred yards ahead. He crouched low and slid into the overgrowth where the brush provided some cover. Placing his hand on the hilt of his broadsword, he moved silently forward, stepping softly to avoid making any loud sounds that would alert the enemy. Duncan glanced at the pre-dawn sky. The slender, silver, crescent-shaped moon, illuminated by the sun's pre-dawn rays, created a stunning effect. In another place, another time, Duncan would have stopped to admire nature's beauty, but the deep indigo and softly hued magenta sky merely served as a warning that daylight was fast approaching, and with it a greater chance for his discovery.

Duncan scanned the distant camp for any signs of danger. Sensing none, he moved cautiously forward, his hand resting lightly on the scabbard of his broadsword, his warrior's instincts on edge. Without his army, Duncan knew he would need to get to Hawkins' tent quietly and quickly. Once Hawkins' men were alerted, Duncan would have only a few minutes in which to accomplish his mission. Hawkins' death was the only end-goal Duncan had in sight ... and he would complete that task at any cost.

Duncan breathed a sigh of relief as he noted the camp was quiet and most of the Order's men were still sleeping off the effects of their drunken revelry the night before. He pulled the dagger he carried from the waist band of his trews, favoring a more stealthy approach than the broadsword afforded him. While adept with a laser gun, Duncan preferred the control and hand-to-hand engagement the blades provided. However, he had to admit the gun's firing range would deliver a definitive advantage when facing Hawkins' horde. He cursed softly under his breath at his lack of judgment.

Pulling himself away from his dark ponderings, he noted the six guards that were stationed every fifty meters along the camp's outer perimeter. He chose the northern most entry point as it was the least guarded and the hillside to the west meant he could mitigate an ambush from behind.

He approached the first guard stealthily and wasted no time slitting the man's throat and penetrating the Order's camp. His kills were targeted ... efficient. He would save his rage for Hawkins. He ducked behind tents, moving quietly throughout the camp; Hawkins' quarters his primary goal. He was within twenty yards of Hawkins' tent when he stopped short, pressing his back against one of the heavily canvassed tents, his heightened sense telling him he had company.

He sheathed the dagger back in its leather scabbard and drew the broadsword, no longer worried that the ring of steel sang loudly over the quiet of the camp and the sing-song lilt of the morning larks. Duncan moved from behind the tent and came face-to-face with a young soldier. He was no more than a boy in soldier's clothing and Duncan felt a momentary attack of morality as his blade swung up to counter the young man's reckless thrusts.

Duncan concentrated on his technique, allowing his body to settle into the rhythm of battle he knew only too well. He parried the second blow and moved swiftly, neatly slicing through the boy's chest. The sickening slurp of skin separating from bone reassured Duncan the boy was dead; another life lost to the Order's repulsive quest for domination. He spun around quickly as he heard another soldier approach from behind. He raised his sword and met the newest assailant head on. They parried for several minutes, each giving and taking ground. However, Duncan had not anticipated an equal in combat.

The air rang with the din of clashing blades and the heavy grunts of both fighters. The Order's men that were close to the fighting groggily shook off the remaining effects of their alcohol induced night and scrambled to join the fight, hastily donning boots, armor, and swords.

Duncan fought desperately, knowing he had to reach Hawkins. If he failed in his mission, Caitriona would be hunted and tortured until she died or became a weapon for the Order's wretched cause. Three more soldiers clambered to the fight, leaving Duncan outnumbered and sorely disadvantaged. He swung quickly left to position his back against Hawkins' tent. Two soldiers lunged and while Duncan evaded the first man's blow, the second soldier's weapon slipped past his defenses and slashed toward his chest. Duncan dodged, but not fast enough as the man's blade opened a six-inch gash across his shoulder.

Duncan didn't pause to assess the damage. He changed hands quickly, slashing at his opponent backhanded in a return blow, favoring the injured arm. He thrust his blade vertically, but the soldier caught it deftly before it cut him in half. Duncan released his blade, the clang of metal against metal rising through the still air and lingering in the soft breeze. Duncan pushed away the sword and spun, raising his sword deftly against the third opponent and catching his weapon high in the air. They stood face-to-face, their breaths mingling as each refused to yield to the other. It was all the delay the other soldiers needed. The man to Duncan's right swung low and sliced his thigh. Duncan's face registered disbelief as his legs crumpled, his body giving up the fight his mind and spirit so desperately wanted to continue.

The soldier he had been fighting stood over him, blood streaming from his left eye to his jawline. A low growl emanated from the soldier, erupting into a scream of rage as the soldier raised his sword high to deal the fatal crushing blow. Around him, his fellow soldiers powered up their laser weapons, the tiny red lights settling on Duncan's chest.

"I want him alive," Hawkins' voice rang out loud over the gathering crowd. The other men parted, allowing Hawkins a clear path to the injured man whose life essence was pooling around him in an inky, congealed mess.

The soldier glared at Duncan, his sword still raised, and yet Duncan met his gaze unflinching and unafraid. The murderous intent in the soldier's eyes left Duncan wondering if Hawkins' orders would be carried out.

Hawkins stepped forward and glared at his prisoner. Without taking his eyes off of Duncan, he addressed his soldier. "Drop your weapon, Corwin," Hawkins growled, "or I will cut you down here where you stand."

Corwin exhaled loudly and lowered his sword, the lethal glare he still fixed on Duncan a promise that the fight was not finished. The other soldiers immediately lowered their weapons, the laser guns' normally low hum eerily silent as all eyes settled on Hawkins.

"I want him alive," Hawkins reiterated calmly as he turned and made his way back to his tent.

Several soldiers grabbed Duncan roughly under his arms and hauled him to his feet, their rough hands digging into the deep cuts across his body. Blood in various stages of drying coated their military style clothing. Corwin handed his sword to a young soldier standing next to him and removed his leather gloves, cracking his knuckles as he assessed the severity of Duncan's wounds.

"You will never win this war, Templar," he spat. "You are outnumbered and no match for our armies. We will not rest until every last one of you is nothing more than blood under our boots." Corwin punched Duncan hard in the stomach, emphasizing his words. Duncan expelled his breath and sucked in sharply as Corwin's next blow landed across his jaw. He spat a stream of blood onto Corwin's boots, before he slumped in the soldier's arms, darkness threatening to engulf him. Corwin's disfigured mouth twisted into a grotesque smile as he expectorated in Duncan's face. The next blow Corwin delivered found its mark on Duncan's temple. As Duncan struggled to maintain consciousness, his last thought was of Caitriona and how he had failed her once again.

Chapter Twenty-Four

I am not afraid of an army of lions led by a sheep; I am afraid of an army of sheep led by a lion.
Alexander the Great

Gawain ran a hand through his greying hair, his brow creasing as he listened to the heated debate of his advisors. The three men seated comfortably at the worn wooden table had been loyal to him and the Templars for nearly three decades. Now, bent over a large map that detailed the Order's camp, the men argued the merits of attacking from the east versus infiltrating the camp from the cliffs. Gawain knew these men would draw their last breath to safeguard the Templars' secret and protect the Seer. Gawain also knew this war would be won only with the aid of magic.

The lines in Gawain's face spoke of his concern and his rumpled clothing bore evidence that he hadn't slept in nearly twenty-four hours. After the Seer had collapsed, Nicolas had relayed the details of her latest vision to Gawain. The older man had listened quietly, the tick in his jaw the only evidence of his rage.

"How many men did Lee take?" Gawain asked.

"He took the Highland army, sir" Nicolas replied. "There's nearly one thousand warriors, most of them blooded. But if the Seer's vision is true, it won't be enough. We need to send reinforcements, blooded warriors who've seen battle."

"Which is exactly what they expect us to do!" Gawain slammed his fist down on the hard table. "The Seer has given us an advantage. We need to use this to our benefit."

Gawain paced the floor, his hand absently stroking the short beard he hadn't bothered to shave. "They will assume we will send reinforcements and that the castle will be left unguarded. I want the castle secured and I want every resident moved to the caves. Station soldiers in the parapets and arm them with laser guns. Tell them to shoot anything that flies too close. No one is to come above ground."

"Sir, the Dwellers don't have capacity to hold us all," said Gawain's first advisor, John McFee. Gawain had known the aging advisor for several decades and was not surprised when McFee willingly opened his castle to the Seer, council and Templars.

"Send word to Rowe. Have her open the tunnels. It might not be comfortable, but no one will be left behind."

"Sir, there are some among us that distrust the Dwellers, and I'm sure there are Dwellers that share that sentiment with us. Without Duncan here to …"

Gawain cut him off and waved away his concerns. "We are out of options, old friend … and time," he said more softly. "There is simply no other way. Have her open the tunnels."

"And if they don't …" John's sentence hung as an unanswered question as Gawain met his eyes.

"Once the residents are safe, I want your castle secured. And send word to Dunrobin. If the Seer is right, Hawkins will end up here with his army. But I don't want to take any chances with Dunrobin. Have them secure those lands as well."

"We're outnumbered," Nicolas said quietly. "Caitriona said the Order's army is vast. There are thousands. The only way we will be able to go in and extract your son is to launch a stealth mission."

"We may be outnumbered, but we have the element of surprise," Gawain spoke quickly, his mind already running through a number of tactics that could be implemented in short order.

McFee cleared his throat. "Nicolas is right about stealth. I'd feel better though if your son had a whole team to back him. When will Lee and his men get there?"

Gawain ran a hand through his hair, lines creasing his forehead as he processed what his friend and advisor was saying. Not waiting for Gawain's response, McFee continued, confident that he had gained the commander's attention. "But even with a team, I don't think we'd get close. If the Seer is right, the Order outnumbers us three to one. A stealth attack might be the only way we can get close enough to kill the bastard. We should let MacKinnon continue with his mission. Lee and his men will be there as back up if it all goes south."

Gawain paced the floor, running his hand nervously through his hair. He nodded his agreement and looked at the Seer's handler, noting the young man's confidence. "Nicolas, we will need your help securing the castle and readying the grounds. After that, you are to take the Seer to the underground chambers and ensure she remains safe. Once the battle begins, you are not to come above ground regardless of what you may hear or what may happen. Her safety is our primary concern."

Nicolas nodded and got to his feet, preparing to leave. "Sir," he said hesitantly, "Caitriona shared this information so we would extract your son."

Gawain sighed, concern clearly etched on his brow. "You know as well as I do that the Order has more sophisticated artillery and weaponry then we do," he said. "If we do not stop them here, they will eviscerate us." He paused, reading the worry in Nicolas' young face.

"Urban battle and covert ops is my son's specialty," Gawain continued, placing a hand on Nicolas' shoulder. "Based on the Seer's vision, a stealthy surgical strike is going to be more effective than numbers and brute force. Hawkins wants us to come charging in … he wants us to leave the castles vulnerable to attack and certainly wants us to leave Caitriona unguarded. If my son's plan for reaching Hawkins fails, we can rally the men for a larger assault, but we've got to let him try."

Gawain knew the pain this would cause the Seer. But her safety and the future of his people depended on his son succeeding in his mission. He had to think of what was good for the majority, and that meant keeping Caitriona safe. They had all risked and sacrificed too much already to bring her here.

Gawain pulled both his hands through his graying hair. He was damned either way … a no win scenario they had trained for in the academy. Sacrifice his son or an army of men and thousands of innocents. He exhaled slowly and nodded to Nicolas. Not taking his eyes from the younger man's striking blue gaze, he made the only decision he could.

Chapter Twenty-Five

The supreme art of war is to subdue the enemy without fighting.
Sun Tzu

"Did ye miss me?" Duncan asked sarcastically as he stumbled forward, collapsing at Hawkins' feet. Blood began to collect in a black-red pool that spread slowly around him as he struggled to get to his feet. Hawkins' men flanked their commander on either side, their swords abandoned in favor of their highly accurate and lethal guns. Duncan knew the odds of escape were not in his favor.

"You have something that I plan to make my own, Commander," Hawkins hissed, his mouth twisting into a sadistic grin. He spat a stream of tobacco that landed near Duncan's boot.

"And what would that be?" Duncan taunted the older man.

"I won't ask again, Commander. I want the witch," Hawkins growled, caressing one of the blades his men had removed from the warrior. An array of daggers, arrows, and a broadsword were spread out on the table before him. Hawkins palmed the dagger and turned again to face his adversary. "The number of blades you came in here with leads me to believe you are working alone." Hawkins spat another stream of tobacco as he ran his finger lightly along the blade. "You don't seem like the suicidal type to me; but then again, love can do that to a man."

"Why don't you tell me who's pulling your strings?" Duncan rasped, the pain in his ribs forcing his words to sound constrained. "We both know you're not bright enough to call the shots."

The muscle in Hawkins' jaw twitched. "We're not terrorists," Hawkins jeered in agitation. "We're patriots, fighting for what we know is right ... no different than you."

"Ye're verra much a group of terrorists that have turned your back on freedom," Duncan said hoarsely. He was ghostly pale and his breath was raspy as he continued to fight off the wave of blackness he knew was coming.

"You couldn't have it more wrong," Hawkins said derisively. "We do what needs to be done—what we've been trained to do—to preserve the New World Order's rightful place in the world." Hawkins spat another stream of tobacco into a nearby container, dragging the back of his hand across his mouth to wipe the brown stain that sat at the corner of his lips. "Without population controls, the world would revert to mass famine, terrorism, and disease. There can be only one master race; you and I both know that. What we're doing ensures peace and promotes perfection." Hawkins relaxed his stance as he placed the dagger back on the tray next to the other weapons. "Someday you'll thank us. Well, not you … you'll be dead."

Blood soaked the front of Duncan's tunic where Corwin's blade had neatly penetrated. He knew the blade had missed any major organs, but he needed medical attention soon or he would likely bleed to death.

"You used to be a patriot, Commander … like us," Hawkins snarled in derision. "Now look at you." Hawkins kicked Duncan hard in the chest and the world went black before him. He fell forward, spattering another stream of blood across Hawkins' polished black boot.

"You chose the wrong side, Commander," Hawkins hissed.

Duncan pulled himself to his knees, gasping for breath; certain Hawkins' last blow had cracked his ribs. "*Tha gach uile dhuine air a bhreth saor agus coionnan ann an urram 's ann an còirichean,*" Duncan repeated the Gaelic words of the Universal Declaration of Human Rights he had spent his life protecting.

Bellowing loudly, Hawkins fisted his hands in Duncan's hair and yanked him roughly to his feet. Duncan stumbled under Hawkins' assault but his gaze remained hard and fixed on the Order's tyrannical leader. "*Tha iad air am breth le reusan is le cogais agus mar sin bu chòir dhaibh a bhith beò nam measg fhein ann an spiorad bràthaireil,*" Duncan continued, his voice strong, the familiar words lending him strength.

Hawkins pushed Duncan back to the ground and walked to the array of weapons that still remained on the table. Picking up the dagger, Hawkins caressed the blade softly, wincing slightly as the sharp knife bit into his flesh and drew a bead of blood. He walked over to Duncan and, pulling his head back, shoved the blade against his throat. "I won't repeat myself again," he ground out each word slowly. "I want the girl."

"She's nae for sale," Duncan snarled.

Hawkins pressed the tip of the knife through Duncan's flesh, drawing a stream of blood that ran unfettered from his throat.

"One more inch and I will bleed you dry," Hawkins growled.

Duncan glared at Hawkins but refused to give any quarter.

"We both know, Commander, the girl was never your wife. A clever ruse but one I'm calling done. Now the question remains, will you hand her over or will I have to deliver your body, in pieces of course, to your beloved? Perhaps if you can't be persuaded, your witch can."

"You'll never get to her," Duncan rasped.

Hawkins laughed sadistically. "That's where you're wrong, MacKinnon. Do I need to remind you that your beautiful witch has already been the benefactor of my … unwavering attention?"

Duncan growled, struggling to get to his feet. He wanted this man dead. No, he wanted this man to suffer first.

Hawkins laughed again and kicked Duncan hard in the face, pushing him to the canvas floor of the tent. Blood pooled before him as he forced his eyes to remain open. He was vaguely aware of Hawkins barking orders to his second in command. Duncan knew time was against him. He also knew Hawkins would stop at nothing to get to Caitriona. The thought left him cold. He could only hope Lee had made it to safety and had delivered the girl to her handler.

Duncan rolled to his side and looked around the room. Hawkins was standing over the weapons, ordering his men to tighten the security around the camp. As they shuffled out to see to his instructions, Duncan thought he saw a flash of his clan's colors. He squeezed his eyes shut and when he opened them again, Hawkins was standing over him.

Hawkins nodded to the two remaining soldiers at the back of the room, who hauled Duncan quickly and roughly to his feet. He pulled against his restraints and was rewarded with a fist to his stomach. Duncan would have collapsed save for the restraints that held him firmly in place. Hawkins slowly walked to Duncan, his thumb grazing the hilt of the dagger he slapped against his palm.

Fisting his hand in Duncan's hair once again, he pulled his head back and ran the blade slowly down the length of his cheekbone. Duncan sucked in air but otherwise did not make a sound. He could feel the rivulets of blood flowing down his face.

"I doubt very much your witch will want you back in her bed once I'm done with you," Hawkins jeered. He drew the blade across Duncan's breast bone, slicing deep. Duncan groaned as the dagger exposed the tender flesh beneath. Hawkins wiped the blade on his pants and set it back on the table. Walking back to Duncan, he stood facing the warrior.

"Let's try this again. Where did you take the girl, Commander?"

"Go to hell," Duncan rasped.

"I thought you might say that." Hawkins ground his fingers into the open wound he had just made, his fingers opening the wound even further, the blood rushing between his fingers and coating his hand.

Duncan groaned and the room swayed before him. He prayed the Goddess would take him soon. He closed his eyes and saw emerald orbs, porcelain skin and full, tantalizing lips. "Caitriona," he whispered. Hawkins slapped him hard across the face and his eyes flew open.

"I want you awake," Hawkins sneered. "This isn't going to work if you're passed out." Hawkins grabbed a fistful of Duncan's hair and yanked his head back cruelly.

The commotion outside had escalated, but Duncan was too far gone to care. He sagged against the soldier's arms, his head lolling before him.

Duncan was vaguely aware that Hawkins had selected another device from his table of torture. This time, Hawkins' weapon of choice was a cat-o-nine tails, the ends of which had been equipped with sharp little barbs designed to dig in and rip through the flesh. Hawkins nodded to the two soldiers, who turned their prisoner around roughly so that his back was presented to Hawkins. The soldiers ripped the shirt from his back, leaving his skin exposed.

A sardonic smile crept slowly over Hawkins' face as he drew back his arm and let the whip fly. Duncan heard the crack before the pain ripped through his flesh. Two more in succession lit his skin on fire. He knew the tails were tearing the flesh from his back. It wouldn't be long before the bone would be exposed.

Duncan sagged between his captors, his warrior instincts registering the skirmish beyond the tent's heavy walls. The whip sailed through the air again and tore at his exposed flesh. He arched against the pain as his body tensed in anticipation of the next blow, which followed in quick succession. He had only one thought before his world went dark … the cavalry had arrived.

***

"Highlander, on your feet. We're going to have company soon and I don't want to be on the wrong end of the sword." Lee shook his friend hard.

Duncan moaned, gagging as he tried to suck air into his lungs. Struggling to open his eyes, he batted at the hands that were trying to drag him to his feet. He was dimly aware of Lee's desperate attempts to bring him to consciousness, but the heavy black cloud that settled around him wouldn't disappear. He took another raspy breath, pulling the air in between his teeth as his lungs protested his efforts. Most likely he had a broken rib or two. As the pain of his injuries began to surface, he fought to remain in sleep. His back was on fire and through the one eye he had finally managed to open, he could see blood on his hands, torso, and the floor. He was a mess.

"Duncan, we have to go now," Lee insisted.

Duncan nodded and swung his legs over the cot, allowing Lee to support most of his weight. Outside Hawkins' tent he could hear the clang of steel, and the cries of men engaged in battle.

"How many men did you bring?" Duncan croaked.

"Not nearly enough," Lee growled. "We ambushed Hawkins' scouts just east of his camp. That's how we were able to find you, but the man is well armed ... and well-guarded," he added.

Duncan nodded as Lee tore the fabric from his tartan trews and bandaged the worst cut across his thigh. He winced as Lee pulled the bandage a little too tight, but he knew it was that or bleed to death, so he remained silent. His body complaining, he strapped the claymore Lee had handed him to his hip and checked the power on the laser weapon his friend had procured.

Leaning on his friend for support, he made his way to the tent opening. Looking out from the tree line where Hawkins had made camp, Duncan could see his men waging war with the Order's soldiers, their claymores covered in blood and their warrior cries a death call in the otherwise quiet Highland hills. A light mist covered the valley, so he knew the bodies of those who'd been slain wouldn't be visible. The smell of sweat and blood brought bile to his throat. Death clung like a shroud, the stench cloying, choking the very breath from him.

With Lee's insistence, he began to move. His body began to complain in earnest again, waking new wounds and sores that had gathered while he had been unconscious. No longer the confident stride of a warrior,

Duncan focused on staying alive. His arms throbbed and his fingers ached as he carried his claymore, the weight of the hilt noticeable in his weakened state. He and Lee climbed up out of the valley toward the cliffs, looking for a spot above the battle where the water would be clean and the air free from the Order's drones.

At the top of the ridge, Duncan stumbled against his friend, his body no longer responding to his will. Lee eased him to the ground, cursing under his breath as he hunted for something to close the worst of his friend's wounds. Duncan could see his men fighting valiantly against impossible odds and knew that unless the Goddess granted them a miracle, his men would not likely see another battle. His heart grew heavy as he shouldered the weight of that burden, but a quiet pride grew as he watched his men fight as one, united in their goal and ready to lay down their lives for the single purpose they so firmly believed would change everyone's lives.

Not like the enemies' troops, of course. They marched in file, turned as one, but only in movement, not in solidarity. Single units melded seamlessly back into the larger company. Company melded seamlessly and smoothly into an army. His clan respected age and experience. His clan marched and organized with respect for that experience. The enemy showed no respect in its ranks.

Lee changed the bandage on Duncan's thigh, using the medical laser to clumsily close the worst of the wound. Duncan grimaced as the laser missed its mark, his eyes meeting Lee's, whose apologetic look spoke volumes. He needed Fiona's steady hand and medical knowledge. Wincing as his friend wrapped the bandage roughly around his thigh, he allowed Lee to pull him up once again. Casting one last glance over the valley's mantle, he watched as one of his men succumbed to the Order's gun fire. His warrior instincts pulled at him and begged him to join his men. But he knew they did this for him … and the Seer. Lee set a brisk pace. As difficult as it was, Duncan knew if they didn't move quickly, the Order would be on them.

As they hurried back toward the castle, an enemy drone seemed to glide out of the fog. Both Duncan and Lee drew their guns and watched as the drone hovered in front of them. Duncan was the first to see the stone rune dangling from the pod's rear legs. The stone had been painted with the Celtic symbol, Algiz. Lee turned to him and they both smiled, holstering their weapons. Algiz symbolized protection.

His men had penetrated the Order's ranks and were providing them a safe way home. The drone hovered another thirty seconds and then the men watched as it disappeared into the tree line. A few seconds later, one of Duncan's men rode into the clearing, leading two of the Order's mounts. Both men grinned, quickly undoing the tethers and mounting the illicitly procured horses. An expression of concern, then decision, crossed Lee's face and both men pushed their horses into the shadows, their path before them clear.

Chapter Twenty-Six

Out of difficulties grow miracles.
Jean de la Bruyere

Caitriona awoke with a start, her eyes frantically searching the darkness for her lover. Shaking the last tenuous threads of the dream from her vision, she hastily left the warmth of her bed, her only need in the pre-dawn hour to find the man she loved.

She raced through the castle's underground passages. The corridors were eerily empty, the castle's occupants long ago asleep. She slowed only long enough to push open the heavy oak door that led to the surface. Her feet were eager to feel the damp earth beneath them. Quickly she climbed the steep passage that led to the main floor and waited until the guard turned his back before she slipped into a secret passage that led to the outer holdings.

The tunnel floor was soft beneath her feet and she moved quickly, fervently hoping she had remembered the way. Castle Lauriston was similar in layout to Castle Dunrobin, but the underground passages still confused her. The catacombs often led to dead ends, forks, and tunnels that turned in maddening circles. She couldn't afford a misstep. Picking up her pace, she turned down one corridor and then another, confident once again in her path. Once outside, she closed her eyes and allowed her mind to drift. She could feel the strange connection she shared with Duncan and knew it wouldn't be long.

Caitriona didn't bother approaching the gates; the guards would merely have detained her and the physical pull she felt was too strong to ignore. Instead, she slipped behind the blacksmith's shop and pushed the stable doors open wide enough for her to squeeze through. She didn't bother to close the doors. One of the horses nickered softly, its breath appearing in a thin mist that reminded her she was clad only in a night dress and bare feet. She barely noticed, however, so focused was she on her task.

She knew Duncan would appear shortly, as her vision had promised. She didn't know how she knew this morning was the right time; she just knew. She could almost feel him pulling her toward him. She made her way quickly to the last stable, dropping to her knees. She pushed straw aside as her hands freed the familiar latch that led to the underground tunnels Nicolas had shown her earlier that week. At first, the passages had frightened her; a cold, dank reminder of the terror-filled world where she was hunted constantly for being different.

Tonight, she welcomed the cold stone beneath her feet and the dark corridors that would shelter her flight from a myriad of spies and guards, bringing her ever closer to her lover. She paused, closing her eyes and trying to remember the direction she should take to move away from the castle. She lowered herself carefully into the passage and set out in a northerly direction, her vision remaining just at the edge of her physical sight.

Several more turns and she knew she was getting closer. The darkness was suffocating, but she pushed her fear aside and focused on reaching her goal. She could sense Duncan's heartbeat, see his torn trews and literally feel the cuts across his thighs, back and chest. And just as surely as she "saw" these things, she knew he would soon appear in the heather.

The tunnels grew narrow until Caitriona felt like Alice down the rabbit hole. The air had become stale and cold, but she barely noticed. She could see her breath in front of her and felt her feet growing numb. Turning a corner, she recognized the steel door that led to the crags just outside the castle wall. Giving the heavy door a good push, she was pleased when it opened easily.

Caitriona's white night dress stood in stark contrast to the pre-dawn light that was just beginning to light the sky. Above her, the stars began to disappear from view as the sun began to herald a new day. Caitriona looked out at the expanse of land before her, the heather silhouetted against the crags, forming bluff-like sentries that waved hello as the wind caught their stems. Recalling the image, she found the now-familiar crag and traced the line to the forest. Peering intently into the dark woods, she strained to see the familiar outline of her lover. She didn't have long to wait. Duncan's men; or rather what was left of his army appeared before he did, their horses galloping toward the castle gate. A slight smile tugged at the corner of her mouth. The castle was already laying preparations for the battle that would, thanks to her recent vision, be met with men that were well armed and well prepared. She watched as the men rode from view, knowing they wouldn't see her from her vantage point. Once out of sight, she set out in the direction from which she knew Duncan would emerge.

***

"Duncan," Lee said sharply, pulling his friend from his almost cathartic state. Duncan lifted his head and peered in the direction Lee was pointing. At first, Duncan couldn't register anything in the dimly lit pre-dawn sky; his eyes were so swollen and caked with blood. Finally, his eyes found her as both men slowed their mounts to a trot.

Clearing the forest, Duncan brought his stallion to a halt, dismounting slowly. He didn't trust his eyes. Lee reined in beside him but stayed mounted. Duncan barely noticed as Lee leaned forward and took the reins from him.

Limping forward, Duncan increased his pace, still not believing his eyes. *She's alive*, he thought, relief visible in the hard lines of his face. *What is she doing out here unprotected? Where the hell is Nicolas?* Realization dawned suddenly and a smile spread across his face. She had already seen this moment.

His smile changed into a grin as Caitriona broke into a run. He opened his arms to her, folding her into his embrace. His lips found hers, his moan forming the shape of her name on his lips. She was his and nothing would change that now. He fisted his hands in her hair, the soft tresses slipping easily through his fingers. He pulled her tight against his hips, his arm sliding around her waist and holding her close. He could feel the anthem of her heart amid the electrical charge that was nearly always present between them.

He scooped her into his arms, his own injuries almost forgotten as he bore her slight weight against him. Memories of an earlier time when he held her close invaded his thoughts and he pushed them away. Her life was still in danger. He had failed his mission and, as a result, she would continue to be hunted by Hawkins and his men. Caitriona was the prize Hawkins sought; if for no other reason than to claim her as his own. But Duncan knew Hawkins' need to possess her went far deeper than that.

Duncan's soul was tied to hers. He knew that now and, if he was being honest, had known it since the first day she came aboard his ship. Their lives were inextricably threaded together. Fate had insured as much. But he also knew Hawkins would seek revenge through Caitriona until the warrior broke; until he handed over the name of every Templar and leader of the Dwellers. She wasn't safe here and never would be.

Duncan crossed the distance to the castle quickly; the sentries ushering them through the gates that moments earlier had received his men. Duncan took the steps leading to the sleeping chambers two at a time. His soldiers were already being helped into the underground chambers where medics would attend their wounds.

Duncan set Caitriona on her feet as he looked around him at the chaos that was erupting. "Gawain has ordered us all to the catacombs," Caitriona said. "He said we will be safer there." Duncan couldn't argue with the man's logic. He knew it wouldn't be long before Hawkins' men descended on the castle.

Taking Caitriona's hands, he pulled her up the stairs and away from the hive of activity headed to the lower chambers. No one paid much attention to their actions, save for a pretty medic who acknowledged their entrance with a knowing smile and an approving nod of her head. "I'll send Fiona right away," she mumbled softly.

Duncan nodded and led Caitriona up the stairs to her vacated bed chambers. He could see the concern for him visible in the furrow of her brow.

"Have ye bonded, lass?" Duncan whispered hoarsely, pushing open the heavy oak door to her sleeping chamber and pulling her to the large bed.

"No," she whispered, shaking her head, his question having caught her off guard. "No," she said more fiercely, the weight of her answer hanging heavily before them.

Duncan released his breath, not even aware he'd been holding it. His eyes searched hers as his mouth once again found her lips. *Mine.* The single word echoed through his head until it bubbled up and tore from his lips. "Mine," he growled in her ear, his tongue tracing the sensitive spot on her lobe until she moaned his name.

She pulled away from him, searching his eyes. Her hand brushed his hair away from his face as he repeated the single word, this time with more urgency. "Mine."

"Yours," she said huskily, nodding her head in agreement, further validating the longing in both their hearts. His mouth found hers again as his tongue teased apart her lips. He sucked gently on her tongue until he could feel her quivering beneath his hands. Breaking the kiss, his thumb grazed her now swollen bottom lip as his eyes got lost in her sultry gaze.

Caitriona undid the buttons of his jacket deftly, her fingers mapping the rough bruises and cuts that covered his hard torso. She sucked in her breath as her fingers traced the outline of a deep cut across his abdomen and she saw the flayed skin hanging from his back. "I'll get Fiona," she said, pushing away from him.

"The cuts are nae deep," he lied; his need to possess her taking precedence over logic. "It can wait." He pulled her to him once again, his hands cupping her breasts and teasing the nipples until they stood in hard peaks, straining against the fabric of her gown.

His muscles flexed and twitched under her touch and when she grew bolder, shifting her palms to his pecs, a low rumble of approval rolled through his magnificent chest. She continued to explore his torso until a gasp of pain from him drew her up short.

"I'm getting Fiona," she said with more resolve, pushing him toward the bed. He reached for her, but she moved deftly away from him, nearly colliding with Fiona as she opened the door. Sighing heavily at his sister's untimely arrival, Duncan locked eyes with his sister, his unspoken words telling Fiona what he knew she feared.

"It's nae as bad as it looks, sis," Duncan rasped, but he obligingly sat still as her instruments quickly scanned his body. He didn't want to alarm Caitriona. He could see the worry in her soft face and wanted nothing more than to send his sister away and finish what had been so abruptly interrupted.

Retrieving one of her lasers from the medical bag, she worked hurriedly to close the largest gashes on his chest and thigh. She ignored the smaller cuts and instead focused on the torn flesh that splayed across his back in ugly crisscross patterns. "These will leave scars, Duncan," she said softly, her hands feather light as she pulled together the torn flesh and used the tiny laser to repair the damage. He smiled wanly at her, fighting the blackness that threatened to swallow him. His battle was short lived. Exhausted, he finally succumbed to the darkness, a pair of emerald green eyes invading his dreams.

***

Fiona worked tirelessly. Caitriona watched, helpless, as Duncan fell in and out of consciousness. The doctor had administered a local anesthetic so that Duncan would be spared the pain of her ministrations. For that, Caitriona was grateful.

After nearly an hour, Fiona stood and surveyed her work. "The worst of his wounds have been repaired," she said gently. "I've pulled the flesh together on the deepest cuts and will see to the remainder of his injuries once I've made my rounds downstairs."

Caitriona pulled Duncan's hand into hers, staring at the pink flesh that was already bearing evidence of the healing process. She pressed a light kiss against Duncan's forehead and squeezed his hand reassuringly when a soft moan escaped his lips.

"I'll come back in a couple of hours" Fiona said, packing her instruments back in her bag. "He'll be fine," she promised when she saw Caitriona's concern.

Caitriona watched as Fiona left the room, then took a seat on the bed next to Duncan. He groaned softly, his eyes fluttering open as his hand found hers, threading his fingers with hers. Tugging gently, he made room for her next to him, her head nestling between the crook of his arm and his chest. They stayed like that for several minutes, each deriving comfort from the other.

Sighing heavily, she pushed herself to her elbows so she could look at him. She could feel the electrical current pulsing between them and suddenly she needed that physical satiation and emotional connection that only he could provide. She fisted her hand in his hair and tipped his head back, her teeth grazing the sensitive part of his neck. The warmth of his touch remained like a brand and she shivered against his touch.

She remembered the way his fingers tasted when he'd touched her face and she suddenly wanted to taste that husky saltiness again. She moved her lips next to his fingers then gently kissed each one, biting the pads of his thumb gently until he groaned loudly. She wanted him to remember her, to never doubt her love for him. Her kiss deepened and he reacted as she knew he would. His kiss was gentle, but firm. He knew her lips.

She remembered the way he had kissed her after he thought he had lost her. That same urgency was here now and she shuddered uncontrollably. He tilted her head back and nuzzled the soft spot below her jaw. He seemed to love exploring the parts of her body that she loved having explored by him. The thought brought an unconscious smile to her passion-swollen lips. She felt the tingle she had been feeling all week begin to grow again.

"I never stopped thinking about you," he said softly.

"I can see that ..." she said, cupping his erection and squeezing lightly. Brazenly, she moved his hand to the secret place between her legs. "I haven't thought much about you at all." A wicked grin lit her soft features.

"Ach, Catie," he groaned, feeling the dampness on her undergarments. "Ye're always ready, lass." Her hand guided his fingers under her night dress to where she wanted him to touch her. He caressed her with the practiced touch of a man, slowly exciting her. He inserted one finger and watched as her lips parted and she began to moan. He caressed her folds and when she moaned again, he inserted another finger, provocatively and rhythmically stroking her exposed flesh.

Her breath was becoming heavier. He removed his fingers and gently took her face in his. She could smell her excitement on his fingers as he kissed her again. His tongue sought hers in an intimate dance that left them both breathless. When he pulled back, he placed his fingers in his mouth and gently sucked.

The man is so hot, Catie thought as she bravely cupped him again and began to undo the ties of his trews.

"Not so fast, *Leannan,*" he whispered, his hand capturing hers. He brought her fingers to his mouth and sucked gently.

"Why not," she pouted petulantly. "What would you prefer?"

"Your incredible mouth," he groaned. "At least for now."

He grabbed both her hands in his and placed them above her head. "Be still," he said gruffly, his gaze penetrating yet challenging. He pushed her gently onto the pillows and parted her legs. She groaned and wrapped her arms around his neck, pulling his face to hers.

He kissed her deeply, his tongue tasting and teasing. "Be still," he said again, pulling away and placing both her hands once again above her head. She undulated softly beneath him and he nipped her ear in reprimand.

"I mean it, *Leannan,*" he admonished lightly. "Be still or I will tie your hands." She stared incredulously at him, but endeavored to keep her hands and body still.

Duncan traced the outline of her jaw, kissing first one corner of her mouth and then the other before pulling her lips into his mouth and bruising the tender flesh with his arduous attention.

He held his hand in front of her to indicate she shouldn't move and then got off the bed. He finished shedding his clothing, the dirty, bloodied garments landing in a heap around him.

"Stay there," he grinned wickedly, wincing as his fingers found more cuts and bruises as he removed his clothes.

Caitriona closed her eyes and imagined his tongue the last time he had explored her secret parts. She remembered their first night together and the way their bodies had climaxed and shattered together... her body grew more excited, her nipples hardening in anticipation.

She let her gaze roam appreciatively over his body, noting the bruises, cuts, and swelling across his chest and face. She pushed away her morose thoughts and smiled wickedly at the man before her, her eyes feasting on the hard lines and muscles that even in his battered state, were all too enticing.

"Thinking of me?" she asked, breaking the silence.

"Only you," he said huskily.

She had heard of injured men who in their lust had taken their women. Their eyes were on fire and all but their most serious wounds hardly noticed. This was different. There was lust. And yet, there was also something more. There was an ever present anchor that connected his heart to hers. She put her hand on his chest and felt the connection grow. This was where his strength—no, their strength—came from. She became lost in the emotion, loving the way the animal in her fought for release.

Duncan undid the ties of her night dress and pushed away the last barrier there was between them. She groaned and parted her legs even more. Once again, his mouth found hers, their tongues dancing to a rhythm only they could feel.

Together they both explored and caressed, each becoming lost in the emotional energy they created. She had felt their connection long before they had parted. It had never left while he was gone and now that they were together - not even his injuries made a difference.

His knee pushed her legs apart and he mounted her, his passion fueling his need. She groaned as he drove into her, his rhythm keeping time to her suggestive undulations and the thrust of her tongue. Her hands caressed his face as she rocked him, moving suggestively against his hard erection. She wanted him. No other man had known this earthy connection with her.

She grew wet with excitement as she began to move faster, keeping up easily with his demanding pace. He came quickly, deeply, and carried her with him as she felt his orgasm and matched his with hers. After a time, she could feel his body relax on top of her. His face lost its anxiety and she could feel the power that kept him going slowly release as the pain from his injuries took center stage.

"Mine," he whispered. "Forever mine."

She still felt the bond; a bond she somehow knew would never leave her. "Forever yours," she whispered, just as she felt the bond begin to fade and Duncan slip into sleep. Yet deep in her heart she still felt the tug of his bond with her. This is where she belonged and, at that moment, she knew she was madly and deeply in love.

***

Caitriona pulled on a dressing gown and slipped quietly from her bed chambers, careful not to disturb the wounded warrior. Although she knew Fiona would be returning, she wondered what could be keeping her. As if in answer to her unspoken question, she opened the door and saw Fiona down the long corridor, her medical bag swinging from her shoulder like the pendulum of an overwound clock. She waited until Fiona caught up to her and briefed the doctor on Duncan's condition. She left out their love making, but was fairly certain the good doctor would be able to piece that together.

"I will be right back," Caitriona said to Fiona. The older woman didn't question her, simply nodded and moved quietly into Caitriona's chambers. Although Caitriona needed to see that Duncan's remaining wounds would be healed, she wanted to speak with Gawain privately. Caitriona felt a renewed sense of purpose as she headed for Gawain's war room. She knew what she had to do to save the life of her lover, even if it was at the expense of her own life. She had always figured that dying in place of someone that she loved would be a good way to go. She just didn't think it would be so soon.

Resigned, she knocked lightly on the door.

"Enter," Gawain commanded.

Caitriona entered purposefully and spotted the elder MacKinnon on the settee by the fire. Two of his guardsmen stood unobtrusively nearby, but otherwise, he was alone. *This is better than I could have expected,* she thought absently.

"Come," he said warmly. "Join me for a drink." He left the comfort of the settee and crossed the room to the serving tray, pouring them each a shot of aged Scottish whisky.

"I can't...I need..."

"That wasn't a question." He capped the 10-year-old scotch and handed her the glass. He watched as she swirled the liquid and then, inhaling the spiced aroma of the amber liquid, she downed the shot, shaking her head as the warmth spread throughout her body.

She handed him the glass and he poured her another. After one more, she wiped the back of her hand across her mouth and waved him away.

"Thank you, sir, for seeing me at this early hour. I would not have disturbed you if it weren't important."

Gawain nodded and motioned for her to sit. "What has you so troubled, child?"

Caitriona twisted her hands in her lap, unsure of where to begin. "Sir, I haven't been entirely honest with you regarding my visions."

Gawain raised an eyebrow, but otherwise said nothing; motioning for her to continue.

"The vision I shared with you was true, but only in part. There is more, but I've been reluctant to share it as I was uncertain of its meaning." She took a deep breath and met Gawain's penetrating gaze with her own. "I think I've figured it out, but I will need your help, and your silence, to save your son's life."

***

Caitriona left before Gawain had a chance to ask more questions or change his mind. He had listened attentively and asked good questions, and together they had hatched a plan. It was bold; if she was wrong, there was a good chance she and Duncan would both be killed. But at length, Gawain had agreed to the plan.

Caitriona walked quickly down the long cold corridor to her chambers, pulling the tartan wool tighter around her shoulders. The pervasive chill of the castle matched her mood. She entered her chambers and stopped short when she spotted Fiona still tending to Duncan's wounds.

"How bad?" Caitriona asked quietly, a momentary attack of guilt over her earlier carnal appetite making her apprehensive.

"He will be fine, Caitriona," Fiona said soothingly as she finished closing the last of Duncan's flesh wounds.

Caitriona gasped as she came closer and saw the ugly welts and red scars that would likely remain even with Fiona's technology and careful ministrations.

"He'll be fine," Fiona said again at the worry on the younger woman's face.

Caitriona nodded absently and brushed Duncan's hair away from his face. He was lying on his stomach, his face turned toward her. His eyes fluttered open and he smiled wanly at her.

"*Ach*, Catie. Dinna look at me as if ye've lost me," he admonished her lightly. "I'm tougher than that, lass."

A sob escaped her lips as she knelt beside him, tears pooling in her eyes. She brushed her lips lightly across his forehead and moaned when his lips found hers. She responded with a need of her own, eagerly parting her lips as his tongue sought familiar ground.

Fiona cleared her throat lightly, reminding the couple they were not alone.

Reluctantly, Caitriona pulled away from Duncan and stood up, the memory of their earlier love making still fresh in her mind. At the thought, a slight flush crept across her cheeks and she quickly averted her face, afraid the doctor would call her to task for her wanton disregard of her brother's health.

"He needs rest, Caitriona."

"Of course. I can stay with him …"

"I've asked a medic to sit with him," Fiona interrupted. She touched Caitriona lightly on the shoulder. "He really needs to rest," she said more quietly, her unspoken words hinting at their earlier tryst.

Caitriona nodded, knowing if she spoke, Fiona would hear the disappointment in her voice.

"Nicolas was looking for you, Caitriona. You know it's not safe for you above ground. I will get the medics to help me move my brother below ground, but he will rest better if he knows you're safe."

Caitriona nodded and walked quietly to the door. Before she could leave, Fiona interrupted her. "How are you feeling, Caitriona? Have you had any headaches lately?"

She shook her head. "I'm fine," she lied. She didn't want the doctor to run more tests or lecture her about the impending bonding.

"Check in with Nicolas. Don't forget."

Caitriona nodded and slipped out of the room, closing the heavy door behind her. In the hallway, she paused and pulled a deep breath of air into her lungs, feeling very much the errant child who had just been scolded. Sighing heavily, she made her way to the lower chambers in search of Nicolas, her heart remaining behind with the man she loved.

Chapter Twenty-Seven

He felt now that he was not simply close to her, but that he did not know where he ended and she began.
Leo Tolstoy

Caitriona was vaguely aware of Gawain and Duncan's heated conversation, the younger MacKinnon now fully recovered from his earlier battle wounds. She knew both men were deeply engrossed in their strategic discussions, given her latest vision that detailed when and where Hawkins was going to attack. The two men had spent the better part of the week securing the most vulnerable parts of the castle. She had also supplied them with the location of Hawkins' army. Because of this, they were able to post scouts and sentries to keep a watchful eye on the army's movements. So far, Hawkins' troops remained at least three days' journey away and hadn't yet mobilized.

While most of the castle's inhabitants still remained underground, Gawain had reluctantly opened the main castle to relieve the burden on the Dwellers. Both sides agreed, however, to keep the tunnels open so that a quick escape would prove possible when the Order attacked. Additional sentries in the parapets kept a vigilant watch on the skies for the Order's invasive drones that, thanks to Caitriona's vision, they knew would arrive hours in advance of the army.

Gawain had also taken this time to send for reinforcements from their allies in the United Kingdom. She knew the army had mobilized just miles from Hawkins' men. And while this gave her some measure of comfort, she also knew Hawkins was very much aware of their movements and troops. They needed a competitive advantage if they were to win this war. And she knew all eyes were on her.

Caitriona strained to hear more of the conversation between Duncan and his father. Duncan had been back only a little over a week and was already talking of battle and leaving. She closed her eyes and inhaled deeply, the smoke from the fire mixing with the heady scent of musk and kitchen spices.

Duncan hadn't touched her since that first night home. Though Fiona had closed his wounds and the bruises were beginning to fade, there was an edginess and distance that was growing between them. A slight blush dusted her cheeks as she remembered their passionate night and how he had claimed her as his. *What had changed*, she thought worriedly.

She glanced up as she saw Nicolas enter the room. A smile stretched across her face as he winked at her and poured himself a drink from the nearby decanter. She could feel Duncan's mood darken as he witnessed their exchange.

The pain behind her eyes that had been building since morning erupted suddenly, and the room swam crazily before her. She could feel Nicolas' gaze and purposely kept from crying out. She crossed quietly to the ballroom's main doors, hoping to make a quiet but hasty exit.

"Caitriona, are you feeling all right?" Nicolas asked, coming to stand beside her. Duncan turned his attention to her, his gaze finding hers, concern visible in his tired face.

"I'm fine, really," she said quietly. "I'm just a little tired and was going to rest." Nicolas nodded, but she knew Duncan could see the effort it took for her to speak, the flush that rose to her cheeks, and the subtle way she tried to shield her eyes from the light.

"I can see you to your room," Nicolas offered, more as a statement rather than a request. She smiled wanly and dipped her head slightly, taking the arm he offered her. She had to remain focused only a few moments longer.

But as they started to leave the room, a searing pain gripped her from the base of her neck and exploded behind her eyes. The pain was so sharp she momentarily lost her vision, as hot agonizing flashes continued to pulse across her forehead. She inhaled sharply and doubled over, clutching her head between her hands. As another sharp stab of pain gripped her she cried out and dropped to her knees, the folds of her thick emerald-green gown swelling beneath her in a glorious waterfall of color.

Quickly, Nicolas knelt beside her, his hands supporting her shoulders as another sharp stab of pain sliced across her forehead and down the back of her neck. Caitriona could hear a woman screaming in the distance and realized, after what seemed like an eternity, that the screams were coming from her own throat. She was vaguely aware of Duncan kneeling before her, smoothing the hair away from her eyes as he whispered softly to her in his native tongue.

Another flash of pain; this one longer in duration and intensity, left Caitriona barely conscious. A moan escaped her lips as she collapsed against Nicolas, trembling and sobbing.

Nicolas' eyes met hers and, in that instant, each knew what the other did not want to voice; she had to bond with him.

Fiona moved quietly into the room and joined the group huddled together on the floor. She ran her medical equipment swiftly across Caitriona's forehead and administered the heaviest dose of laudanum that she dared. Caitriona registered barely any relief as another sharp pain tore across her skull. She groaned and pressed her hand to her forehead, willing the pain to disappear.

"I've done all I can," Fiona said softly, looking between Nicolas and Duncan.

"Caitriona," Nicolas spoke her name softly.

"No," she whispered, trying to push away from him and the fated outcome he offered. "No," she said, sounding much stronger than she felt. She pushed again and was successful this time in struggling to her feet, ignoring the help Duncan offered. She pressed the heel of her palm against her forehead as she let loose another scream that echoed across the massive room.

"Caitriona," Duncan implored. "Ye have nae choice, lass."

"There is always a choice," she sobbed; the words he'd said to her many months ago now being thrown back at him. "I would rather die than live in shackles, no matter how invisible the bonds might be." She bit her bottom lip and stared defiantly at Duncan, tears coursing down her cheeks. She knew this was a battle she would likely lose.

The next flash of pain tore the breath from her. She would have collapsed had Nicolas not supported her weight. She lolled helplessly in his arms, death no longer a frightening missive but a welcome relief from the torrents of pain that wracked her body.

"The pain will kill her, Duncan," Nicolas said harshly. "I have to do this now."

A low growl erupted from Duncan as the weight and finality of

Nicolas' words hit home. Caitriona slumped in her handler's arms, her face ghostly pale, her eyes lost to this world.

"Do it," he growled, the pain of his decision evident in the hard lines of his face.

Nicolas wasted no time. With one arm supporting Caitriona, he used his other hand to pull the dagger he kept sheathed at his side, and quickly made a four-inch incision above his right breastbone. The cut was deep and the blood ran freely, turning his crisp white shirt a gruesome shade of red. He kissed the top of her head as he whispered, "Forgive me, *Caterine*," before he plunged the dagger into her left breastbone and sliced downward, creating a four inch cut that matched his own.

She inhaled sharply, her eyes snapping open and staring in horror at the blood that flowed down her chest, staining her emerald dress a dark grisly red. Nicolas dropped the dagger and hooked his fingers under her chin, forcing her to look up into his eyes.

"Stay with me," he whispered. "There's nothing else right now but you and me." His thumb grazed her lip.

Caitriona's eyes locked with his, their lake-blue depths warm and full of concern. Her breath was ragged and hoarse as the finality of what he had done sank in.

"Open your mind to me, *Caterine*. Just like we've practiced."

She shook her head, her eyes never leaving his. She wondered absently if he would be able to complete the bond if her mind was not open and receptive. With her last bit of strength, she held her shields in place. She would not, could not, allow this union.

Acutely aware of the metallic smell of blood that permeated the air around them, Caitriona felt the sticky warmth of her life essence mixing with that of her handler's. She choked back a sob as she glanced down and saw the blood running down her chest.

"I can make the pain go away," Nicolas promised; his voice husky and full of emotion.

As if on cue, another searing block of pain gripped her body, tearing a sob from her throat. She wanted to collapse, to curl into a ball and hide from the pain, but she knew there was only one path to relief.

"Open yourself," Nicolas said, mentally pushing against her mind.

"I can't," she cried.

"You can," he pushed harder. "You are one of the strongest women I've ever met. This bond will not define you." He brushed her hair away from her face, his finger tracing the tear that fell across her cheek. "No, I'm not ready," she rasped. "I can't do this."

Caitriona was acutely aware that Duncan and Gawain had left the room. Fiona had remained behind, but had distanced herself from the pair; on hand to administer medical support, yet relegated discreetly to the shadows to give the two the privacy they needed.

Caitriona felt another wave of pain begin to build behind her eyes. The loss of blood left her nauseous and weak. She leaned into Nicolas, allowing the strength of his arms and gentle touch to buffer her. She whimpered as the pain threatened to immobilize her.

**

Nicolas knew he had to act quickly. He pulled Caitriona tightly to him, the blood mixing and providing the channel he needed to complete the bond. He could feel the slow but steady beat of her heart keeping time to his. Nicolas opened his mind to Caitriona's, feeling her pain and fear. He could also feel her resistance and her shields. He had hoped to have more time to prepare her; to have her accept him and the relief he brought. But time was not kind to either of them.

Mentally, he pushed her again. He knew he could force this if he had to; but he so badly wanted Caitriona to accept this … to accept him. He caressed her cheek, noting how pale she had become. He knew he couldn't be patient much longer. She would soon drift into unconsciousness and would be lost to him forever.

She cried out again and he pressed his lips to the top of her head. She was so vulnerable, he thought absently. He focused on her heartbeat and wrapped them both in his energy, allowing his warmth to surround them. He could feel her visibly relax. His eyes pleaded with her one last time. Suddenly, she released her shield. Her visible intake of breath was his reward. He immediately felt her body go lax and he mouthed a *thank you* to the Goddess.

**

Once Caitriona released her shield, warm energy spread throughout her body, replacing the pain with a comfortable security she hadn't experienced since coming to this world. She could feel Nicolas' heart beat; steady, reassuring, as he stroked her hair and lightly kissed her brow. She was aware only of Nicolas; his even, slow breathing and the energy that cocooned them both.

"Blood to blood," he whispered softly. "Our minds become one. Your soul to mine until our lives are done." Nicolas spoke the ancient words that sealed their bond. She knew the words weren't important. The bond had been forged when Caitriona released her shield, but the words gave her strength derived from love and finality.

Nicolas tucked an errant lock behind her ear and smiled at her. She could feel the waves of energy roll across her and wondered if Nicolas felt the same. The pain that only moments before had wracked her body was blissfully gone. She looked at him, eyes wide. "The pain is gone," she whispered incredulously. "But how? Why?"

"Your magic is created by energy," he said simply. He palmed her cheek, skimming his thumb over the soft outline of her cheekbone. "Unlike a caster, you have nowhere to displace your energy once you've tapped into it. Because I'm an empath, I can absorb your unused energy and keep you grounded," he paused slightly and then added, "and keep you safe."

Caitriona's cheeks flushed. "I don't want your protection, Nicolas" she said. "I don't want any of this." She dropped her gaze and sagged in his arms as a stream of blood coursed down her chest.

"I know this isn't what you wanted, *Caterine*," he whispered hoarsely, interrupting the silence between them, "but I make this promise to you - for as many tomorrows as the Goddess may bless me, I will serve and protect you with no regrets. I will stand beside you, share your pain, your sorrow and your joy, and spend every day loving you if you will have me."

Caitriona tensed in his arms. "I don't know what I want anymore," she replied quietly. "I feel like I'm drowning. I don't know how to navigate this world," she confessed.

"Lean on me, *chéri*," he said. "I will help you navigate, in turn, we will share a life together."

She stared at him, the silence growing uncomfortable between them. She was acutely aware of a physical need that was building in her. She wondered if Duncan was at the heart of that need or if it had something to do with Nicolas. She closed her eyes, trying to feel for the connection she shared with Duncan. She felt nothing. She pushed her physical needs aside and stared blankly at Nicolas, wondering what her life would be like now that she was connected to this man. He tucked an errant curl behind her ear, his hand softly caressing her cheek before he dropped it to his side.

Nicolas kissed her forehead lightly and, hooking his arm behind her knees, pulled her into his arms. She stiffened and then relaxed as he settled her against him.

"There's so much blood," she said, her voice barely above a whisper.

"A necessary side effect, *chéri.*" He nodded to Fiona who quickly crossed the room to assess her patients.

"Let's get you both upstairs," the doctor said. "The wounds aren't deep, but they should be closed, and you will both need some rest to recover after the blood you've lost."

Nicolas allowed Fiona to push open the heavy oak doors as he bore his slight burden up the stairs. Caitriona registered the look Duncan gave them both as they passed. She nestled deeper in Nicolas' arms, aware that she was in his arms and now in his heart.

***

Duncan allowed Gawain to pull him away from the sight of Caitriona's bloody and limp body being carried upstairs by Nicolas. *Mine.* The word echoed in his head, until he thought the emptiness would consume him.

Gawain pushed open the doors to the drawing room and ushered his son inside. Crossing the room to a tray that held glasses and an assortment of whiskies, Gawain quickly selected an amber colored scotch and poured a generous amount for Duncan, before pouring one for himself. Duncan took the proffered drink readily, and downed the fiery liquid in one shot, his anger barely kept in check. He wanted to go to Caitriona and gather her in his arms and tell her everything would work out … that he would find a way for them to be together. But he knew that would be yet another promise he wouldn't be able to keep.

Duncan slammed his fist down on the large wood table, watching as the glasses teetered precariously under his assault. "*Damnu,*" his voice thundered across the room as he fought to control his anger.

His father poured him another shot of the decade-old scotch and motioned for him to drink it. Downing the second draught, Duncan set the glass back on the table and swiped the back of his hand across his mouth. He ran a hand through his hair, mentally recalling Caitriona's bloodied body cradled in Nicolas' arms. *Mine.*

"Let her go, son," Gawain said gently. Though not biologically Duncan's father, the older man had fostered Duncan from the time he was brought to his hold at the age of eight. Duncan had immediately formed a kinship with the older man, whose fiery passion for helping the Lessers obtain equality influenced Duncan's own ideals and values.

Duncan stopped pacing and faced his father. "I dinna ken how," he growled, anger boiling inside of him. "She is as much a part of me as the verra air I breathe, and I'll be damned if I watch while Nicolas shares her life."

Gawain didn't speak for several seconds. "Do this for her. You know she belongs with Nicolas … with her own kind."

Duncan's head snapped up and he glared at the older man. "What are ye saying?" Duncan growled, his blistering anger boiling just near the surface.

"Duncan, she …"

"Just don't." He waved away his father's objections. "She's done everything we've asked to help us win this war. Where is this coming from? This isna like ye."

Gawain closed the communications plan he had been studying and sat down, gesturing for Duncan to take a chair opposite him. Duncan shook his head. He didn't feel like sitting, but Gawain merely nodded to the empty chair, his expression indicating he wouldn't take no for an answer. Duncan sat down and sighed heavily. He put his face in his hands, his hair falling across his shoulders. After several seconds he sat up taller and faced Gawain.

For all his independent ways, Duncan longed for a partner who could love him, stand up to him, stand by him and soften his hard lines. And by all accounts, Caitriona seemed perfectly suited to that task, but it seemed the Goddess had other plans for him. He groaned, running his hand through his hair.

"There's too much at stake, Duncan. Let her go."

"Dinna ye think I ken that?" Duncan asked hoarsely. "I take neither my position nor my responsibilities lightly. The Goddess knows I have tried in every imaginable way to let go of her, but I simply canna. It's as if there is a magnet between us and I am being constantly pulled toward her." He poured himself another drink and downed the amber liquid quickly. He could feel the warmth spread throughout his body; the immediate numbing giving him the relief he sought. Gawain watched as his son poured another.

"The council has agreed to test the girl in five days," Gawain said softly. Duncan's head snapped up, fury visible in the hard lines of his face.

"If she passes their scrutiny, I can ask that she and Nicolas are moved to Cawdor Castle where she will be well guarded and well protected. If she doesn't pass their tests ..." Gawain let the unfinished sentence hang between them. Duncan didn't need to be reminded of the fate that awaited the young woman if she was not able to call her visions at will.

"No," Duncan thundered. He got up and began pacing, his agitation barely held in check. "She will be ready," he finally said quietly and without a hint of anger. He walked to the large oak door and started to leave. Not bothering to turn around, he spoke over his shoulder, "And regardless of the outcome, she stays with me at Castle Dunrobin." He pushed open the large doors and exited the vast room, the weight of his words settling like lead in the immensity of the great room.

***

Gawain sighed and poured himself another drink, settling comfortably into the oversized chair that was positioned near the fire. He was accustomed to his son's unexpected and often hot temper, but he had never seen him this rankled and agitated before. So much was riding on this young girl's ability. He couldn't allow their feelings for each other to come between the work they were all entrusted to do.

Gawain stared intently at the embers in the fire that were nearly extinguished. He was suddenly very tired; the day's activities and challenges weighing heavily on his mind. He pulled a wool tartan blanket across his lap and chest and closed his eyes. He would make a point of speaking with his son tomorrow. He also needed to weigh the information Caitriona had shared with him earlier. Once he had a chance to review all the pieces, he'd make his decision and ensure his orders were carried out, knowing that someone would most likely be hurt.

***

Caitriona's eyes fluttered open as Nicolas laid her gently on the over-sized bed. She was dimly aware of her handler and his concern. She knew she should be angry, but she wasn't. Nicolas had saved her life and had done it as unobtrusively and gently as he could. She touched his arm and allowed a soft smile to light her face. Her eyes felt heavy and she struggled against the sleep that threatened to keep her.

Caitriona heard Nicolas move away from her as Fiona bent to cleanse the incision he had made. After using the microscopic laser to close the wound, she placed a cool cloth across Caitriona's forehead. Caitriona blinked several times, panic rising in her as she realized she could no longer feel her connection with Duncan. Pushing the cloth from her face, she looked around and saw Nicolas sitting quietly in the large leather chair closest to the bed. He had built a fire in the hearth and was now staring intently into the young flames, watching as more wood caught fire and added fuel to the growing warmth.

"I should see to your wound as well, Nicolas," Fiona said quietly. He nodded and started to rise, but she motioned for him to stay where he was. He pulled his shirt over his head, his eyes never leaving Caitriona's. Quickly, Fiona washed away the now crusted blood and closed up the wound. She started to administer the laudanum, but Nicolas grabbed her hand and just shook his head. She replaced the vial and packed up the rest of her equipment.

"You both should get some rest. On our way upstairs, I asked one of the kitchen maids to bring some food and water." Nicolas nodded. Caitriona struggled against the drug-induced sleep the laudanum would bring. She wanted to go downstairs and find Duncan. She was hurt and felt betrayed. The last time they had been together he had told her he loved her. Clearly, she was naïve to think she meant anything to him. And she still wasn't sure what this latest development would mean to him. She didn't feel any different, except that the headaches were now blissfully absent. And where was Duncan? She was hurt by his easy dismissal of her. She sighed softly, wondering if Nicolas would always be able to feel her emotions.

"If you'd like, I can get her out of her gown and into her night clothes," Fiona said hesitantly. He nodded again and turned his back to her. Caitriona watched as he found the poker and stirred the flames to life. The flames leapt higher with the infusion of oxygen.

Fiona rummaged quickly through the large dresser drawers until she came across Caitriona's night dress. She undid the bodice of the ruined gown and slid Caitriona's arms out of the garment, pushing the damaged dress down over her hips. Caitriona was too numb and too hurt to care. In a cathartic state, she watched from somewhere outside her body as Fiona pulled the night dress over her and tucked the bedding in around her. Her last thought before sleep took her was of steel grey eyes locked with sorrow-filled green.

***

Sometime later, the kitchen maid returned with a tray of fruits, meats and cheeses, some brandy, and a pitcher of water. Nicolas gestured for the girl to set the tray down on the night stand, and once again settled his gaze on the flames that leapt and danced in a frenzied rhythm. Behind him, he could hear Fiona settling Caitriona into the bed and dared a glance in her direction. Fiona was just pulling the covers around Caitriona and he knew he would soon be left alone with the most powerful woman his century had ever known.

He squared his shoulders and ran a hand through his thick locks, his gaze settling on his charge. The enormousness of what he had done, and what he would do, was not lost on him. Not only was he tasked with keeping the Seer safe, but he was also charged with her magical development, as well as her emotional and physical wellbeing. He had spent years training for this role, yet now that she was here, he suddenly felt inadequate and certainly not up to the task ahead of him.

"She simply needs rest at this point," Fiona said quietly.

Nicolas nodded and walked her to the door. "You need rest as well, Nicolas," she said. "I know your thoughts are focused on Caitriona right now, but she will need you to be strong in the days and weeks ahead. Use this time to rest and prepare."

Nicolas nodded again, the dark circles under his eyes underscoring the stress and responsibility he bore. He wondered if Fiona resented him for what he had done. He knew her brother was grieving, that he needed time to come to terms with this newest, but not unplanned, development.

She touched his arm, "Please," she stressed. "Get some rest."

Nicolas watched as Fiona quietly left the room, his heart heavy with concern. Caitriona groaned softly in her sleep and turned on her side, kicking the covers from her as she did. Nicolas crossed the room and gently lifted the covers back around her shoulders, noting the delicate curves of her body as he did. Without thinking, he brushed a silky strand of hair from her face, the tips of his fingers skimming her delicate cheekbone.

She sighed again in her sleep and he brushed the back of his knuckles softly across her cheek. Confident that she was once again resting comfortably, he walked back to the fire and stared myopically into the growing flames. All of his training had not prepared him for the overwhelming emotion he felt once he had bonded with this powerful woman.

Nicolas pulled the oversized lounge that was placed near the window close to the fire, intent on making the lumpy chair his bed. He angled the chair so that he was close to the fire yet had an unfettered view of his powerful charge. He poured himself a small glass of brandy from the decanter the serving maid had left behind before easing himself into the chair. He was uncertain what the day would bring or how Caitriona would react once she woke up, but right now, he was confident that the uncertainty would surely be his undoing.

Downing the fiery liquid in one shot, he swiped the back of his hand across his mouth and set the glass back on the serving tray. He watched as Caitriona winced slightly in her sleep. Opening his mind to hers, he mentally reached across her mind and felt the hidden recesses of her fear. He was on his feet in an instant and crossed the room quickly, concern etched visibly on his face. She cried out, pushing the covers once again from her body, her night-dress tangling around her legs. Nicolas sat down on the bed next to her and pulled her into his arms. She stiffened, her eyelids fluttering open, but she relaxed visibly when she saw him.

"Shh," he whispered softly, his hand brushing her hair from her eyes.

"I wasn't dreaming?" The question was more of an affirmation. Her hands fluttered to the almost healed scar across her breastbone. Nicolas shook his head slightly, his eyes searching hers.

"I can feel your sadness," he said hesitantly, afraid she would push him away. Instead, she nestled closer, burying her face in his hard chest. He released a sigh of gratitude and continued to stroke her hair, his emotions raging their own war as he battled his need to physically connect with her. After several minutes, he could feel the deep, even breaths that told him she had drifted back to sleep, and once again he mouthed a silent prayer to the Goddess.

He guided her gently back to the mattress and slipped his arms out from under her. Her eyes fluttered open and a momentary look of panic crossed her face.

"Don't go," she whispered hesitantly.

He brushed a hand through his hair and sat back down next to her. "*Caterine*, I will be right in that chair all night." He gestured to the oversized chair that suddenly felt cold and remote. "I promise I won't leave you."

"Please?" The word was more a plea than a question as she scooted awkwardly to the other side of the bed and patted the space beside her, the laudanum making her movements slow and clumsy.

Nicolas sighed and stretched out next to her, keeping the covers tucked around her so there would be no physical contact between them. He could feel himself growing hard but did not want to take advantage of the girl's highly sensitive physical state. The physical connection was as much a part of the bonding as the emotional connection they shared. While a physical bond was not necessary, the emotions created by the initial bonding fueled a physical need that, if left unsated, became increasingly uncomfortable for both participants.

"Sleep, *chéri*. We will have lots of time to sort this out tomorrow."

She nodded and rolled away from him, snuggling deeper into the covers.

"Son of a bitch," she suddenly groaned loudly, rolling onto her side so she could face Nicolas. "Can you read my thoughts?"

"Language, *chéri*" he admonished softly. "And no, your thoughts are safe. I can only read your emotions." There was a comfortable silence before he continued. "But emotions often say more than words." He let the unanswered questions sit between them.

Caitriona sighed, visibly relieved and rolled back on her side away from Nicolas' intense gaze. "Rest, *chéri*" he implored again.

Nicolas folded his arms under his head and stared vacuously at the ceiling. The day's events unfolded in his mind and he once again cursed and praised the fates that had brought this woman into his life. He knew he had a long way to go to gain her trust and he still wasn't sure how rooted her feelings were with MacKinnon. He watched as the embers in the fire crackled, knowing he should stoke the fire one last time before succumbing to sleep. But for the first time in a long time, he welcomed the cold.

***

Caitriona pulled the covers tightly around her shoulders and pressed herself against the hard body that was curled around hers.

"*Caterine*, please stop that," Nicolas groaned hoarsely, his growing hardness evidence of the effect she was having on him. "You will unman me if you keep that up, and I am not certain you are ready for that."

Caitriona's eyes flew open in horror as she realized where she was and that the hard man-wall next to her was not Duncan.

"Oh," she groaned; a flush creeping steadily across her face. She kicked off the covers and sprang to her feet, wanting to put as much distance between herself and Nicolas as possible. She was acutely aware of the flush that spread across her cheeks and of her own body's growing betrayal. *What was happening to her*, she thought wildly.

"I'm sorry…I don't…I shouldn't have…" She didn't know what to say. Her usual wit and sarcasm seemed horribly inappropriate given the situation. She only stared blankly at her handler.

"I know this isn't what you want, *Caterine*," Nicolas said softly. "I wish for your sake it could have been Duncan."

As do I, she thought sadly, her eyes meeting his.

Nicolas disentangled himself from the covers and got to his feet. Caitriona was startled by what she saw in his eyes and, for an instant her eyes dipped lower, taking in his hard erection that strained against his pants. She couldn't stay in the room any longer. Summoning her resolve, she ran to the door and into the cold hall.

"*Caterine*, wait," Nicolas called after her.

Caitriona didn't stop. She disappeared quickly around the corner and scooted down the servant's stairs, knowing Nicolas would be right behind her. She needed time to think, time to unscramble her feelings and sort through the raging emotions that were consuming her. The stone floor was cold beneath her bare feet, but she didn't care. She practically leapt down the stairs, the stairwell creating a cold draft that cut through her thin night dress. She was glad for the early morning hour and the fact that most of the castle's inhabitants were still asleep or below ground.

When she reached the bottom level, she pushed open the outer door and entered the courtyard. The sun was just beginning to dot the horizon and, for a brief moment, she tilted her face to the morning dawn and allowed the cool breeze to wash over her and cool her flushed cheeks.

Hearing footsteps behind her, she was reminded that she was never alone. Moving easily through the courtyard, she was aware of the guards and soldiers that watched vigilantly for dangers in the air and on the ground. One of the sentries on the parapet spotted her and saluted before bending a knee. She tilted her head in acknowledgement, uncomfortable with this new level of respect that so many of the soldiers and civilians had begun showing.

"You shouldn't be out here, mistress, especially not alone," the soldier called down. Those standing near him turned to see who he was speaking to and, when they saw Caitriona, each bent a knee.

"I won't be long," she called back. "I just need some fresh air."

"Commander MacKinnon has given us strict orders that you are not to be left unprotected." He signaled to two men below him who then flanked Caitriona as she stood in the courtyard. Sighing heavily, she smiled at the men who had joined her. She looked up at the soldier and once again nodded her thanks, knowing it was pointless to argue with the guards. Everyone knew who she was and why she was here. And though the guards remained respectful and polite, every one of them was deeply, innately interested in her and the hope she brought to so many.

Caitriona started walking toward the stables, uncertain why she had selected that as her destination. As she walked, she felt herself begin to relax and the morning's embarrassment with Nicolas began to ebb. Once at the stables, she found herself inside and stroking Marcie's nose. She wished she had some carrots or an apple for the gentle horse. After a few minutes, she sat down on a bale of hay and put her face in her hands. She could hear her guards several yards away, vigilant in their shared responsibility.

"Can we talk?" Nicolas' question broke her meditation as he caught up with her inside the barn.

She groaned but pulled her hands away from her face and motioned to the seat beside her. Nicolas sat down next to her but didn't say anything for several minutes. Finally, when he spoke, he was almost apologetic.

"I'm a man, *Caterine*, and you are a beautiful woman." His gaze raked her body appreciatively.

She blushed profusely, aware that his voice had become deeper.

"I love him," she whispered.

"I know."

"This feels like such a betrayal."

"It shouldn't," he said simply. He nudged her playfully with his shoulder. "We share an emotional bond that is nearly impossible to separate from a physical one." At her look of concern he quickly added, "A physical attraction neither of us will act upon."

She laughed softly and grinned. "Clearly easier for you than me," she mumbled in chagrin.

He smiled at her. "I like that sound." She arched an eyebrow quizzically at him.

"Your laughter," he continued, seeing the question in her eyes. "It's been far too long since you've allowed yourself that one small indulgence."

They both sat together in comfortable silence for several minutes.

Caitriona eventually leaned her head on his shoulder, and she could feel him smile. He took her hand and rubbed it between his palms trying to chase away the chill.

"We'll figure this out together, *chéri, oui?*"

She nodded, her head still resting on his shoulder. "I never thanked you," she said quietly.

Nicolas stopped rubbing her hands and pulled slightly away from her.

"You've given up so much," she continued. "I haven't been fair to you. I've been so focused on my own needs. I'm sorry. You don't deserve this."

"*Caterine*, you are not a burden. I would choose you and this life a million times over. I know you have been thrown into this; your destiny chosen for you, asked to fight a war that was never your fight. But I can be the friend you need. I'm not asking you to embrace it all right now, but give me a chance."

She nodded slowly, not trusting herself to speak. She pulled her lower lip between her teeth, fighting back the emotion that remained just near the surface. "I can do that," she said softly. "You deserve at least that." She smiled at him as he slowly released his breath.

Kissing the back of her hand, he got to his feet. "Shall we start back?" She smiled and got to her feet, Nicolas tucking her hand into the crook of his arm.

"Let's go win a war, *chéri.*"

Chapter Twenty-Eight

Two people don't have to be together right now ... in a month ... or in a year. If those two people are meant to be, then they will be together somehow at some time in life.
Anon

Duncan paused outside the library when he heard the lilt of Caitriona's laughter echo through the west hall. His already dark mood grew even more discordant when he realized the source of his charge's; the Seer's, he corrected himself, amusement: Nicolas. Pausing only briefly, Duncan stormed into the library, his fury causing both occupants to abandon their game of cribbage and acknowledge the powerful man who stood before them.

Nicolas was the first to break the stony silence, meeting Duncan's cold, steel-grey eyes without hesitation or fear. "Is there something we can do for you, Commander?"

"Leave us," Duncan spoke to Nicolas dismissively, gesturing to the large oak door.

Nicolas remained seated, watching the visual exchange between his charge and the Commander. Slowly, Duncan tore his eyes away from Caitriona and met Nicolas' icy blue gaze. Taking a deep breath, Duncan closed his eyes. When he was certain he had regained control of his emotions, he opened them and spoke directly to Nicolas. "I need to speak to Caitriona... alone," he added.

Caitriona gave a slight nod of her head to Nicolas. Pushing back his chair, Nicolas leaned over and squeezed Caitriona's hand. "We shall finish our game later," he said softly. Caitriona nodded, her eyes never leaving the steel grey ones that were locked intently on hers.

Nicolas had barely left the room before Duncan's temper erupted. "Are ye mad, woman?" he growled.

"Duncan, I don't understand," she said softly, trying to diffuse the tidal wave of anger that was coming. "Why don't you sit down?"

Duncan ran a trembling hand through his hair, shaking his head in exasperation. Turning, he fixed Caitriona in his cold stare. "I spoke with Gawain," he said tersely. At her bewildered look, he continued. "He told me about your plan, Caitriona. What are ye thinking? Do ye ken what these people are capable of?"

"I think I have a pretty good idea," she retorted tersely, turning her palms up so he was reminded of the wounds the Order had inflicted.

Duncan winced at the harsh reminder that he had been unable to protect her. While he had closed the distance between them physically, he could still feel the emotional barriers that she held firmly in place, and he knew that he was partially to blame for her withdrawal.

Caitriona moved to the settee, pulling the silk-like coverlet around her shoulders. Duncan placed another log on the fire, instantly warming the chamber's dark walls and deep rugs. The fire hissed and popped, sending a few rogue sparks to the stone hearth as Duncan sat down in front of the fire. His dark, brooding thoughts provided no invitation to anything other than darker ponderings.

"Why would ye do this, lass? Why would ye even suggest using yerself as bait? Goddess, Caitriona, does Nicolas ken?"

She shook her head. "Only Gawain."

Duncan got up and paced the floor. *What wasn't she telling him*, he thought. *Why would Gawain actually entertain this idea?*

"Ye're hiding something," said Duncan flatly.

Caitriona didn't say anything. She just stared blankly at him. "I don't want to discuss this with you, Duncan," she stated tersely, finally breaking the unyielding silence.

Duncan glared at her, the storm visible in his eyes. Caitriona got up and moved away from him slowly. He knew she had never seen him this angry but he couldn't tell her how he felt. Not with so much at stake.

"And why not?" he growled at her. "*Damnu*, Catie, I willna let ye do this. I dinna ken what game ye are playing at but tis goin' tae stop here." Caitriona winced as Duncan's fist slammed against the table.

"This is a conversation I will have only with Gawain," she reminded him. "In fact, I'm irritated that he pulled you into this at all."

"Pulled me into this?" he stated incredulously. "Everything about this," he stressed the last word, "affects me. I am the leader of the resistance army, Caitriona. Do ye think any strategic military maneuvers would not be run past me, lass?"

"I suppose not," she retorted haughtily. "But, honestly, what difference does it make, Duncan? If my plan succeeds, we will have brought Hawkins down. If we don't succeed, then I'm one less problem you'll have to deal with." Her eyes were daggers of green, daring him to cross her.

"*Damnu*, Caitriona. Ye are nae goin' tae do this. I willna allow it!"

"I have your father's support, Duncan. This time you don't get to call the shots."

"That's where ye're wrong, lass." He paced back and forth, his anger barely contained. After several seconds, he stopped pacing and fixed her with his steel-grey gaze. "Tomorrow ye meet the council. I suggest ye find yer handler and prepare."

He crossed the room to the door but, before he could leave, Caitriona's icy response stopped him. "Gladly. At least I know he won't abandon me."

Duncan took a deep breath and closed his eyes, his own emotions for the young woman at odds with his warrior's duty. Saying nothing, he slipped quietly from the room and the only woman he would ever love.

Chapter Twenty-Nine

The first duty of love is to listen.
Paul Tillich

Caitriona closed her eyes and took a deep breath. She concentrated on this simple task as she pulled the air in through her nose and exhaled slowly through her mouth. When she had released her breath, she opened her eyes and scanned the room before her. She saw a hundred or more pairs of eyes focused intently on her every move. She was, after all, new and different and powerful.

She was acutely aware of Nicolas, who stood slightly behind her as they entered the underground meeting hall. She knew he was scanning the room for any signs of danger, his hand resting casually, yet ready, on his sword. This gave her a small measure of comfort despite the accelerated beating of her heart. She also knew he had a gun tucked into the waistband of his trews. He'd never use the weapon in the caverns unless her life demanded it. There was simply too great a risk of the underground passages collapsing if a soldier missed his mark.

She was stunned by the vast number of people who had crammed into the large, cavernous area. The air was thick and fetid with the odors of so many people. She hesitated, no longer sure of her commitment to this plan. She knew that Nicolas, attuned to her feelings, felt her trepidation. Placing his hand on her elbow, he reminded her gently of the important role she played. With another deep breath, she continued resolutely forward, meeting the stares of the people before her with determined strength. Through the hordes of people, Caitriona remained silent, moving gracefully by her handler's side and ignoring the veiled, speculative looks of the occupants as the two passed among them.

At the opposite end of the room, a long table was arranged with twelve seats on one side that faced the audience of men and women, many of whom crowded near the table, presumably to get a better view. The crowd parted for them and Nicolas guided her to the table. When they reached their seats at the center of the table, Nicolas pulled her chair out for her and motioned for her to sit. She refused to meet his eyes or acknowledge his assistance, but took her seat quickly, smoothing the folds of her russet and gold gown in a gesture that belied the tension in the room. She fidgeted nervously with a long auburn curl that had come unwound from the perfectly coiffed hair she had undergone with less-than-patient ministrations earlier that day. Her pure, ivory complexion was flawless, with the exception of the large, nearly-faded bruise that was visible just below her right eye.

Caitriona had a good idea how this day would end. The vision that had haunted her since childhood visited her again last night. She had awoken in terror, drenched in perspiration from a battle she never won. Nicolas, sensing her fear, was immediately in her chambers, a welcome reassurance in a world where everything was a threat and her terrifying vision an ever-present reminder of the fate that awaited her.

Nicolas took the seat next to her and cleared his throat rather softly, a subtle reminder that she needed to stop fidgeting and find something more appropriate to do with her hands. He poured them each a glass of water from the tall carafe that was placed before them before raking a perfectly manicured hand through his neatly trimmed, jet black hair; a small bead of perspiration on his upper lip the only indication of his frayed nerves. Today, the council would test her skills. And they would likely find her lacking. She shuddered at what that would mean or how it would impact her plan with Gawain. Damn Duncan, she cursed silently, but her heart ached for him all the same.

Gawain eyed the pair quizzically but took his seat as the cacophony of voices around them swelled. Brushing his thick, wavy gray hair from his face, he looked out at the sea of faces, scanning the room. Deep lines etched the older man's face and dark circles gave away the fact that he hadn't slept well for months.

Caitriona mentally noted the absence of several of her guards and said a quiet prayer for the men and women who had given their lives to ensure this historic moment would one day arrive. Now, after countless centuries, these people were closer to their goal than they had ever been. The world would soon know their secret and the battle for freedom would elevate them all: a battle born of tyranny and the New World Order's unjust persecution.

The nine council members all took their seats at the long table, some nodding to Caitriona as they settled themselves for what would undoubtedly be a long, heated evening. The usual hum of conversation was decidedly absent as the council members focused their attention on the pair before them. Today marked a turning point in their century-long war; after decades of preparation and planning, the Templars were on the brink of unleashing her magical powers that would tip the scales in their favor and, with any luck, bring an end to the bloody and costly war. She merely had to pass their tests and prove her gifts.

The torches on the wall cast eerie shadows across the room. Two young girls pushed their way through the crowd to bring pitchers of steaming coffee to the seated council members. The carafes were placed on the table next to trenchers of meat and cheese. A few members eagerly began filling their plates, but most remained focused on Caitriona and her escort seated at the middle of the table.

Gawain rose slowly and placed one hand on Caitriona's chair, the tide of voices which earlier had rushed through the room fading as he was given their full attention.

"My friends," he began, "for centuries our brothers met in secrecy to ensure the preservation and freedom of all life. Our ancestors watched as genocide, sanctioned and protected in the Global 2000 report and approved by the US President James Earl Carter, reduced the world population in 2050 by more than three billion people. As we are continually reminded, The Committee of 300, created and sanctioned by the New World Order, has called many of our ancestors "useless eaters" and has promoted the practice of genetic selection to further their own political agendas." He paused, more for dramatic effect than for loss of words, before continuing.

"Our populations have remained silent while genetic selection has grown rampant and has now made us captive to the technology we all once enjoyed." Caitriona looked anxiously around the room, noting the affirmative nods as the older man set the stage like a gifted playwright.

Swiping a calloused hand across his eyes, he took a sip of water. Caitriona noted his confidence, acutely aware that he had the full attention of the men and women in the room. "For generations we stood by, helpless, as our Pagan brothers and sisters were persecuted and slaughtered for their beliefs; claimed by the Church as heretical practices before they burned hundreds of thousands at the stake." He allowed his voice to rise to a shockingly loud crescendo before continuing with his next thunderous statement. "But our day is now here! We can no longer sit back in silence. We must act! Our people are counting on us to bring about change!" He took a deep breath and paused again before continuing. The audience grew more excited.

Gesturing to Caitriona, he touched the back of her chair, placing his hands slowly on her shoulders. She remained still, her eyes fixated on the faces before her. Gawain nodded to Duncan, who had taken a seat next to Nicolas. Duncan nodded his head slightly but otherwise remained expressionless and immobile. For not the first time since she was introduced to her handler, Caitriona marveled at the stark differences between the two men. While physically smaller than Duncan, Nicolas was striking with his jet black hair that fell in soft waves across his head. He was every bit as sculpted as Duncan, but whereas Duncan's legs and arms were thick muscle, Nicolas was more lean and defined. Nicolas also had an easy, carefree manner that others found charming and were easily drawn to. In short, the man was utterly enticing and charismatic without one ounce of effort.

Duncan, in contrast, was dark and brooding, a storm cloud of emotion that always lay ready to erupt. And beneath the surface, there was that ever constant electrical pulse that connected Duncan to Caitriona in ways Nicolas never would. Only she hadn't felt the pull in several days. A deep frown creased her brow.

Her musings were short lived as Gawain delivered the confirmation they were all waiting to hear. In another rising crescendo, he emphasized his next words, "Commander MacKinnon has succeeded in bringing us the Seer! We have confirmed her genetic line is pure and we will prove to all of you today that she is truly gifted and the one named in our prophecies. We will bring an end to the Order's tyranny." There was a unified cheer as those gathered at the table excitedly whispered to one another and nodded to Caitriona, who remained impassive. Those seated near the Commander extended warm handshakes or hearty pats to him.

In front of the older gentleman, unable to see his face, Caitriona stared blankly ahead, green eyes ablaze with fury. She said nothing and only Duncan could read the fury in her eyes. Pushing back his chair,

Duncan stood abruptly, causing the room to grow quiet. All eyes were on him as he swept his gaze around the room. Turning, he left the cold chamber. Caitriona released her breath, her eyes following him from the room and from his heart.

***

Caitriona watched as Duncan got up and left the room. Beside her, Nicolas reached over and found her hand. Squeezing softly, he nodded his head, a knowing smile tugging at the corners of his mouth. She returned the affection as she pushed her chair quietly away from the table. Gawain glanced nervously at Nicolas, who remained seated, calmly meeting the gazes of those around him.

Standing, Caitriona met their stares look for look, challenging them all in that single moment. Picking her skirts up in her right hand, she ran from the room following Duncan's earlier path. Outside the door, she could hear the crescendo of voices and Gawain's own surprise echoed in his words.

"Duncan, wait," she called, racing to catch up with his naturally long strides. "Why are you doing this?" she demanded as she caught up to him, her green eyes locking instantly with steel grey ones.

"Ye ken why," he stated tersely. "Because I, and others like me, believe that ye alone have the power to save our world."

An uncomfortable silence followed and Caitriona dropped her gaze, a bright flush rising to her cheeks. Duncan touched her arm. She thought she felt the familiar tug, but it was subtle and she wondered if she only imagined it. He cupped her chin in his hand and raised her face gently so that she was looking into his eyes. His hand pushed a stray strand of hair from her face, the backs of his fingers caressing the side of her cheek. Caitriona sighed and leaned into him, her hand encircling his neck and drawing him close.

"Ach, Catie, why do ye tug so at my heart?" His hand moved to the small of her back and pulled her in close, his lips brushing a light kiss across the top of her head. "This ... us ... it canna continue." He pulled away from her but took her hand in his. "Ye have a life ahead of ye; ye can make a place for yerself here. Nicolas ... he's a good man, Catie." He paused, the anguish he felt evidenced by the hard line of his jaw and the sharpness of his eyes. "He will care for ye and keep ye safe. He can ground yer energy and help ye develop yer gift. I canna do that for ye, lass." The last was spoken almost in a whisper.

"Duncan, I don't care about any of that. Don't you see? I can't imagine a world without you in it. All this," she gestured at the council chambers behind her, "my gift, is only because of you. I want to live in your world. I will fight your war. But with you, not without."

"Ye dinna ken what ye are asking. I swore an oath to my people, to the Templars. I canna abandon ..." Duncan's thought was cut off as a large explosion rent the air, the force of the blast pushing them both against the cold stone walls.

Shaking off his brief disorientation, Duncan quickly scanned the Seer for damage. "Are ye hurt?" he growled.

She shook her head. He reached for her hand. "This way," Duncan barked, clasping her hand and pulling her with him.

"Nicolas," she cried, pulling him back toward the council's chambers.

"Nay. We have to get out of here, lass," he stated when he saw her hesitation.

"I can't leave him," she cried, already moving toward the council chambers. Another explosion, this one more shallow, shook the walls. The sconces that once lit the darkened passages swayed wildly.

"It's not a request, *Leannan.*" He grabbed her arm, the strength of his grip evidence that he did not intend to let her go. Casting one last glance at the council's chamber that now lay filled with rubble and smoke, Caitriona said a silent prayer that Nicolas was all right, and that he would forgive her for abandoning him.

Duncan led them both through the narrow underground halls. The force of the explosion had doused the lights and the darkness was impregnable. Her heartbeat accelerating into a short, fast staccato, Caitriona gripped Duncan's hand tightly as he led the way through the labyrinth of passages and shadowed, empty rooms. Behind her she could hear muffled cries and anguished moans as survivors of the blast sought to escape the battle that was coming.

Duncan led her to one of the unused rooms at the top of the first landing and, pushing hard on a stone panel that was covered by a heavy tapestry, he motioned her inside the narrow passage. "Stay here," he commanded, slipping quickly into his command mode. He turned to leave.

"No!" Caitriona pulled at his hand, memories of his disappearance at the cave washing over her. "I'm staying with you."

"Ye're safer here," he said. "I'm going tae find my men and will station guards until I can get word tae Nicolas where ye are."

"No," she said again. Her green eyes softened as she met his gaze, but the determination remained in her steely resolve. She recognized the determined set of Duncan's jaw but knew he would never feel comfortable risking her life. She knew he couldn't take any chances. Not now.   Suddenly, he pulled her to him and his lips found hers. His tongue slid lightly across her teeth, seeking the sweetness she offered. Capturing her tongue, he gently sucked until he heard her moan. He pulled away slowly, grazing his thumb across her now swollen lip.

"*Damnu*, Catie! This is not a request. I canna risk yer life."

"Because I'm your best weapon?" she paused, trying to rein in her temper. "Or because you love me, Duncan?" The last was spoken in an almost hushed whisper.

"How can ye ask that?" he questioned, fury lacing his tone. "Ye dinna think it does nae tear at my heart every day we're not together? How do ye think I feel watching Nicolas care for ye, laugh with ye, touch ye?"

Caitriona shook her head. "I thought ... I didn't know," she whispered breathlessly. "You are so committed to your mission, to ensuring my visions will give you the edge you need to win this war. How was I to think I would ever be anything to you other than an asset in your war?"

Duncan looked genuinely hurt at her words but didn't have time to expound further. Another explosion rent the air and sent them both tumbling to the ground, debris raining down on top of them. Duncan clambered over to Caitriona and covered her body with his, bearing the brunt of the fallout. When the air stilled, he pulled himself from her, checking her for injuries.

"I'm fine, Duncan," she said pushing hair out of her eyes.

"Change of plans," he said gruffly. "Ye're with me until I can find yer handler and some men tae safeguard ye."

Caitriona didn't argue, knowing she had no intention of leaving his side.

***

Nicolas spun around as he heard someone call his name. Trying to see through the smoke and debris, he reached in front of him for familiarity in the now charred ruins of the underground chambers. He took a few hesitant steps forward, stretching out his fingers into the ashy, inky darkness and, finding nothing, dropped to the ground to find cleaner air.

His lungs burned and a sharp pain in his left shoulder reminded him he was alive, which was more than he could say for many of the men, women, and children who'd been trapped in the underground cavern when the bombs exploded. *Where did it go wrong?* he wondered. *Why hadn't Caitriona predicted this?*

At the thought of Caitriona, he called out for her in the darkness. His cries were met with the moans of the injured and dying; their voices echoing the lost hope that exploded when their world was shattered. Somewhere above him he heard gunfire, and he drew himself instinctively into a ball, covering his head with his arms.

He stayed like that for several minutes before once again inching his way through the dark, knowing he had to find Caitriona. Given the number of explosions that had blasted through the caverns, he was surprised the entire system hadn't collapsed. Using his hands as a guide, he crawled along the ground looking for something familiar, something that would help guide him above ground. He finally bumped into what remained of the castle's food stores. The heavy stone doors that had been used to keep the cellars dry and cool now lay in two pieces against the ruins of the lower tunnel wall. "Caitriona," he rasped. His voice sounded muted and hollow in the debris filled tunnel, but he tried again.

Hearing nothing but the cries of the injured, he opened his mind and reached out for her now familiar impression. Panic gripped him as he realized he couldn't feel her mind. He tried several more times, but always with the same, hollow result. *It's possible she survived the initial blast and found safety,* he thought, pushing his own fears aside. He continued to pick his way through the debris, the inky darkness swallowing him. He helped the injured as best he could; wrapping bandages around the more serious injuries and assisting those that couldn't walk.

After several hours, the smoke began to clear and the earlier sounds became more distant, muffled or lost. At regular intervals he stopped and repeated his search for Caitriona, casting as wide a circle with his mind as he could. He was growing more concerned as his efforts proved futile. He focused on making his way top side, knowing that if the Seer was still alive, she would likely be above ground and looking for shelter. *Or she was unconscious or dead,* his mind screamed.

He picked up his pace, the pain in his shoulder slowing his progress and reminding him of his own injuries. He was finally rewarded for his tenacity when he saw stars through a small hole in the debris that filled a rarely used corridor of the tunnel. He moved quickly to the small opening and started pulling rocks away, his efforts hampered by the use of only one arm. At length, he created an opening that he could squeeze through. Not sure of what he would find above ground, he pulled himself carefully through the opening and into the unknown.

***

Duncan gave the order to attack at first light. Taking the stone steps three at a time, he quickly closed the distance between the heavy, barricaded gate and the approaching army. The Order's army vastly outnumbered the band of refugees and exiles that Duncan had bravely led into battle. His only hope was the trap they had laid in place and the information he had retrieved from the Seer.

The thought of how he had used Catie to polarize his own political agenda sickened him. "*Damn!*" He yelled into the brisk morning air, gazing out at a sea of faces that continued to fight despite the odds and the cold and fatigue that had long ago set in.

As light began to dot the horizon, Duncan scanned the battlefield, noting the fallen soldiers and burned structures; a stark reminder of the decisions he had made. Around him bodies lay strewn in gruesome positions that belied the brilliant rays of the sun just starting to warm the day. The landscape he so dearly loved was now blackened as far as the eye could see. Entire forests were reduced to leafless, charred trunks, farmland to ashes, and homes reduced to piles of collapsed rubble.

The Order's army was vast and well equipped. Their technology gave them a military advantage that left the Templars and their band of Dwellers, Lessers and fugitives at a distinct disadvantage. Despite this, Duncan's men had managed to drive the Order's army back, largely due to the visionary advantages the Seer had supplied him.

After the explosions had nearly leveled the west wing of the castle and torn apart the upper chambers of the underground caverns, Duncan had secured the remaining tunnels and the three entrances. Survivors and wounded were escorted to the underground chambers where they were given medical attention, food, and shelter while the war raged on above ground.

Duncan then ordered four soldiers to guard the Seer at all times. While she had protested at first, the visions had increased with such frequency that they left her tired and shaken and with very little energy to protest her confinement. Her visions had allowed Duncan's army to remain one step ahead of the Order's troops, setting traps, avoiding heavily infiltrated areas and running reconnaissance to the Order's methodical movements.

He sighed as he spotted one of the messengers Caitriona had been using to convey her visions. He hoped she was sending information they could use to ambush the Order's army and drive a substantial shift in their favor. His men were tired and morale was declining as the Order's troops took more lives and continued their unrelenting advance.

"Commander," the young messenger saluted briskly as he approached his commanding officer. "The Seer says you must withdraw your men that are fighting in the east. The Order's men are regrouping and planning a coup to the North. She says you need to act quickly. Your men must be repositioned by nightfall."

Duncan saluted the young messenger and removed a secure communicator from his pocket. After punching in a series of commands, he pocketed the device, confident that his orders would soon be carried out.

"How is she?" Duncan asked softly. He had ordered all communicators at the caves to be removed in case Hawkins was tracking the signal. He didn't want to take any chances that Hawkins would find Caitriona.

"She is well, but the visions come more frequently now," the young messenger said.

"But she isna in any pain?"

"No, sir. She just seems tired."

"And LaFelle? He has recovered?"

"Not fully, but the doctor plans to check on him tonight and administer the last of his treatments." Duncan nodded but his thoughts were on the auburn haired beauty who was being kept hidden and safe within the cave's numerous caverns. He wanted—needed—to see her. He was brought out of his musings by the messenger's throaty cough. "He insisted on the others being treated first," the messenger continued.

A rusty weathervane that had long ago been abandoned atop a cottage outside the castle walls creaked noisily as the wind gusted across its broken vanes. Duncan ran his hand through his hair, his eyes watching the vane's rhythmic spinning, his thoughts returning to the earlier attack on the chambers and the lives that had been lost. Caitriona hadn't predicted the disastrous events. *Why?* He thought, his agitation growing at his inability to untangle the thread.

"Sir?" Duncan's thoughts were interrupted by the messenger's persistence. "I asked if there was a message you wanted me to take to the Seer?"

Duncan stared out across the land at the charred landscape and piles of rubble. He wanted to tell her that he loved her, that he wanted to forego his oath and take her away from all this death and destruction. *She's better off without me*, he thought resignedly.

"Sir? A message?"

Duncan shook his head and saluted. The messenger returned the courtesy and left.

The communicator began vibrating in his pocket and he quickly pulled the small device out, noting the incoming message. The Templars were marching toward the North. He acknowledged the message and closed communications. Pocketing the device, he shifted the broadsword on his side, and slinging a larger gun over his shoulder, set out in the direction of his men.

***

Caitriona paced the Great Hall, pausing every few minutes to glance nervously at the door. Duncan still had not returned. The last messenger had arrived two days earlier and had indicated Duncan was moving north according to the Seer's instructions. She sighed heavily, feeling caged and helpless. Without communicators she hadn't talked to Duncan in days, and the last messenger from him returned with no personal message to her, only military instructions for Gawain.

"We need to look for him, Nicolas," she implored. "You know he's in trouble. I've as good as given you the location. You need to send some men. We can't just sit here and do nothing."

"He's fighting a war, *chéri*. He knows the stakes. The battlefield is no place for you."

Caitriona winced as she was reminded that she had failed to warn the Templars of the attacks on the chambers. In fact, some of the Dwellers had even implied she was a spy for the Order and had deliberately withheld the information so as to murder the men, women, and children who were there below ground.

Caitriona sighed and plopped down on the brocade covered settee nearest the fire. "I don't know what's wrong with me." She twisted an errant lock of hair around her finger, frowning as she glanced again at the door.

"There's nothing wrong with you, *Caterine*" he said, sitting next to her and wrapping his arms around her. "There's nothing wrong with you," he whispered again, kissing the top of her head.

"Why can't I see anything? Why didn't I predict the explosions?"

"I can't answer that, *chéri*."

"I can't just sit here. I am tired of being locked up like a rare bird in a gilded cage." She got up and moved quickly to the door. Before she could leave, Nicolas was across the room and placed his hand over hers.

"You can't leave, *Caterine*. It's not safe."

She turned, piercing him with her eyes. "I'm going. I need some fresh air. Maybe it will help clear my head. So you can either come with me or stay behind. It's your choice, but I am going."

"Don't make me restrain you, *chéri*."

"You wouldn't." She stared at him through long lashes, daring him to carry out his threat.

"Your safety is the only thing I care about," Nicolas replied sternly.

"Fine," she replied tersely. "I won't go any farther than the edge of the castle. You can have the guards come with me and I promise to turn back at the first sign of the Order's men. But I need to be above ground. Maybe it's what I need for the visions to come." She knew she was reaching with that last statement, but she had to convince him to let her go above ground, if only for a moment.

After several seconds he finally acquiesced. "Four guards, no less, and I'm coming with you. We turn back at once if I even think there is a hint of danger. Is that understood?"

She nodded and hugged him tight, eager to be outside. Pulling a heavy wool tartan shawl across her shoulders, she opened the door and made her way above ground.

Chapter Thirty

Only the dead have seen the end of the war.
George Santayana

Caitriona's scream rent the air as she realized they had been ambushed. Her guards sprang to action but were quickly outmatched by the Order's numbers. Side stepping one of the Order's men, she spun quickly and landed a back kick to the man's jaw. He stumbled back and she took that opportunity to run. She knew she would lose in a foot race but dared not lead the Order's troops to the tunnels. Spotting some dense underbrush that would likely provide some cover she grabbed her skirts in one hand and ran as fast as she could. She could hear the tintinnabulation of the guards' swords as they fought to protect her. Hearing gun fire, she gasped and fell to the ground, her breath leaving her in a rush. Next to her, an unsuspecting shrub became the victim of the Order's gunfire as the plant disintegrated in a flash of smoke and crackle of fire. She gasped and inched her way forward, using her elbows and legs to make limited progress.

Another round of gunfire brought her to an abrupt stop, her heart beating at a fast clip as smoke made visibility nearly impossible. She covered her head with her hands as yet another round of gunfire erupted over the clanging of swords. Breathing heavily, she started to raise her head when strong arms plucked her from the ground. She started to scream when a hand clamped over her mouth.

"*Chéri*, silence," Nicolas said in a hushed tone. He released her and she spun around, noting the deep laceration that ran across his left bicep.

"The guards…"

"Dead," he stated tersely. "I've requested reinforcements but I lost contact with command shortly after I sent the communication. My only concern right now is your safety," he told her for the second time that day. At the look of concern on her face, he added, "We will make it out alive, *chéri*. But I need you to follow orders, *oui*?"

She nodded and covered her head when another round of gunfire reminded them both that they didn't have the safety or luxury of discussing their next move.

"See the outcroppings and cliff over there?" Nicolas pointed to a protected area three hundred yards in the distance. She nodded again. "We need to make it to those outcroppings. That should give us the protection we need until the Templars reach us." She nodded again as he pulled a gun from the holster he wore on his hip and fired toward the approaching horde. "Go!"

Caitriona gathered her skirts in her hands once again and bolted toward the shelter. The smoke burned her lungs and she struggled to find a deep breath. Behind her, she could hear Nicolas firing his weapon. *I have a bad feeling about this*, she thought.

Caitriona stumbled and fell headlong into the heather. She remained there, panting, for what seemed like several minutes when she finally rolled over and stared up at one of the Order's soldiers. He leered crazily at her and placed his meaty hand around her arm, hauling her to her feet. She screamed and he kneed her hard in the stomach. She fell forward, gasping for air. *Where is Nicolas?* She thought, as panic gripped her.

Her abductor grabbed a fistful of her hair and dragged her painfully forward. Emerging from the expanse of growth, she saw Duncan, surrounded by a dozen of the Order's men, fighting his way toward her. *What is he doing back here?* She thought, panic gripping her again. She cried out in pain as the soldier pushed her roughly to the ground.

"Duncan!" she screamed as she tried to drag herself away from her abductor. The soldier kicked her hard in the stomach, forcing her to give up any notions of escape. She fell face forward into the dirt, rolling herself into a ball to protect her vital organs. She didn't know how long she stayed there, but she became aware of the eerie silence that now dominated the charred highland landscape. She raised her head slightly, trying to see through the smoke that clung heavily in the air. Not encountering any resistance, she pushed herself up on her knees.

She gasped as rough hands once again hauled her to her feet. She tried to strike out but the soldier held her tight. He spun her in front of him and she got a good look at eyes that stared out at her from hollow sockets and a dirty, blood-smeared face. Her assailant grinned wickedly, showing missing teeth. Laughing, he pinned her against him while his hand fumbled clumsily at the bodice of her gown. Ripping the fabric, he grabbed her breast, pinching the tender flesh until she cried out. His other hand covered her mouth, stifling the scream that was on her lips.

Her world grew dark, the sour breath of the soldier a vile taste in her mouth. She tried to twist away from his vise-like grip when she suddenly felt a sticky warm substance coat her face and neck. She watched in horror as the soldier slumped to the ground, an arrow protruding from his skull. She stumbled back, where strong arms pulled her against an equally hard body. She started to scream but recognized the calm voice near her ear.

"Keep still, *chéri*," Nicolas said in a hushed voice. His arm curled around her waist, pulling her close against him.

Caitriona wanted to run but knew the danger was still very real. She nodded and pulled the ripped fabric around her chest, hiding her breasts from Nicolas' sweeping gaze.

"Keep low and follow me, *oui?*" She nodded and took his hand, allowing him to lead her from the Order's soldier who was now staring at her from vacant, lifeless eyes.

Within minutes they reached the outcroppings that were their original destination. Kneeling down behind a large boulder, Nicolas tugged her down beside him, his eyes assessing her injuries. He brushed the hair from her eyes and pulled her close against him. "We will get out of this. I promise," he whispered reassuringly.

Caitriona nodded, but there was no conviction in her eyes or her nod. They were flanked by soldiers on all sides and the Order's drones were sweeping the air. She shivered and hugged her body tight. She acted selfishly in insisting they come top side and now there was a very real chance she had placed her handler and the Templars in danger. "Stay low and stay out of sight," Nicolas whispered to her. She watched as he cautiously raised his head above the rock to better assess their situation. The look of horror on his face told her everything she needed to know.

Chapter Thirty-One

The fear of death follows from the fear of life. A man who lives fully is
prepared to die at any time.
Mark Twain

Duncan was kneeling in front of Hawkins, his wrists bound behind his back and blood streaming down his face.

Caitriona gasped. "No," she croaked. "This can't be happening." She struggled against Nicolas' grip, but he held her tight against his hard body. She had underestimated his strength. By a lot. She stopped struggling and stared at the gruesome scene before her, her earlier vision a knowing prelude of what was to come. "You know how this will end, Nicolas," she whispered. "We have to stop this."

Duncan lifted his head, the cords in his neck straining, the muscles in his arms flexing and rippling with power that she had witnessed first-hand. Her heart stopped. *Had Duncan heard her?*

Nicolas turned his charge so that his body was a shield. She choked back a sob and buried her face in his shoulder. She heard the ring of steel and started to cry out but Nicolas clamped his hand over her mouth, his hold firm enough to bruise. Tears streamed from her eyes but Nicolas' orders were clear; protect the Seer and get her to safety... at all costs. She knew he wouldn't deviate from his orders. She gripped his hand, trying to peel his fingers from her mouth, but they remained like steel.

Ceasing her struggle, she did the only thing she could think of. She bit. Hard. He cursed and dropped his hand. Caitriona moved quickly, freeing his dagger from the scabbard hanging at his side. He reached for her, but she stood up and moved quickly from his reach. "Stay down," she hissed.

She turned and ran toward Hawkins, once again facing the man who had tortured and enslaved her. Waving her arms to get his attention, she yelled his name. To her credit, the Order's men stopped and stared at her, their weapons suddenly trained on her and their eyes hungrily devouring her exposed flesh. She walked slowly forward, ignoring Nicolas' hushed pleas.

"Let him go, Hawkins," she said, her voice more authoritative than she had thought possible. She swallowed hard, the knots in her stomach expanding. Outwardly, she knew she had to appear in control.

"It would appear I have gained two rewards this day," Hawkins sneered, his lips curling as his eyes raked across her body and the tender flesh that was still exposed. Duncan pulled at his restraints, the cords in his muscled arms straining with his effort. The soldiers powered up their weapons and Caitriona watched as the red lights locked on her heart.

"I will say this only once," Caitriona growled. "Let. Him. Go."

"Ah, my young jewel, what you fail to realize is that you are not in a position to bargain." He nodded to the soldiers closest to him. "Seize her!"

The soldiers sprang forward but before they could close the distance, Caitriona brought the dagger to her throat, pressing the tip against her jugular.

"Don't think I won't do it, Hawkins," she hissed through clenched teeth. "I'm no good to you dead and you and I both know that." For emphasis she allowed the tip to nick the delicate skin, a small bead of blood forming where the knife had punctured.

Hawkins raised his arm to stop his soldiers. "Come now, my pet. While I do so admire your ... spirit, we both know you won't do this."

Caitriona continued to slowly walk toward Hawkins. She hoped her performance was convincing. Her heart was beating so loudly and so fast she felt certain Hawkins could hear it.

When she was ten yards from Hawkins, she stopped walking and motioned toward Duncan. "He walks away, as do his men, and I will go with you. Without argument or resistance. If I even think he is followed or harmed in any way, I will slit my throat and you will have to explain how your jewel slipped through your fingers," she said, emphasizing the word jewel.

"As I've said, chéri, you are not in a position to bargain." He walked toward her, his palms out indicating he was unarmed. He motioned to the soldier holding Duncan and the man released him. "But I will give you this. I am feeling rather generous where you are concerned." His eyes openly raked her body, lingering on the bare flesh of her breasts. He licked his lips appreciatively.

"His hands." She nodded at the iron shackles that bound Duncan's hands in front of him. "Remove the irons." Hawkins nodded again and the soldier held a small device near the clasp until an audible click indicated Duncan was free.

"Put down the knife," Hawkins purred.

"Not until I'm sure he's free." Caitriona's gaze remained locked on Hawkins, but she could feel Duncan's eyes on her.

Still keeping his hands where Caitriona could see them, Hawkins turned slowly and faced Duncan. "Make one move, Commander, and I will have you killed. So don't be a hero. The girl is mine." He chuckled sadistically. "It would seem that you have lost ... again."

Hawkins spun back around to face Caitriona. "I will enjoy breaking you," he leered at her, licking his lips as his eyes ogled her curves. He closed the distance slowly between them, his eyes never leaving hers.

Caitriona tentatively took a step back. Fear gripped her as memories of the man's torturous abuse came rushing back. She gasped, her hands trembling as she realized she was no match for this sadistic man. It was all the hesitation Hawkins needed. He moved quickly, his snake-like reflexes surprisingly agile. He pulled her deftly against him, at the same time twisting her hand until she released the dagger.

Caitriona yelped as her fingers betrayed her and she released her vise-like grip on the weapon. He leaned in close to her ear, "I will forgive this first transgression, my pet. But don't disappoint me again." His breath was sour and foul against her skin. She tried to pull away but he merely tightened his grip and laughed. "You can save your squirming for when we are alone and under the covers" He licked her ear and blew hot, sour breath across the wet trail.

Caitriona closed her eyes and tried to get control of her nerves. She was vaguely aware of Duncan's attempts to escape his jailers, his struggles ineffective against the highly trained soldiers. His voice sounded small and far away as he tried to negotiate for her release. She knew his threats were not empty promises. Duncan would kill Hawkins.

Getting control of her panic, Caitriona stopped fighting Hawkins and looked up to see Duncan staring intently at her. And suddenly she understood. It was as if the last few pieces of a thousand-piece jigsaw puzzle had fallen into place and she was left with a simple truth:

Duncan would never let her fall into the hands of his enemy. She was too important to his cause, his people, and the war he had spent years fighting.

She closed her eyes, the vision that had haunted her since childhood playing out in her mind. The tattooed stranger with arresting grey eyes finally became clear. This was how she was going to die; at the hands of the man she loved. *It wouldn't have mattered who we brought forward in time. This war must still be fought. And it must be won. At any cost and at any sacrifice.*

His words came floating back to her, their intent made even clearer with the finality of her situation. She stiffened, no longer afraid of the vision and what it meant. She had arrived at this moment - all her fears of the tattooed stranger and her death leading up to this one final crescendo, a situation she created of her own actions.

She locked green eyes with grey. "I forgive you," she said softly, knowing that his genetically enhanced hearing would register her declaration. She blinked as tears coursed down her cheeks. Sobbing, she sagged against her captor, her head lolling to one side. Glancing once more at her lover, she released her breath as the blade left Duncan's hand.

***

What in the hell is she doing here? Duncan thought, panic gripping him. He pulled hard against his restraints, the animal in him coiled just beneath the surface and wanting to spring. He could see her terror and fought harder against his bonds.

"No," he croaked, his hands clenching into fists. Raising his head he locked steel grey eyes with Hawkins' dull brown ones, fury cascading from him in sheets. "Let her go, Hawkins. This is between you and me. She has nothing to do with this."

"On the contrary, MacKinnon, this has everything to do with my dear, sweet Caitriona," he hissed, his hand caressing Caitriona's hair. He fisted his hand in her hair and inhaled deeply. Duncan's fury boiled to the surface of his barely held restraint. His eyes narrowed as he watched Hawkins unclench his fist and allowed Caitriona's silken tresses to slide through his fingers. Hawkins pulled Caitriona tighter against him and grinned when she tried to twist away from the bulge in his pants as he pushed roughly against her.

Duncan continued to watch, helpless, as Caitriona closed her eyes and took a deep breath.

"I will kill you, Hawkins," Duncan yelled. "Let her go."

Hawkins laughed wildly and pulled Caitriona tighter against his groin, grinding himself suggestively against her. She gasped, clearly horrified at the turn the negotiations had taken.

Duncan's struggles became more menacing, his muscles straining and his veins standing out against his skin. He locked eyes with Caitriona and heard her soft whisper. The soldier next to him relaxed his hold just briefly as he shifted his position. It was the only break Duncan needed. As the soldier shifted his stance, his hip where he kept his dagger was within Duncan's reach. In the blink of an eye, Duncan deftly removed the dirk, the startled soldier too slow to respond to this newest threat. Duncan's wrist barely flexed with the effort it took to throw the blade with deadly accuracy.

***

Caitriona felt something warm and sticky hit the side of her face. She had assumed there would be more pain and that death would be instantaneous. She opened her eyes as she felt Hawkins' hold on her release. She spun when she heard Hawkins hit the ground and gasped when she saw the hilt of Duncan's dagger sticking out of Hawkins' temple. Blood poured from the gash where Duncan's dagger had found its mark.

Caitriona fell to her knees as Duncan's men emerged from the forest, their shrill battle cries a welcome sound as the fighting erupted around her. She had to find safety. She took one last look at Hawkins, his vacant eyes staring back at her, and crawled away. Next to her, one of the Order's soldiers fell, his hand reaching for her as he lay twisting in his own blood. She gasped and scrambled farther away, the ground cold and unforgiving against her hands and legs.

***

As Hawkins fell, everything around Duncan slowed. He was acutely aware of the gunfire that blasted several of the Order's soldiers closest to him. His eyes quickly traced the hills to find Lee firing his weapon in rapid succession. Templars began pouring from the hills, cutting their way to the duo below. But Duncan had eyes only for the Seer, who crumpled to the ground once Duncan buried his blade in Hawkins' temple. Caitriona was crawling away from the fighting, but he was still too far away to get to her. One of the Order's men swung his broadsword, but Duncan deftly moved to the side, avoiding the fatal blow. Spinning, he nearly took out Nicolas, who was engaged in battle with two of the Order's men. Nicolas stabbed his first opponent and swiftly removed the blade, bringing it around and connecting with the second man's armor. He stepped back, bringing his sword above his head to meet the other man's deadly thrust. Nicolas danced back, his sword locked with the other man's deadly steel.

Duncan turned his attention to the soldier closest to him. Wrapping the remnants of his irons around the soldier's throat, he squeezed hard. The man dropped his sword and Nicolas wasted no time in delivering the fatal blow. Picking up the fallen sword, Duncan somersaulted into a roll as gun blast crumpled the outcroppings just ten yards in front of him.

"Get Caitriona," Duncan yelled to Nicolas over the cacophony of fighting and gun fire. He spun to his left and narrowly avoided one of the Order's soldiers barreling down on him. Side-stepping the soldier, Duncan bent low to avoid the man's blade, his gaze spotting the horde that was advancing from the valley below...

***

Caitriona looked furtively around for any sign of Duncan. She spotted Nicolas making his way toward her, his progress hampered by the Order's men. Another blast of gunfire brought her quickly to her knees as she covered her head with her hands. Almost immediately, something heavy landed against her, driving the breath from her in a loud huff. She pushed at the obstacle, unsure of this new threat.

"*Caterine*, it's me," Nicolas croaked.

She gasped and rolled to her side, effectively pushing Nicolas off of her in the process. "Duncan," she cried. "I have to get to him."

"No, *Caterine*" he said, his tone clipped and commanding. "You will only distract him. You cannot help him now."

Caitriona pushed herself to her feet, crouching once again as shrapnel rained from the smoke-filled sky after a nearby blast tore the earth. Nicolas was right beside her and reached for her hand when she turned toward the fighting.

Putting his arm behind her knees, he hefted her quickly across his shoulder, stopping her defiant behavior. Caitriona gasped, caught off guard, and began to beat against Nicolas' shoulders demanding her release. He ignored her pleas, making his way quickly from the battlefield toward the relative safety of Castle Lauriston.

Only after Nicolas could no longer hear the battle did he set his charge on her feet. Her face was streaked with dried blood, tears and dirt, and a large bruise was already beginning to form below her jaw. Her bodice had been torn, exposing her bare breasts. Nicolas removed his shirt and handed it to her. She took it graciously, turning from his gaze and using the oversized shirt to cover herself. The shirt hung nearly to her knees and extended beyond the tips of her fingers, but the warmth caressed her skin. Blood was pooling from a nasty cut across her forehead and a longer cut along her left thigh made her wince as the cold breeze danced across the open wound.

"How did you think this was going to end today, *Caterine*? Did you think these people would just turn Duncan over and let us all walk free?" he asked heatedly.

Caitriona's anger gave her a sense of bravado she didn't possess. "Maybe not," she said haughtily, "but I couldn't just sit back and do nothing." She stood glaring at her handler, her arms akimbo as she refused to back down.

"*Caterine*, you can't continue to be this reckless," he said, deliberately enunciating each word. "You could have been killed today," he said more softly.

Startled by a loud commotion near the castle's gate, she and Nicolas both turned, fearful the Order's horde had advanced their position.

Caitriona gasped as she spotted Duncan and his men. "He's alive," she whispered breathlessly as she watched the war-weary men make their way toward the castle. Gasping softly, she ran towards her lover, a fierce need to connect with him and touch him overwhelming her. Behind her she could hear Nicolas' soft admonishment, but she knew he wouldn't follow.

Caitriona covered the distance quickly and threw herself into her lover's arms, relishing the hardness of his body. He dropped his weapons and wrapped his arms around her, burying his face in her hair. He inhaled her scent, the subtle hints of lavender and lily mixing with the heady earthiness that was so distinctly her. He tilted her face to his and skimmed his thumb across her lips.

"I thought I'd lost ye today," he said softly, his breath warm and caressing against her skin.

"I know," she confided, leaning into him. "I was so certain of my vision, so certain of how I would die. But I've never been more wrong."

"*Leannan*, you are the verra air I breathe. My world begins and ends with ye." He took her mouth, at once demanding yet caressing. She felt him harden as an answering ache grew between her legs. Caitriona leaned into him, the world and all its horrors and complications simply falling away. She groaned as he deepened the kiss, his tongue grazing her teeth as his hands cupped her face.

Duncan moaned and broke off the kiss first. He tilted her chin and bent his head down to hers, nuzzling her cheek before kissing the top of her head.

"Where do we go from here?" she asked against his chest, fearing his answer.

He pulled away from her. "I dinna ken," he replied, honestly. "Ye dinna deserve this life, lass. But I canna change what has been done. Nicolas can give ye the kind of security and stability ye deserve. The only thing I have tae offer ye is a violent, bloody war, a life of uncertainty, and a target that would be forever painted on yer back."

"Duncan, I am yours and will forever be yours in every way imaginable. Don't push me away."

"Ach, Catie. My first duty is to this war, to the people who will sacrifice their lives for basic freedoms. I canna turn my back on them."

"I'm not asking you to," she replied softly, unshed tears lurking at the surface of her emotions.

"I canna promise anythin' beyond today. And that is nae a life I'd wish for ye."

At her protests, he shook his head and pulled her close against him. "Every fiber of my bein' tells me tae leave ye be; tae leave ye to another… but I canna." He hooked his finger under her chin and forced her to look at him. He could see the tears pooling in her eyes.

"*Tha gaol agam ort*," he said softly. A sob tore from her lips as the tears fell unchecked down her cheeks. "I will find a way for us tae be together, lass. I swear it. By the Goddess and your God, I swear it to ye." Any further protests were silenced as his lips found hers. She clung to him, the emotions of the past several days finding release in the man whom she loved equally.

Breaking the kiss, she brushed the hair from his face and ran the back of her fingers across his cheek. He looked so vulnerable, his emotions visible and bare to her soul. "We are in this together," she whispered. "I promise."

But each knew it was a promise that would be tested.

Chapter Thirty-Two

The bud of victory is always in the truth.
Benjamin Harrison

"Caitriona, you have saved our century from its own short-sightedness and we will forever be in your debt," Gawain said, kissing her lightly on the cheek. He raised his glass to those gathered in the room. "To Caitriona," he said loudly.

As those gathered in the room raised their glasses and provided their own heartfelt toasts, Gawain leaned close to her ear and spoke quietly, "You have brought my son home to me. Your courage and loyalty have not gone unnoticed."

Caitriona smiled, but it didn't reach her eyes. "I have delivered the visions you needed and have measured up to the council's scrutiny," she said in a whisper, her breath brushing the hairs on his neck. "I trust you will find an appropriate way to thank me."

Gawain dipped his head, his eyes meeting hers. Caitriona started to say something else but was interrupted by Nicolas' hand on her shoulder. She turned and looked into his startlingly blue eyes that were so much like Eric's. She felt a momentary stab of nostalgia at a life that now seemed a distant memory. Nicolas squeezed her shoulder, bringing her out of her melancholy mood, and handed her another glass of wine.

"I'm still angry with you," she teased lightly, a smile tugging at the corners of her lips.

"Something tells me you won't stay that way for long," he teased back, his eyes dipping appreciatively over the curves of her body that were accentuated by the rich, decadent sapphire blue gown she wore. The dress was cut high in front, showing delicate calves and legs before cascading in a pool of silk behind her. The décolletage was cut low, revealing the dip between her breasts. White, embroidered leaves were sewn to a nude-colored bodice appearing to be suspended on her bare arms. Her hair had been pulled away from her face by five small braids that met at the nape of her neck before blending with the rest of her thick tresses. A crown of white beads sat low across her forehead and ringed her head delicately. The effect was stunning and had captured the attention of more than one man in the room.

"Probably not." She teased back. She was uncomfortably aware of his growing interest in her.

"And you," Duncan admonished Caitriona lightly, having joined the trio. "From now on, no more secrets, aye?" He brushed a soft kiss across her forehead and draped his arm around her shoulder possessively.

A radiant smile lit her face. "Only if you promise not to treat me like a prized bird that you want to keep locked in a gilded cage," she replied petulantly. She knew she needed to diffuse the growing tension between the two men. Nicolas' growing attachment to her clearly bothered Duncan, but at the same time he often encouraged the two to spend more time together. It was clear that Duncan was at odds with the relationship between her and Nicolas, but was trying hard to find a way to be part of her life, despite the emotional bond she shared with her handler. And while she admired his loyalty and conviction to his cause, a part of her also wished selfishly he could put aside honor and duty.

Gawain interrupted her thoughts, placing an arm lightly on her shoulder. "Let's not talk of secrets. Tonight, we eat, drink, and celebrate the victory that is ours." He smiled at the trio, also aware of the tension between the two men.

Hearing the first strains of a fast, modern tune, Gawain nodded toward the grand ballroom, indicating they should join the party. "It is good to be home at Dunrobin, no?" he said to his son as he clasped him on the shoulder. Duncan smiled and Caitriona saw his eyes light up as his gaze swept the beauty of the castle. The older Castle Lauriston had been nearly demolished during the battle. Caitriona knew it would be a long time before its inhabitants would be able to return to the historic building and lands. Gawain had graciously opened his home to his long-time friend and Castle Lauriston's occupants. Despite the increased number of guests, Dunrobin was able to accommodate the new arrivals with ample room to spare.

Watching the two MacKinnon men exit the room, she slowed her pace so she could talk to Nicolas in private. "I can't believe you told Duncan about my recurring vision," Caitriona said to Nicolas as soon as she was confident the older MacKinnon was out of ear shot. "I told you that in confidence."

"And had I not told him, *chéri*, last week's battle may have had a very different outcome." He pulled her hand through the crook in his arm and covered it gently with his. "When will you learn your safety is my only concern? The Commander needed to know that I would not let anyone," he stressed the last word, "harm you."

Caitriona arched an eyebrow at her handler, not missing the underlying meaning in his words. Duncan's earlier words onboard the ship came back to haunt her once again, "*It wouldn't have mattered who we brought forward in time. This war must still be fought. And it must be won. At any cost and at any sacrifice.*"

They entered the ballroom and Caitriona was pulled from her musings by the grandness of her surroundings and the infectious music. Her earlier misgivings were pushed aside as she took in the lavish embellishments. She sighed appreciatively as she looked around her. The ballroom was an elegant rococo in rich golds, reds, and browns. The mirrored walls glittered brilliantly with the light that reflected from several grand chandeliers, sconces, and candelabra. It was a stunning effect that left Caitriona nearly breathless.

On the parquet floor, there were easily two hundred people, though the room was so large it could have held five times as many. Several couples were gliding effortlessly over the dance floor, the women's gowns and men's tartans providing a kaleidoscope of color against the otherwise elegant backdrop of the ballroom. She was equally pleased to see Genetics and Dwellers alike mingling on the floor. *Perhaps there is hope for this century after all*, she thought as she saw Rowe moving gracefully across the dance floor with a Genetic she recognized from Gawain's Cabinet. Caitriona's feet tapped slightly to the hypnotic beat of the modern music and she couldn't help but smile at the grandness of it all. It was hard to believe that these people were embattled in a bitter war.

When the music came to a stop the dancers and guests applauded, the twenty-one piece orchestra moving right into their next piece; one she recognized from the nineteen forties.

"Frank Sinatra?" she questioned Nicolas when she heard the familiar words to "*S'posin*" being sung by a handsome young man who clearly bore evidence of the Order's genetic engineering.

"All for you, *chéri*," he said nodding to the small band. "I believe you said you are a fan, *oui?*"

A grin lit up her face as she leaned in and pressed a light kiss against his cheek. "Thank you," she said simply, yet sincerely. "It's wonderful."

"May I have the honor of this dance, *chéri?*"

She nodded and allowed him to lead her to the dance floor, her sapphire blue gown catching the air and floating behind her as she walked. Nicolas pulled her effortlessly to him, his right hand resting lightly at the small of her back, while his left hand covered hers over his heart. She placed her left hand on his shoulder and allowed him to move her gracefully around the room.

Nicolas was a confident and skilled dancer and Caitriona soon found herself caught up in the pulsing, rhythmic music. As the song came to an end, Nicolas spun her so that her back was to his front. She laughed and turned to look at him, noting the longing in his eyes that she hadn't noticed before. His gaze locked with hers and, after several seconds, she finally dropped her eyes, an uncomfortable silence settling between them.

She was brought out of her trance by Duncan's hand on her elbow. She turned to face him, dropping Nicolas' hand and moving away from their intimate position. Feeling like an errant teenager who'd been caught in a compromising position, she felt the heat rise to her cheeks. A scowl framed Duncan's chiseled features and she could see the storm brewing just below the surface of his emotions. *Oh shit, he's mad*, she thought tiredly as she tried to gauge his latest disposition.

"May I?" he asked, but his hand was already reaching for hers, pulling her tight against him as the soft refrains of "*When I Fall In Love*" floated across the dance floor. Caitriona leaned into him, inhaling his masculine scent. At his touch, the trickle of electricity that had been absent turned into a flash of sudden, raw need. Caitriona looked up into his steel grey gaze and saw her need reflected in his intensity. Her nerves were awake and singing and they wanted only one thing; him.

Caitriona dropped her gaze and settled her head against Duncan's chest, allowing him to move her slowly around the dance floor. The fiery need that had suddenly consumed her passed and she almost wondered if she'd imagined the connection. After several seconds had passed, she raised her head and locked green eyes with grey. A slight smile tugged at the corner of his lips as he took in the appreciative swell of her breasts beneath the thin fabric of her gown. He moved them deftly to the outer edges of the dance floor and, when the song had finished, guided her to the outside terrace.

The gardens were cast in shadows save for the occasional torch that provided some light in the inky dark night. Caitriona's heart beat faster as she realized they were alone. Once again, she felt her need surface at his prolonged touch. He took her hand and led her to a small gazebo at the edge of the upper garden. She shivered, as much from anticipation as from the cold.

Seeing her shudder, Duncan removed his jacket and wrapped it around her slim shoulders. She pulled the jacket closed across her bosom, not wishing to break the comfortable silence that sat between them. Duncan's movements were decisive and sure and Caitriona reveled in his masculinity. His white shirt stood in stark contrast to the dark night, his kilt lending him an even greater air of authority. He removed his sporran, setting it on the bench beside them, and pulled her close once again, kissing the top of her head as she nestled against him.

She moaned softly and he tilted her face to his. He kissed the hollow of her hand, every nerve singing in the wake of his warm touch. His mouth found hers in a crushing intensity, reaching so deep that she whimpered, her hands curling into fists beside him. She returned his kiss with a fiery passion of her own, hungry for him as she always was. Her skin prickled and she felt the weight deep in her belly and the wetness between her legs.

Duncan broke the kiss first, his eyes searching her brilliant green depths. "I thought I had lost ye last week," he said finally. "How could ye be so reckless with yer life, Catie?"

She shook her head, unwilling to have this conversation with him but knowing she needed to if she were to ever clear the air between them. "I told you before that I would stay here and fight your war, but with you in my life, not without," she said softly. She hesitated slightly before continuing. "We are connected somehow," she said cautiously. "I don't know how I know this but I do. And I think you feel it, too."

"Aye, lass. But with the war, I dinna have the luxury of acting verra often on my feelings." He brushed her hair from her shoulders and bent to place a feather light kiss on the exposed skin. She shivered, the kiss a promise of something more.

Nicolas emerged from the shadows and cleared his throat. A flush crept across Caitriona's face even in the cool night air. For the second time that night, she felt like an errant teenager. "Gawain is looking for you both," he said tersely. "Come, *chéri*," he offered his elbow to her. Caitriona tucked her small hand into the crook of Nicolas' elbow, her eyes never leaving Duncan's. "We will finish this later, *Leannan.*" He stressed the last word which she knew didn't escape Nicolas' attention. Caitriona's heart accelerated as she recognized the endearment for what it was: he was claiming her as his. Duncan scowled at Nicolas but otherwise relinquished her back into the hands of her handler.

***

Duncan waited several minutes, his eyes scanning the shadows for any signs of danger. Convinced there was none, he followed the two back to the ballroom. Slipping past Nicolas and Caitriona, he quickly spotted his father having a heated conversation with one of the council leaders.

Making his way over to his father, Duncan watched as Nicolas and Caitriona shook hands and greeted several of the late arrivals. Duncan acknowledged his father's oldest council member with a nod of his head, not wanting to interrupt the conversation. He knew Ian Fraser well and knew the older man was passionate about only two things; his children and a stalwart belief in genetic research. Unfortunately for his father, tonight the older man was sharing the monotonous details of his latest research.

Duncan shifted his weight, his attention wandering to where Caitriona still stood with Nicolas, greeting guests. She shifted her gaze and met his eyes. He wanted to lose himself in her. His mind drifted to the last time they made love and he felt himself grow hard. There was no denying she was beautiful, but there was something more, some deeper connection that continued to bring them together.

Duncan was dimly aware that Gawain had excused himself and had motioned for Nicolas and Caitriona to join them. Not taking his eyes from Caitriona, Duncan watched as she and Nicolas moved toward him. He could almost feel her fear as he saw her stop abruptly and draw in a sharp breath.

Duncan glanced at Nicolas, each so accustomed with Caitriona and her gift to recognize the familiar vacant stare that always accompanied one of her visions. Duncan hurried to her side, but it was Nicolas' hand that rested possessively over hers.

"It isn't over," she said quietly, when Duncan brushed the hair from her eyes and kissed her forehead. He knew she wasn't with him but he also knew she needed to feel his presence. He wasn't wrong. The simple gesture brought reassurance and she relaxed visibly. She looked beyond Duncan, her eyes taking on the ethereal, other-world look that was an appurtenance of her second sight.

Gawain raised his arm, signaling for the band to stop playing. His council advisor frowned, seemingly confused by what was happening. As the band stopped playing, the crowd grew silent, each eager to bear firsthand witness to the young woman's vision.

"Nay, lass," Duncan said in reply. "We've defeated Hawkins and we've turned back his army. We've had confirmation from nine of the sixteen cities that the Order's armies have been defeated."

Caitriona continued, seemingly unaware of what he was saying. "Power of three." Her words were harshly accentuated and crisp. "There will be a price to pay in blood," she said, her voice rising in panic. "Blood on the moon; trouble soon follows." She gasped loudly as he saw her eyes lock on a picture only she could see.

Caitriona shuddered as the vision left her. Duncan was acutely aware of the eerie silence that had settled across the room and the hundreds of eyes that were upon her. She blinked several times to restore her sight and sighed softly when Duncan scooped her into his arms and quickly exited the room, her now familiar entourage in tow. Duncan pushed open the door to the library and deposited her on the small but comfortable settee.

Nicolas poured her a glass of water and handed it to her, indicating she should drink. She took a sip and handed it back, her hands trembling. Duncan knew she didn't need water. She needed him. He felt it in every fiber of his being; in every way he could imagine, she needed him. Sighing, Caitriona sank back into the oversized settee and shivered. Duncan pulled a tartan shawl around her shoulders, and she smiled at him. He kneeled in front of her and took her cold hands in his. Kissing the back of each of her hands, he ignored the look Nicolas gave him.

"What is it, lass? What did ye see?"

Caitriona looked into Duncan's hard grey eyes. She squeezed his hand and took a deep breath, her eyes never leaving his.

"Hawkins is alive."

Epilogue

Hawkins fumbled for the lone cigarette he kept tucked away in his shirt pocket. He placed the flattened stick of tobacco loosely between his lips and, holding the match between his thumb and forefinger, struck hard against the crumbled outcropping. The flame sprang to life and he quickly lit the pungent stick, his fingers shaking. The cigarette end glowed brightly in the darkness as he took a deep draw, blowing thin pale smoke rings into the inky blackness that surrounded him. His mouth twisted into a sardonic and cruel jeer as he allowed the nicotine to work its magic.

With his good arm, he felt gingerly for the gash above his eye, his fingers trying to discern the damage. The cut was deep, but he would live. He flinched as his fingers pressed a little too hard.

He closed his eyes, an involuntary shudder brushing across his body. After MacKinnon's blade had struck him, his world went dark and the ground rushed up to meet him. He stayed there for several minutes before he felt the blast and the wave of heat and flame that nearly engulfed him. He remembered thinking that he was going to die without ever having fucked the red-headed beauty that was an aberration of everything he believed. The blast expelled him away from the crumbling outcroppings and burning buildings and into a sheltered, dense patch of brush where one of his men had eventually found him. It was the blast that had saved his life.

He winced as he recalled how his men had scampered like roaches in a brightly lit room once the fighting broke out. *Where had it all gone wrong*, he wondered as he ran a hand through his matted hair, blood from his head wound coating his fingers. *At least I am alive*, he thought distractedly. He took another long puff on the cigarette and exhaled the smoke slowly. Of course, he hadn't quite escaped injury: his head was bleeding profusely and his left arm hung useless at his side.

But MacKinnon and his witch had underestimated him. Again. He laughed hysterically, the sound a raspy, hoarse snigger that turned into a violent cough. He crushed the cigarette out beneath his boot and spat a stream of bloodied tobacco juice into the slick dirt. Next time he would be ready. He chuckled mirthlessly and then winced as the pressure in his head grew. Again, he gingerly touched the deep gash over his eye and cursed loudly.

When he saw the Seer again—and he would see her again—he would make her pay for his defeat. And she would pay dearly.

The End

About the author

Karlene lives in the beautiful Pacific Northwest where she practices and teaches marketing, chases sunshine, and dallies in wine and coffee. Karlene has published articles in *Appaloosa Journal*, *Performance Horse* magazine and several newspapers. She blames her obsession with conspiracy theories on her sister who still maintains we never sent a man to the moon. When not writing, Karlene can be found plunking away at the piano, rafting the white water of the Wenatchee River or enjoying a good cup of coffee, or wine, depending on the hour.

Coming soon from Karlene Cameron

Dark Gathering

Latest titles from Black Velvet Seductions

Their Lady Gloriana by Starla Kaye
Cowboys in Charge by Starla Kaye
Holly's Big Bad Santa by Starla Kaye
Her Cowboy's Way by Starla Kaye
The Love She Wants by Mila Winters
Punished by Richard Savage, Nadia Nautalia & Starla Kaye
Accidental Affair by Leslie McKelvey
Right Place, Right Time by Leslie McKelvey
Her Sister's Keeper by Leslie McKelvey
Playing for Keeps by Glenda Horsfall
Playing By His Rules by Glenda Horsfall
Sympathy Dance by Sue McConnell
The White Spider of Savignac by V. L. Smith
The Stir of Echo by Susan Gabriel
Rally Fever by Crea Jones
Behind The Clouds by Jan Selbourne
Trusting Love Again by Starla Kaye
Runaway Heart by Leslie McKelvey
The Otherling by Heather M. Walker
First Submission - Anthology
These Eyes So Green Copyright by Deborah Kelsey

See more of our titles at
www.blackvelvetseductions.com

Our titles are available from:
Amazon
Smashwords
LuLu
Nook
and other retailers

Find Black Velvet Seductions on Facebook
And follow BVS Books on Twitter